To Megan and Mikle for their everlasting love
and constant support

ARIELLA PAPA

lives and works in the great, courageous
city of New York. She has been writing since
she was three. When she isn't writing prose or
screenplays, she works as a television writer
and producer. She'd like to give a shout out to
all the assistants out there who'd rather be doing
something else. *On the Verge* is her debut novel.

On
the
Verge

Ariella Papa

**RED
DRESS
INK**
™

First edition July 2002

ON THE VERGE

A Worldwide Library/Red Dress Ink novel

ISBN 0-373-25017-7

© 2002 by Ariella Papa.

Visit Red Dress Ink at www.reddressink.com

Printed in Canada

ACKNOWLEDGMENTS

Although they did not realize it,
many people helped me to write this book.
I would like to thank all of my friends,
family and co-workers. I would especially
like to thank the following people for the
little extras that influenced me so much.

Grazie to Anne Marie for calendars and cheese.
Thanks to Becky, Beth and Jimmy for Big Chill nights
of debauchery and a world tour to come.
To Cav for access to his mom's potatoes.
To Cheryl for the outfit and resonance.
To Colleen for apartment searching. To Corby
for Portuguese men. To Dolvie for his funny little
songs. To Erica for Christmas party memories.
To Josh for cinematic toasts. To Kristy for the womb
to the Lodge and beyond. To Maclin for
remembering everything and a night in 1986.
To my editor, Margaret Marbury, for holding
my hand through this crazy, amazing process.
To Matt Wood for translating legalese
in a not-so-quiet bar.

Thanks to the Papa family and the Botte/Leislle
family. To Ratha (snooky!) for being a constant source
of cheer and kindness. To Rick for L.A. To Riz for
Otis Spunkmeyer cookies. To Romolo for Italy.
To Snappy Cohen for never wanting to sit upstairs.
To Travis for not being like anyone in this book.
To Zoe for mayonnaise and sanity.

Most of all I would like to thank my father,
Rocco Papa, for his unconditional love
and for the best chicken cutlets in the world.

Prologue

Sometimes I think I should have just had my nervous breakdown and gotten it over with. In high school, okay, maybe it would have been a little dramatic, but in college? I know I could have done it then. Lots of people did. I could have created a small but forgivable scandal. Nothing bad ever really happens to girls who take "time off." It's cool. I could have gone from gossip for a week to a point of reference for depressed women in future semesters. I kept waiting for the right time to give in to my depression, but I was too busy holding everyone's hair as they puked up cafeteria pesto and Natty Lite.

I plan to talk to my bosses about doing a little writing for the magazine. Mind you *Bicycle Boy* is hardly what I had in mind when I spent those four and a half years not breaking down in college, but it's a start, right? Something for my portfolio. Something my mom could boast about to her cronies who couldn't care less, "Yeah, a journalism degree and she just did an exposé on helmet straps."

A few months back I wrote a totally fabricated piece on a man who fell off his bike as a child and refused to ride. In the story, my character, the narrator, had become a surgeon, only to feel something was missing. He had no release after extracting all those hearts, until he returned to his first love—cycling. The fresh air calmed him, he shed pounds and reconnected with the outdoorsman he yearned to be. I wrote it from a thirty-two-year-old guy's perspective and it was complete bullshit, but I was appealing to the demographic. I mentioned it to my bosses and they said we could talk after that month's deadline. We never did.

Unfortunately one of our major advertisers, a water bottle manufacturer, is under investigation. Seems some guy in Dearcreek, Montana—no doubt one of our readers—got very sick after a twelve-mile trek. He claims the water tasted funny and some scientists are thinking this brand may not be the most hygienic. Luckily, it hasn't been publicized, but you can well imagine it isn't the best time to broach anything with the big men.

I comfort myself with the knowledge that the interns think I'm cool. They respect my power because I provide the supplies and order lunch. If they're nice to me it's a plethora of Post-it notes and maybe even a slight fat content in the bland vegetarian lunches I am forced to order. Also, one of the interns is exactly a year and three months my senior. She would kill for my job.

I have been working as an assistant for this magazine for almost seven months. I was temping for the large magazine conglomerate that owns this and many others, Prescott Nelson Inc.—I'm sure you know it. Right here in the crossroads of the world, Times Square. Although I harassed the human resources department to let me work for their feminist magazine, *Angry Beavers,* they assured me *Bicycle Boy* was a great place to be. I sucked it up, because I noticed a cosmetic ad or two slipping into the back pages of *Angry Beavers.* This allowed me to create the line, ''Well, I wanted to work for *Angry Beavers* but I question their agenda. Fabian Nail Products has some shady investors that smell right wing to me.'' This usually got the desired nod of understanding to the slackers or barflies I was explaining myself to. I was anything but a sellout.

The barfly I happened to be explaining myself to on the night the water bottle scandal erupted (well I guess ''scandal'' might be a tad exaggerated, but this is New York and I am all about image) was not just your average white shirt and khaki accountant that dressed down for a night of fun. This guy told me he had perhaps one of the coolest jobs in the city—he was an A&R guy, or at least reported directly to one. He alluded to a lot of things as he plied me with vodka collins (my drink of choice; I had switched from gin and tonics three months ago—too college).

I noticed, as he was explaining the hype over a new trip-hop artist who only pretended to be British, that he had chest hair curling out from his black T-shirt. I found it strangely attractive, a sign that I was indeed maturing. His name was Zeke and we were just beginning to do the drunken lean-in when Tabitha, whose place I was crashing at, staggered over to us and slurred her desire to leave. It was with great reluctance that I agreed.

I knew it would be uncool to do any kind of deed with him so early in our relationship (listen to me naming our children) but I must admit my plan to take over the city wasn't quite going as expected. This might be largely in part to my lack of a power partner. I needed the kind of man who could help me, support me, be my date to all the too urban charity functions and who secretly aspired to be a filmmaker. I wanted a guy I could feel comfortable referring to in my essay in a trendy online magazine. A guy who, like me, was on the verge.

My head was spinning in the back of the cab. Tabitha was slumped over on my shoulder snoring softly (alliterations are my forte). I wondered if I would have to carry her up the six flights of stairs to her apartment. Maybe she'd do a nap by the toilet and I could snag the bed. I shirked any pleasantries with Yaleek, our driver, who was competently zipping along, and thought of Zeke's promises. He had said we should go out sometime for sushi, sake and cannoli. I knew it was wrong, but I didn't dare hide my delight. This was the life I wanted to be living. Who knew that this midtown watering hole could prove to be so fruitful? In a daring temptress of a move I had taken his number and not offered mine. I was golden, this was the start of it. I was taking Tabitha's bed. There was no stopping me. I was going to be running the magazine soon enough.

September

What you really want to know is what happened with Zeke. Well, so does Tabitha. Although I only met him on Thursday and spent all weekend with her partying, recovering and watching *Valley of the Dolls,* she wants to know if I disobeyed her dating mandates.

"Tab, what was the last thing you said to me on my way home yesterday?"

"First off, I'm Tabitha, not Tab. I'm neither calorie conscious nor from the eighties." She loves that line. "Secondly, I know what I told you, but who knows, once you crossed state lines the Jersey girl in you may have come out and disobeyed." Aggh, as always, the Bridge and Tunnel stigma rears its ugly head. If only I lived in Manhattan, I could squelch it once and for all.

"You said wait three days. I'm waiting more than three days. Above and beyond what is required. Although, I know he's beyond those boyish games."

"Why, because he wasn't an ex frat boy? You don't even know that. He just impressed you by knowing what chopsticks were. The fact that you took his number means he probably thinks you are a feminist, which you are, but as far as he's concerned that means you like weird sex. The moment you call he is going to start polishing the cuffs and the dog collar, which is fine if you like that sort of thing, but you know you are strictly a first date missionary style 'take me to a place I've never been before' girl."

"Do you ever take a breath?"

"Don't have the time. Oh, shit!"

"What?"

"The Big C has the Prada suit on. She's going to assert some power today."

"I thought Prada meant she had her period and was retaining water."

"That's the black suit. Don't call me today. And remember, wait till tomorrow to call the musician."

"A&R guy..." I say as she hangs up on me.

Lorraine, my supervisor, is standing by my desk when I hang up. She hates the city, but is always asking me where the hot spots are. If only I was as cool in reality as Lorraine's husband and dogs must think I am. Lorraine gives me data to input in the assignment grid. This is what I am paid eighteen fifty an hour to do. Other people stand over hot grills making French fries for a quarter of what I make. I type names into slots of stories that are being published over the next few months. Who is working on the bike of the month, what is the best bike seat, and, for fun, what books have significant cycling scenes in them. (Like any of our readers ever get off their bikes.)

Inputting this data is tearfully boring, and since I have a week until it is supposed to be in the system I put it off as long as possible. I can do it ridiculously quickly and it is my only real responsibility. The Internet only occupies so much of my time. I spend a lot of time staring at my screen saver, which is really just the standard stars that come with Windows. It was left behind from the last temp, whom I'm sure also spent a lot of her time staring at it. I know I could be using this time a lot better. I could be writing. I could be coming up with freelance articles and researching them (I have unlimited phone calls after all), I could be trying to contact other magazines to get a new job. But, for whatever reason, I spend a lot of time just sitting here. But, it's all good— it's New York.

For the past eighteen years, September has meant change. I looked forward to the fall because it meant new clothes, new classes, a new year. There is always that hope from kindergarten to my very last extra semester in college that something new and wonderful was going to happen. That anything bad that had happened in the past year was going to be magically wiped from the slate.

I've been working since February, when I finally graduated and moved home. Despite a couple of storms, it was a mild winter. Mild enough to keep me deluded into thinking that maybe this was all some big summer vacation that was eventually going to end in either another leg of my academic career or fame and fortune. There is no way this, the tedium that is my life as an assistant, could be (gulp!) my life.

As we reach the middle of September and I am still doing this nine-to-five rat race thing, there is no denying it—this is it. I couldn't ignore the fall fashions and back to school sales. My sister, Monica, the perpetual student, returned to Massachusetts for her third master's degree, this time in Women's Studies. No doubt about it, I'm stuck here for a while, but I intend to work it.

The fact is I love New York. The image. The way my friends from school are envious of me only because I work for Prescott Nelson. The people I meet around my parents' house (someday I *will* have my own place) are always sort of shocked that I commute to the big city. Granted, they're from New Jersey—they're impressed by garage door openers.

When I forget about all the good stuff, the thing that bugs me is the absolute stagnancy of the routine I've fallen into. The fringe benefits are cool, but each week means more of the same. No one else on the crowded elevators really seem to have these thoughts. I suppose it's cool enough for them to be a part of this great publishing empire, even if they are just nothings. They, like my friends from school or the people in my hometown, are impressed by the name and the possibility of something that no one can quite identify.

But I try not to think about it that way.

One of my greatest sources of relief is Tabitha. She is one of the few friends I have at work. Best of all, she lives in the city and knows everything about what's cool and what's not. Tabitha and I met in the temp pool, on our very first day. I arrived, ready to start my career, ready for that lucky break. I was wearing what I like to call my Jackie-O suit; retro yet respectable.

Tabitha is a big girl from Texas. I know that oversimplifies her, and she would hate to be referred to that way. Robust, Rubenesque, statuesque—striking, these are the words Tabitha would use. Tabitha isn't fat, well, maybe she is, but only by Calvin Klein standards. But it doesn't seem to stop her and she has no intention of changing.

I find all kinds of men are attracted to Tabitha, despite her size. She mostly dates foreigners: Italian businessmen, Argentinean soccer players, and I think there was even Kuwaiti royalty. Foreigners are instantly drawn to her. She says they're safe to date because "if they're here, they can afford me."

Everything about Tabitha is image. I have watched her spend a fortune on clothes. I have yet to figure out how she does it, she pays New York City rent and makes the same amount as I do.

"I just know what to prioritize." She always says this at the occasional times when I can't afford to go shopping with her. She always dodges the issue of finance. I wonder if she's got a trust fund? Since she hates to shop alone, she usually tries to bribe me into going with the promise of presents. If I don't go, she's liable to buy anything she finds in my size that she thinks is cute. Tabitha is generous, but I think it's more about the way she wants her friends to look. She wants to run in stylish circles, so everyone around her must be stylish. (Sadly, I don't think I've ever lived up to the promise of my Jackie-O suit.)

The best part about Tabitha is the perks that come with her job. A lot of the fringies that enable our image making are courtesy of Tabitha's job. The glamour gods were smiling down on her when she got her temp assignment. She is assistant to the editor-in-chief of, if you can believe it, *NY By Night.* Yes, we own that, too. That "we" being Prescott Nelson Inc. Uncle Pres, the founder of our great company, has got his hand in everything. *NY By Night* covers all the N.Y. happenings: film premieres, gallery openings, club life, celeb birthdays, charity functions, and the random publicity events that only people in the "biz" go to so that they can photograph, write and read about how much fun everyone is having being that much hipper then the rest of the population.

Tabitha's boss is Diana Milana. Tabitha likes to call Diana the Big C (and you can imagine what the C stands for). The Big C is very well known in this industry. She told Tabitha, the first day she started, "I like to get things done." But due to the Big C's hectic schedule she has very little time to attend all the events she is supposed to as the head of the "pulse of the heart that never sleeps" or whatever *NY By Night*'s slogan is. So, when the Big C can't get one of her equally pressed employees to attend these events, guess who winds up with several engagements in one evening? Sometimes, we travel for an entire night, staying for exactly an hour and fifteen minutes at each event. (Well, that happened twice.) Tabitha gets to expense all the cab receipts, and on nights when she meets the right immigrant, she sends me home in a company car. Thanks, Uncle Pres!

I would give anything for a job like Tabitha's, but at least I still get to experience the perks. I don't know how I would survive my parents' house in Jersey without it. There are weekends when I basically live with Tabitha in her box of an apartment starting on Thursday. We usually get our nails done on Thursday at lunch to prepare for a night of craziness and bouncer schmoozing. We can barely function through Friday, catching a quick nap before we go out again. Then, everything becomes a blur up until Tabitha is sipping strong coffee and reading me the Styles section of the *New York Times* on Sunday afternoons. If we're lucky, we make a brunch and have some hair of the dog that bit us. I stumble back to New Jersey and catch *60 Minutes* with the 'rents and wonder how come it always seems like Sunday night and how I am going to get through the next four days.

Monday is a great day to make excuses. I could screw everything up on Monday and shrug it off with a "Monday Morning." No one notices anything on Monday.

On this Monday, at least, I have another distraction—the napkin Zeke wrote his name and numbers on. He wrote Zeke in big bold letters, your standard male handwriting, slightly wobbly from alcohol intake, and then the numbers. The most interesting thing about the napkin is the way his sevens are crossed. My Italian grandmother used to cross her sevens like this. How Euro. I have the urge to call him tonight, but how desperate would that seem? On the other hand, would he be annoyed that I am playing the phone waiting game with him? I'm certain he is above those things, but alas, I cannot be.

But Tuesday, I have an actual dilemma: which number to call and when? If I call him at work, he may be busy promoting some amazing new artist and have to go abruptly, which will sour the whole experience. I also may not have a chance to give him my number, which will mean I have to gauge whether or not he was really busy or if he finds me physically repulsive and whether or not to call him back.

If I call him at home, I will get his answering machine. He might wonder why I'm calling him at home when it's a weekday.

If I beep him, he might not recognize the foreign number and not call, forcing me to beep him again or call another of his numbers, which ruins everything, because again I seem desperate. Or, he might call every number he sees on his beeper because it could be a business beeper, in which case, I'm sort of forcing him to call me, which I don't want to do.

But I definitely don't want to talk to him, so I have to call a number where I think I'll get a voice mail. I can try calling him during lunch—but what if he is too busy to take lunch and answers the phone? Of course, I could always hang up if someone answers, *but* what if he has caller ID and he calls me back and I have to answer and he thinks I'm in junior high? I think about calling Tabitha, but I would no doubt slip from adolescent to pre-pubescent levels.

Okay, I'll call him at home. Now, what to say? I drop my voice an octave. (God, I wish I smoked and drank a fifth of vodka a day to get a sexy Kim Carnes voice. How can I project sexiness when I sound like your average unattached twenty something?)

Possible messages: "Hey, Zeke, it's Eve, I have an urge for sushi and I was wondering if the offer still stands." But, what if he doesn't remember our supposed date? Does that sound sexual? Might he think I'm comparing his penis to raw fish?

Or: "Zeke, it's Eve. I've been thinking about your chest hair, if you've been thinking about my chest, give me a call." Maybe that's a little much and besides, I want to be loved for my mind.

Or: "Zeke, Eve. We met on Thursday. Here's my number. Give me a call." The Thursday might sound too interested, like I've been thinking too much about that night in the bar. Like I've been x-ing off the days in my Filofax.

Or: "Hi, Zeke. It's Eve. We met this weekend. Please give me a call." Please? How bad is that? I might as well say, "My life depends on you calling. I haven't been on a date in three months, let alone had sex, and I'm about to put out a personal ad under Anything Goes in the *Voice* just to have some human contact."

Or: "Hey, Zeke, it's Eve, from this weekend. Just calling to see how your weekend was. Call me when you get a chance." Reasonably neutral. I write it down and dial. It rings three times and then the wretched voice mail…with a *female* voice. *Hey, Heather and Zeke aren't here right now, but our answering machine is.* Beep.

I hang up. He lives with someone. How could he? Who is this Heather—and what kind of name is Heather?

"An overused one," says Tabitha when I join her on a smoke break.

"All those promises, I was already practicing eating seductively with chopsticks."

"Well," says Tabitha, exhaling, "it might just be his roommate, a platonic friend."

"C'mon 'our answering machine' implies togetherness. Items owned together is surely not a sign of platonia."

"Platonia? Whatever. If they were together, he'd probably leave the message."

"I told you he wasn't like that. He was different, special. Now, he's gone."

"Tragic, really. Look, Eve, just call him at work. It will come up. Don't mention the home phone call and pray he doesn't have Caller ID." She stubs out her cigarette and we start to walk in. "But whatever you do, give him your work number. You don't want to specify area codes. You don't want him to know you're from Jersey.''

I wait another day, and finally I dial the number quickly before I can stop myself. *Voice mail, voice mail, voice mail,* my mantra.

"This is Zeke." Shit.

"Zeke?"

"Yes."

"Hi, it's me, it's Eve, from this weekend."

"Oh, Eve. Hi, Eve. I was hoping you would call." (Hoping? Did he actually hope? The cockles of my heart are warm, my stomach is turning, other parts are reveling in the possibility of finally getting some attention.)

"Well, I meant to call yesterday, but I had a hectic day. You know how it is." I can hear Tabitha applauding me. My weekend was obviously too intense and already full, my job is taxing and challenging.

"Yeah, of course, this is one time I'm actually at my desk." Inferiority alert! His job is actually taxing and challenging. "All weekend I had to check out these horrible new acts and get schmoozed by their wanna-be managers, who are totally clueless types from Long Island or Jersey or something."

"Ick."

"Exactly," he laughs. A nice laugh, a warm, masculine laugh. Heather has to be his sister. When Zeke and I are each established in our careers and ready to make the plunge, I will make her a bridesmaid. "So, Eve, are we going to go out together or what?"

"Sure. I would love to."

"How about tomorrow?" Tomorrow? Probably too short notice, but before I can put him on hold to consult Tabitha, his other line beeps so I agree and he says he'll call me with details.

I arrive at the restaurant five minutes late. I am perfumed, I am blow-dried, I am waxed in all the right places. ("Just to be safe. Don't let it make you a slut," admonished Tabitha.)

The place is exactly what I envisioned—a trendy little East Village spot full of beautiful people. I'm trying not to be impressed but wait a minute, he isn't at the bar. Curses! If he gets here later than me, he'll think I got here early. Maybe he is sitting already. I ask the beautiful woman in the kimono if there is another room and she gestures toward the back into a traditional Japanese dining room where shoes are not allowed. Thank God I let them grate off the dead skin at the pedicure.

He waves me over from one of the low tables. His shirt brings out the green flecks in his eyes. There is an awkward moment as I slip my shoes off before entering the room.

"Hey," I say, kneeling at the table.

"You look beautiful." Wow! Am I going to blush?

"Well, thanks, you're not so bad yourself." He reaches across the table and touches my chin. I hadn't expected the physical contact so soon, but I lean into it.

"I ordered for us, the first round, at least. Then, we'll see what you want."

"Great." He pours me some sake. I drink it, it's very warming. I pour some more. He smiles.

"I have a very high tolerance," I say.

"Is that right?"

"Yeah, I was never very popular at frat parties." He has a disconcerting habit of just staring at me smiling. I gulp some more sake. "What?"

"You are just breathtaking."

"You're embarrassing me, really. So tell me about your job."

He starts to talk about the people his company represents and although he doesn't tell a lot of stories that involve him, it's interesting enough to entertain me. He gets a lot of CD promos and has two thousand CDs.

"I have a thirty-disk changer. It puts me to sleep."

"Oh, is it just you in your apartment?"

"No, I have a roommate. A friend's ex-girlfriend. What a bitch." I have this aversion to hearing a man call a woman a "bitch." It's overused and I think very distasteful. Zeke seemed like a sensitive enough guy in my alcohol-affected impression, so I am about to give him my views on this in a nonthreatening manner, but the sushi arrives. It's lovely and multicolored. I love sushi. Zeke pours us more sake and presses his hands together, pleased with his selection. There really isn't anything sexier than a man who knows how to order.

"You start." I get to it.

"So, Zeke, where are you from?" He chuckles a little.

"Well, I've basically lived all over California, Maryland... I live way over on West 12th." That's sort of hip, but, I bet he's lying about where he's from, I bet he's from Long Island. As long as he doesn't turn it around. "Where do you live? Where are you from? Tell me everything, Eve."

"Oh, I'm crashing with a friend who lives on the Upper East Side. I know, awful. We're looking for another apartment." Time to deflect, I will not admit to living in Jersey. "Good thing you got two of everything. I love yellowtail."

We eat for a while and I always feel less awkward when I'm stuffing my face. I am so into eating that I don't realize he is staring at me again. I set my chopsticks down and wipe my mouth.

"Don't stop. It's nothing. I just like to watch you eat. It's very erotic."

"Maybe you should just concentrate on your dinner."

"That would be like masturbation." I practically spit my sake onto the remaining sushi. I cough. I might be choking, the waitress brings water and Zeke reaches over to thump me on the back. I regain my composure and take a deep breath. Is he for real?

"I didn't mean to offend you. Really. I'm sorry. I can't help who I am. I'm a very sexual person and I'm enjoying this very much. I want you to relax."

"Oh, I'm relaxed." The sake pitcher is empty. I nod for more, "Completely."

When Zeke isn't cataloging my every chew, he does a lot of talking about himself. Well, he does a lot of hinting about himself, he hints at things. A possible summer home, an expensive college education, a book he might want to write, friends who work in independent film. It sounds too good to be true. And also, (try not to wince) he has a tendency to refer to himself in the third person. Example: "Zeke thinks that every woman should be up on a pedestal." Believe me I'm sparing you the really bad dialogue.

For whatever reason, I agree to go to Veniero's with Zeke. By this point the sake is making me really loopy. We get shots of grappa "to help us digest." I stop him before he can force me to lick the cannoli cream off his fingers.

"You know the thing is, Eve, a woman's pleasure is more important to me than my own. Her pleasure," he says, interlacing his fingers, "is worth more than her pain."

"Well, Zeke, that's a very admirable ideology."

"Do you really think so, Eve?" I can tell he's really pleased with himself. "It's been a long time since I've indulged in satisfying my senses so completely. I'm having such a great time. I feel like growling. I feel so basic, like an animal." He runs his fingers through my hair and growls. Yes! He actually growls! The old Italian men at the table next to us look over. Maybe they'll rescue me. Does this actually work? Am I having a drunken hallucination? Is he really saying this?

"Let's talk more about you, Eve. What are the things you like? I want to know you."

"Oh, boy, Zeke. You know, I'm pretty complex, it might take a while."

"I've got all night. We've got all night." I need to get out of here. I want my own bed. I wish I had a car voucher.

"Maybe we can save that for next time, I'm burnt, all the excitement and, you know, I have a big day at work tomorrow. Deadlines and such. The crazy world of magazine publishing." I can't believe I got a bikini wax for this.

"Oh, Eve, sure, well, let me hail you a cab." Luckily, there is a cab right there and I'm hoping to expedite this awful goodbye.

"What an extraordinary night. We'll have to do this again." I offer him my hand, but then he is passionately kissing me against the cab and it's not a bad kiss.

Now, maybe it was the sake or the way he's rotating his pelvis into mine in the middle of East Eleventh Street, but I'm not exactly proud of what happens next.

"Well?" asks Tabitha first thing in the morning over the phone. I am so hungover. The freshly squeezed six-dollar orange juice and toast isn't doing a thing for my head.

"Well, let's just say it's a good thing the Gap is open at nine."

"Oh, how scandalous and low down! Was it great? How big?"

"No, awful, well, not awful in the satisfying of mutual desires way, but awful in the how desperate I am and what lengths I will go to merely get laid."

"So tell me everything—actually skip the sushi and start with the sex." Sometimes Tabitha's alliterations are on par with my own. I make a mental note.

"Well, made out the entire cab ride back to his place. The driver's name was Numbi, very discreet, I would have liked to speak to him, but—"

"Eve. Please."

"So we got back to his place—"

"Where?"

"Meat-packing district/West Village, pretty cool apartment. Roommate who he lovingly calls a 'bitch' away on business."

"Convenient. Are there two bedrooms?"

"Yes. That was the first thing I checked."

"Thatta girl. So then he took off your clothes?"

"No, then I had to pee. All the sake. Anyway, I do my thing."

"Some stuff can be spared."

"Right, and when I come out the lights are dim and he's got what I assume is the thirty-disk changer going with some R&B 'make love to your woman' music and he's lying on the couch in his Calvin Klein briefs, well, you know the boxer brief things, and Mr. Pokey is struggling to get free."

"Wow! The bod?"

"Well, let's just say he should have gotten the wax."

"No!" She practically shrieks into the phone. "How bad?"

"Shoulder hair."

"Mother of God." She is really excited now. "You are lying!"

"This is a story I could not make up, and you should take it down a notch before the Big C talks to you about volume control."

"Shit, you're right. She just scowled at me—doesn't do much for her crow's feet. I'll call you back in two. Must smooth this over. Don't go away. I gotta hear the rest."

She hangs up on me.

Two minutes turns into three hours and finally I get up to go to the bathroom. I run into the big boss, my boss, on the way back to my desk. Herb Reynolds, the man who handles all the editorial work for the magazine. He has the smug look of a man who has never had to work too hard for anything. A man who believes in the integrity of his writing and honestly believes his "work" (that is, detailing his struggles to find independence on the open road, just a man and his bike, the importance of physical activity for the American Spirit, et cetera) is somehow furthering American journalism. I find Herb a tad ridiculous and intimidating at the same time, but he's a good contact to have.

If I even entertain the idea of him publishing my reformed biker doctor story (it sounds like a B-movie, doesn't it?) or anything else, I'll have to kiss his ass more than I do already. I am supposed to be his assistant, but he has a corner office on the other end of the floor. Our phones aren't even connected. My only true contact with him is when I make his travel plans or when I need to get someone's expense report signed.

"Hello, Eve," he says with his usual pompous smile. "I was meaning to stop by."

"You were?" Did someone finally tell him that he has an amazingly gifted writer whose talents are being virtually wasted in a thankless position? Finally, on the verge of my big break. A testament that a little sex puts the world in a whole new perspective.

"Yes, can you check my schedule and put together a meeting with Lacey Matthews?" He gives me her card.

"Oh," I say, "and what is this about?"

"She's a freelance writer. We're going to see about her doing some work for us. Appeal to the lost female demographic." (Well, it is called *Bicycle Boy,* after all.)

"Great," I say as I consider ripping up her card. "I'll call today."

"Yes, when you have some downtime." As if my job isn't defined by downtime.

"Okay, great."

Great is how I usually answer all requests. A hypothetical:

Person of dubious authority: "Eve, why don't you count all of the paper clips in the entire department and then divide them into seven equal piles."

Me: "Great. I'll get right on it. That'll be great."

Sometimes, when I feel I'm being especially artificially cheery I run into the bathroom, stare into the mirror and alternate between smiling my fakest most "entry level" smile and making my face as ugly as it can possibly get. I rival anyone in the ugly face department. I have lots of ways to make myself look absolutely monstrous. You probably think that's really weird and freakish, but believe me, it makes me feel a lot better about being so low on the corporate/creative food chain.

When I get back to my desk, my red light is blinking; a message from Tabitha. She is annoyed that I wasn't there and insists we go to The Nook, our company cafeteria, so she can hear the rest of the story. I call her back and we plan to meet in twenty.

Of course she's late. I have to wait at the designated meeting spot, just outside The Nook and fend off the advances of the lecherous security guard. He likes Tabitha better, but today my less womanly body will do. As he asks me if my husband (I made one up) knows how to make love to me, he gets a call on his impressive walkie-talkie. He scans the area and assures the other concerned party that it's all clear out here.

"Except you of course," he smiles, flashing his ugly teeth at me.

"Yeah, I'm a real danger." I study my Employee ID intently, hoping he will stop talking to me.

"The big guy's coming out."

"The big guy?" Is he being dirty?

"You know," he points up to the sky. Is the second coming happening here in The Nook? Then it clicks, it's even better. Tabitha is going to be so jealous. Sure enough, within seconds, none

other than *The* Prescott Nelson turns the corner with an assistant
and a few beefy bodyguards. He is limping, which everyone knows
is from the time, as a young man, he bravely saved three people
in a mountain climbing expedition gone wrong. Other than that,
he looks quite spry for a man over seventy.

Then, something amazing happens. It is so amazing it almost
happens in slow motion. Our eyes meet and I smile and he smiles
back and walks by and gets on his elevator up to the top floor.
Almost immediately after his elevator door closes, Tabitha gets off
an elevator coming down. I try to compose myself to protect her,
but I can't.

"Wow," says Tabitha, "you're really glowing from it."

"It wasn't that," I say, "it was him."

"Who?" I put my hand on her shoulder. She is going to take
this really hard.

"Him." I point up.

"Him?" She's confused, but then realizes. I know because her
lip starts to quiver.

Tabitha is on the verge of hysterics all throughout our tortellini
salads. Apparently the real travesty is that she wore her Hermes
scarf today and the great Prescott never got to see it. She keeps
asking me the same questions.

"Are you sure he was smiling at you?"

"Our eyes met. If he was thirty years younger it could have
been magical. Scratch that, it was magical anyway."

"You know, it's her fault, don't you?"

"Is it?" I ask, knowing that the Big C is indeed the root of all
evil.

"Yes, she had me printing out all this stuff for her 'supposed'
power lunch. Now, it's common knowledge that unless it's on my
SchedulePlus, it ain't happening. I suspect an afternoon tryst at
the Marriot. It's DKNY today, a dead giveaway. But she has to
have these documents and she keeps making changes and what
the fuck? Is she going to read them while her whoever is going
down on her?"

"Well, that's probably how she got so far."

"Anyway, I'm just happy for you, Eve, even though you aren't
as big a fan as I am and it's hard for me to be so charitable."

"Tabitha, you're doing an admirable job."

"Thank you." She is quiet for a while. I wonder if she's going
to be okay about this. I really want to tell her the rest of my story,

it's so rare that I have something juicy to tell her. This and the Prescott thing are almost too much. When it rains it pours.

"So about the primate..." Now, that's the Tabitha we love.

"Yes," I say, leaning closer, it's not exactly lunch room gossip. "Where was I?"

"The sex music on, he's half naked and hairy." She really does listen. I take a dramatic sip of my iced tea.

"Right, so I am sort of wobbling in, because, let's face it, I've had too much sake and I know it. 'Hi,' I say, because I'm kind of surprised, you know, and it's not too often you walk into a room and find a half-naked hairy guy."

"Of course not," Tabitha says, understanding, "but it's dark?"

"Well, the lights are dim, so I stand there like an idiot, the room is sort of spinning, you know, and, Tab, I'm kind of in the mood, despite the hair, the body's pretty good and he does know how to order sushi." She nods, not minding the "Tab" because she is so intrigued.

"'Do you want to sit down?' He's all Barry White like or maybe it's the R&B, so I go over to the couch and sit on this little edge by his feet, he puts one in my lap and starts, well, touching me with it." Tabitha looks slightly disturbed. "It was actually kind of nice. So I close my eyes to try to make everything stand still and next thing you know we sort of wind up on the floor. Hardwood."

"Nice, but, uncomfortable."

"Exactly. He pulls a blanket off the couch and puts it under me."

"Very thoughtful."

"So we're kissing and he's not a bad kisser. Except, I think he might have been kissing me to the rhythm of the music, although, all my impressions could be blamed on the sake—"

"Even the hair?"

"No, that was very—real. Next thing you know, some of my clothes are off—"

"Of course you had the decency to get your unsightly hairs removed."

"Right. And the condom comes out—"

"Where does it come from?"

"Well, unfortunately it's in another room."

"At least he wasn't too prepared."

"Right, but I'm hoping that I don't pass out while I'm waiting— I'm pretty drunk."

"I can imagine."

"Right. So he gets back and you know we continued from where we were—"

"How's the hair playing into all this?"

"Not bad, it's actually sort of something to hold on to."

"In the absence of a headboard or say, a car seat."

"Right. Well, sort of. And I must say, he's a great kisser, great with his hands, not shy about the things that matter." We smile and nod at each other knowingly.

"And the act?"

"Not exactly memorable."

"Ick."

"Exactly, and I'm kind of surprised when he's done."

"Because you're not, um, satisfied?"

"Precisely. So he looks at me and says 'That was beautiful.'"

"He did not?"

"He did. You have to understand, he's been saying stuff like this all night."

"Mother of God."

"So I realize that means he's done, and in spite of myself I say, 'Oh'."

"Just like that?" She giggles.

"Yes, and I feel sort of bad because even in the dark, I can see he's crushed, but you know, we've come so far and all, it seems a shame not to actually get it right."

"Of course, you were hoping to go on the journey with him."

"Right. So, I tell him what he can do and he does it and he does it well, and it works and we conk out on the floor and it's a little awkward in the morning, but not too bad because he had to rush out, because he was late and we were both sort of rushing around and I couldn't find my bra. But, it was fine."

"Did you kiss goodbye?"

"Um." I have to think about this one. "I think so, probably just on the cheek, it was all so rushed."

"How did you leave things?"

"Give me a call."

"Do you want him to call?"

"I'm not sure."

After giving it a lot of thought, I decide I don't want him to call. I mean, I don't need a dead-end relationship right now. At least I got my fix. It had been a long drought, but I just don't know if I could stand to listen to him refer to himself all the time

and watch me eat. Every time the phone rings, I take a moment
to prepare my Zeke speech, but it's never him.

"Eve Vitali." I answer my phone a week later. This time it's
Roseanne, one of my best friends from college.

"Hey, Eve. What's going on?"

"Not too much. Just hanging out. Dodging phone calls from
some guy." Roseanne will appreciate this, as she is known for
having sketchy encounters with what I like to think is a lower-
caliber guy. I give her the details.

"Oh, my God." She is laughing over the hairy shoulders. "But
at least he's got a cool job. I've been meeting a bunch of conve-
nience store workers up here." Roseanne lives just outside of Hartford. She got a job in some random finance department right out
of school. She's been there for a year. She finished school in four
years.

"So how's work, Ro?"

"Well, it's kind of boring."

"What? Finance? I can't believe it."

"No, I've been giving some thought to what we talked about."

"Oh," I say, trying to remember. Roseanne has an even better
tolerance than I have. She's Irish. "What do you mean?"

"You know, about living together. Remember?"

"Well, I don't really want to move to Hartford."

"No, kookhead—" a classic Ro term of endearment "—I'm
moving to New York."

"Really? Do you have a job?"

"No, but I'm a woman in finance. I'll get a job. Besides, I've
got savings."

"Rent is pretty expensive." I'm not sure why I'm not thrilled
about this. I don't know why I'm being held to a drunk promise
I can't even remember. I love Ro, really I do, but she's from some
cheesy town in Connecticut and besides, finance.

"I know that I'm prepared, besides, aren't you dying to move
out? Isn't this what you want?" She makes a good point, it is time
to move out of Victor and Janet's house.

"When were you thinking of moving down?"

"Two weeks." I swallow my iced cappuccino. "I can look for
a job and an apartment at the same time. We can move in by
November first." It's almost October.

"It might take a while to get something."

"C'mon, didn't you tell me that night that it's all about being
ready to just jump off the cliff and decide that you're ready on

the way down?'' Did I say that? ''Well, I'm ready. I want to go
to movie premieres, hobnob with celebrities, make the big bucks.''

''Ro, I think you need to be realistic.''

''Yeah, yeah, I know. I will be, but if I don't do this now, I
may never do it and I want to. It's good for you, too, it'll light a
fire under your tail.'' My tail? How can Roseanne expect to move
to New York when she can't even say the word ass?

''Well, okay.''

''So do you think I can stay with you for a couple of weeks?''

With that, it's basically settled. Roseanne has made up her mind.
She is moving down and I am moving out. I suppose I should see
this as a good thing. Roseanne can be a lot of fun. She likes to
party hard. While her taste in men can be a little, shall we say,
juvenile, she's a good person.

There would be definite advantages to moving out. Commuting
was taking a lot out of me. Once I move to the city, everything
will be different. As it is, I spend an hour on New Jersey Transit.
I live in Oradell, quaint but sickeningly suburban. My parents have
a four-bedroom, two-and-a-half bathroom house and three-car garage. My father owns a plumbing business and my mom is a part-
time travel agent.

I wish I could hate my parents, but they aren't all that bad. I
mean they seem perfectly contented with their suburban life. Although my mom gets great deals on airfares all over the world,
they usually take their vacations to Florida. Their biggest concern
about my job is that I don't get benefits. I wish I had a worse
childhood, sometimes, I think my childhood was too average to
ever have the type of life I would want. Plus, I'm from Jersey.
The stigma is unbelievably harsh. When I move into the city I will
never again admit my roots. I will be rootless. Rootless is cooler.

''How was work today?'' My mother asks me this every day
during dinner as she passes over whatever vegetable we're having.
One thing about my mother, she insists we eat together. Mom
basically holds the family together with her chatter.

''It was okay.'' Living at home after college is a lot like being
in high school. Every day your parents think that some tiny item
of your day will catapult them back to the happier days of their
youth. What they don't understand is that the actual events I could
possibly share with them (which excludes drinking, boys and general debauchery) have become as mundane as theirs. It's tough.

After dinner, I sit in the family room and watch my dad flip through the stations for a while. My mother asks me for help with the Bergen Record Crossword. It's times like this when I know I need an apartment in the city. I finally go to bed when Leno comes on, but I can't fall asleep. I guess what is concerning me is that I will lock myself into a situation with Ro and there will be no way out. I think I have a fear of commitment. In college, it took me a long time to declare journalism my major. I had to keep taking intro business classes to keep my parents happy. I skipped most of them and got passing grades, until it seemed to be apparent that I wasn't going to be a stockbroker.

Another issue is that now my life was going to be scrutinized by the likes of Roseanne. What if it just didn't measure up? Did I care about her reporting to the crew from college about my New York life? Of course, a finance job couldn't possibly live up to the excitement that was my high-powered publishing job. Ridiculous as I knew it was, I could always manage to impress people with working for Prescott Nelson Inc.

The biggest thing would be breaking the news to Tabitha. She was weird about new people and I'm not sure what I had told her about Roseanne. I sometimes have a tendency to exaggerate stories when I think the parties involved will never meet. I'm sure I had done that with Roseanne. If they hung out would their impressions of each other in any way affect their impressions of me? But, I was getting ahead of myself. I probably never mentioned Roseanne, except in passing.

"You mean the one who gave the guy a blow job in the bathroom of some dive?" Even over the blaring ambient music, she's a little loud. I've waited a week to tell her. We are at a party for some female poet who just published a book. An old friend of the Big C's. I break the news to her after we are both nicely toasted. Some obnoxious looking guy smirks at Tab at the reference to oral sex. She glares at him. "What? Is that a term you've never heard? Anyway, is this Rhoda girl gonna really come down?"

"Roseanne. I forgot I told you that story. I think you'll love her. She's lots of fun." Tabitha seems unconvinced, she puts some truffle pate on her plate. "Is the Big C coming?"

"Probably for about ten minutes. I know she's got her yoga class and then she is getting her eyebrows shaped. She rolled her eyes when she got the invite. This food is awful."

"She has always yearned for the bohemian lifestyle of a poet."

"Yeah, I think it's just the word poet that the Big C likes. I think this one's sort of an academic flake." She looks over at the

guest of honor, who already seems a bit drunk. She is surrounded
by a group of people who are trying very hard to look sincerely
fascinated as she describes her plans for a book tour. "She really
should have worn a bra with those droopy boobies. The Big C
will be validated."

"Well, that's a relief. Let's get another drink." The bartender,
Luis, is a really cute Spaniard who makes me a Kettel One gimlet.
He likes Tabitha, so it's pretty stiff.

"So," says Tabitha, eyeing our new friend as she speaks.
"What does Ronda do? Finance, right? Fascinating," says Tabitha, just as the annoying guy squirms his way over to me. I feel
him standing a little too close. I don't even have time to give
Tabitha the red flag when she's all over it. She glares at this poor
sod.

"Excuse me. Do you think she would ever want to talk to you?"
I look at the guy sympathetically, he really is no match for her.
"Okay, then."

He cowers away, cursing under his breath. Luis is impressed by
Tabitha, although he can't really understand the harshness of her
words. She smiles at him. They begin to talk, well, shout over the
music. The best part is the broken English and sign language that
goes along with their communication. I can see Tabitha mouthing
the word "fabulous." When he has to make someone else a drink,
Tabitha bombards me with questions about where "Rowena" and
I are going to live.

"I'm not sure."

"Maybe you should live on Wall Street." She never takes her
eyes of Luis.

"Tabitha, stop being so testy and go play conquistador with
your new friend."

"He's busy, serving."

"Well, I guess he better get used to it." She glares at me.

"This is the thanks I get?"

"What, for saving me from the evil swine? You know you
enjoyed that more than anyone. C'mon, if you're good I'll go make
the excuses for the Big C's absence for you."

"Well, I guess she really isn't coming. It is two-thirty. She has
an eight o'clock breakfast. She's certainly not the spring chicken
she used to be. It probably looks better for her not to show up.
What a great image she cultivates." Deep down Tabitha admires
the Big C.

"But, she's not as good a friend as you are."

"All this flattery! I assume you want a car voucher?"

"Well, I'd hoped to stay with you, but I forgot Thursday is Matador Night."

"Brilliant. Let's do some kind of crazy Spanish shot and then you can put your spin on my dear employer's absence. I guess this means no Krispy Kreme tonight."

"Well, I'm sure you can get some special sweet treat." We motion to Luis who gives us a double shot that looks a lot like a lemon drop. We clink our glasses and swallow down the tasty goodness.

"Tabitha," I say, swaying a little. "We will always go dancing."

"We rarely go dancing now."

"Well, you know like from that movie about the people in Seattle when she meets the guy from Spain and thinks she's going to marry him."

"Whatever." She looks around at the thinned-out crowd, the men who have been pretending to drink so they can schmooze, the love connections that have been made for the evening and then the classic Tabitha, "Oh the carnage!"

"Do you want to live with us?" Perhaps, that wasn't the best way to phrase it. Tab would never admit to wanting to live with *us*.

"No."

"Well, at least be happy. It will be fun, a new place to hang out."

"I guess. I'll have to." She hands me the coveted voucher.

"It's true what they say."

"Which is?"

"You are a queen among women." I kiss her cheek.

"Be gone!" She waves me away with a hand. "This party totally thinned out and I need to look ready before our little Latin friend makes other plans. Don't incriminate me with Elizabeth."

"Oh, right, that's her name."

"She uses lowercase, if you can imagine the obnoxiousness of it all."

"I can't. Enjoy." I wave to Luis. He comes over, kisses me and calls me something in Spanish. I call my car, which should be here in fifteen. Enough time for me to pee and make Tabitha's excuses for the Big C. Lucky for me, the poet elizabeth is on line for the bathroom. Two birds with one stone.

"You really shouldn't have to wait on line, you're the guest of honor.'' (Now I know that seems like ass kissing, but I want to think that if anyone ever threw a party for me, I could avoid the whole bathroom line thing.) She laughs.

"I think I might pee on the floor."

"Do you want a glass or something? I have a dance I like to do in these situations."

"I'll try to hold it. Are you an artist, too?"

"Yes,'' I say, "I am a writer. I often freelance for Diana Milana's magazine.'' The great thing about these things is no one will remember specific facts the next day. "I know you two are old friends. She was really hoping to make it tonight, but we've got so much going on."

"Oh, Diana, she's great, isn't she?"

"Oh, yes, great.'' There's that funny word again.

"She must be such a joy to work for."

"She's pretty intense,'' I say, intending to be ambiguous. (It's not easy to gauge if my intentions are actually coming across when I've had all this good vodka.) "What was she like in school?"

"We didn't go to school together. We knew each other through her ex-husband. It's a long story. Diana doesn't have much education. She just worked her way up. Started as an assistant on the lowest level. Some rag magazine. Who knows what she did to get this far.'' Talk about ambiguous.

The bathroom door opens and three people come out. I look at elizabeth and shrug. I extend my hand for her to go in. She puts her hand on my shoulders and puts her face a little too close to mine.

"We could go in together if you want.'' As boozy as elizabeth is, I catch the sparkle in her eyes.

"Gee,'' I say (this is the speech I reserve for women and men wearing tube socks), "I'm awfully flattered, but you know I'm sort of out of that stage. Thanks for asking.'' Lesbian experimentation is so passé.

"Have a great night—'' she smiles up at me "—and be sure to pick up the copy of my book."

On the ride home, I chat with Dwight for a while. He's a sweet old guy whose got no problem with speed. This I like in a driver. Dwight has it together. "The best part is at the end of the day, or the end of the night, it's over, you know,'' he says. "I never take it home with me. No baggage. I get my life.'' Very interesting.

Another nice thing about Dwight is his obvious respect for the city. You know this about a driver by the way they handle the view right when you are about to go into the Lincoln Tunnel. There's a dip right before you go under where you can see the city. At this late hour, the city really is beautiful. Dwight doesn't talk incessantly over that view. He sees me staring at it from the rearview mirror and he seems to enjoy it, too.

"I know how you feel, kid, gets me every time, too. All that life going on." Well said, Mr. Dwight. (Hang on! I'm not getting cheesy just because I crossed over to the Jersey side and I'm not too drunk. You check out a view of the city at 3:30 in the morning with just the right amount of free alcohol floating around in your system and I bet a tear or two trickles down your cheek.) Dwight knows all these shortcuts to get to my doorstep. I bid him farewell and climb up my stairs, trying not to make too much noise.

As I'm passing out, I think, for as long as it takes the room to stop spinning, about all the things people know about each other that they probably shouldn't know. Tabitha knows the select portions of Roseanne with that guy in the bathroom and I know that the Big C doesn't have an education. I wonder how much people know about me. Maybe I don't have too many secrets. Maybe I should cultivate some.

Also, it's reassuring to think that the Big C started out as an assistant and now she's wearing fabulous clothes and skipping the coolest parties, just because she can. I have to remember to tell Tabitha all this stuff. She will love it.

Hungover again. The terrifyingly long ride into the city did not help my throbbing head. As it is, I'm a half hour late for work, but of course, I still get into work before everyone else. Perseverance is the only way to the top. Of course it would be a lot easier to get into work early and catch the proverbial worm if I only lived around the corner. More motivation to start looking for a pad.

First, I send an e-mail to everyone who works for the magazine. This is really against what our internal e-mail is supposed to be used for, but if people can send porno and the Top 10 Reasons Mondays Suck and all those wretched chain letters, I can use the system for myself.

Hi all,
I am going to need to leave the nest pretty soon and I would prefer not to be homeless. If anyone out there knows of the much coveted "available New York apartment" please let me know and save another soul from the streets. Thank you!
—Eve

I get a couple of sympathetic warnings about apartment perils and a few people e me names of their brokers. Marketing Adam e-mails his standard biblical reference.

Eve,
Just stay with me forever in our garden. I promise to put on some clothes.
—Adam

Since paper is old news, (I know, I know I work for a magazine. Shame on me! Whatever.) I check the Net for real estate. Even one-bedroom apartments are at least fifteen hundred plus the broker's fee, which is fifteen percent. I have been the sympathetic shoulder to cry on for enough of these loony health nuts I work with to know a few things about finding apartments. First, I am supposed to locate a neighborhood and stick to it. Second, it helps to have a roommate to split the cost of incidentals. And finally, apartments are a lot cheaper in the outer boroughs. Now, I may have limited funds and I could probably get a palace in Brooklyn or Jersey City for the price of a closet in the city, but, I refuse to continue my stint as a Bridge and Tunnel person.

It's Manhattan or bust.

I find a great apartment, right on University Place in the Village. The ad says perfect for students. Well, we were once students. The student thing implies that it's cheap, but, it's really $1550. It's a converted one bedroom with a big living room. There's an open house tomorrow. The best part is that the ad says it's no fee. I call the number. It doesn't hurt to jump on these things. It rings about eight times before a woman answers.

"Hi. My name is Eve Vitali, I'm a student at NYU and I was calling about the apartment on University Place. I was wondering if I could see the apartment a little early because I have class at that time." Pretty crafty, huh?

"Sorry, honey, the apartment's already taken."

"But, the open house isn't until tomorrow."

"It's amazing. Someone found out about the apartment and came by with three months' rent in cash and offered another six more."

"Wow, so you are definitely going to let them have it?"

"Well, of course, wouldn't you?" No, I would give the apartment to me, because I really deserve the lack of hassle in my search for an apartment.

"I guess. Are there any other apartments available in that building?"

"Well," says the lady who obviously thinks she has better things to do, "you would have to call the management company for that."

She gives me the name of the management company. When I call them they tell me that I will have to send thirty dollars for myself and anyone who I would be living with so they can run a credit check. I also have to go to their offices on the ultra Lower East Side and fill out applications. If everything goes okay, I can get myself on a waiting list and maybe, just maybe, I will be able to afford one of their apartments. I tell the receptionist I will consider it.

The next place I call sounds too good to be true. I don't know why I didn't call there first. It is a two bedroom on Avenue A for $1450, also no fee. I call and it turns out to be one of those places that you have to pay $200 and they fax you this listing every day until you find an apartment. What a disappointment.

Since we at Prescott Nelson are so self-contained, we have some kind of special deal worked out with a real estate agency. It's no great bargain, just a ten percent fee instead of the usual fifteen. When I call, the lovely real estate agent, Judy, doesn't laugh when I tell her what we're willing to spend. She is hopeful that the market may change. In, like, eighteen months. Maybe. I'm screwed.

"Well, Eve, this is New York," says Tabitha, informatively. I am standing outside the dressing room in Lord and Taylor. She hasn't been very helpful at all. She's pretty cranky about the whole thing. It seems she and Luis are having trouble communicating. She's hoping her lingerie purchases will help them understand each other better.

"Tabitha, no shit it's New York, but you'd think I could find an apartment."

"Don't get testy, Eve." Imagine her saying this to me. "People kill for apartments here. Literally. Maybe you should check the obits. How depressing."

"Maybe I should break down and find a real estate agent."

"Okay, so you're gonna get an apartment you can't afford, plus a fifteen percent fee." She holds up a tiny black lace bra. "They make this shit for supermodels. Will you go try to find my size?"

Tabitha is really pissing me off with her attitude. She wants me to fail in my search for an apartment and here I am trying to get her a slut bra. Aren't I always her sympathy blanket? It's a thank-less job. I start searching for Tabitha's size. I even open up those little drawers beneath the hanging bras. The saleswoman hurries to help me.

After an eternity she comes back with the bra in red. Tabitha wanted black, but I take it back toward the dressing rooms. Tabitha is already on line and the cashier is wrapping a pretty large pile of lace. I notice the total is one hundred and twenty dollars.

"Hey—" I hold the red bra out to her "—they just had red, what did you get?"

"Red is too trashy, although it might have the matador and bull affect. No, I'm tired of catering to him." She tosses the bra on the potpourri rack and takes her bag of unidentified goodies.

"So what's that?"

"Just some undies."

"Seems like a lot of undies."

"You know I hate to do laundry. We better get back. Do you want to go to some advertising party Luis is working tonight? I know it sounds mundane, but I want someone to hang out with." We walk along, ignoring the stares and whistles of the construction workers who have taken over Times Square. Tabitha stops to flip one off when he comments about her showing him what's in the bag.

"I've got to cool it on the drinking during school nights and besides, tonight is Operation Leaving the Nest."

"I hope Victor doesn't have a stroke."

"Tabitha, my father's health is nothing to joke about. Besides, it's Janet who has a tendency to overdramatize." Tabitha thinks she's got my parents pegged, but she rejects all invites to see for herself how the other half lives.

"Have you devised your tactics yet?"

"I'm just going to appeal to their sense of reason."

"They're not going to be able to handle it."

"I know, but I've got to try. Have fun at the party."

"Too bad we can't switch places."

"Yeah, like *Freaky Friday*, or all those weird eighties movies." Tabitha nods disinterestedly and gives me a kiss on the cheek.

"Yeah, Eve, exactly like that."

We reach the office, and part to our respective elevator banks.

I have waited to tell my parents about Roseanne's arrival until days before she actually arrives. I know you probably think that's not a fair thing to do, but believe me, my parents work best under pressure. Theirs was a shotgun wedding.

I wait until after dinner. The only notable thing about dinner is the way my mom keeps fussing over me and mentioning how nice it is to have me home, because I'm never home and all that mother guilt babble that mothers love to dish out. They were just getting over my sister Monica being a perpetual student and now, this. I'm debating whether or not to give in to the tears caused by my mom's ambitious attempt at Cajun cooking. Maybe it will work in my favor and they won't be so heartbroken when I break the news. Janet is not the best cook and she's certainly not shy with the spices.

I decide straightforward is the best approach for delivering my news. I've never been a very good actress. I can barely fake an orgasm. (Not that I condone that in any way.)

Mom is just stacking the dishes. She does this with a sense of urgency the moment she senses we're done. She hasn't made a single comment about Dad not finishing his whole piece of blackened chicken. This is a good sign. Dad takes out his first cigarette. His health problems are the real thing. He has only just quit smoking during meals; that is, while he eats. My mother is waiting for me to bring the dishes into the kitchen, so I seize my moment.

"Mom, Dad." That's how they always started stuff like this on *The Brady Bunch.* "Roseanne is going to be coming down for a while. Is it okay if she stays with us?"

"Of course, honey. We love Roseanne. How's her job?" My mom likes Roseanne. She's my mother's example of how much happier someone is when they listen to their mother and finish school in four years—*and* she majored in business.

"Well, Mom—" I'm choosing my words carefully "—she's actually not very happy with it. She'd like to be doing more."

"She's a smart kid," says my father, puffing away.

"Is she coming down for the weekend?" My mom already suspects something.

"Well, she's coming down this weekend. But I thought she might crash here for a while, because she is going to relocate to New York." My parents look at each other. They have some kind of telepathic conversation. When my mom turns to look at me she is speaking for both of them. It's amazing how they do that.

"Honey, we are very happy for you that your friend wants to move down. We know you miss college a lot and you're a little lonely." Are they talking about me? Do they have any idea what they're saying? "But, you know, we are not a hostel. We had our share of that with Monica."

When my sister got her first masters—in philosophy—she decided that she and seven of her closest friends were going to practice communal living out of my parents' basement. It lasted two weeks, until one of her friends declared, after my mom made them French toast with store-bought syrup, that she couldn't live "like a pauper" anymore. She ran hysterical from the house and had her family's chauffeur pick her up at a 7-Eleven. He drove down from Connecticut. All those ideals shot away by the lack of Vermont maple syrup. It gave Monica something to think about.

"Mom." I feel myself starting to get excited and I am not going to succumb, especially since I haven't gotten anywhere near dropping the real bomb, yet. "Okay, Mom, you know Roseanne isn't like any of Monica's pseudo-intellectual, pseudo-hippie friends. She's only going to be staying here until we find an apartment." Shit. I shouldn't have said "we."

They don't even bother to have their telepathic conversation this time. My mother mouths the word "we" and shakes her head. She is a lot easier to read than my dad. Her mouth turns into a nasty line and she gets a frown in the middle of her brows. My father is his stoic self, although his face tightens a bit.

"Why do you want to live in that dirty city? With those people, those dirty people?" I can't imagine who these dirty people might be.

"Mom," I say, as if she were my two-year-old, "I understand all of your concerns, but really, the only person I'm going to be living with is Roseanne. No dirty people." Of course they don't need to know about the ambiguous "dirty" encounters I might have.

"Why would you want to leave here? I can't understand you or your sister. Your father and I give you everything. Everything. We would never charge you rent. We don't beat you. I cook all your meals. Maybe I should have breast-fed." I can see my mother slipping into hysteria so I turn to my father who is on his third cigarette.

"Everything, you get everything. It's like a vacation for you two. It's like…" He's struggling here to think of a place. "It's like the Rivieria." Ick. I think I understand now why my father lets my mother do all the talking. She may be emotional, but she puts a much better spin on things.

"Dad!" I start to say that the closest he has ever been to the

Rivieria is Epcot, but I have vowed to be calm. I look at both of them. Desperate situations call for desperate measures. I take their hands. In my mind I hear the triumphant score of a million made-for-TV movies. I take a deep breath and try to blink up a tear.

"You know, I love you guys, I do. You've given me everything. You are the best parents ever." I make eye contact with both of them. Parents love this stuff. "Monica and I (well, not really me) have been draining money off you for years. Dad, you went out on your own at sixteen, don't you always tell us that? Mom, it wasn't easy for you with two screaming kids but you made ends meet, didn't you? Now, I want to give you guys a break. I also want you to be proud of me. I want to support myself. It's important for me. I promise I'll get the safest best apartment I possibly can. I just need your love and support. And I need your help."

Have I pushed it too far? Did I lay it on too thick? Have they seen through me? I look back and forth to each of them and then...my mother starts to cry. At first, I'm not sure if she's crying because she's genuinely moved by the whole thing or because I've just given her the biggest pile of bullshit she's ever heard. I look to my father who seems really uncomfortable with all the emotion, fingering his pack of cigarettes and contemplating another smoke. My mother squeezes my hand and wipes a tear. What a scene!

"Honey, of course we will help you. I'm so proud of you." She gets up to hug me. I hug my dad. What a happy family.

"I guess I'll get the daybed out of the garage," says my father, pushing his chair away from the table, poised for escape.

When my mom finishes gushing I head upstairs and call Rose-anne to tell her we are all set.

I spend the rest of the night in the bathroom making ugly faces.

October

To be fair to my parents, I spend all of Friday cleaning the house in anticipation of Roseanne's arrival. Tabitha was really annoyed that I didn't go to this chi-chi West Village gallery opening with her. She also didn't appreciate it when I said I'd offer her a twenty for every straight guy she encountered. She got off the phone all huffy.

Rosie got to my place around eleven on Saturday morning with her rented Ryder truck. Sometimes I forget how blond she is. She looks like a cross between Reese Witherspoon and a country and western singer. She had a little too much lipstick on for the hour, but I wasn't going to be catty. She noticed my hair right away. I was pleased.

"Eve, you cut your hair. You look so..."

"Urban?"

"Well, I guess." I could barely hide my delight. My dad and I helped Roseanne move her stuff in. Four hours later, my mom insisted we come in for risotto. She was trying to outdo herself for Roseanne.

I think I've forgotten to mention what an amazing cook Roseanne is. I guess this tidbit is not as sensational as the blow job in the bathroom. When we were in college she would make elaborate meals in our toaster oven. When we moved out of the dorms, she would organize dinners and throw themed cocktail parties. She used to craft little place cards for everyone and make pastries. We'd tease her about having her own brand of linens to sell to a major department store. My mom loves to pump her for little cooking tips.

"You know, Roseanne, my risotto never comes out the way it tastes in the restaurants."

"Well, Mrs. Vitali, I think it's delicious. It's all in the stirring. You have to stir constantly."

"I know, I did, but it still tastes blah." Aggh, my ever descriptive mother.

"Well," says Rosie, obviously scanning the recipe file of her mind. "For a cheese risotto like this one, you might want to throw in a few golden raisins just for a little sweetness." Who would think of that? Golden raisins? Only Roseanne.

"Would that be good? I mean I'm sure you know best." My mother is practically drooling over the happy homemaker Rosie has the potential to be.

"Just a few would do the trick. Remember risotto really is just sexy Rice-a-Roni, so play with it." My father clears his throat. The last time "sex" was spoken at the dinner table was when Monica was getting her master's in Social Thought and dating that guy who said he was an anarchist. It wasn't pretty. My father excuses himself and makes his way to the garage to look at the lawn mower.

"Thanks, for all your help today, Mr. Vitali," Rosie says sweet as pie. My dad nods and heads out to the garage.

I had made plans to go into the city and hit a downtown bar with Tab, you know give Rosie a little taste of the city, but by the time Rosie and I get finished organizing my (now, our) room, we are ready to collapse. Tabitha is not happy.

"Again?"

"Tabitha, we're tired."

"Isn't she a marathon runner or something?" God! I've really said too much.

"Not exactly. I'm really tired. Call Adrian."

"I can't deal with another night of the unbridled lust of a bunch of gay men."

"Luis?"

"That's an in-person story. I don't see how you can stand to spend an entire weekend out there in dump land."

"Okay, we'll meet you for brunch tomorrow. Okay?"

"I wouldn't want to pull you away from the hairspray."

"Tabitha!"

"Fine, fine. Let's go to the place on Spring with the nice mimosas. Around one. Will that be enough beauty sleep for you?"

"I'm going now." When I get off the phone, Rosie is painting her nails red. This is definitely going to be culture shock.

What an understatement. The next day, we arrive at the place and order mimosas. Tabitha is late as usual. Rosie is taking it all in.

"Wow, it's amazing."

"Yes, they do a lot of photo shoots here. It's a real beautiful

people crowd.'' Everyone is kind of giving Roseanne a dirty look
because she is not wearing black.

''Is your friend Tabitha like that?''

''Yeah, she's very glam.'' Rosie nods, mulling this over.

''She sounds a little snobby to me.'' I will never learn to keep
my mouth shut.

''No, she's great. She's not like anyone we went to school
with.''

''Can we go to FAO Schwartz?'' I pretend I don't hear her.

Forty-five minutes pass and Tabitha still hasn't arrived. She isn't
trying very hard to make a good impression on someone she's
hopefully going to be spending a lot of time with. Rosie checks
her watch, but we keep ordering more mimosas. ''Doesn't this girl
know about the half hour rule?''

''I know, Ro, but it takes a while to get down from the Upper
East Side.''

''She might have accounted for it when she left the house.'' Not
a good sign. But, before I can defend Tabitha's honor, Herself
shows up. She's a vision in brown this morning—and where did
she get that leather jacket?

''Sorry, I'm late.'' This to me and an extended hand to Rosie.
''Tabitha.'' They shake hands and eye each other. Does it really
have to be this strenuous? Can't we all just get along?

''Was it a rough night?''

''You could say that.'' She hasn't yet removed her sunglasses.
''I went out with Ahmed.''

''What about Luis?'' She looks from me to Rosie and back to
me.

''I just can't date people in the service industry. You should
have seen the restaurant he suggested we go to.''

''I'm sure it was hideous.'' This isn't doing much for her image.
The waiter comes over, but Tabitha, still undecided, waves him
off as she ''needs a minute.'' I try not to see Rosie roll her eyes.
I sigh.

''C'mon, Tabitha, I'm starved.'' I am really trying to keep it
together.

''You could have ordered.''

I grip my mimosa glass. ''We didn't. We waited.''

''Fine,'' says Tabitha. She closes her menu and takes out a
cigarette. Rosie absently waves some smoke away. The waiter
takes our order. Tabitha smirks when Rosie orders an egg white
omelet with grilled vegetables.

"The omelets are great," I say, making an attempt.

"Of course you never get egg whites. Wanna cigarette?" Rosie excuses herself to go to the bathroom.

"Is she going to puke?" I hope I didn't tell Tabitha about Roseanne's former eating disorder.

"Tabitha, what's your problem?"

"What problem?" I shake my head. The waiter pours us more mimosas. These drinks are never stiff enough, but usually I'm still slightly toasted from the night before. I snag one of her cigarettes and smoke fiendishly.

"And that outfit," she rolls her eyes, "high fashion."

"Tabitha. Maturity. Come on."

"Fine, I'll play with your little friend." When Rosie returns, Tabitha stubs out her cigarette and removes her glasses. If you were a student of Tabitha body language like I am, you would think this was a good sign. We'll see.

"So, what field are you interested in?"

"Finance. I was a finance major and I worked for a small consulting firm in Hartford."

"Do you have any leads?" Our food arrives and the waiter mistakenly puts Roseanne's food in front of Tabitha. "No, *this* is not for me."

"Well, I've written some letters and I have two interviews set up for this week. I'm also in contact with an agency."

"Those agencies are such a pain." Tabitha shoves a huge forkful of eggs Benedict in her mouth. I think she is flaunting her appetite, if you can believe it. "It's pretty admirable of you to just hop on down without a job or any hope of one." (Is this a compliment?)

"I figured it was the only way to get motivated." Tabitha asks the waiter for more bread.

"You know." She pauses to get our attention before she speaks again. "I do have a friend at Deutsche Bank. Remember Johann?" I nod, remembering the awful fashion sense.

"Is he still talking to you?"

"I stopped talking to him. *Danke.*" Rosie smiles at that. "Anyway, see how your other interviews go and if nothing comes, give me a call and I'll call Herr Johann. If you want." Is she being helpful?

"Thanks." Rosie is genuinely grateful, but of course this happy moment of togetherness can't last. "I can't wait till we find a place and then we can join a gym."

"What fun," Tabitha outdoes herself on the sarcasm and excuses herself to powder her nose. I stare down at my Belgian waffles.

"Is she always this...way?" Rosie asks.

"I know, I know, I know. She just takes some getting used to. She doesn't mean to be abrasive. Really."

Tabitha returns at the same time the bill arrives. Rosie reaches for it but Tabitha grabs her hand.

"Hey, I got it." We protest, but it's really hard to change Tabitha's mind, also, she who pays has the power. I am starting to breathe a sigh of relief that this all seems to be going smoothly and we are just about to embark on Phase 2: shopping. Then Roseanne sees one of the actors from some series on the WB. It isn't pretty; she starts to hyperventilate. At first we aren't sure what's going on. Rosie extends her hand as this quasicelebrity walks by. She turns red and starts saying over and over "star, star, star, star." We quickly lead her out of the restaurant to calm her down. Tabitha smokes and shakes her head. I think it's going to be a long, tough period of adjustment.

Rosie and I don't get back until 7:30 just in time to catch the end of *60 Minutes* with the 'rents. Luckily my mom has saved us her leftovers of Thai Chicken Satay. Rosie refrains from making any suggestions, perhaps she feels it's hopeless. And again another Sunday night in a life full of Sunday nights.

The woman I presume is Lacey Matthews shows up at work as I'm on the phone with Roseanne reading her a list of apartment possibilities. She's been searching for apartments and jobs nonstop. No luck, but it's still too early to worry. Besides we've been having fun. Lacey has to be in her thirties, but she's got the young chic going. If there was a juniors department of the designers she likes, she'd shop there, but instead she's wearing Betsey Johnson. She has this huge bag and it's moving. I get a flash of Zeke, but that's dirty.

"Call me back, Ro, after you see the two-bedroom on Columbus." I hang up and smile at Lacey and eye the bag. "Can I help you?"

"I'm Lacey Matthews." It doesn't take much more for me to decide that I don't like her. Just the way she pauses after she says her name, to let it sink in, annoys me. I'm usually a lot friendlier but I forgo the "greats" because I know I'm being sized up. One of those funny woman things.

"You have an appointment with Herb, don't you?"

"Yes." She smiles, she definitely has had dental work.

"What's in the bag?" The lost maternal instinct comes out. Lacey, who moments ago was all hard-core New York, gets one of those stupid high-pitched voices reserved for babies and kittens.

"Oooh, its just Maxie. Maxie! Maxie?" I peer into the bag. A puppy all right, not exactly my type. This one acts too much like a cat. Lacey continues with her excited voice. "He's so little, too young to leave at home with his siblings."

"Your kids?" I ask, already knowing the answer will make her look down at her belly. All those crunches and the trainer? No, abs as flat as a board. She is reassured. I am just a naive little assistant who doesn't understand what kids would do to all her ab work.

"No kids, not yet." Yes, of course, she is still hoping to meet the right breeder. That hope will kill her. You need hips for the mothering thing. She has body sculpted hers off. Besides, New York is not exactly a place for the unattached. Luckily, I've got age on my side. Nope, poor Lacey is lucky if she gets one of her homosexual friends to donate some sperm. But, I digress.

Herb has a nasty habit of wandering off and not telling me where he is going. Since I am supposed to keep his schedule I wind up looking like a big ass when people ask me where he is. Tabitha has a homing device on the Big C, but I have no idea where Herb is until he comes back—usually all sweaty and smelly, having just taken an eight-mile jaunt around the city "to get my blood flowing." Apparently deodorant inhibits his creativity somehow.

I kind of wish he was returning from a bike ride right now, because I think I would enjoy watching Lacey pretend Herb's creative man scent didn't bother her. Instead, Lacey is sitting in his office listening to his stupid sitar music while I track him down.

Herb is two floors down talking with Jarvis Mitchell, one of the big guys. Jarvis handles all the sporty type magazines Uncle Pres owns. He gives me this weird look when he sees me as if he is surprised that he would have someone like me who has to keep track of him.

"Sorry to interrupt." I always say that when I interrupt him and I wait for him to accept it like most people would, but he never does. "Lacey Matthews is in your office."

"Lacey?" It is obviously too much for Herb to keep all of his expanding creativity in his head along with the name of the person he asked me to call.

"Mike Greaney's friend," Jarvis Mitchell reminds him. So that's how Lacey gets to write for us. Mike Greaney is another big guy.

"Oh, right," says our fearless leader. "I guess I better go be an interrogator." Now, I stand awkwardly as Jarvis and Herb say their goodbyes. I'm not sure if it would be rude to leave, so I wait. I say goodbye to Jarvis as Herb is walking out, but he doesn't acknowledge me. Herb and I walk up the stairs (he wouldn't dream of taking the elevator).

"So I left Lacey in your office with—" I imitate Lacey's long pause "—Max." I'm setting this up to wow him with a witty comment about dogs now that I know Lacey isn't a friend of his.

"Oh," says Herb so that I know he isn't paying attention to me at all. When we get to his office Lacey is all smiles and I leave them to their introductions and their cooing over Max. Whatever.

When I get back to my desk, there are three messages waiting for me. The first: "What's up, it's me." (Tabitha) "Guess who is going to be reviewed in the *Times* this weekend? If you guessed your lost love elizabeth, you are right. Aggh, what could have been, had you only had one more drink."

I delete that one, sending it to the message graveyard, never to be heard from again. The second: "Eve, hey, it's Zeke. I know I haven't talked to you in a while. I was out of the city but I'm back now. Wanted to take you out for some tapas." (Yes, he says it with the correct Spanish accent just like a newscaster.) "Give me a call."

I forward it to Tabitha's voice mail. Finally: "Eve, where are you? I am so sick of sitting in Bryant Park between interviews and telephone calls. I talked to a Realtor about that place in the alphabet section." (City, she means, this is a girl who loves *Rent*.) "It sounds really good. She gave me the name of a bar to meet at, it's called Bar on A and it's on Avenue A. Ooh, I guess that's easy. Can you try to meet us there at 6:30?" My other line beeps. It's Tabitha.

"Want to meet me and Adrian for dinner in Chelsea tonight?"

"I can't, I have to meet Rosie to see an apartment in Alphabet City."

"Oh, how Bohemian." Tabitha knows Ro likes *Rent*. It's come out in the past two weeks that among other things Roseanne thinks the soundtrack to *Rent* is really "real." I would have liked to keep that quiet for a while; Tabitha still hasn't gotten over the celebrity sighting.

"What time are you going to be there?"

"Probably not till eight."

"We'll try to meet you there."

"Don't forget to give her Valium in case Regis Philbin walks down the street."

"Let me ask you this, Tabitha, what happens to Adrian if he leaves Chelsea? Is there some kind of electromagnetic field that electrocutes him?"

"Meow! Remember that Mexican place on Eighth."

"How could I forget the twenty-dollar margaritas?"

"You are going to be no fun until this whole apartment thing is settled, aren't you?"

"Yes, and I appreciate you being so supportive."

"Mother of God. So will I see you later or what?"

"If you can behave yourself."

"I'll certainly try."

"Great," I say and hang up.

I meet Roseanne at the bar. She looks a little red. It must be all the sun she's getting pounding the pavement. She's been here since 4:15. It's quarter of seven.

"Are you drunk?"

"No." Okay. That's reassuring.

"How was the interview?"

"I'm not going to get it."

"How do you know?"

"No chemistry."

"Where is the Realtor?"

"She is talking to someone at the table over there. We were waiting for you. The bartender bought me a drink." I order a gin and tonic. Rosie gets me back to my bad college habits.

"Do you want to meet Tabitha and Adrian for dinner after this? Mexican."

"I guess."

"We don't have to."

"I'm concerned about money. I have a feeling it's going to take me a while to find a job. Also, I haven't seen an apartment for under $1600. That doesn't even include all the stuff we'll have to get or the darned Realtor's fee."

"Well, I know you've had a lot of time to think about this, but honestly, you've only been looking for two weeks. That's eleven business days. No one could get a job that quick.''

The Realtor interrupts us, a woman named Kate who has a really husky voice. She can't stop raving about the area—she lives here, it's changing, it's safe enough to raise her daughter. She talks so much in the short walk over that I feel dizzy when we get into the apartment. Maybe it's the walk up four stories. The moment we get into the apartment, Roseanne leans against the wall in the kitchen and refuses to look at anything else. I think she may be a little drunk.

"Why is the shower in the kitchen?" Roseanne asks.

As I walk around the apartment (which is really just three tiny rooms) I hear Kate explaining the charm of washing your naked body in the kitchen. There is only one closet and the door opens into the disgusting, showerless bathroom. Kate assures me that the bathroom will be cleaned and they will actually put in a sink before we move in. I could barely fit my double bed in here. The wood floors are nice though, maybe I could sleep on them.

"So what do you think?" Kate asks. Roseanne is peculiarly quiet. I ask again how much it costs.

"Only $1300." I add in the $1000 broker's fee, and we owe Kate $2300. I look at Roseanne, wishing we had my parents' telepathic gift. Her face is unreadable. I know there is no way I want to move into this apartment, but does Rosie? I wait for her to speak, but she doesn't.

"It's a great apartment," I lie, "but, we need to think about it."

"Do you want to leave a deposit? We are also going to have to do a credit check and make sure we have a guarantor because you are so young."

"I think we should talk about it first and maybe give you a call tomorrow."

"Fine." Kate seems a little disapproving. "I just want to advise you that apartments like this don't last long in New York."

I thank Kate and Roseanne manages a smile and we are back on the streets. I don't say a word for a while, giving Ro the chance to mull it over. We cut through Tompkins Square Park and ignore the drug pushers.

Roseanne says nothing, but looks like she is in pain. I try to make casual conversation. "So, um, what did you think of the palace?"

"I would sooner cut off my right arm than take a shower in the kitchen.'' Well, that settles that. The idea of being alone in my house with Roseanne repulses me, so I offer to buy her dinner.

We meet Adrian and Tabitha at the Mexican place on Eighth Avenue. It overlooks the street at all the beautiful boys walking by. The worst thing about Chelsea is that feeling of being in the best bakery in the world and having your mouth wired shut. There are no men as attractively unattainable as the ones in Chelsea. They dress well, have cuddly dogs, and probably awesome jobs and money in the bank, but you don't stand a chance unless you have a penis.

Adrian lives in Chelsea. He's one of those mouth-watering boys, but I know him so I've gotten used to it. He also works for Prescott, and has a job he actually enjoys. He works for *Little Nell,* the kids magazine based on a Saturday cartoon character with that annoying theme song. I guess it embarrasses him a little, but he's a graphic artist, which is cool no matter how you look at it. He and Tabitha go way back to the days when they temped for MTV.

As soon as we order, I take Tabitha into the bathroom and give her the lowdown; Roseanne's going nuts from all these dead-end interviews and ridiculous apartments. I am having trouble being positive. Tabitha seems focused on applying her MAC lipstick.

''Are you listening to me Tabitha? She's getting really upset. I purposely walked by the Life Café, you know, the place in *Rent,* and she said nothing.''

''You mean she didn't hyperventilate again.''

''Oh, Tab!'' I say, just to be a bitch, but she doesn't take my bait. She is too busy studying her eyes. She did them up from a picture in a book by this great makeup artist that she loves.

''What do you think, too much kohl?''

''Well, not if you are going for that Cleopatra look in blue.''

''I wish he would let me know where he gets his liquid eyeliner.''

''Who?''

''Kevin.'' The makeup artist, of course. ''It's sweet though, you know he isn't selling out to anyone, he's tight-lipped about who he gets his cosmetics from. No exclusive contract, not yet anyway. How admirable.'' Whatever.

Back at the table Adrian and Roseanne are laughing loudly. There is an empty margarita glass next to Roseanne. I told you she could suck it down. Anyway, I have to hand it to Adrian, he's definitely taking some of the edge off. Thank God.

''I mean, I wasn't raised to live in a place like that,'' Roseanne says. She quiets down when I sit. "Imagine showering in the kitchen."

"Imagine," Tabitha says. I think she's pissy because Adrian and Rosie are getting along. Adrian is a god to Tabitha. Rosie ignores Tabitha and we actually have a great dinner. Of course Rosie and I get drunk and when the bill comes I'm not psyched about paying for Rosie's portion and it hurts me to turn her down when she offers to pay, but I keep my word.

While Rosie is in the bathroom, Adrian suggests we go to this gay dance club. "Adrian, the last thing I'm going to do is go to another meat market with you. If I want to see that kind of hormonal display I'll go to the Upper East Side and get lucky with a frat boy."

"Listen to Miss Thing," says Adrian, laughing. He looks at Tabitha. "And you?"

"Well, I'm certainly not ready to go home to the 'burbs." She smirks at us.

"Meow," Adrian and I purr together.

"Your friend Rosie is nice, we should try to hook her up with a job." What a sweetheart Adrian is. Let that be a lesson to Herself. Tabitha rolls her eyes.

"What's next?" asks Rosie, back at the table. I know she's tanked.

"Next is a whirlwind of an evening on the bus. I can't be hungover again. You can sleep late."

"You could always stay over, Rosie," Adrian offers, and I feel Tabitha kick me under the table. She would absolutely die.

"Well, thanks, Adrian," says Rosie softly, "but I don't want Eve to go back by herself."

"Of course you don't," adds Tabitha definitively. She could just give me a car voucher, but I've got no legitimate cause to ask for one.

We take a cab to Port Authority and catch the bus home. I plan on sleeping the whole way home. Rosie wants to talk about Chelsea.

"I think we should live there, Eve. All those guys, I mean, I know they aren't your type, but they all seem so built and cute—and did you notice all the dogs? That's the kind of guy for me." She must be kidding, but she isn't. It only gets worse.

"And Adrian, what's his story? He's so cute and nice. He's a designer for Prescott Nelson, well, of course you know that, but how cool is that? Why didn't you ever tell me about him? Did *you* like him? I kind of wanted to hang out, but I didn't know. Are he and Tabitha together?''

The worst part is, she's serious. I mean, Adrian isn't flaming and he doesn't really fit what people would stereotype as gay, but isn't it obvious? Does one need to be singing the show tunes to be clear about their sexuality?

The trip turns into a harsh education for Rosie. I thought it might upset her more, but she actually takes it well. She laughs with me for the first time since she started looking for a job.

Need I remind you again that it's only been eleven business days?

Tuesday morning is our staff meeting. I am mildly hungover. The staff acts like these meetings are the greatest things since the Times Square Shuttle. How much fun can you make articles about cycling? You get a real feel for what exercise geeks these writers are—they sometimes read questions that are sent in to the ''Dear Biker'' column and laugh about the ignorance of readers. Today is a special treat, we are watching a promotional video for some biking company that wants us to cover their newest brand.

Everyone is on the edge of their seats, mesmerized by the amazing angles the cameraman got on the bikes. Everyone except Lorraine and me. Since Herb has seen all the footage, he manages to be even more smug than usual, like he created the bikes or something.

I do a lot of eye rolling at Lorraine and she shakes her head. She leads the business aspect of the meeting; who is supposed to be doing what assignment, what kind of budgets the writers have and gives us feedback from different departments, lines of business as they are called. Herb does a lot of interrupting during Lorraine's part. It amazes me that he does it with such ease. He makes the stupidest jokes and people will laugh. How does someone get the confidence to do that? Is it just by being the boss? If I ever tried that I think everyone would look at me as if I had eight heads and maybe I would get a good human resources ''talking to.''

The meeting concludes with people reading select excerpts of their articles. There is a separate meeting called the Feed Meet, to get feedback before the articles are published, but this is reading the articles after they are already in the magazine. If we really cared we could just grab a copy of this month's issue, but Herb insists that certain writers should read their articles during our staff meeting. There is no escape, not even in the fresh-squeezed orange juice and bran muffins. After the ''special'' writer finishes, we all have to applaud.

After the meeting I bring the carnage of the picked-over breakfast by my desk. This means that all day long, I'll have all of them coming by looking at the leftovers as if there might be some new healthy snack that just appears. They also make goofy jokes about how the food is breaking down and are inspired to talk about how many miles and at what speed they have to bike in order to burn off a certain number of calories. Then it always deteriorates to fiber jokes and bathroom humor. Like I said, exercise geeks.

''Do you need any help?'' Brian, the new semester slave, asks me after the meeting. I'm in the midst of e-mailing Tabitha.

''No, I'm fine for now.'' Brian lives for these meetings. The bad thing about interns is they remind you of how little you have to do, and thus, how little you can pass onto them. Brian is going to be with us all semester, which means that I have him to look forward to until Christmas. ''Why don't you check out some of our old issues?'' Brian is one of those interns who thinks if he asks enough questions and kisses enough ass, he'll get a job here. When Brian isn't slaving away or kissing ass, he is harassing me. He seems to think that part of the so-called learning experience is being involved in every aspect of the office.

''Hey, Brian. This—'' I cover up my monitor ''—is personal. It's not some important job secret that is being kept from you.''

''Oh, okay.'' He goes back to sit at his makeshift desk. I guess I should feel bad for the guy. At least I get paid.

He comes back fifteen minutes later under the pretense of getting a different issue. This time I'm on the Net trying to find Roseanne a recipe for gumbo. This is getting annoying. I quickly switch my computer back to the desktop and pretend to find it amazing. He decides to address me anyway.

''You know, I'm thinking of trying to write an article.'' Mother of God.

''Great, Brian.'' I don't take my eyes off the screen, but I'm surprised how annoyed I am that Brian thinks it's that simple.

''Did you ever think about trying to write?''

''Bikes don't really interest me.''

''But still, it's a great opportunity you have here.'' I think they must brainwash them at the intern orientation. ''I mean, you don't want to be a receptionist all your life.''

''What?'' This time I actually turn and look at him. Now, I have a very long desk that is sort of in the middle of a bunch of offices and cubes, but the receptionist sits in the elevator lobby. "I am not a receptionist! I am a department assistant. Big difference!" Brian walks away with his head hanging. Good riddance. But this raises another more serious question, do I really seem like a receptionist? Image is everything. What if I give off a receptionist image? I call Tabitha.

"If you seem like a receptionist, I seem like a receptionist, and I am certainly not a receptionist." Tabitha has the same desk that I do and sits in almost the exact same position.

"Do you think it's the desk? Is that what makes us seem like receptionists?"

"Hey, Eve, don't clump me into the reception pool. It's this shitty intern who is ignorant of the ways of Prescott Nelson. Don't let it bother you. That's the problem with these interns—they waltz in here with these ideals and think they can run the company."

"Well, Tabitha, so do we."

"Well, we can."

"But here is the question, is there any more dignity in being an assistant than a receptionist?"

"Ah, the conundrum," says Tabitha as my other line beeps.

"Hold on." Tabitha sighs as if by putting her on hold I have ruined her day. "Eve Vitali."

"Eve, Zeke." Wow!

"Zeke! Hold on, I'm on the other line."

"Is this a bad time I could—"

"No, I'm just finishing. Hold on." I click back to Tabitha, who is incidentally singing a Spice Girls' song, although she stops quickly when she hears me. "Hey, Slutty Spice, that's Zeke."

"Return of the Ape Man."

"Thanks for consoling me about the receptionist thing." I click back to Zeke. "Hi." I will be strong. He can't just decide not to call me and get away with it.

"Oh, Eve," he growls. I might weaken a little. (I know, I know, but remember, I have needs, too.) "God, I've missed you."

"Really."

"I had to go to L.A. to check out a band." I reminisce about why I first liked him. Say 'bye, 'bye receptionist, my carriage awaits. I can get over the hair, I know I can.

"How was it?"

"Oh, you know L.A." I don't, but someday I'd like to. "It's good to be home."

"Yeah."

"So, Eve, can I see you?"

I agree to meet Zeke for Jamaican food. I must admit that he has a knack for picking restaurants. Tabitha thinks this signifies a chronic dater, but she gave me her blessing, because I might as well keep on getting some after my long drought. Roseanne wasn't thrilled about spending the night alone with my parents watching "Nick at Nite," but she agreed to corroborate my working late story. This being the only reason my mother would accept for not being a proper host to Roseanne.

Anyway, Zeke has on a dizzying shirt. It has black and white swirls and I wonder if he thinks it will hasten my drunkenness. Again, I intend to stand firm.

"Eve." He gets up and kisses me (yes, on the lips). It's not one of those gushy kisses—it's worse. It's one of those "we have something that won't be cheapened by saliva, so let me take your face in my hands as if it is an exquisite jewel and kiss you with just a hint of the passion that will hopefully not explode all over the dinner table" kiss. You know the ones? Anyway, it's troubling.

"What's up?"

"Nothing. Everything," he says, shaking his head. "It's great to see you. You look beautiful."

"Thanks." Standing firm. Unsinkable. We sit down.

The waitress arrives and places Jamaican beer in front of both of us.

"I ordered for us," he says, taking my hand. "I hope you don't mind."

"Uh, no." Well, I guess I don't mind. What I mind is the way he is sniffing my hand.

"You smell good, Eve, real good." I have to wonder if my life just got scripted by soap opera writers. I look around for a camera.

"Are you looking for someone?"

"No."

"Good, because I just want us to focus on each other."

"Well, I'm starved. Let's check out the menu." I break free from him. I feel him watching me, but I ignore it. I take a sip of my beer.

"Eve," he says. I look at him. He looks intensely at me and smiles. "I can't wait to taste you again." Yes! He says that. I feel yucky. I have a serious uh-oh feeling.

"Okay." Straight back to the menu. I get the jerk chicken.

When the food arrives Zeke is telling me about the book he is writing. He is writing it from the perspective of a thirty-five-year-old, Korean-African-American single mother.

"But, it's different, very stream of consciousness. Very...I don't know, how do I say it...?" he pauses as if thinking. Something tells me he has given this very same explanation a hundred times. "...well, I like to think poetic."

"That's interesting, Zeke—" I take a bite of my chicken and chew almost as thoughtfully "—but I thought the idea was to write what you know."

From Zeke's expression, I assume no one has ever discussed this with him before.

"Eve, that's so oppressive. Why should I let my writing be defined by limits, by archaic rules. I understand this woman, I feel I've gotten her. That's what being an artist is. I feel a side of me opening up. It's an amazing release. It transcends everything."

"Does it?" We eat our meals for a while. The waitress brings more beer. I'm pacing myself. Zeke is really quiet. No amount of sexual eating will pull him out of it. He's not even watching me. The silence is so awkward, I actually run my tongue over the chicken before I put it in my mouth. It does nothing. When he isn't talking, I kind of enjoy looking at him, and what the hell, I'm horny. (Yeah, yeah, I know what I said.)

"So, what should we do now? Do you want to get a drink?"

"Eve, I think I am ready to get the check and call it a night." What?

"What?"

"I just don't think it's going to work between us." Really.

"Really?"

He takes my hand again, this time almost pityingly. "You just don't seem to get my work."

"The A&R stuff? What's to get?"

"No, Eve, not my job. No, my writing, my art."

"What, that book?"

"It's a huge part of me, and it's clear by your ignorance that you'll never understand." Is he being serious? "I cared for you, Eve, but I realize you will never support me and that is a big issue." The big issue I think I am starting to realize is that I am not going to have sex this evening and who knows how long it will be again.

"Zeke, maybe you're getting a little excited."

"That's just it, Eve! You don't understand!" He actually slams his hand on the table when he says this. Several diners turn to

look at us. The waitress hurries over to see if she can get us the
check.

"Yes, get the check." I offer Zeke money, but he won't take
it. I was going to head to Tabitha's, but in the absence of a good
lay, I think I want nothing more than my own bed. Zeke gives me
a quick kiss on the cheek and hops in a cab.

I ride home alone on the bus, because I missed the train. Again.
This pathetic feeling is reason enough to move out.

My parents and Rosie are circled around the TV. I assure my
mother I took a car home and Rosie seems a little too smug,
knowing my date must have gone dreadfully wrong.

I go up to my room and feign sleep when Rosie comes in. She
says my name, but I ignore her. Wasn't I beautiful? Didn't I taste
delicious and eat sexily? What happened to all that? One blast of
reality and Zeke is a goner.

We should have gone for Italian, I would have done wonders
with spaghetti.

I don't talk to Roseanne about Zeke for a few days. She's got
her own problems stressing about a job and searching for an apartment. I found this one on the Net and convinced her we should
go after I got out of work. I've taken a new policy of "don't ask,
don't tell." If she gets a job she will undoubtedly tell me. Until
then I will neither inquire about her search, nor offer constructive
criticism about things like not wearing such a glossy lipstick or
how much nicer her black pantsuit looks than the cotton-lycra skirt
set.

The Realtor, Craig, gives us a little attitude about being late for
our appointment. There was a subway delay. I give him attitude
right back. Roseanne says nothing. I hope she isn't this quiet and
miserable on job interviews, but remember, I am beyond advice.

The apartment is not exactly near the subway, but I guess it's
still considered "in the vicinity." Craig is very elusive about this
apartment. Since Roseanne won't talk (again), I have to be the
spokeswoman. "So how is the place?"

"It's great and so charming." Okay, small—I gathered that
from the ad. And I am sure the advertised EIK (that's Eat In
Kitchen, for you nonresidents) is minuscule. Craig chats up the
apartment all the way there. He must feel guilty about the ridiculous fee that Realtors charge and somehow hopes to feel like he's
earning his money. Whatever.

We turn onto this nice block. I'm not jazzed about the Upper

East Side and the only reason I'm checking out this place is because I feel bad about making Rosie do all this work in her fragile state. Despite all the telltale signs from the ad that it would suck (EIK, charming, 1BR converted, prewar), I suggested we check it out so I could put in some effort.

We stop at a really nice brownstone. I am fighting that hopeful feeling but, I can't help thinking that this could be it. I look to Rosie, who is staring at the cracks in the sidewalk. I didn't want to do this alone. I take a deep breath.

"Okay," says Craig, stopping in front of the building, beginning his hard sell. "Now, it will be painted before you move in." Don't get too far ahead of yourself there, buddy. But, wait, he is headed downstairs! Downstairs? No one said anything about a basement apartment.

He opens the door to one of the tiniest apartments I have ever seen. Maybe if Rosie and I were Siamese twins we might have an enjoyable life here, but we'd probably also have a book deal and do the talk show circuit and could afford to live somewhere else. One bedroom converted? Converted to what? Two tiny closets? Yes, you can eat in the kitchen. The kitchen, the living room and the "converted" bedrooms are one big room. If you plan on eating in the apartment, you will virtually always be in the kitchen.

"Feel free to look around," says Craig encouragingly. There is nothing I need to look at; the entire apartment is right in my field of vision. Including the bathroom. Craig must read my mind. "They're definitely going to put the bathroom door on before you move in."

That's reassuring. I look at Rosie. She is turning a color I've never quite seen before. "There is no way in hell I will ever live in this doody apartment." Rosie starts out slowly, but I can see it getting worse. That's pretty crass for her.

Craig looks shocked—as shocked as I am. "Excuse me?"

"You heard me, this is ridiculous. How much are you charging for this place? Fourteen hundred? The worst part is some schmuck is actually going to pay." I note her use of "schmuck."

"Listen, miss, I don't where you're from, but this is New York."

"This is garbage!" Wow! Craig can't believe it, either. He sweeps his arm around the tiny apartment and up toward the barred window that is barely street level.

"Where in New York do you think you will get a view like this one?"

Rosie shakes her head and physically grabs me and pulls me
out of the apartment. As we're out the door she turns back towards
him and shouts.

"Up your ass!" Those are the harshest I've ever heard from
those lips. I am holding on to the wall of the brownstone, so I
won't fall over laughing. What balls! The well-dressed people
walking by will probably have us arrested for loitering, but I can't
stop laughing. My stomach starts to hurt and I am about to cry
from the hysteria. I look at Rosie, expecting the same, but she
really is crying, sobbing and it takes me by surprise.

"Roseanne." I touch her shoulder. "Are you okay?" She
doesn't speak for a while. She shakes her head and keeps trying
to stop.

"I've gone through two thousand dollars in three weeks."

"How?"

"Little things—drinks, food—I swear I've only bought like one
skirt and it wasn't that. Just little things. It wouldn't be a big deal
if I were working, but what if I go through my entire savings and
still don't have a job? We are going to have to put a deposit down
on the apartment. What am I going to do?"

"You are going to get a job."

"No one has called back for more than a second interview. I
was even thinking of putting in a résumé at Prescott."

"Well, you should. I believe sooner or later everyone works for
Uncle Pres."

"And I just roam around the streets of New York all day, which
would be great if I were on vacation, but I feel guilty, like I'm
not doing what I'm supposed to be doing."

"I know." But I don't.

"And today, you know how it rained this morning? Well, I went
to The Virgin Megastore and I was reading and I just sort of fell
asleep. One of the employees woke me up and told me I wasn't
allowed to sleep there. Like I was freaking homeless or something." Wow! What do you say to that? There's really only one
thing.

"Let's get a drink."

We wind up back in the Village in a dark little bar. There is
nothing like drowning your sorrows in the creature. I foot the bill.
It's the least I can do. I opt not to call Tabitha, although she loves
this place and she'll kill me if she finds out we're here without
her. I attempt to console Roseanne. "We just have to keep a positive attitude."

"I know, but, I can't stand another dead interview and I can't stand another 'charming' apartment. What the heck is prewar, anyway?"

"No idea. But, there's a guy looking at you." Okay, I'm lying, he's not. But Roseanne is pretty in that All-American way, which really means Northern European. (I only know that because of my sister's Social Politics master.) She also is an exercise junkie. Anyway, I know I shouldn't have, but if she just makes eye contact with this guy, it might work wonders for her self-confidence. Besides, he looks real cheesy and Tabitha thinks that's totally Rosie's type. I tend to agree.

"He is not." She checks him out quickly. This is called setting the bait, he definitely saw her. These meat market games are so freshman year, but times are tough. The girl needs love. Within minutes, said guy comes over to us with his fat friend. They buy us drinks.

Roseanne and I play good cop/bad cop for a while getting Brad's (of course) employment history out. It figures he works in advertising. Rosie is into it. I can imagine Tabitha smirking as we are in the process of picking up the cheesiest men in the bar. That is, Rosie is. I am not interested in Paul, the fat friend.

"So you work for a publishing company," Paul asks, smiling at me with bad teeth.

"Yeah."

"You girls got an apartment here in the city?"

"No, we are visiting from Tulsa, and we'll be leaving tomorrow." Roseanne shoots me a look. It's amazing that she can hear me so clearly with her back to me yet she needs to lean so close to Brad's lips to understand him. I correct myself, for her sake. For the sake of love, if you will.

Anyway, we imbibe quite a bit. So much so that at one point I must mistakenly give Paul the go ahead to kiss me (maybe it's just the example set by face sucking Roseanne and Brad), but I quickly put a stop to that.

Roseanne walks away with a business card and a date for next Thursday night (props to her). Luckily, it's the night I'm going to the Fashion Awards with Tabitha. Once again we are back on the bus, but this time we get to pass out. I wake up just in time for our stop and note that Rosie has a smile on her face as she sleeps. It warms the cockles of my cold heart.

* * *

"I found it!" Roseanne says when I pick up the phone. Herb happens to be standing near my desk, talking to one of the writers.

"What's that?" I try to sound professional.

"The most wonderful apartment!" Let me just say that ever since her date prospect, she's been a little happier, but finding the perfect apartment is nothing to joke about. I feel my heart start to beat. This could be the new beginning.

"Where?"

"Chelsea. Right on 7th Avenue. It's amazing. The landlady's cousin showed it to me. She says they're making their decision tomorrow. Eve, there were like thirty other people there."

"How much?"

"Only fourteen. Only? Gosh, I never thought I would say that. Shit, I'm becoming a New Yorker. Eve, I am serious, we have to get this apartment. Have to. Call the landlady and schmooze her. You're good at that." Really?

"Okay, give me the number." She gives it to me. Her name is Mrs. Yakimoto. "How many bedrooms?"

"Well it's just one bedroom with this alcove and a sleep loft. The bedroom and the loft aren't that big, but the living room and everything else is huge. It's unbelievable, it's amazing. Eve, I haven't seen an apartment this nice. Oh, shit." Roseanne is getting real accustomed to this cursing thing. She is loving her new New Yorkness. It's actually rubbing off on me and I find myself wanting this apartment sight unseen.

I hang up the phone. I smile up at Herb, who just sort of stares at me, like I am somehow representative of a generation of young women that he would never want to attempt to understand.

"Searching for an apartment," I say.

"I hear it's tough these days." I smile and nod, hoping he will go away so I can make personal phone calls.

"Can you send this out for me, Eve?" He hands me a big puffy envelope full of stuff. Now as I said, Herb is a very self-sufficient man, but little things like "sending stuff out" are beyond him. This man has published books and had honorary and real degrees from all over but can't figure out the Prescott Nelson mail system. Basically, our mail system entails just dropping it in a bin for someone else to come and take care of postage. It's wonderful. My mother gives me care packages to send to my sister all the time. No one questions anything. All it takes is a *Bicycle Boy* or Prescott Nelson label. Since Herb has already written out the address, all I have to do is put the package in the mail bin next to my desk. It's easy enough, and the nice thing is it makes both Herb and I feel like I am earning my title as "assistant."

I take the package from him. I ooze efficiency. "Great. I'll do it right away."

I call Mrs. Yakimoto. She lives on Long Island. Her son answers the phone. He can't be more than six. He screams for his mother to get the phone. She answers and speaks in slightly accented English.

"Mrs. Yakimoto, my name is Eve Vitali. My roommate Rose-anne looked at the apartment today."

"Yes, I think my cousin mentioned her. There have been so many calls today." Mrs. Yakimoto sounds a little stressed. I can hear her kids in the background.

"Well, we are really interested in the apartment and we are really hoping to get it."

"I know, but I wasn't expecting to rent to two people and you haven't even see the apartment yet. I never expected to even have this apartment to rent. My cousin decided to get married and now she wants to move uptown. She said she would handle it, but I still have to talk to all these people. Do you believe people are offering me six months' rent?"

"Yes, I do. It's really tough to get an apartment in the city." I hear one of Mrs. Yakimoto's children bawling and she yells at them in another language and gets back on the phone with me.

"Are those your kids?"

"Yes, I have four."

"Well, Mrs. Yakimoto, I'm sure the last thing you want to do is worry about all of this. I just want to tell you how great my roommate Roseanne thinks the apartment is and how much we would really love it."

"Well, I have to talk to my husband about this. You girls seem very nice, but it's a lot to decide. I will call you back tomorrow."

"Okay, but Mrs. Yakimoto, we are really interested in the apartment. We'll be great tenants. Really."

When we get off the phone, I get an idea. I call Adrian.

"I was wondering if you had any extra Little Nell toys lying around."

"We've got tons. Come down and get some. I could use a visit."

It's always nice to visit Adrian, because he notices things that most men wouldn't. Today he said my lipstick was glam and very

New York. He's so cute. I can understand why Rosie had her little crush on him.

Not only did he give me a bunch of Little Nells, he gave me all kinds of cartoon T-shirts and some promotional toys from *Little Nell*'s advertisers. I look up Mrs. Yakimoto's address on the Net and FedEx all the stuff to her with a note telling her (again) how much we'd like to live in the place and hoping her kids enjoy the stuff.

I can tell Tabitha is impressed with my cunning and maybe a tad jealous that I will live in a much cooler area plus be closer to Adrian *and* Krispy Kreme donuts. I neglect to tell her about my night out at the bar and the guy Roseanne kind of picked up. I am too tired to go out tonight, but I promise to go out tomorrow night, Friday, to kick off what might be one of the last warm weekends of the year.

She bugs me again about what I am going to wear to the Fashion Awards next Tuesday. Again, I say the same black Bebe sweater and some skirt I got in Soho for really cheap. I can tell Tabitha isn't all that excited about it. All we are doing is seat filling. She finds the whole thing a tad beneath her. She wishes we had actual tickets instead of having to hop around from seat to seat whenever someone vacates. She is also dying to find a post event invite, but the Big C only got one.

"Eve, you're a real peach today."

"I'm just worrying about the apartment thing."

"I'd worry, too, especially if only Roseanne has seen it. You're giving her an awful lot of responsibility, don't you think?"

"Well, I trust her, Tabitha."

"What are you gonna do if she can't get a job?"

"She's been looking for three weeks. Only three weeks. She'll get one."

"As what? An aerobics instructor?" I don't say anything for a full twenty seconds. I count it on my phone's time display.

"Look, Tabitha, just give me a call tomorrow when you decide what you want to do this weekend."

"Maybe try to scout out some more pseudo celebrities. Roseanne will like that. I hear there's a bar where old cast members from the *Real World* are put out to pasture."

"Whatever." I hang up. That's something I never do to Tabitha. I just can't take the excess drama.

My parents are delighted about the apartment possibility. Well, I'm exaggerating, my mom dabs her eyes a little and congratulates us in her typical martyrish way and my dad makes some comment about Chinese people. I remind him that Mrs. Yakimoto is most likely Japanese, but it doesn't seem to register. Thankfully my sister Monica isn't around to start a political correctness war with them.

Roseanne describes the entire apartment to me. The things she keeps raving about are the hardwood floors and all the space. It's unbelievable that it's so cheap. There are only two other tenants in the apartment building. One above us, one below. We have the entire floor. It sounds too good to be true.

And we definitely need to get out of Jersey.

I call Mrs. Yakimoto first thing in the morning. A different kid answers this time, this one is probably nine. I ask to speak to Mrs. Yakimoto and he starts screaming.

"It's the lady, the toy lady!" Mrs. Yakimoto comes to the phone.

"Eve?" She sounds weary.

"Hi. Mrs. Yakimoto."

"Thank you for the stuff. The kids love it. They told me to give the apartment to the toy lady."

"Well you should," I say, pleased.

"Well, Eve, to be honest, my husband isn't thrilled about the idea of giving it to two girls. What if something breaks? We're just not sure about girls." We're women, thank you. I will get this apartment one way or another even if I have to sue her for sexual discrimination.

"Well, Mrs. Yakimoto, we're very self-sufficient women. Actually, my father owns a plumbing business. He's really handy. So, really, we'll never ask for anything."

"But, you're so young, and how do we know you can pay the rent? We have a lot of other interested people."

"I know, but we love the apartment. It's our dream. We will be the best tenants ever. Really." Mrs. Yakimoto laughs. "We will definitely be able to pay the rent."

"What about Roseanne, she doesn't have a job?" Damn!

"Yes she does." Shit.

"Really?" Fuck.

"Yes, actually she got a job working here, working for..." Help! Help! "A different magazine, she just found out last night." Mrs. Yakimoto is silent for a long time.

"Well. I would like to see a copy of your last pay stub and I need something from Roseanne. Can she get a letter from her employer?'' That Mrs. Yakimoto is sharp, depressingly sharp.

"Of course, I'll send it right over."

"You can fax it to my husband's office." The awful Mr. Yakimoto once again standing in the way of all that is rightfully ours.

Shit! Shit! Shit! I call Roseanne. She has just returned from a grueling run that she starts to tell me about. I cut her off right away to tell her the news.

"What are we going to do?" She sounds like she's on the verge of tears. Why must I always be the pillar? I don't have time to start wondering why; instead I come up with a brilliant plan. "Roseanne, I'll call you back." Immediately I call Tabitha.

"What's up?" she says, obviously still a little miffed from yesterday. "Wanna have a cigarette?"

After a lot of begging and pleading and many allusions to how much more I like Tabitha than anyone else in the world (i.e. Roseanne). I get her to agree to be Roseanne's boss. An idea that I'm sure would be dangerous were it a reality. The letter I type on *NY By Night* stationery reads like this:

To whom it may concern,
Roseanne Sullivan has been hired as an editorial assistant for *NY By Night* magazine as of November 1. Her expected salary is $38,000 for this year after which she will renegotiate her contract. Call me with any questions.

Sincerely,
Tabitha Milton
Vice President, Creative Development, *NY By Night*

It is a vision. I call Roseanne to let her know what her new job is and remind her to be very very nice to Tabitha the next time she sees her. Sure enough, within an hour of getting the fax, Mrs. Yakimoto has called Lorraine, my reference, and left a message on Tabitha's (fortunately) unincriminating voice mail.

Although she is pretending to be huffy about it, Tabitha likes the idea of all of this. She calls me and then conferences with Mrs. Yakimoto. I keep my phone on mute so I can hear. Mrs. Yakimoto answers for a change. Tabitha is all professional. "Mrs. Yakimoto, this is Tabitha Milton. You left me a message?"

"Yes, I wanted to know about Roseanne Sullivan."

"Oh, right, she's our new hire. I wrote up a letter..." Tabitha is doing her Big C frazzled impression.

"Yes, is she going to make $38,000?"

"Yes, and probably a bonus that she doesn't know about." Wow, we never discussed that, what an actress!

"Really? Do you know Eve Vitali?"

"I know of her, but she works at a different magazine. I think she's a writer, too." Tabitha will be preparing her Oscar speech after this.

"They're so young, how did they get these great jobs?" Good question.

"Just talented I guess. Is that all your questions?"

"Yes, thank you." Mrs. Yakimoto is as impressed with us as I am. We all hang up. I call Tabitha right back. She sees my number and answers on the first ring.

"You owe me so big."

"Tabitha that was great. I'll buy you a drink tonight—ten drinks, whatever. I'll never stop repaying you."

"True enough," says Tabitha. "But hopefully there will be men buying me drinks, thank you."

"There will be. You are the coolest. I am gushing."

"Now let's hope she gives you the damn apartment."

"She has to. She just has to."

"Okay, I'm going to leave you alone with your emotions. Come to my place after work and we'll head downtown."

"Okay! Um…"

"Speak!"

"Roseanne?"

"Whatever. She can come, I guess. Just tell her to go easy on the perfume or better yet, change it."

This means Tabitha is warming up to Roseanne. It's only a matter of time.

Roseanne is just as excited about the conversation. I don't think she can quite believe that Tabitha would do that or that Tabitha wants her to come out tonight (so, I exaggerated a little, I'm giddy).

I call Mrs. Yakimoto before I leave for the day. She tells me that her conversation went well with Roseanne's future employer, but she still hasn't made a decision. She is going away for the weekend with her family and she will let me know on Monday if we can have the apartment. Apparently it is down to one other guy and us.

"Well, Mrs. Yakimoto, I hope you make the right choice. We really hope to get the apartment."

"Believe me, I know. You are definitely persistent."

"Thanks," I say, not sure if it's really a compliment, "and have a great weekend."

The bar we go to is, of course, dark and trendy. Tabitha and Roseanne seem to have resigned themselves to each other a little more. Baby steps, that's really all I ask. Roseanne was super gracious and Tabitha waved it off with a hand, like an old pro who commits fraud all the time.

Tabitha situated us in the perfect spot, as usual, on low couches in the back, very close to the VIP room. She sits there in her new outfit and puffs away on her Dunhills. She always winds up getting a light from men at the bar. She dismissively thanks them and continues being aloof and attractive. I am wearing one of Tabitha's sweaters over the black pants I wore to work. Roseanne, who notes daily how she is becoming more and more of a New Yorker, has put on some sexy black dress that I've never seen. She's going minimalist on the makeup today (honestly she doesn't need all the foundation) and she looks good—starstruck, but good.

I bum one of Tabitha's cigarettes and Roseanne shakes her head. Hey, I'm a social smoker and it looks so cool.

"Can we go back there?" says Roseanne, motioning to the VIP room. Tabitha and I shrug at each other.

"We have to assess the situation." Translation: a few more drinks before we try to schmooze the bouncer.

"Interesting," says Tabitha, looking over my head, "but don't look now."

"Who?" I say as Roseanne whips her head around, irking Tabitha incredibly. I cringe.

"One of the fashion show designers. We profiled him. He's French, Jaques something. Shit." Tabitha hates when she can't remember these important factoids.

He walks by, and it's classic Tabitha. She exhales a puff just as Jaques something or other passes. It goes right in his face. He looks down at Tabitha, who smiles up at him coquettishly and shrugs. Then, he's off to the VIP room.

"Wow!" Roseanne says, and Tabitha just smiles. The next few minutes are sort of a waiting game. There is no sense talking to Tabitha because she knows that soon she will have the prize.

Sure enough, someone brings us a round of drinks and tells us we have an invite to the VIP room. Total class, I think. It's major points with Tabitha and me if a guy who is interested in one of us gets the other a drink for the hell of it.

"Well, should we go back?" Roseanne is all anxious to get the fun under way.

"Not yet." I smile at Tabitha. She's sweating the Frenchman out. She drinks slower than the rest of us. We tap our nails waiting for her. She makes us get up and hit the bathroom where she reapplies makeup for what seems like forever. Finally our entrance. Tabitha casually gestures to the Frenchman and the super-slick bouncer lets us in.

I scout the place. The only celebs are the Frenchman and some guy who looks recognizable from an independent flick or two. The rest are suits, probably industry people, and their nondescript model girlfriends. Among all the skin and bones that call themselves women, Tabitha stands out. She has mastered the art of getting attention. We go up to the bar and order our drinks. Tabitha keeps her back to Jaques the whole time. He makes his way over to us. I think it might be nice to score this exchange with some music and sell it to the Discovery Channel.

"Is dees your fwend?" he asks me, because I am the only one looking at him. I nod. He screams over the music. "Tell your fwend I like zees eyes."

"He likes your eyes," I say to Tabitha.

"No, no, no, no." He shakes his hands at me. Then he makes a circular motion with his arms. "Dee size, dee size."

I don't translate. Jaques turns to go back to his table, where he is sitting with other artsy French types. Tabitha smiles and follows him. Roseanne looks at me, confused. It's the last we see of Tabitha for a while although we keep giving her "you go, girl" looks whenever we can catch her eye.

Roseanne starts talking to some long-haired guy who is a guitarist on tour with some woman who has just released a single. He says her name, but neither one of us has ever heard of her. He points over at an attractive Asian woman.

"Oh, yeah, I saw her picture in the Virgin Megastore." Roseanne is all over knowing this obscure person.

"She spends a lot of time in Virgin." I tell this guy whose name is Q (hey, he's a musician).

"Yeah, it's a cool waste of time. Shit, the rest of my band is leaving. Gotta run, too." He shakes my hand and winks at Roseanne. When he's gone Rosie looks pissed.

"He was so cute, I wish he asked for my number. And you? I

can't believe you told him all I do is hang out in Virgin. He is lost forever."

"Can you really take a guy named Q seriously?" I say.

"Yes." She's miffed. She usually doesn't go for these long-haired types. I look over at Tabitha who is smiling drunkenly as Jaques strokes her hair and whispers in her ear. I also see the Asian singer that Q (the horror!) works for.

"If you are that into him, why don't you just give that woman your number?"

"You don't think that would be—" she searches for a word "—too much?"

"No."

"What should I say?"

"Here's my number. Give it to your guitarist. Tell him to call me. I think your new single is great."

"You always know the perfect thing to say." She kisses me. I feel like Tabitha. She scribbles her number and bounds off, leaving me to stand with my proverbial dork in my hand, sort of wishing at least the bartender would ask me for my number, so I could refuse. He doesn't. I can no longer feel my nose. Tabitha comes to my side.

"Bored?"

"A little." She pulls out the car voucher.

"Not too many more of these. You'll have to start taking cabs once you move to the city. Drunk?"

"Completely. How is Jaques?"

"Incohesive," she says, but I know what she means.

"It's kind of hard to hear anyway with all this Portishead playing."

"Guess what? You have a ticket to the Fashion Awards after party. Well, we both do, but I also have an October hookup."

"Awesome." I hug her like she just won the peace prize.

"You know, Eve, I was so impressed with your little scheme today. Fabulous! You guys are definitely going to get the apartment." We hug again, boozy floozies.

"It will be great, really we'll have so much fun." She nods almost tearfully. All this emotion makes perfect sense after six Kettel One and grapefruits. Roseanne comes back over to us and I swear that she and Tabitha might hug, but I'm just drunk and it doesn't happen.

* * *

"So what are you wearing to the Fashion Awards?" Tabitha calls me first thing Monday morning. I am just about to call Mrs. Yakimoto.

"Tabitha, c'mon, didn't we clear this outfit up last week?" She sighs.

"Yes, but I had trouble sleeping last night and I thought it over. I have a dress for you. It's a BCBG, very stretchy, so it should fit you." Not be too big, she means. "We have tix to the post party." She's been saying this for days.

"Are we going to hang out with a bunch of production assistants and talent people?"

"Well, aren't you Ms. Savvy about these glam events. This *is* the Talent party. Jaques would never have me mixing with the techies. This dress is much better for this kind of event."

"All right, I'll borrow it." End of conversation.

"Hi, Eve," says Mrs. Yakimoto, not sounding very enthusiastic when I finally reach her.

"Did you have a nice weekend?"

"Yes, look Eve, I don't think we can give you apartment."

I am crushed, I have never wanted anything more than this apartment.

"Why not?"

"Well, I spoke to my husband and we really didn't want to rent it to two people. What if you get into a fight? Who pays the rent?"

"Mrs. Yakimoto." I take a deep breath. "Roseanne and I have lived together for almost four years. We are very good friends and we never fight, but if we did fight we would resolve it very quickly and not let it ruin our time in the apartment. We wouldn't move out. Do you want me to call Mr. Yakimoto?"

"No. No. Eve, you seem very nice and I wanted to give it to you, but my husband thinks I will regret it."

"You won't, Mrs. Yakimoto, believe me, you won't." Slowly, I think I will lose every shred of dignity I possess solely to get an apartment that I have yet to see. "I think the fact that I haven't even seen the apartment and I am fighting this hard based on what Roseanne says is a testament to how much I trust her." Mrs. Yakimoto doesn't say anything for a while. It's creepy. Finally, I can no longer stand it.

"C'mon, Mrs. Yakimoto, don't let Mr. Yakimoto tell you what to do. You're the one that holds the family together. I know you are sick of this apartment thing. Has Mr. Yakimoto handled any of it? No, it's been all you. So, c'mon, Mrs. Yakimoto, trust your instinct. Let us have the apartment."

"Well," she breathes again, "my kids would be happy."

"They know—" I am triumphant! "—they know."

"Oh, I guess."

"Really?" I can't believe it. Yakimoto might be toying with me.

"Why not?"

"Thank you, Mrs. Yakimoto, thank you."

"You're welcome. Just don't make me regret it."

I want to do a little dance, but at the same time, I'm in shock. I never thought we would find an apartment this quick. I can't believe it. I call Roseanne, who is in the middle of an elaborate calisthenics routine, and she screams when I tell her. I wish I were away from this office, so I could celebrate. I still haven't seen the apartment myself and I certainly hope I won't regret it.

Thursday, Tabitha and I are putting our dresses (well, Tabitha's dresses) on in the bathroom stalls on my floor. (She didn't want the Big C to see her before the event.) I had been trying to hide my hands from Tabitha all day, but she finally saw them and had a hissy fit at my chipped nail polish. She ran right downstairs and over to the Duane Reade and bought nail polish remover.

She's starting to calm down now, but I'm still reluctant to complain about anything. Putting stockings on in a stall has to be the most difficult thing ever. I suffer in silence. I have no idea how the dress Tabitha gave me ever fit her. It feels painted on. "Tabitha, I don't know about this."

"Let me see." I step out of the bathroom, sort of smiling at the other women who are there for a reason. I hear a couple say "Wow." Tabitha opens her door a crack and peeks out.

"Looks pretty good. Except lose the bra."

"I don't want droopy booby."

"Eve, just take it off. You've got good boobs. Pull it down a little to show them off." I do as she says and stare at myself in the mirror, clutching my breasts. I'm not so sure about this.

Tabitha fully emerges from her stall. She is wearing some shiny gray dress that's almost sheer. She puts her hair up and reapplies her makeup. I compare our reflections in the mirror. Tabitha may be a lot bigger but she fills her space up well, while I think I'm sort of grasping for a "look."

"You look fab, you're really doing it, Mommy," Tabitha says catching my eye in the mirror. She turns toward me her lip pencil poised. "I just want to redefine. Your lips are really your best attribute, Eve—well your lips and those perky boobs. We should go.''

I bounce all the way down 7th Avenue.

The Fashion Awards are kind of a snooze. I mean it's cool to hobnob, but when there is no alcohol involved and the dialogue is this poor, it's kind of a letdown. The nice thing is wherever I look there's celebrities, but you really can't want to interact with them without seeming like the biggest star-struck loser. It's only fun to look at them for so long.

Being a seat filler is solely for the purpose of making an event appear to the viewing audience as if it is the most populated happening in history. Most of these award shows are attended by industry people, and if they manage to lure celebrities, the celebrities only want to stay for a little while. They are kind of like us, they just want to get to the party.

I know I get on TV a couple of times. That will make my mom happy.

The party is at some club I've never heard of. My presence doesn't stop Jaques and Tabitha from being overly affectionate with each other. Just as I was afraid of, this party is more for production people. There are some low-level celebs and models, but no one to really freak out about. I am here to keep Tabitha company while Jaques schmoozes with the producers to insure that he will be styling the awards next year. We have the bartender make us something extra special, which turns out to be Absolut Currant and cranberry juice. We have three. Suddenly Tabitha starts quasi-hyperventilating. In fact (and she would hate for me to point this out), she looks a lot like Roseanne did at the fateful brunch.

"What? What? What?" I say, while motioning to the bartender for more.

"It's him, it's him." I look around. Who could it be? "It's Kevin. C'mon." She pulls me with her, practically spilling my new drink. It's Kevin, the stylist whose book is her bible.

We hover close to Kevin, who is talking to some TV actress. It's hard for him to ignore us because Tabitha is breathing down his neck. He smiles at us.

"Hi," says Tabitha—whom I have never seen like this—"I think you are great. I love your book. You are truly an artist. Oh, I'm sorry. I'm Tabitha.''

Kevin extends his hand, very humbly. "I'm Kevin." Wow! Then, he turns to me and smiles warmly. He takes my hand.

"Eve," I say, wishing Kevin could be my best friend.

"Nice eyebrows."

"Thanks," I say, but not being enough of a fan to gush I feel kind of stupid. Tabitha drags me away, although I know it's difficult for her to remain calm.

"Isn't he amazing? So nice. Introducing himself like we didn't know who he is." We sigh and have another drink to celebrate the glowing goodness of Kevin.

Eventually, Tabitha has to hang out with Jaques and I wind up talking to some production assistant who tells me that his name is Moose. Moose talks to me as if I am about five. Even though he has opted to wear sunglasses inside, I can still pretty much tell that he is staring at my breasts.

"Have you ever been here before, Eve?"

"No, have you?"

"No." He enunciates every word like he's my preschool teacher. Maybe he's really stoned or just used to talking to four-year-olds. He is so repulsive, but I'm bored and I'm kind of enjoying just toying with him. I guess correctly that he is from Staten Island and I think he thinks I want to go home with him.

"You know it smells there. Do you know where the bathroom is?"

"No," he tells my chest. "I said I was never here before. Why would I lie to you?"

"I don't know," I say, adding, "Moose." And then he just stares, blatantly stares, at my boobs. I look around for Tab, but she is cuddling with Jaques. She is to blame for my lack of bra. But wait! No matter what, I don't deserve this. Why should I be gawked at or talked to like a child, by the likes of Moose? I've had enough.

"So, Moose—" I crouch down to crotch level and speak to his fly "—are you having fun?" I'm not quite sure Moose gets it. He would most likely swear I was seconds away from giving him a blow job. Tabitha must think the same, because she and Jaques rush over and decide to send me home in Jaques's car. They are going to go to some party for a designer that will certainly be more star-studded. I protest that I want to go too, but Tabitha will not listen. I wave goodbye to the dickhead Moose, who is still trying to guess my tits' address. I only hope Kevin didn't see my display.

At work the next day, I don't hear from Tabitha until she calls at noon (when she finally rolls in) thinking I am going to be a wreck, but, it is she who is moving slowly. I ask her about the rest of her night. Despite the presence of several "fabulous celebs," she is really most excited about the Kevin meeting and his kind compliments. Of course, she has to take some credit.

"Remember when I told you how to shape them better?"

"Yes, Tabitha, I owe it all to you."

"Well, it really all goes back to Kevin. I mean, I got the idea out of his book. But, you know I can't help feeling a bit envious. First you meet Prescott and now this. Two of my personal heroes you manage to charm."

"I didn't exactly meet Prescott, or charm anyone. It's really thanks to you that I know who both of them are."

"Well, I guess you're right." Everyone feels a lot better now.

I was so undrunk last night that I had a long talk with Roseanne when I got home. She had waited up for me after her short-lived disaster date. Apparently her breasts also were in the spotlight. She had just sat down for a nice dinner with Brad (okay so the tipoff should have been when he took her to a midtown tourist trap) when, feeling a little hot, she slipped off her blazer.

"Wow," he gasped. "What a set of jugs." Needless to say, Roseanne considered getting a doggie bag for her dinner and bailing, but she stuck it out through Brad's leerings and boring descriptions of his ad accounts, specifically a tartar control toothpaste and how they made the tartar look especially gross.

"Yuck," I said.

"Worse, when I got back, I wanted to go for a run, but your mom was up and she forced me to discuss portobello mushrooms."

"How bizarre. Poor you."

Just as we were falling asleep, we realized that we only had four more days until we moved in and became true New Yorkers.

I have to deposit the check Roseanne gave me. She handed it over a little nervously; apparently she's down to her last three hundred dollars after I cash it. We have to send in our first month's rent and deposit. Somewhere along the line Mrs. Yakimoto raised the rent to fifteen hundred and in all the excitement, I agreed. I am keeping this from Roseanne until she gets a job. Not fun.

I head to the bank at lunch and hand the bank teller my money and the deposit slip. She's a really attractive British woman. I wonder why she's working in a bank.

"Eve Vitali?" She looks up at me, questioning.

"Yes, what?"

"That's your name." I nod. She smiles at me, a perfect tartar-controlled smile.

"Well, that's a grand name—a telly name. I'm charmed by it. Absolutely." Wow! I love British people.

I walk back to the office. It's cool out, really perfect weather, and I just feel like everything is working. Ever have one of those days when you just feel perfect, unsinkable, nothing can touch you, because it's just going to roll right off? It's all going to fall into place finally. The apartment, my job, everything. I wanted the apartment and I got it. Didn't Kevin say I had nice eyebrows? I feel like I'm floating. A telly name? Imagine that. Thanks, Mom and Dad, you've made me destined for greatness, just by choosing the perfect name.

When I get back to the office Lorraine looks at me strangely. I am so cheery, so far from being fake. I am a strong woman, I can do anything.

"Um." She looks so uncomfortable. "Lacey Matthews got the job."

"How wonderful," I say. Not great, wonderful, and I mean it. We walk together to my desk. Good for Lacey Matthews. Nice name, not a telly name, but I wish her all the success in the world.

Lorraine still seems uncomfortable, she should just relax. She's awkwardly holding a stack of napkins. "Herb took her out to lunch." Lorraine takes my arm firmly before I get to my desk. "She brought Max in. You know, the dog?" She looks down and I follow her gaze.

For the rest of the afternoon, me, my perfectly shaped eyebrows and telly name mop up the floor and try to ignore the disinfectant smell mixed with the dog piss.

November

I race up the stairs the moment we get the key, early Saturday morning. Roseanne follows behind me (she can usually run faster, but she is giving me the lead). We both kind of take a deep breath before I open the door.

I was expecting a palace, but what I find is just a really nice average-size apartment. Anywhere else it would be worth less than half of what we are paying. Here in New York, it's a place I want to call home. The floors are amazing. Roseanne, seeing that I don't hate it, starts pointing out more features. I follow behind her, looking at the windows, the bathtub, the brand-new stove.

"So?" she asks.

"Wow!" I grab her arm. "Good job."

"Dusty," says my mother, before sneezing.

"Where should I put these?" asks Phil, one of my dad's buddies, holding up a box of my clothes. My dad says nothing.

The room I get is pretty big. It's a washed-out dingy white, which eventually we will have to change. The closets are huge. Rosie's cranny, as we call it henceforth, is a smaller alcove next to the kitchen with a sleep loft above the kitchen. In the alcove, she has space for a desk and maybe a bureau. It's actually kind of cute.

I'm really happy that my dad's friend Phil is helping out, even though we see a lot of his butt crack. My dad is still on hyper-speed, he's rushing up the stairs with everything, but thanks to Phil, there is a lot less for him to take. My mom cleans the whole time. She brought her super-duper vacuum and vows to buy us a small vacuum so we can be "on the ball about cleaning." The thing about my mom is she keeps giving me these hugs and saying "my little girl" like I'm getting married or something. My father stands on the fire escape, which we will henceforth call either the balcony or the veranda, and smokes.

The whole process takes about two and a half hours. Phil goes to the store and gets a bunch of sandwiches and some beer. Then, we sit around on the hardwood floors eating. I look at my dad to make sure he is not going to have a heart attack, but he is happily gnawing away at his pastrami and swiss with mayo.

"So," asks my mother as she leaves, "are you coming home for Thanksgiving?"

"Mom! I'm not living in Alaska! Of course I will, it's only an hour train ride."

"Okay, honey! Remember you can always come home."

"Okay, Ma, okay." As my father leads her out, I hear her start questioning whether or not the lock is safe.

Rosie and I work steadily for a while. We put up shelves, hang a few posters, unpack clothes, arrange the bathroom. By the time we get the apartment closer to the way we want and make a list of the things we need, it's almost nine o'clock.

We stand out on the veranda and look out over 7th Avenue. If we turn to the right we can see all the way up to the lights of Times Square. "Tired?"

"A little—" Rosie leans against the stairs "—but I wouldn't mind a drink."

We don't even bother to shower. We (I) invite Tabitha, who agrees to go out with us, but informs us that she is "not in the mood to excess." Adrian declines because he has a date.

Tabitha arrives with puffy eyes. She refuses to talk about Jaques. He left for Paris a few days ago. She surveys the place. "Not bad. This is a loft."

"Thanks, we knew that," Rosie says, getting up to finish putting on her makeup. You'd think in their times of need they could be nice to each other. Wrong.

"How do you plan to fill your days?" Tabitha yells toward the closed door.

"C'mon on, now," I plead with her. Tabitha looks like she might start crying again at any minute. "What are you doing to-morrow?"

"I've got a tennis lesson."

"Tennis?"

"Yeah, I need something to fill my time away from Jaques. The circles I want to run in are full of people who play tennis. I would encourage you to look into it."

"No thanks, I like to be sedentary."

"Even with Ms. Jazzercise, here?" Ms. Jazzercise herself opens the door to the bathroom and emerges with an obvious foundation line. There is no way she needs to wear this much makeup. Maybe

I should buy the Kevin book and leave it open to a page that talks about minimalism. I look at Tabitha and shake my head.

"Okay let's go, ladies." I clap my hands together like my mother.

Tabitha wants us to go to this lounge all the way over by the river.

"C'mon, there's so many other places. Both of us are a little weary. We just want to sit and drink and not have to worry about anyone looking at our breasts." Roseanne nods in agreement, probably too scared to say anything.

"Why not?" Tabitha is confused.

"Tabitha, at least think of Jaques. We don't want a meat market."

We wind up at Peter McManus. It's an Irish pub with a kickass jukebox. This is the type of place that I would think Tabitha would hate, but she gets up and puts at least two dollars in the jukebox. She keeps telling us we are going to love her selections. When each song ends we pause and look to Tabitha for a word on whether the new one is one of her choices. It's always a good one, but never one of the ones she picked.

We drink a lot while waiting for her songs to come on.

While Rosie is in the bathroom, I ask Tabitha if she'll call Johann, the German banker.

"Eve, what about my feelings? I'm just getting over one European."

"Tabitha, you don't have to date him, just give him a call."

"You never tire of testing me. Oh, God." She gets up. "Shit, shit. This is it. My song." I leap up, too. It's "Suspicious Minds" by the King himself. We start dancing and dancing and when Roseanne comes out she starts dancing, too. Some of the regulars look over at us and laugh. They sing along, but it's just kind of us, fucking up the words, making up dance moves. It's a good drunk.

Next is Marvin Gaye singing about getting it on and we make up some serious Motown moves. I've never seen Tabitha shake her ass so much. Her selection surprises me: the Stones, Men at Work, Aretha Franklin, Blondie. We dance to them all and she warns us about a "song for Jaques." It's that "Michelle...ma belle" song from the Beatles and we sing it to Tabitha, twirling her around. Then we collapse at the table and order another drink.

This is probably the most unhip bar I've ever been to. There is not a single guy I want to hook up with, there's barely a guy under thirty-five, but it doesn't matter. It's not that kind of night. The bartender buys us some drinks.

"I gotta go," says Tabitha finally. "I have to call Jaques. He went to a party tonight, but he should be in by now." We walk her out. The cab is waiting and she leaps into it like she's making a getaway, but she rolls down the window before she goes.

"Auf wiedersehen," she shouts, and winks at me.

"That was actually fun." Roseanne is surprised. I nod and we both smile the whole way home.

After we get back and wash up, we call to each other from room and cranny. "Good night," we say like the fucking Waltons. The room is spinning, but it's my very own spinning room right here in the heart of New York.

When the room finally stops spinning, Roseanne is shaking me awake. I have no idea where I am, but then realize that something has to be wrong. "I found something. Come look."

It's 11:00 a.m. I need more sleep than this on a Sunday. I did physical labor yesterday. I follow her into the kitchen, cursing. It smells really good in here. She has obviously gone shopping and was making some really awesome breakfast treat when tragedy struck. She points to the floor by the oven.

"I was so happy because I found this terrific little gourmet shop and I was going to make a portobello goat cheese omelet and surprise you, but then I found this." I have no idea what it is. It looks like dirt. I shrug.

"Eve, it's a turd, a rat turd. We have rats."

"You've obviously been brainwashed by my mom."

"Eve, what if we have rats? I'll be sick if we have rats."

"We don't have rats. It's just dirt."

"No, it's turd." I look closely at the "turd." I'm not convinced. Roseanne begins talking crazy. "We should call your mother. She would know what to do."

"We are not calling my mother! It is day one of New Apartment. Of New Exciting Life and you want to call my mother?"

"Well—" Rosie swallows "—yes."

"Look, let's just eat this delicious-smelling meal you made and calm down."

Rosie sighs. "Fine, let's eat, but I can't just close my eyes to this. I won't live with rats."

"Don't worry, Scarlett, you'll never go hungry again."

Even though we have an EIK (once again, Eat In Kitchen), we opt to eat on the couch in the living room. Roseanne also made

Cajun homefries and turkey bacon. It's a small feast that I would like the pleasure of enjoying in my happy home, but Roseanne keeps sighing and looking over into the kitchen.

"Okay, after breakfast we'll get some traps."

"I won't touch them. I'll be sick."

"Jesus Christ, Rosie! We don't even know if there's a fucking rodent. Can't we just enjoy the first day in our new home!" Roseanne slumps into the chair, muttering about how she is the one who is going to be stuck at home with the rats.

Begrudgingly, I dress to go hunt for rattraps with Roseanne. There's a deli right under us that seems a little dirty, but it's got this funky lighting. We christen it the "Dirty Disco Deli." We decide the only safe thing to buy from there is sealed beverages. We head over to the river and down to Chelsea Market. The cool food shops temporarily distract Roseanne. We sit on the docks. It's just starting to get chilly, but it's still warm enough to hang out. We stop for coffee and people watching. Rosie keeps reminding me that we have to get the rattraps, but at least she is not mentioning my mom anymore. I remind her how lucky we are to even have a place to live.

"I won't share my life with rats." She stares at me over her latte.

We make our way up to K mart and buy some sponges, a bath mat and so much rat poison that the cashier asks me if I am planning on killing someone.

"You see," I say to Roseanne, who apparently does not, so I point to her and nod at the guy, who might take me seriously.

"That isn't very nice, Eve. I'm protecting you."

Roseanne suggests we get to know our neighbors. She really just wants to find out if they have rodent problems, but I'll allow her to think she is being friendly. Our first stop is the woman below us. Her name is Marie. She seems a little spacey. She works in a public relations firm. She tells us that we should make sure we have a covered garbage can and though she hasn't seen any rats, she also has three cats so maybe that's why.

"Are you two students?" It's a loaded question; Marie is trying to gauge how much trouble we'll be. Most people don't want to live with students.

"No," says Roseanne. "We've been out for two years now. I work in finance and Eve is in the publishing industry."

"Oh." Marie is now trying to gauge if we are together.

"If you ever hear us making too much noise, just let us know."
We head up to the top floor.

"Maybe I should have made something."

"Like what? A pie. Forget it, Ro." We knock a couple of times,
but no one answers. It seems we will have to wait to uncover his
rodent experiences. So far, it's looking pretty good for the case
against rodent presence.

"Let's just tend to the matter at hand. Shall we?"

When we finish covering the edges of the kitchen floor in poison, Roseanne makes a delicious pineapple barbecue chicken. I
am going to gain about ten pounds just from living with her.

"I'll sleep much better knowing that we are fighting the furry
ones." Great.

"I do not want to go to work tomorrow." I feel kind of bad
for saying it because I know Roseanne wishes she had a job to
dread, too.

"I wish David Letterman was on tonight." Okay, here's some-
thing I haven't mentioned. Roseanne has this strange (dare I say?)
obsession with David Letterman. Anywhere she goes, she buys
Top 10 Reasons shirts (University of Michigan Top 10, Top 10
Reasons to Love New York, Top 10 Reasons Fishing is Better
Than Marriage, Top 10 Reasons to You Name It). Thank God
Tabitha has not seen these! In college, Roseanne would always
recite the actual Top 10 the day after they aired.

Once when we were especially drunk, she explained to me her
fascination with David Letterman. I guess when Roseanne's parents got a divorce, she had a lot of trouble sleeping. She used to
creep downstairs to her basement and watch his show. She'd have
to sit really close to the TV, because she didn't want to turn it up
too loud. She said he always made her feel better, and a lot of
times she'd wake up on the floor in the basement. Sweet story,
right? Definitely is, but, it gets a little strange.

The night she told me about this we were at a party. At some
point, when we were super drunk (it was Saturday night and Sat-
urdays were a big booze night for Roseanne because she wouldn't
have Dave as an interruption), we had to use the bathroom. As
usual, there were a lot of people on line for the bathroom. We
went out into the woods in the back. It was freezing, but Rosie
was in no rush. She asked me if I found Dave attractive. I thought
she was kidding, but she told me about how she yearned to put
her tongue in the gap of his teeth. All I wanted to do was get back
inside, but I had to crouch there and imagine Dave's gap.

"Don't you have some episodes on tape?" I ask her now.

"Yes, but I need new Dave, fresh Dave, unadulterated Dave."
It really was hard on her that my parents liked Leno.

"Mmm." I have to try to discourage this kind of thing. "Let's
see what's on Fox."

It isn't that hard to get up on Monday. I lie in my bed for a
while thinking about my week. Every Monday I dread the work
week, but I intend to change my attitude. This week, in celebration
of my new New York life, I'm going to talk to the big guys about
my bicycle story.

The walk to work is great, it takes me twenty-five minutes. It's
double my walk from Penn Station, so I'm used to a lot of the
same faces, but it's different south of 34th Street. I see the same
people I usually do, but at slightly different points on the street.
This is the closest New York comes to being a small town; those
same morning faces. It's like I'm getting a whole new view of the
city.

I vow to be happier at work. After all, is this not a dream place
to be? Everyone keeps telling me that so I have to start believing
them. I mean, as everyone also points out, I could be working in
the service industry, making fries.

I smile at everyone in the elevator. They give me dirty looks;
no one likes a good mood on Monday. I should respect that, but
I will not be deflated. It's Lacey Matthews's first day. She's waiting at my desk when I get in.

"Good morning, Eve. I don't have a computer."

"Oh, yeah. Well, I called last week and they are going to try
to bring it up today."

Lacey leans closer and swallows in case I am not quite sure of
how imperative this is. "But, I was hired to be a writer. In order
for me to write, I need a computer."

"Look, you over-aerobicized, dog-loving, talentless, nepotism-
profiting floozy, I spent all last week cleaning up the smell of your
dog's piss. I had a lot more important things to do than to order
your goddamn computer." (Okay, I don't say that, I'm just keeping
you on your toes. How quickly you forget about my new positive
attitude.)

"Okay, well, I'll try to get it up here as soon as possible. They
are just a little crazed right now." I find it's great to have a "they"
to pass the buck to, no one ever investigates who the "they" are
and what "their" story really is. It's a benefit of being the middle
man. It's like when I worked in the drugstore all through high

school. People, especially the elderly, would think that whatever wasn't sitting on the shelf was hiding out in "the back." I was always pretending to check the magical back, but there was nothing but cleaning supplies and a big closet where we used to smoke pot. Sometimes, you just have to indulge people.

Lacey hands me a long list of supplies that I am to assume is equally as important to her ability to write. Apparently, she can only write with the most expensive pens in the catalog and only schedule with the hundred and fifty dollar calendar.

To be annoying and to waste Lacey's valuable time, I send out an e-mail about anyone needing anything.

Hey folks,
I am going shopping in the stockroom. If anyone needs any more supplies, please let me know before the end of the day. Please do not request rubber bands for non work-related activity. Remember our company policy on hall sports. Thanks.
—Eve

I immediately get about eighteen replies for Post-it notes. Adam responds,

Eve,
Can you get me an apple? Thanks.
—Adam

I think Adam just may be my favorite person in the department. I also suspect he might be serious about thinking we have some kind of biblical destiny together, but I've been holding him at bay. It's wrong to date people from work.

I have lunch with Tabitha and tell her about the rodent Lacey and the rat we might have in the apartment. I think she is about to offer me some very meaningful advice because she looks so contemplative as she chews her mesquite turkey wrap.

"Maybe I should move to Paris." Forgetting about my own vermin problems momentarily, I spend the remainder of my lunch hour telling Tabitha about my own new attitude and how if she can make it here, she'll make it anywhere.

"What'll you have to look forward to in Paris except a bunch of snotty French people?" I have to act quickly if I want to talk some sense into her.

"Jaques is a snotty French person." I have never seen her like this before.

"I can't believe you are gonna let some man play you like this. Seriously, Tabitha, you are getting too wrapped up in Jaques. Didn't you always tell me about your dream to live in New York, that you weren't going to leave until you had made something of yourself? Until you had a mention in *Vanity Fair?* Come on now. Why the drama?"

"Because he hasn't been returning my calls in a timely fashion. I wonder if he's got another mademoiselle in Paris. I've been trying to find the file we had on him for that little story we did. We used some fucking freelancer and we don't have any records. Damn." It's always easier to blame the random temp pool. Tabitha and I are perma-temps.

"Well, he is an artist." I know this will get her.

"You know, you're right. I shouldn't be so selfish, his art was always more important. Better his art than some French floozy. I've just been so bored lately."

"Tabitha, he left a week ago. I thought you had fun this weekend."

"Fun in a base way. It didn't push me along to my destined greatness. I can't slip up and have too many lost weekends like that."

"All weekends are lost, Tabitha, eventually."

"I just need to do something fabulous soon. I should call Nicole." Nicole is this absolutely horrid girl who works for some casting agency. She thinks Tabitha is a lot bigger deal at *NY By Night* than she really is. Even though Nicole has the worst personality ever, Tabitha tolerates her because she usually knows of even better parties than Tabitha.

I loathe Nicole, especially the way she gets calls on her cell phone in the middle of bars. She constantly talks about all her connections at Miramax and rich friends who are going to help her start her own film company. Tabitha buys it, too. I hate to think of Tabitha as holding on to anyone's coattails, but she is. She thinks someday Nicole will be a power person and we'll be able to milk her for something.

"Ooh," she says, looking across The Nook. "I guess there are some reasons to stay in New York." She's referring to a dark-haired guy by the condiments, maybe a new intern. He's really well dressed and really cute.

"He's definitely decked out for an intern. Maybe that's the secret." I myself am wearing upscale Zara.

"Eve, that's Robert King." I shrug. "God, you've got to start reading the trades. Robert King is the guy they brought in to shake things up a bit to change the look of some of our magazines. He's some kind of marketing guru."

"What is he? Twelve?"

"No, probably thirty, making his mark young, if you will. A hint to us that we are approaching our prime and thus, close to being past it."

"I am already way past my prime."

"Oh, the carnage. Anyway, that Robert's a cutie. He parties with the jet set. Dates models. Needs no sleep. The typical bio. But look at him, he's having trouble with the catsup thingie. Who has trouble with that? Deep down you know he's just a loser and here he is being 'brought in' to help our company, which is doing amazing."

Whatever. I am just happy that Tabitha's little talk has revitalized her. She intends to be one of the movers and shakers. She knows she can stay in New York now, because of the catsup thingie.

"Did you call Johann yet?"

"Yes, Ms. Broken Record, for your information, I did. I left a message. He was away from his desk. He might not call me back and if he does I'm only going to tell you once that I will *not* prostitute myself for your friend. Okay?"

"Fine. Just let me know what happens."

"I will."

"You know, Roseanne could be your friend, too. She is a lot nicer than Nicole."

"That's arbitrary, Nicole is more of a contact than a friend."

"Whatever."

"I've got to get back. I think the Big C is premenstrual."

When I return from lunch, Lacey is at my desk once again. They still haven't delivered her computer. "I am paralyzed without it! I am wasting the company's money, by not having it. I am sitting there doing nothing."

Welcome to my life. Doesn't she have any phone calls to make? Should I suggest she look at some of the old issues? I try another approach. "Do you have a laptop?"

"Yes, of course, but I didn't bring it. I didn't know this was going to happen."

"Well, I'm doing my best to get you the computer." She looks at me like she doesn't believe me. She is doing everything in her power to ruin my positive attitude.

"Well, I am going to go to lunch with Herb right now. Do you think it will be here when I get back?"

"That's really not for me to say. We can only hope…and pray." I smile. She shakes her head and goes off to her fabulous lunch.

I head down to the underbelly of Prescott Nelson with my list of supplies. Just below the lobby is a whole mess of rooms that no one but assistants seem to know about. There you will find the mailing room, the Express Mail guy, the messenger service, the supply room, the copy shop and the catering service. If I were to ever rise to the great heights at Prescott Nelson that Tabitha imagines for us, I think this knowledge would be a part of my success. Tabitha hates coming down here, but I am amazed that all of these people exist in even more thankless, yet tremendously more important jobs than I have.

It's mostly guys down there, and they're all so nice. I guess it's because I'm nice to them, when so many people don't even see them. It's like a network, a secret society that I feel I could call on at any time. In my most bored moments (usually, just when I've messengered something) I imagine scenarios where the future of our magazine hinges on getting something mailed out, tracing a messengered package, or making thousands of copies with a five-minute turnaround. It is only my knowledge of the inner workings of Prescott Nelson that saves the day. A corporate superhero with my own league of justice. This is my aspiration.

Down in the supply room I hand my list over to Roger, the Caribbean guy with dreads who calls me "honey." He gives me the few items he has, which are all the Post-its, some hanging folders, those giant desk calendars, three-ring binders, message books and some notebooks.

"You got all that, honey?" he asks, piling the stuff up in my hands. I reach up to steady the Post-its that are slipping off. "I could send a guy with a cart, this afternoon."

"No, I'll be fine, really. Actually, can I also get a pack of whatever pens you have around?" I want Lacey to have some form of writing utensil, so she doesn't have to "waste the company's money" anymore. I get a pack of the cheapest pens.

I walk slowly back to the elevators. I wish the elevator would just express it back to my floor, but of course, it stops at the lobby. A guy gets on. He smells good.

"Hey, whoa, need a hand with that?"

"No—" I peer over my supplies to his forehead "—I'm fine."

Of course the elevator has to stop at every floor and no one gets in. "Does this happen a lot?" The good-smelling guy is trying to talk to me. If only I could see his face.

"Well, sometimes," I say. He must be new. "Looks like we got the local." Aggh, elevator humor. I can't believe I've stooped so low.

"Yeah, right. Where can I get some Post-its?" A new temp. Has to be.

"You just go down to the supply room with your finance code and a list." It's my floor.

"Oh, here, let me help." He gets out of the elevator, swipes his ID, and opens the door for me.

"Thanks." That was really nice. I take a look at him as he is waiting to get on the elevator. It's the first time I get a good look at him. We smile.

I opt not to call Tabitha and tell her that my sweet-smelling Good Samaritan was that Robert King guy, the catsup thingie incompetent. Not as big as Prescott or Kevin, but a marketing guru, nonetheless.

I have a message from my sister when I get to my desk.

"Hey, Eve. It's Monica. I just talked to Mom. Why must that woman have so many issues? She places no value in anything we do. Could you call me please?" I delete her. My sister gives new meaning to the word drama.

I call my apartment and Roseanne is not there. I take it as a good sign. We haven't figured out how to check our messages externally yet, so I have no clue to her whereabouts. If I wasn't so bored, I wouldn't be compelled to call my sister, but I am, so I do. At least this way, it's on Prescott's dime.

"Hello?" How does my sister manage to sound so frazzled in just one word?

"Hey, M."

"Oh, my God. Is Mom losing her mind or what? Have you talked to her lately?"

"Yes, Monica, up until two days ago I lived with her." It doesn't occur to my sister to ask me anything about my move or my new apartment. She does tell me that my mom is a nervous wreck about my "unsafe" neighborhood. Then she launches into her own tirade about my mother not respecting her work at all. I start to absently play computer hangman, since conversations with

Monica usually only require sounds in the affirmative. Also, an occasional disgusted agreement like this...

"Can you believe them, Eve? Can you believe we hatched from such absolute weirdos?"

"Absolutely not."

"Anyway, I'm in love." (I don't say, "again?") "He is amazing, he's a singer."

"Not a student?"

"Eve, he's forty-three." It's enough to make me give my poor hangman a leg.

"Isn't that a little old?"

"Ageism is one of the most innocuous forms of discrimination." My sister always says shit like that. I wish I had started a list of her phrases. "I wonder why our family has such a problem with it."

"Maybe because he's seven years younger than dad. It's kind of an issue."

"He also less than fifteen years older than me. What does that mean? Nothing." She also likes to ask and answer her own questions. I think it comes from doing so many papers all these years. I try to reverse it.

"Monica, do you do this to give Dad a heart attack and make Mom go into a panic? I think so."

"Eve, why do you let Mom brainwash you? I guess without me she's quite formidable."

"Monica, look, sleep with or 'love' whoever you want, but until you've got a ring on your finger or a bun in the oven, don't tell them about it. Do you think Mom or Dad gives a shit about your love life? They want to forget we know the definition of sex."

"Why do you choose to live a lie with them? It's so they'll think you are the good one. Not me. I live my life honestly. I have integrity. Besides, Chuck could be the one."

"You are going to marry a forty-three-year-old singer? I don't think so." I can get used to talking like this.

"Yes, he is principled. He sings folk songs, from the sixties. Songs about change. He has quite a following around here. He has ideas and beliefs that are stronger than most of the guys my age. He's an activist. We've lost that, Eve. Our society has moved away from those ideals to an empty one. Our generation has nothing. It's an empty MTV generation." Here we go. She won't stop.

"I love everything he represents. For the first time ever, I am in love with a man and at the same time in love with his politics."

Wow! I am speechless. I cannot even imagine answering my sister in one of my two tried and true ways (sounds in the affirmation or disgusted agreement in case you forgot), I guess it's best to ignore her. I see Lacey Matthews striding over to my desk.

"Listen, Monica, I have to go. I have someone at my desk." Lacey is already mouthing something to me. She is blind to the phone at my ear.

"Okay, Eve, I want to talk to you soon, honey. I want to find out about your apartment. I miss you. I love you." Not only is my sister a big time sap, I'm starting to think she's bipolar.

"Me, too. 'Bye." I hang up and turn to Lacey. She's got a yucky crease between her eyebrows. "My sister."

"Still no computer." Lacey is not taking the sister excuse, she is just not having it. "This is getting ridiculous."

At some point during Lacey's *brief* tenure, she stopped seeing me as the departmental assistant and began to view me as her own personal secretary. I think I should start being less efficient.

"I think you might have to wait until tomorrow. It's already 4:30. I seriously doubt they're going to come up now."

"Well, I don't want to have another day like this tomorrow. Can you have them up here first thing in the morning?"

"It's not something I control. I have already called them four times today. You see how much it did." In reality, it was only twice, but she'll never know.

"Maybe you're not being aggressive enough." Is she out of her bird? My expression must register, because she starts one of those phony office apologies that people give when they are totally insulting, but can't afford to offend you. "I mean, maybe they just can't recognize the importance of it. After all, I am wasting money and productivity. It's a big deal."

I am starting to sense that to Lacey everything (with the exception of indoor canine urination) is a big deal. Hasn't she ever had a first day before? First days are all about bumming around trying to figure out your place and getting a feel for the environment. Not much work gets done on first days. They aren't supposed to. In fact, first days are suspiciously similar to my job.

"Well," I say, trying to remain cheery (she is really testing my new stance on positivity), "if you want to give them a call, you certainly can."

"Well, I don't know if I would have the impact you would." I thought I was just accused of not being aggressive enough.

"So, what would you like me to do?" Lacey looks like a little girl who has to go to the bathroom, except her face is too put together. She twists a little and fidgets.

"Can you call them again, please?"

"Oh, sure." Just go away. She stands there waiting for me to call. "Now?"

"If you could." She smiles. Jesus. I dial Tabitha's number. She can tell it's me from her caller ID.

"Hey, Eve."

"Um, hi, my name is Eve Vitali. I've called several times today about getting a computer for Lacey Matthews."

"Is that the bitch with the pooch?"

"That's right. Well no one has yet come up to install her computer."

"What is this? Is she right there?"

"Yes, and I mean basically Ms. Matthews has been stagnant all day. It is really a waste of her tremendous talent." I smile at Lacey and nod. We are on the same side.

"Mother of God."

"I mean she can't write without her computer."

"Why don't you tell her to go fuck herself."

"Oh, I've already tried that, but I still haven't gotten a response."

"This woman is going to kill you. You shouldn't even indulge these sick fantasies."

"Yes, I know that. Do you have a supervisor I could talk to?"

"Why, am I not being helpful enough?"

"Oh, he left already."

"Why would you assume that he was a guy? See how sexism is ingrained?"

"You know that's exactly what someone I spoke to earlier said—it usually takes a day to process." Now Lacey is enjoying cheering me on. She is mouthing something to me about deadlines. "I mean, really, she is on a deadline. This *is* a magazine company."

"Nice touch. She's used to the sound of her clock ticking. This, too, shall pass."

"Yeah, well what do you expect her to do?"

"Maybe get laid instead of walking her barbaric dog, so she can get off your back. It might work wonders."

"I'm not even sure that would do it."

"Most likely not, but I think you can be a little snottier. Show me who's the boss."

"Yes, I understand and I want you to know how imperative it is that we get this computer as soon as possible."

"You know, next she'll need help wiping her ass."

"I'm certain that would be the next step."

"There you go. Keep that witch tone going."

"Now give me the absolute latest it will be installed. This woman needs to start cranking."

"That's not all she needs."

"Okay, we definitely need to have it before then. I don't want to have to get our supervisors involved in this."

"Oh, no, anything but that." Tabitha uses this Southern accent and I almost lose it.

"Okay, so I have your word? What's your name?"

"What are you going to do, ho? Call my supervisor? Haven't I been helpful? Haven't I bent over backward? You want my name? Okay, fine. Zeke."

"Great, Luis. Thanks for all your help."

"Fuck you."

"Oh, you, too. Thanks again." We hang up. I smile at Lacey. She seems genuinely impressed. I hope I haven't started a trend of doing her dirty work for her.

"Thanks, Eve. So what did they say?" Lacey thinks that if she uses my name I will think she sees me as a person, not just someone to literally piss on.

"Well, Lacey, they think tomorrow afternoon, Wednesday the absolute latest. It's a mess down there. He told me about all these people they had to service first. Totally unorganized. I suggest you bring in your laptop, just in case." Lacey sighs.

"Well, okay. Listen, Eve, I really appreciate it." She switches into some phony British accent like that is supposed to be friendly or something. It's stupid.

"Fine, Lacey, anytime." I wave her off. Don't give me too much praise.

Moments later the computer guys show up and ask me who needs their computer set up. There's two ways to play this. I can freak out because I insisted to Lacey that they were backed up or I can make it my moment. The danger is that Lacey will think her nagging is ultimately responsible and she will continue to hound me whenever she needs something done and that will, as my sweet grandmother would say, "drive me to an early grave." I don't want to start that trend. I stride over to Lacey's desk with the computer guys in tow.

"Look who's here, apparently the person I spoke to was misinformed. They were already on their way, because of all my earlier harassment."

"Oh, how wonderful!" Lacey looks like she is going to have an orgasm. I flit back to my desk and call Tabitha.

"Stellar performance."

"I do my best. The computer guys came to put a muzzle on her."

"Now wasn't that quick turnaround? You see the speed in which I operate."

Lacey comes to me before she leaves. She gushes with thanks and tells me she is so glad she got so much accomplished on the first day. Of course it's never enough. "So what about the other supplies?"

"At least two days."

"Of course we thought that about the computer." I am definitely going to sit on the other supplies for at least a week if they come in before that. I should try not to do my job too well. "Well, have a good night."

"You have a great night."

It's not easy to be positive on Mondays.

When I get home Roseanne is sitting on the couch in her sweats watching Jerry Springer in his fourth run today. I don't ask her if she's seen the first three. The house smells good though, like food. She must've gotten up off the couch at some point.

"How was your day?"

"Well, no sign of our furry tenants. I watched a lot of talk shows. Made mango-glazed pork chops and garlic mashed potatoes for dinner. Joined a gym, well actually I signed us both up for one. It's right on 8th."

"A gym? How much?"

"A few hundred down usually, but it was two for one so it's like one hundred and change for each of us. Then it's seventy."

"More?"

"A month." I am certain she is going off the deep end.

"Roseanne, I really don't have that kind of money right now. I wish you discussed this with me first." Is everyone in cahoots to drive any positive thoughts from my head? Remain calm. Smile and nod.

"Eve, our fitness is important. There'll always be a tomorrow. We need to start now."

"What is that? Is that in the ad? Where are you getting this? I like being unfit. I drink too much to be fit. So do you."

"That's why we have to do this. If we are going to enlarge our livers we have to enlarge our muscles, too." She is undoubtedly reading too many pamphlets.

"Well, fitness is expensive, Ro, and I prefer to spend my money on my vices. Besides, how are we going to afford this?"

"I got a job." What? "Yep." She gets up and goes into the kitchen. I follow her and watch her pour wine, then put our feast on the plates. She has set our tiny kitchen table, so we can actually eat in our kitchen. Just like the ad.

"So we're celebrating."

"Yes—" she takes a sip of wine "—we are celebrating fitness."

"No, your job. Aren't you excited about your job?"

"Well, I guess. It's in some boring old firm. Don't you get all out of hand, it's very, and I mean very, low level."

"How did you get it?"

"I answered an ad. I suspect they just wanted a woman, but I got it."

"That's fabulous." I hold my glass up to her to toast. She clinks mine, reluctantly. "What's wrong? Not enough salary?"

"Actually, it's more than I ever dreamed of. They pay lots in New York. I don't know, though, I mean, do I want to sit around and play with numbers all day?"

"I could never understand how you did it in school. Those classes were awful."

"Yeah and I was so jealous of you when you got out of that major. I figured I was good at it so it would have to get better, but it didn't fascinate me like your job fascinates you."

"My job does not fascinate me. Not in the least."

"You get into it—and you yourself said it's a foot in the door. Plus the things you want to do are more exciting."

"If I could figure out what it was. I question that 'foot in the door' stuff. The good thing about all those business people at school was that they seemed to have a definite plan. There's something calming about that. I mean you graduate from college with your business-related major, you line up a job for September, you travel, getting it out of your system, and then boom you're on a track to success, to all those attainable American things. Shit! One talk with my sister and this is how I start to think."

"No, you're absolutely right. But I don't know if I want that. I don't want it to be predictable. I want something, I don't know. I guess it is nice to have your life planned, but when the actual life is so boring and has to be lived in uncomfortable hell it isn't as cool."

"But it is good. You got a job."

"I guess."

"How's the salary?"

"45." I think I'm going to choke on my pork chop. Can she mean forty-five thousand? "But, Eve, they're buying my life from me."

"Well, at least for a good price."

When we finish eating I do the dishes. It's a familiar college pattern, she cooks, I clean up. It's only eight o'clock, I feel like there is so much more time left in the evening. We decide to walk down into the village.

Then we visit Adrian. It's just 9:30 and I still can't get over all the time we have in a day. We walk up 8th Avenue and ogle all the pretty boys. Adrian's friend Cliff is visiting. I think there's something up between them, but whenever I try to get Adrian's attention to mouth stuff to him, he looks confused. We convince Roseanne to have a drink, although she vows that she is totally revamping now that we have joined a gym.

"C'mon, hon, just a drink." Adrian is already up and in the kitchen. I follow him.

"What's the deal with Cliff?"

"He's a total Rice Queen, not into my occidental stuff. Did you hear who Miss Thing was going out with tonight?" Adrian does a mock salute and says, "Frankfurter."

"Johann? No, sir."

"Yeah, she just called. He invited her out for a late dinner. She had tried you at your place. She assumed you were out running with Roseanne. That girl has issues."

"Shit. She's going out with him to help Roseanne get a job. Rosie just got one."

Adrian assures me that these small acts of generosity are something we should try to encourage in Tabitha. I know he's right, although I am concerned that she will hold this, too, against Roseanne.

We drink at Adrian's for a while. I suspect Cliff may like him, despite what Adrian said. If I was a gay man, I definitely would. I may, despite my hetero state, have a crush on him anyway. (It'll be fine, I'm used to disappointment.) Cliff doesn't leave when we do. Adrian walks us down.

"I think you might just get some booty," I say as I kiss him.

"We'll see about that." He kisses Roseanne. "Take care, ladies. My love to the mouse."

We walk back to our place. I look up at it from the street. I find my main worry is that someone will break in and take my stuff. Monica would have a field day with the fact that my material belongings are my most important concern.

"Eve, do you think I've got the New York Kiss down?" What is she talking about? "You know, everyone in New York seems to kiss each other. Sometimes. I mean you never can tell. The other night at the bar you kissed the bartender. You didn't kiss Brad's friend. You kissed Brad. We both just kissed Adrian. Sometimes you kiss Tabitha. You never kiss me. What's the story?"

"Wow! I didn't realize you were keeping such good tabs on who I was kissing. I guess it's just like a regular kiss, there's no hard and fast rule. Just whenever. Like a handshake or something. No rules. I mean, I guess you go with the other person."

"Okay. Let's look for droppings." Roseanne's new pre-Letterman pastime is the rodent patrol. She forces me to look around the kitchen on my hands and knees for curious particles that may or may not be rat dung. I find nothing, but she insists that a piece of dirt is a dropping. I try to reassure her, but it doesn't work. Luckily it's 11:35 and I can coax her over to the television. She sighs, sitting on the couch. She isn't quite ready to give up on the rat thing, but Letterman lulls her into a calm. I make my escape right before the first commercial break. Before I fall asleep, I note that she stomps into the kitchen twice and flings the light on. I will not be roused and brought into this war.

At about 3:30 a.m. the phone rings. I scramble to get it, disoriented. It's a drunk Tabitha. "I hope you're happy."

"Oh, Tabitha, what is it? It's late." My heart is beating so fast. I think I was dreaming Adrian was a samurai.

"I went out with Johann. I had to eat lots of gross German food, but some good wine. He doesn't know of any jobs, but he'll take Roseanne's résumé."

"Great, Tabitha, thanks." I think I might fall asleep on the phone. I'm not even going to tell her about Roseanne's job. I'll save that reprimand for tomorrow. "I'm going back to sleep now."

"Well, he definitely lost some hair since we last went out, but he still wears leopard bikinis." Of course.

"Well, Tabitha, at least it wasn't a complete bust—you got a November notch on your hooking-up post."

"My heart belongs to Jaques." I'm really going back to bed. I cannot deal with another lament about the Frenchman. "Besides, I'm not sure if Johann counts, since we already hooked up last March. Of course I had also hooked up with Romolo in March. Can the same guy count for two months? Can I hold over a guy if there's more than one in a month?"

"Tabitha, the regulations are definitely something we can discuss tomorrow."

"Yeah, okay, good night."

As usual the days seem to fly by and drag at the same time. For a while, I can't help feeling that I have all of this time. My nights seem so full. I let Roseanne drag me to a couple of step classes and I try to run each night on the treadmill for fifteen minutes. I'm a baby about exercise. I hate it. Roseanne keeps telling me about the hard New York bodies she sees and she's got a point, but I just can't get into going to the sweaty, yucky gym. Tabitha laughs at me in the mornings when I tell her how much pain I'm in. She says she would go to a spa if she cared about "that stuff."

"Well, not everyone has your trust fund, Tabitha." As usual, she ignores any talk of money.

On Friday, I decide to blow off the whole gym thing and go out with Adam and Joe from marketing for some drinks. I try to coax both Tabitha and Roseanne to come out. Neither is very compliant.

"Thanks to you, I'm going out with Johann. He's taking me to some ridiculously expensive hot spot that has yet to find its way into our illustrious mag. I want to get while the getting's good."

"As I'm confident you will."

"Well, I was certain you'd be raquetballing or something tonight."

"Touché. I can't go to the gym. I draw my line at the weekend."

"Okay fine, give me a call tomorrow." I sigh. "Well, if you must leave me a voice mail tonight. If you go somewhere good."

Roseanne is dissing, too. She is compelled to work out, even on this most sacred night of the week. Of course Friday means nothing to her now, but give her a week of working and I know she will abandon this fervor.

"Roseanne, it's Friday night. Can't you just exercise now and get it over with?"

"Eve, until I am making money, I don't want to be spending money."

"Never mind the small fortune we spent on the gym. I'll buy you a drink."

"That's only going to last so long, Eve, but I do appreciate it. Really."

"Roseanne, come on, there's going to be boys there. Don't you want some loving?"

"I'll pass thanks. Speaking of loving, I looked up Pete Twist today."

"Shit! What's his story?" Pete's a guy who used to live on our dorm floor. Roseanne had the biggest crush on him. He's real quiet. We were both better friends with Todd, his roommate, whom I suspect had a huge crush on me.

"You know he's in New York, right?"

"No, how did you know?"

"Todd told me. Pete is bartending and trying to be an actor." I can't believe Todd called her and he never calls me. "He's on the Lower East Side."

"Cool. Are we going to see him?"

"I'm meeting him for a drink tonight after the gym." Now it all makes sense. I can tell that means she doesn't want me to come.

"What's Todd up to?"

"He's doing well. He still works for the same clothes company in Atlanta. He travels around a lot—to India mostly, sometimes Hong Kong. He actually checks the factories."

"When did you talk to him?"

"I've had a lot of time on my hands."

"You didn't tell me. Did he ask about me?"

"In a roundabout way. I told him to give up his infatuation with you for once and for all."

"Really, c'mon!"

"No, relax, I'm sure he's in love with you, the same as ever." I know it's wrong, but it's nice to think that someone out there likes you, especially if you aren't hot for them. It means that somewhere out there you have an advantage over someone.

I only wanted to have one drink with Adam and Joe, because I think it's wrong to get drunk with your co-workers or date them.

Of course I wind up loopy sitting between them in the back of a cab heading to a going-away party for one of their friends in finance. I am leaning a little too close to Joe, a sexy Latino whom I am super attracted to, while Adam tries to take my hand. I can't feel my nose.

"It's cool hanging out, being one of the guys."

"Eve, you're too pretty to be one of the guys," Joe says, throwing his arm around me. I will not hook up with him. We work together. I won't. I borrow his phone to call in Tabitha for backup.

She shows up at the farewell party. Her date was a bust, and she's almost as drunk as I am. We have no idea who the party is for and we spend the night telling everyone bon voyage. The boys laugh at us and dance with us and I might almost kiss Joe at one point, but it's all kind of a haze.

Finally, the DJ tells us it's the last dance. Tabitha and I bid good-night to the boys. We all kiss. I start laughing and saying "the New York Kiss" over and over. I get the "pity the drunk girl" look from everyone, which makes me laugh even more. I have to pee—it was definitely a bad idea to drink so much with work people. Tabitha says she wants to stop at Krispy Kreme before we go home. It's open late tonight.

"Shit," I say to Tabitha in the cab, "you know I meant to tell them about my story this week, but I never got the nerve up to do it. We should start our own magazine. We could self-publish, we could do it for people like us. That would be cool, but it would take a while. I guess in the meantime, I should try to make the best of this. I guess I'll talk to them about it next week. Always, another week. But seriously, Tabitha, maybe we should think about that magazine. It could be awesome. I don't want pipe dreams." I look over at her in the cab, but she has already fallen asleep. Although, we're only ten blocks to my place, I have the taxi driver go up the F.D.R. and drop her off at her place first.

No Krispy Kreme tonight.

I get home just as Roseanne does. She is fiddling with the keys in the front door. I realize that she is totally smashed, so for safety's sake I tell her sleep in my bed and I'll sleep in the cranny (I can't have her falling off her sleep loft). She holds on to the walls in the apartment and asks me to come in so we can replay the evening's events with her. She really just wants to know if I think she shouldn't have "New York Kissed" Pete.

"His lips were really soft, just like his voice." Whatever. She has her eyes closed and her face is kind of scrunched. I hope she

is going to be okay. "Eve, will you put the trash can near the
bed?"

When I come back with the pail from the bathroom, she is
already out. I roll her onto her side. I promise myself when I shut
the light off for bed that I will talk to Herb about my article this
week.

It takes me until Wednesday to get the courage up to e-mail
Herb about having a talk.

Hi, Herb,
If you have some time soon, I would like to talk. Thanks.
—Eve

I spell check the e-mail at least four times. I hesitate. I get it
out at the end of the day.

His reply is waiting for me when I get in on Thursday.

sure, stop by. lets takl.

So I am sitting in his office, which smells of incense, and he is
nodding. I tell him about how much I think I have to contribute
to the magazine and how important it is to have different voices
represented (without implying that all of the writers on the magazine are too much like him).

"You see, this article—" I point to the copy of my story about
the surgeon who turns to biking "—is totally fabricated, but it's
an example of my work. I have a degree in journalism and I wrote
quite a few stories when I was an editor for our college paper. I
put a few in this folder for you to read."

I can't really gauge Herb's reaction. In meetings he says the
first thing that comes to his mind, but now he is not saying a word.
I am wondering if I have something in my teeth.

"Well, Eve, I really can appreciate your interest in writing."
This sounds like the beginning of a rejection letter. "Right now,
we just hired Lacey. Hopefully, she will help with the workload."
He stops. Maybe he's waiting for me to tell him that Lacey has
no idea that you can use paper to write, too. I stare at him. I am
not going to speak.

"So what does that mean for me?" Damn! I suck. I can never
stick to my guns.

"I'm not sure. You've been here for how long?"

"Almost nine months. Long enough to have a baby." I have

no idea where that came from, even though, yes, I said it. He thinks I'm an asshole. There is no doubt.

"Maybe it's time we gave you a raise." A raise? That's great, what about writing? Shit.

"Well, that's great, but what about the writing?" I will stand firm. I will not falter. I am roaring. He sits back again in his chair. His silences are killing me.

"Well, we usually don't do this, because frankly, our writing is so important to us. I guess if you wanted, if you weren't too busy with...your other...stuff, you could attend the Feed Meet every now and then. We could see how that works."

"Great, that would be great." Oh, boy, invite me to the meeting. Even the fucking intern, Brian, gets to go to the Feed Meet. Whatever. "And will you read my stories?"

"I'll try. Sometimes I get a little crazed." He smiles at me.

"Well, thanks, Herb—" I then remind him "—and thanks for the raise."

"You're welcome." He believes he is doing me a favor. "And it's every Wednesday at—"

"One. Yeah, I know." He looks surprised, as if the Feed Meet was a national secret. "It's in your schedule."

"Oh, right."

Fast forward to Bloomingdale's, two hours later. Tabitha and I are, as usual, shopping in the underwear section.

"I mean, he doesn't even realize I keep his schedule and when he finds a new appointment, a meeting, it's because I put it there. Can you believe it?"

"Yes. I'm telling you the Big C has no idea how I make her life work. Right down to how many tomatoes are on her whole-grain sandwich. They know my order at the deli! It's ridiculous. I'm telling you, Eve, I can do about six more months tops as an admin, then I swear I never want to answer another phone again. What do you think of these?" She is holding up a pair of cream-colored lace panties.

"They're fine, but you have a zillion underwear. I thought you were shopping for going out clothes."

"You're right. I saw a top here that I think you'll like."

"So what do you think of the Feed Meet?" I'm putting on this retro dress with a low cut bodice, and calling to Tabitha, who is in the next dressing room trying on another pair of black pants.

"I think it's cool that he let you in on his secret society, although, I know it's probably going to be more of the same shit you get at your staff meeting. Now, there's pressure to perform. Let me see that dress.''

"No, Tabitha, it's too tight. What do you mean, pressure?''

"Let me see it. I'm coming over. Pressure because you talked to him—I'm opening the door—about writing. Give him a story. Eve, that looks so good on you. You must, must get it. How are these pants?''

"Nice, but you have a zillion pairs of black pants. I guess you're right about the story. I feel like this just delayed my inertia. Really I can't get another going out dress, I need everyday clothes. And we have to get back—we've been lunching for an hour and a half.'' She just shakes her head and I know I'm about to spend too much money on an impractical dress.

"So how much of a raise are you going to get?'' We are getting on the elevators. Tabitha is coming to my floor to pick up a sweater that I borrowed. She bought the pants, five pairs of underwear and a strapless bra. I, of course, got the dress.

"I'll probably make twenty an hour. Every little bit helps to pay for all the shit you make me buy. I don't even have a bra to wear with this. Let me see the one you just got.'' I get it out of her bag, before she can tell me I don't need a bra with the dress. It's huge. "Tabitha, you have the biggest boobs. One boob is bigger than my head.'' Since we're alone in the elevator, I put one cup over my head. Tabitha laughs, crouching over like she is trying not to pee and the door opens and I am staring at Robert King and a bunch of good old boys in suits. Robert King smirks at me.

"Oh, hi.'' I say stepping back to let everyone on. Shit! If only I worked on this floor. Tabitha grabs her bra off my head and stuffs it back in the bag.

"I think red would be a much better color for you. It would set off your dark hair.'' Robert King is smiling down at me.

"Thanks.'' I mean, what else can you say to that, especially when half the board of Prescott Nelson is on the elevator?

"Can you get those in the supply room, too?''

"No, this is a special order.''

"I see.'' He nods, starts talking to the old guys, who keep looking at me. Tabitha pulls me off the elevator when we reach my floor. As she is swiping her card, I turn to meet Robert King's eyes. What a cutie.

"What was that all about?'' I don't want to get into it, so I shrug.

"Hey, I got connections.''

* * *

Wednesday's Feed Meet gives new meaning to the words "waste of time." We spend the first hour discussing the potential harm in letting your children of the opposite sex bathe together and the weather in San Francisco in November. This was the top secret meeting? Maybe I wasn't supposed to come because Herb feared I would tell someone what a waste of time and lunch this is.

Finally, we get down to the writing. Let me say that I have never, not even in stupid college writing courses, experienced a group of more sensitive people. When Gary, one of the senior writers, finishes his piece on a trail in Montana, Lacey argues the use of several words. She wrote them all on a piece of paper while Gary was reading.

"Lacey, you haven't been there. I spent months out there last year. I reached a clarity that you have to experience, which I was hoping true riders would through this article." Oh, veiled references at Lacey's being neither a cyclist nor a boy. I love a good fight and certainly an opportunity to diss Lacey.

"Well, I may not be an experienced cyclist, but I am an experienced writer, and those phrases don't work." Wow! "Go back to the top and read those sentences again."

As Gary is reading, Lorraine is writing notes to me on her stack of schedules and assignments. I have been trying to distance myself from her, to sit among the writers, but they scowled at me when I walked in. I am an infiltrator. I only got halfhearted applause when Herb said I would be attending the meetings occasionally. He stressed occasionally. Lacey smirked. Whatever. Lorraine thinks this meeting is absolutely ridiculous, but she has to attend. She does busy work throughout the meeting and half listens to make sure everyone is meeting their assignment requirements.

Herb intercedes the battle between Lacey and Gary and everyone nods at his words. He smiles at them, like a dad, like a wise parent. He makes a stupid joke about Gary's two months in Montana and what exactly he found. Everyone laughs. I wonder how I would feel if everyone laughed at every single stupid thing I said. The debate is resolved and the group claps for Gary's piece.

I should probably comment, too, but I don't think anyone would take too kindly to anything I said. I don't ride, I haven't written and I'm far from being a boy. After a while I start to feel like I'm at a very boring college lecture. I tune out and just clap at the appropriate moments. After two and a half long hours, the meeting is over.

I promise I'll find a new job.

"I can't believe I ever wanted to go to this meeting. In a word, it sucks. How big should I cut these?" I am cutting up potatoes for Roseanne, who is making fresh gnocchi.

"That's fine, we're not reinventing the wheel here." I grab the cup off the fridge and hold it out to her. "I don't have a dollar. I promise, I'll put it in tonight."

We made an agreement that every time she says something stupid that she gleaned from work she'll put a dollar in a jar. From the moment she starting working, she came home using expressions like "marry them together," "take it to bed," and "give me the heads up." She is trying to avoid turning into a corporate slug. She claims her job is awful. She gets in at eight and leaves at seven. They buy her breakfast and lunch, so she will be most productive. If Roseanne has kids, she will be supermom, because every night she comes home and makes an awesome meal. Then she waits an hour and heads to the gym. I hope all this energy doesn't last, because I can't handle all the guilt I feel about never going to the gym.

"They will applaud anything. Someone reads two sentences about a bike chain, everyone applauds."

Roseanne chimes in, "All the people I work with curse and complain about carpal tunnel syndrome. I found out I have to work the Wednesday before Thanksgiving. How much does that suck?"

My mother calls while we are eating. She sounds upset. My mother calls every other day and she always suspects I'm home when the machine picks up (sometimes, I am). It's like she has a camera in my room, which wouldn't be too bad because of the lack of booty I'm getting.

"What's wrong, Mom?"

"Are you coming home for Thanksgiving?"

"Mom, didn't we talk about this already? Of course, I am."

"Monica isn't coming home. She is feeding the hungry with what's his name."

"Oh, God! She is such a volunteer. Actually, what *is* his name?"

"Chuck. What kind of name is that for a thirty-eight-year-old?" Monica has deliberately misinformed my mom. She should really let me know these things before I slip up. "Eve, can you talk some sense into her?"

"Mom, I can't make Monica do anything. She'll get even more stubborn if I try. Just act like you don't care and she'll come home."

"How can I not care? When you have kids, let's see how you don't care?"

"Okay, Mom, I'm not saying don't care. I'm saying *act* like you don't care."

"Is Roseanne going home? She can come over, too."

"I'll ask her."

"Is she there now?"

"No, Ma, I'll call you and let you know." I hold my finger to my lips so Roseanne won't make a sound.

"Okay, honey, let me know as soon as you can, because I have to cook, love you, honey."

"Yes, Mom, love you, too." Roseanne is waiting for me to ask her about Thanksgiving. I was certain she wouldn't want to come over. I mean it's one thing to live at someone's house for a month and another to celebrate the holidays with their extended family.

"Do you want to spend Thanksgiving with us?" I am hoping she'll realize that it's not such a good idea, that she ought to go see her family.

"Is it okay?" No!

"Yes."

"Well—" she is acting like she is thinking about it, but I know her answer already "—I guess I'll go." Great. Suddenly a calm Wednesday night is thrown into commotion by an event two weeks away. Roseanne leaves her gnocchi and runs to the kitchen to look through her books (I take a few extra gnocchi—I cut the potatoes after all). She starts calling recipe ideas to me from the kitchen.

"I'll make sweet potato and pumpkin pies. Someone else will probably make pumpkin. Pecan, yes pecan. I hope no one is allergic to nuts. I'll make some potato gratin and bruschetta. That'll go over well with the Italians, right? Oh, and here—caramelized root vegetables. That'll be great. Okay, I'll write this down so you can tell your mom." She winds up skipping the gym to go through some more recipe books. I eat the rest of her gnocchi and watch Fox.

"So what are you doing for Thanksgiving?" Tabitha asks the Sunday before.

"Not too much, going home. Roseanne is making a feast."

"Roseanne is going home with you?" She is annoyed.

"Yeah, why?"

"Nothing."

"When is your flight?" She says nothing. "Tabitha. You are going back to Texas for the holidays, right?" More silence. "Do you want to come home with us? I'm not sure you'll have fun with my family."

"Oh, but Roseanne will because she is making the turkey?"

"She isn't making the turkey. Please come, I mean, you're always invited. My mom would really love it."

"No thanks."

"Well, why? What are you going to do? You can't be alone on the holidays."

"I'll find something to do, believe me. Have a great Thanksgiving."

She hangs up before I can say anything else. Bring on the holidays.

I try calling Tabitha again Thanksgiving Day, before we leave to head to the 'burbs. We are sitting on the couch watching the Macy's parade, although Macy's is only about ten blocks away. It's kind of cold and Roseanne is exhausted from all the cooking she did last night. We just can't exert any energy—other than painting our nails, fielding the calls from Roseanne's family, and watching the awful parade announcers. I get Tabitha's machine when I call. I leave her a long message, begging her to come.

Roseanne holds out her hand to inspect the frosty purple polish she used. "Any minute I thought you were going to offer to digest her turkey for her."

"Ro, the holidays are a very tough time for everyone. Don't you ever watch those news shows. Suicide rises."

"I doubt we have to worry about Tabitha. Really."

I'll spare you most of the details of my Thanksgiving. Everyone loves everything Roseanne made, my aunt actually passes my uncle the potato gratin when he asks for it, and in the middle of the quietest most reflective moments of our feast, my grandmother, who's going totally senile, leans over to my mother and says, "Do you hear them, too?" My mom shakes her head and my grandmother goes back to chewing loudly.

Roseanne and I spend two days on the couch in my living room, literally. We sleep there because my bed is in the city. We don't even bother to get the bed out of the sofa; I sleep on the sofa and Roseanne sleeps on the recliner. Roseanne doesn't even go for a run, which I was certain she'd try to drag me to within moments of eating. On Friday night, we go to a local bar.

"These look like the people who work at my firm," Roseanne says, repulsed. There is an awful lot of cheesy, high hair around. I realize how far Roseanne has come. We have a drink and walk home (yes, I had my dad drop us off, thinking we would have to take a cab home).

I call Tabitha from the couch on Saturday. She picks up during my message. "How's the Shore?"

"I don't know, I'm nowhere near it. Not all of Jersey is the shore. How's your weekend going?"

"Boring. Jaques hasn't called at all. When are you and Roseanne coming back?" Because she includes Roseanne, I tell her I'll call her back.

"Hey, Ro." Roseanne is working on her toenails now, a very respectable red. "Wanna go home early?"

Tabitha has an urge to go dancing Saturday night. She is happy we came back early. She calls up the club and uses the old MTV thing. She temped there for about three weeks and held onto her ID. Now whenever she wants to go somewhere it's either the standard *NY By Night* line or she pretends to be a producer from MTV scouting locations. Occasionally, they have asked for credentials and the ID does it, but usually if you're dressed well enough, they'll believe anything.

We get our own special reserved section. Someone obviously wants an MTV segment shot here, because we get drinks on the house. Roseanne is particularly impressed.

"Do you come here a lot? It's so cool."

"I need to be in the right mood," says Tabitha, reminding me that it's all about her whims. She is still a little bitter about Thanksgiving. I am not in the mood for the abuse.

"Should we dance?" I ask, wondering if Tabitha would prefer to sit and sulk.

"I'll dance," says Roseanne. I raise one of my nice eyebrows at Tabitha, who glares at me. She just should have come home with me. Then we could still be on the couch, instead of sucking our guts into impractical dresses.

"I am not nearly drunk enough to start dancing."

"Well, Tabitha, it's totally dead and no one is talking to us. I don't want to sit here all night, hoping they'll buy us drinks so we won't have to spend eighty million dollars."

"Fine. Let's go dance. I'm loving it now." She gets up and hurries out to the dance floor, where she starts to dance near a guy whose girlfriend jumps out immediately, and all but pees around him to mark her territory.

"Eve, I can't deal with her anymore. Why is she such a witch?" Roseanne grabs me before we get onto the floor. I, myself, am not nearly drunk enough to dance.

"Okay, c'mon, she's just pissy. She's warming up to you. Really. Remember how she tried to help you get a job?"

"What an honor." I lead her onto the dance floor. We dance next to Tabitha, who ignores us. We're all pretty uninspired. The dance floor is not nearly full, so our silly shuffles seem even more ridiculous. Finally, Roseanne and I shrug at each other and decide to head back up to our couch. Tabitha is so annoyed, she follows us. Unfortunately, two Amazon über women take it up. They're spread all over what is rightfully ours; the couch and Tabitha's jacket. We hover nearby, glaring at them. Tabitha is clearly livid.

"Well, eventually, they have to get up and get more drinks," I say, trying to be positive. They certainly are managing to suck down their drinks and avoid us. When they start slurping on their straws, I think we are pretty much all set to pounce. But then, in an unbelievably sneaky move, the bustier one pulls out her cell phone and calls the bar (which is twenty feet away) to bring them drinks. Oh you have got to be kidding me! Of all the low down moves!

"This is ridiculous," says Tabitha, loud enough for them to hear. "I am not going to be ignored by some catalog models who are barely this side of over the hill. Look at those awful heels." The heels don't look that bad to me, but I can tell the models are a tad self-conscious. Tabitha has hit a nerve. Shit! The last thing I need is a confrontation.

"Bitch!" sneers one of the models at Tabitha.

"Get off my jacket!" Tabitha yells.

"Whatever!" The other model yells, not moving.

"Did you get those shoes at Sears, you whore?" Oh, my God! The blonder model's eyes narrow.

"Why don't you lose some weight?" Curses! I should probably be right up there to get Tabitha's back, but I move a little slow (okay, so I'm chicken).

Roseanne gets right up in their faces and says, "Hey fuckface! Why don't you get some dick?"

Then, drinks go flying, words get hurled and then the bouncer is escorting the women out and apologizing to us for the trouble.

We settle back into the couches and sympathize with Tabitha about the damage she claims has been done to her jacket. The waiter comes over with the drinks that the models ordered via cell phone. He tells us they're on the house. I defer them to Tabitha and Roseanne. They truly deserve them for all their hard work. I have to admit that in the thick of things, I remained untouched. (I'm a lover not a fighter!) Hopefully, this battle will solidify Tabitha and Roseanne's friendship.

I get up to get a drink. I have to walk past the evil duo, who are still complaining to the bouncer and manager about being kicked out. They look awful and disheveled. The heel on one of the women's shoes is broken, which I think is total props for Tabitha. The manager is shaking her head, not listening to any of their arguments.

I can't begin to describe the satisfaction I feel when I hear the manager say, "I'm sorry, but I mean, they are with MTV."

December

On the first workday in December, there is a huge evergreen tree in the lobby of the Prescott Nelson building. There's a lot to look forward to—people on vacation (Herb is taking two weeks!), special Christmas goodies and most importantly the notorious Prescott Nelson Christmas party.

The Christmas party buzz starts around mid-November. People always refer to it in a sort of threatening way. "Make sure you have the presentation perfect or we'll pull out those pictures of you at last year's Christmas party." It was one of the things that they brought up at my orientation. Yes, even we serfs could go.

I'm dreading my first corporate holiday party. I can just feel I am going to do something stupid. (If this isn't foreshadowing I don't know what is.) I see myself twirling around the dance floor, shamelessly flailing my arms. I think this floozy behavior will only be intensified by the Christmas party. I don't think it's a good idea to date *or* drink with co-workers.

Tabitha thinks the party is going to be lame. Actually, she thinks it is going to be in a cool space but with "lame snoozers." She tried to tell me that no one at any of the cool magazines (like hers) was going. Invitations to the Christmas party are coveted, which makes Tabitha popular with all her friends in higher places that work for other companies. I think she's starting to come around. If there's one thing Prescott doesn't believe in skimping on it's the Christmas party. Despite her misgivings Tabitha calls me moments after I arrive at my desk.

"Have you gotten any promo presents yet? I just got a gazillion bottles of wine from one of the restaurants that we reviewed favorably. The Big C got two baskets. One was totally healthy, I think she was secretly bitter at the implications. Nevertheless, she gave me the naughty one. I'm eating Belgian chocolate breakfast wafers." She crunches loudly to prove it. "Did you hear the latest about the party? Hammerstein Ball Room."

"No way."

"One can dream. I heard they ordered five hundred pounds of sushi for it. Imagine. I love the season of giving. My season. Any thought to how we are outfitting ourselves?"

"No, I'm surprised at how long it's taken you to ask me."

"I think it's time to pull out the beaded." Now Tabitha is talking crazy. The beaded dress is this vintage dress we found on a shopping expedition. It's red, flares at the knee, and has a supertight bodice. I had to have this dress, and paid 175 bucks for it. I couldn't have created a better dress for my body. I feel like there is some power attached to it, like I will be irresistible to mere mortals in it. I vowed to only pull it out when I was down and out.

"I've hidden that dress in Jersey. I can't wear that to the company party."

"Why? It's fabulous! You thought I had forgotten about it, didn't you?" Lacey comes over and stands by my desk.

"Tab, you are an elephant." I knew it would make her hang up on me. I turn my attention to Lacey. "What's up?"

"Eve, I heard an awful rumor." She pauses, like I have some idea what the rumor is. "I heard you have to be working here for six months to be allowed to go to the party. I've only been here a month."

Did you ever read those cartoons in *Highlights* magazine, "Goofus and Gallant"? Gallant helps his elderly neighbors rake up their yards, Goofus runs through the leaf piles. I loved those. Anyway, it's true you *do* have to be here six months before you can get an invitation, but since we have a large freelance population what with all the writers we use, all you have to do is be on a list that says you contributed to an article in the past six months. Gallant tells his annoying, self-absorbed fellow employee not to sweat the invite, she can get as respectably sloshed as she wants if she speaks with Lorraine. Goofus tells Lacey that the rumor is in fact true, and she should hang out and see if anyone isn't going that will give her their invite.

"But, I just have to go."

"I'm sure it isn't as exciting as everyone says."

"Does that mean you aren't going?" Fat chance.

"Oh, I have to, I make it my business to load up on as many free things as possible. Really we'll see what we can do." As if on some kind of sick psychic sibling cue my sister Monica calls at that exact moment. I tell Lacey I am having a personal family issue and won't she please excuse me. She walks away, crushed.

"Hi, Monica."

"How did you know it was me? Oh, you have one of those caller ID thingies. Why are you so happy? I hope you're being careful, Ma will flip if you get knocked up."

"I can't believe that expression is still in your vocabulary. For your information I have not been naughty in quite some time. Too long. Thank you. I can't just be happy merely to talk to you, my flesh and blood?"

"Are you on drugs? No you're allergic to aspirin. Well, whatever it is, I guess it's good you're happy. What do you think about Ma totally not calling me on Thanksgiving? She must be going through the change or something."

"I think Ma realized you were dead set on rescuing the downtrodden."

"Funny. I was thinking of not doing Christmas this year." I know when my sister is trying to get a reaction. There is nothing that makes my sister happier than the one time of the year when my father actually raises his voice and gets involved in family dramas. Every Christmas morning, right after I get a better gift, she makes some liberal comment to try (invariably successfully) to get a rise out of him. This sets off a whole chain of events—Grandma spewing forth a whole bunch of Italian, Mom running into the kitchen and coming out with plates of rock-hard biscotti and me sizing up the gifts under the tree, desperately trying to figure how much more loot Santa got me and how long it'll be until I can open it. I know how to handle her. I know how to appeal to my sister's socialist principles to the part of her that rejects what she believes are the downfalls of American society: materialism and commercialism. I take a deep breath and clutch the phone like a champ.

"That's fine, Monica. More for me." I can hear her breathing, dying.

"I guess I can't do that to Dad. I can't ruin their holiday like that."

"They seemed okay on Thanksgiving, despite your absence."

"Yeah, but Grandma's sick. It wouldn't be right."

"Awfully considerate of you, Monica."

"Besides, I wanted you guys to get something special for Chuck."

"A new Porta Potti for his van?"

"What is that supposed to mean?" I can't help it; I imagine this guy as a Grateful Dead loving hippie.

"Nothing. Keep in mind, nobody knows him yet." Or wants to. "When will you be home?"

"The thirteenth. Can we go shopping right away?" Hold those horses, honey.

"That is the night of the party."

"Oooh, the Prescott Nelson Christmas Party. I saw something about it on TV. Can you get me a ticket...?"

Lacey went straight to Herb about not getting a ticket and he instructed me to unearth every stone to make sure there's an extra one for her. I am serious, he said "unearth every stone." Well, actually he e-mailed it to me. People have a tendency to get a little overzealous when e-mailing. I saved it. I want a record of this ridiculousness.

It's another instance of blaming the illustrious "them," but since I already know the solution, I decide to hang out and sit on my info for a while.

"I'm getting the runaround. No one is sure who to ask. Maybe you should try calling," I say to both Lacey and Herb when they ask what the ticket status is.

They both say, "Well, why don't you keep trying?"

With the big P (party) approaching, my mother comes into the city and brings The Dress with her. She also brings a shawl that she refers to as a "wrap," that I can wear over the dress, as well as some apartment supplies: toilet paper, paper towels and a box of rubber bands.

She's actually in town because she has a doctor's appointment.

Her appointment is at 10:30 on the Upper East Side, so I suggest we go out to breakfast. My mother calls me before she leaves home (I'm still asleep), when she gets into Penn Station, and once on the corner. She's neurotic like this, because one early morning when my parents came to visit me at school, I wasn't alone. I opened the door up at crack and suggested they should probably wait in the car. My father's mouth did not move from the straight line it was in for the entire day.

I take my mom out to breakfast on 8th. I'm aware that every man in the place is gay and I keep trying to gauge if my mother notices, too, but she keeps chatting on about my dad and my sister and what I want for Christmas.

"So are you doing okay here, honey? Don't you miss us at all?"

"Of course I do, Ma, but living here is more fun and close to work.'' An appeal to practicality and a stitch in time saving nine will always win big with my mother.

"So are you going to this party I keep reading about?''

"The Prescott Nelson company party? Yeah. I doubt it's going to be that big a deal.''

"Well, it seems like it's going to be at a nice place and you'll have fun.''

"No one knows where it's going to be.''

"Well, I was reading an article in *Daily News* that it's going to be at a place right near here. I think it's near the Hudson River on 15th or 14th.''

There is no justice in the world if my mother knows the location of the Prescott Nelson party before the employees. We actually have a nice time, then I put mom into a cab and head home.

That night, Roseanne is making her Christmas cards. She is painting trees and reindeers and abstract Santas on each card, personalizing them for their receivers. She holds up a card. "Eve, look.''

"That's pretty, I want one like that. The red nose reminds me of one too many drinks.''

"No, my arm, my arm! I haven't been to the gym in four days and look—the muscle is turning flabby.'' She smacks it a little, nothing happens. "Oh, my god, disgusting.''

Roseanne had an eating disorder sophomore year, now she has learned through counseling to love food. She has forced herself to enjoy it and that's why she gets so in to making it; she's in control. I think she's just replaced her food issues with other body issues, and thus her fanaticism with exercise. I tell myself that a lot as I watch her on the treadmill for fifty minutes, while I sort of circle the machines trying to decide which one won't bite.

"Roseanne, your arm looks fine. Really, what's more important, sweating off a few hundred calories at the smelly gym or the pleasure you'll give all the people you love when they receive your Christmas card and cookie plate?''

"Don't forget, I'm also making ornaments.'' It's hard to live with Roseanne sometimes. As her cheesiness slowly erodes, I am left with a woman who can do everything. It's not easy being inferior.

"So, Eve, can I get the heads up on this party? Oops! I'll put a dollar in when I get up.''

"I have no idea where it is except what my mother told me. I'm actually dreading it.'' I'm waiting for Roseanne to ask me why and assuage my fears by telling me how charming I am, how I can show a little restraint and have a great time. Instead, this: "Just try not to publicly embarrass yourself. I mean try to at least find a dark corner with your chosen victim of the evening."

"What kind of slut do you think I am?"

"Well, it has been a while."

"Thanks for reminding me."

"So, any hope of getting me a ticket?"

"What do I look like? Besides, aren't you having your own company party? The Kirsch Christmas Company Craze?"

"Yeah, at a bar near the Seaport. It's the worst." I appreciate Roseanne, she amazes me everyday as she leaps and bounds away from all that is New England.

"I really don't think I can get you in. They have guest lists and everything." Roseanne looks at me and rolls her eyes. She is absorbing too much. Just the other day, she listened, captivated, to Tabitha's speech on charming bouncers and evading the velvet rope. She is not accepting the power of a Prescott Nelson list. I used to think of Roseanne as my fair lady (Tabitha said she was my Frankenstein), but now its gotten out of control.

"What's with that dress your mom brought? It's nice."

"I'm thinking about wearing it, but I might switch to basic black, always the acceptable choice."

"No, try it on. It's really pretty." I don't really want to try it on, but *Law and Order* is over. I figure I should decide whether or not I am going to wear it, so I can determine how to deal with Tabitha if I opt not to.

I look at myself in the bathroom. It's great. I mean it's powerful. It could make anyone look spicy. If only I could flatten my abs. Roseanne calls for me to show her. When I come out, she starts nodding her approval.

"I think it's cool, but then there's this." I point to my stomach.

"What? You have to use it while you got it. And what is 'this'?" I stick out my stomach more.

"Your tummy. It's fine. It's not flat, but it's better. It's your poochie."

"My what?"

"Your poochie. When we were juniors and I was still dating Billy, I was hanging out at his place with Jake, Liam, Cav, and Carlton. I was outside the living room and they were watching some guy thing, maybe football. During the commercial they started talking about girls. It was amazing how they just jumped into it. They all started talking about how important it was to find a girl who wasn't too skinny. Jake said, 'Yeah, you know, Vitali, she has my perfect body.' Carlton said, 'Yeah, she'd be warm to sleep next to,' and Liam said, 'She's got a great ass.'''

"You are lying! What did Cav say?"

"'Let's smoke the resin out of the bong.' But all those guys agreed you had this great body and I thought, Wow! Eve doesn't even try, she just is."

"Well that's profound. I wish I had known about Jake, I always thought he was a cutie." Roseanne and I share a moment of regret.

"So are you going to wear it?" I stare at my poochie again. I can learn to love it. I will love it. I nod. I'll do it. I pity the man that stands in my way.

The invitations come in a manila envelope addressed to the department assistant—that's me, folks. Someone must have smelled them because everyone gathers around my desk like vultures, waiting for me to tell them where it's at. In the time it takes me to get the tape off the envelope, five of them have placed bets. I am feeling a little claustrophobic. Herb comes over and suggests that they give "my assistant some room to breathe." He is, in affect, huddling like the rest of them, only disapprovingly.

I rip open the manila envelope and look around at the staff's expectant faces. I may never have so much power. I start tantalizingly pulling the invites out. Chris, one of the writers, plays along and starts making burlesque music sounds. Everyone laughs, even Herb. I fully enjoy the moment for the split second it takes me to get the invitations out of the envelope. I hold one up for inspection. It's a hologram that says "Holiday Party" and morphs to Prescott's face. A definite collector's item.

My mom was right, the party is all the way over on the river at 15th Street. How does she know these things? No one has really heard of this place except Lacey, whose friend "in the business" shot a video over there.

When everyone has seen (with their eyes not their hands), I put the invites in my drawer. By law I am supposed to hold on to the invitations for another two days. Don't ask me why. I am supposed to lock my drawer every time I get up. It takes me all morning to find the key to the drawer and by the time I do I have to pee so bad I am thinking about using a Prescott Nelson cup.

I meet Tabitha at one o'clock in front of The Nook. She is having serious wardrobe issues. Before I get a chance to say a word, Tabitha holds out a bunch of Polaroids and a picture she ripped from a magazine. They are all of Tabitha in different dresses. The magazine dress is a Badgley Mischka. I hold it up to her. "I think you're getting a little crazy."

"I'll get noticed."

"No one will recognize the designer but a couple of old women and gay men. Plus, you'll spill beer on it." I'm doing salad today. I want to love the poochie less.

"What do you think of this one?" On most people this dress— feathers—would look like they were dressing up as a drag queen, but I'm almost certain Tabitha can pull it off.

"It's out there, but cool. Wait a second, what's this foot?" Behind Tabitha, I can barely make out a naked male foot. "Who is this?"

"No one." She takes the pictures out of my hand. "It must be someone at the store."

Except I also recognized her bed frame and bureau. Whatever, Tab. We sit in our usual spot in the center of The Nook as she gives me the plan for the party. It's another week away and I am certain that both the plan and Tabitha's dress will change about eighty times before we actually set foot in the door.

Tabitha, Roseanne (yes, I got her a ticket) and I arrive via cab to the party. One of the attendants opens our door and directs us in. As we rehearsed, both Roseanne and I have invites, but not IDs. We need both, so we have to go up to someone with a list. My ID is at the bottom of my bag, just in case they really won't let me in. The woman lets me and Roseanne in with Lorraine's invite (that's how I got Roseanne here) and right away the three of us get a Polaroid photo. Tabitha gushes awhile and Roseanne suggests we get before and after shots to have evidence of the results of alcohol. I just want to check out the space.

It's great—huge with high ceilings. The best part of the place is that one whole side is just windows overlooking the Hudson River. Tabitha has a drink in my hand before I can get too carried away by the beauty of the place.

There is a ton of sushi. It looks good, but Tabitha and I decided beforehand not to eat until we'd been at the party for forty-five minutes. We vowed to be strong when the other faltered. At this point we are talking Roseanne down. Given a chance, I suspect she would push the knife-wielding Japanese chef out of the way and slice herself a huge roll.

Roseanne is sporting basic black, Tabitha has this light brown number on with a feather boa (the one that would make most people look like a drag queen) and I am trying really hard to keep the beads on my dress and to suck in my poochie.

Joe and Adam find us right away. They are with two friends, Anthony and Kristen. All four of them already seem drunk. I think being drunk might take the edge off, but it might also lead me down the road to my dastardly deed.

"What's up, Eve? You look a little pale," says Adam, leaning close to me. "I like your dress."

"Thanks, Adam."

"It's so beady." The last thing I need is to see Adam make a fool out of himself. I will not let my dastardly deed be hooking up with Adam. I excuse myself to get a drink and wind up taking everybody's order. Roseanne comes with me.

"Eve, what's up with you? Let's do a shot, it will put some color in your cheeks." Rosie's cure-all. We order two kamikazes and knock them back.

"See, don't you feel warm now? This place is awesome. Eve, are you okay? I thought you would be more into this. You've been dying to go to this since June. I remember you called me and told me all about it. That's when we decided I should move to New York."

"I just have a weird feeling. Do you remember the last time I had a weird feeling."

"You always have weird feelings—no offense."

"It was the night we went to Rick's party, remember? I kept telling you I felt weird, but I drank anyway."

"You wound up doing the walk of shame the next day with the guy who lived next door to Josh's dorm."

"That wasn't the worst part, the worst part was—"

"That he was a math major. I know. That was bad." I nod. "Well there are obviously no math majors here. All the boys here are cool."

"I don't know about that."

"C'mon, Eve, I don't think you have some kind of psychic power. What you do have is willpower. Look how good you're being about the sushi. C'mon." She gives me a hug. "Let's do another shot and go forth in sin. We've got people waiting."

I've got to hand it to Roseanne, she makes a good point. I do the shot with her and I feel my brain starting to flood. It's a good feeling. We bring the drinks back.

"It's about time," says Tabitha. I am told that Kristen went off with some guy in Media Development so we have an extra drink. I wind up holding it, because I could put it down, but eventually someone is going to want to drink it and that someone turns out to be me. I am done with it by the time everyone is finished with that round, so I have Adam and Joe bring me another Stoli gimlet.

"Well, Anthony and Roseanne seem to be getting along." I look over to see Anthony offering Roseanne a cigarette. I bum one from Tabitha. "Maybe she'll get lucky."

"With any luck. This place is cool."

"Yeah, Prescott doesn't skimp. Wonder if he'll show."

"Doesn't he have to?"

"No, he's a little old, so it's understandable." Tabitha loves to make excuses for Prescott.

"He's not in the box yet."

Tabitha laughs and fake hits me. "That's blasphemous. Look at all the guys from shipping dancing."

"They've actually got some good moves."

"All your friends. Kinda makes you wish you lived underground, too. I know I'm terrible, but I look good. Look who it is—your friend in high places." I look over at Robert King. Adam comes over a little too close to give me my drink.

"Here you go, gin and tonic and roofies."

"Don't even joke about that, Adam." I'm serious. Joke references to roofies are like references to snuff films—always in poor taste. I hope I'm not going to think less of Adam after tonight.

"Hey, Eve, chill, I'm just kidding."

"Some things aren't funny."

"Sorry." Adam's head hangs as we walk over to the table where I guess we are supposedly based. He is a fifth wheel, because Anthony and Roseanne are getting closer and Joe is hitting on some Latina.

"Nice going." Tabitha exhales a bunch of smoke in my ear.

"Well, I don't find date rape jokes funny."

"Neither do I, but I'm talking about dissing your power man." I stare at her confused. "Rob King just waved at you and you ignored him."

Shit, he must have waved just as I got my drink. He's not there anymore. I look around for him. Nowhere. Maybe he was just putting in an appearance. Tabitha hands me another drink and suggests we get some sushi. We stop by the table and see if Roseanne wants anything. She shakes her empty glass, so we'll bring her more alcohol. She gives me a little smile just to make sure everything is okay and I smile back; she doesn't need to know about my missed opportunity with Robert King. Wait! What am I thinking? No, I will not entertain the idea of him. I am just buzzing.

Tabitha and I go and stockpile our plates with goodies. The food looks delicious—salads, chicken, steak and portobello mushrooms. As Tabitha puts each thing on her plate, she says, "Thank you, Prescott, thank you." I know I'm getting drunk, because it's funny every time.

We get a separate plate for sushi and meet Adrian at the sushi line. After a round of kisses, we decide to scarf up our food and dance. We grab Roseanne, the crew and more drinks and start shaking it to the disco songs that come on. Adrian is a great dancer (surprise!) and he takes turns leading the three of us around.

I drink up. I am starting to get over my ominous feelings, but that may be a part of the danger. I will be strong. Roseanne comes up to us looking sulky, maybe the bad feeling is passing to her. I would be secretly glad if it is. (That doesn't make me a bad person—it is my company party after all.) Tabitha (who has suddenly become the better friend) asks her what's wrong. She points over to Adrian and Anthony (!) getting their groove on. This deserves a hug.

"Adrian can be such a slut."

"No, Tabitha." Roseanne shakes her head like a scorned woman. "Anthony can't help how he feels. They make a cute couple." It's true they are dancing away like they've been doing it (dancing, that is) forever. I decide to be helpful. After all Roseanne is *my* roommate, I should be responsible.

"I know it seems like all the good men are gay, but look around, there's got to be some straight ones you can find." Unfortunately, the Village People come on right at this moment and we realize we are standing in the center of some of the most beautiful least attainable men.

"But, what does it say about me?" Roseanne asks. "This is the second time I've been attracted to a gay man. Now they are both dancing together."

"It means you're a lesbian." I am trying to make a joke. They both glare at me. Sorry, Wonder Twins, can't anyone take a joke? I need another drink. I must have telekinetic powers because just then a waiter comes around with frozen margaritas. He has one left. Victory! I take it. Tabitha shakes her head. Fine. I hand it to Roseanne. Why does everyone love each other more than me?

Some really cool Latin music comes on. I want to dance. I see Joe and give him a smile.

"Hey, Eve. Want to dance?"

"Yeah, but I don't know how to dance to this music. I'm betting you do."

"C'mon, I'll show you." Before I can say no, Joe is leading me onto the dance floor. He puts his hand very low on my back and tells me that when he presses it I have to turn. At first, I feel like a spaz following his moves, but soon I get it and my hips sort of move on their own. He's an excellent dancer. He is totally in control—and you would never think it was such a turn on. Wow! I could marry Joe. We dance for three songs and then he thanks me and kisses my cheek. I go back to Tabitha and Roseanne, who clap for me.

"You looked like you were in a movie."

"That dress fit right in, it looks so Spanish."

"I never knew your hips could move like that, girl," Adrian yells.

I turn back to my Latin Love, Joe. He is now dancing with the Latina he was talking to earlier. She really knows how to dance, too. Her hips are moving like mine never could. She is putting my pitiful attempt to shame.

"I feel like Tony in *Saturday Night Fever* when he gives the prize to the Puerto Ricans, because they totally deserve it."

"Well, Eve, it looks like she already has the prize," Tabitha says. I see Joe kiss the woman as they dance. I am heartbroken.

"Ladies, what say we get another drink and check out the room where the big boys are?" I am starting to get that wobbly feeling and as usual, when Uncle Pres pays, I don't know when to say when. It's bad.

Anyway, there is no official bigwig room. But just like The Nook, the bigwigs manage to isolate themselves. They are all in a room off to the side of the main floor. It's real stuffy in here, but for whatever reason those with the power, the board members, the execs, and most of the editors-in-chief are hanging out here chatting merrily away, content to be separated from the peons. We see the Big C right away. I rarely get to see the Big C; she's always in a meeting when I go visit Tabitha, so seeing her in the flesh is kind of an event. She looks good, I mean well put together, but that's all. She's just a really attractive woman in terrific shape, but it all seems so forced. She spots Tabitha and comes over and kisses her. Talk about forced.

"These are my friends, Eve and Roseanne."

"Lovely to meet you." The Big C shakes both of our hands firmly.

"We've already met," I say as she pumps my arm. She smiles and nods and I know she has no idea who I am. She chats with Tabitha, but all the while her eyes check out who's here. Maybe that's how she stays on top. You would think after all these years in this business, she could let the party come to her.

Finally, as if she allows herself exactly ninety seconds with everyone, she excuses herself by saying. "Well, I've got to find my boss. Remember, Tabitha, we have billing to do tomorrow." Tabitha nods, and I think it lacks class on the Big C's part to remind Tabitha about work at an event like this.

"I bet she doesn't show up before noon," Roseanne says, trying to comfort Tab.

"No, she will be in at eight. That woman is hard core."

"Well, Tabitha, she severely lacks tact. She's on a power trip." This helps a little, so we decide to get another drink. (Are you keeping track? I've stopped.)

Anyway, what before my wondering eyes do appear? Herb, obviously drunk (Healthy Herb?) chatting away with shitty Lacey Matthews. She is doing a good job of throwing her hair back when she laughs. I get pushed into Lacey (I swear it was unintentional—the bigwigs are restless) and she spills her drink a little. What is she doing in here in this room anyway?

"Hi, Eve." Herb has such a condescending way about him.

"Hi. Sorry about that, Lacey." Lacey gives me a tight smile and turns back to Herb, but he addresses me.

"Are you having fun at the party, Eve?" As if he planned the fucking event and I am lucky enough to be here.

"Yes. It's great."

"You're quite the dancer." Shit.

"Oh, thanks, I was just learning."

"Well it's good to give new things a try," Lacey chimes in. "I've been ballroom dancing for ten years, but that's the first time I've seen Latin moves like those."

"Rob King is a fan of yours," Herb says.

"Really?" Lacey and I say together, and I smirk at her.

"Yeah, he couldn't remember your brother's last name."

"My brother?"

"Well, isn't that how you know him? From your brother's soft-ball team?"

"Yep, from around the neighborhood. Uh-huh." I think about sticking a "great" in for good measure. If I weren't getting loopy this would be a lot easier. "Well, have a great night you guys."

Did I just call Herb and Lacey "you guys"? I can't believe they saw my dancing debacle (which moments ago I thought was cool). I also cannot believe Rob King is a "fan." Wow! I have to get a drink and find the girls. I get half of my plan accomplished when I feel something cold on my back.

It's Rob King's drink attached to Rob King. He looks like a twenty-something club kid who somehow got to swim with the big fish. I can feel my face flush and I know I am all teeth.

"I heard you're a big fan." Thanks to alcohol I can be this brash.

"I had to think of something to find out your last name, Ms. Vitali. By the way, I'm glad you took my advice about the red, but I miss the hat."

"That was, I don't know—elevator shenanigans."

"Oh, really." He smiles. I am going to die. I just have to keep being cool. "I'm also a big fan of elevator shenanigans. You know, you're quite the dancer."

"You saw that? It was kind of embarrassing. I don't really know how."

"Coulda fooled me. Want to get some sushi?" This is seriously a bad idea. I am not ready to run in these sushi-eating circles. Doesn't this guy date models? I can see Roseanne, Tabitha, Adrian and Anthony gesturing about us from across the room. I don't even know Anthony, but already, he's involved in the scandal.

"Okay." I am awful. I am drunk. It's going to be a slow burn.

"Let's go downstairs." Oh, sure, away from the big guys.

"What's wrong with here?" As soon as I say it I know I sound like a child trying to prove something.

"Whatever you want. There are comfy couches downstairs." Uncle Pres is paying this guy the big bucks to say "comfy"?

I agree to go downstairs and he hands me a big plate by the sushi bar. He starts piling pieces of sushi up on my dish. I thank him after each piece and he ignores me, until he has about twenty-five pieces.

"My pleasure," he says, and gives me a seductive look. Now, I'm in trouble. I have totally lost the girls and I know (I knew!) I am going to do something regrettable.

"You're not going to feed me, are you?" I ask him as we sit on one of the couches. These couches are off to the side behind some gauzy lounge curtains. Apparently, we have reached the designated hook-up area. The couches are already full of smooching couples. I try not to recognize anyone.

"Not unless you want me to."

Some truck is blocking me as I try to pick up five hundred pounds of sushi with a forklift. I decide to back up, because Prescott is waiting. When I take a look at myself in the rearview mirror, I notice I have a red bra on my head and Tabitha and Prescott are in the back seat. Both of them are wearing Tabitha's underwear.

"You better hurry up," says Tabitha.

"I'm trying!" I scream, but immediately feel bad about losing my cool.

"Why don't you answer the phone?" says Prescott.

"What?" I ask, trying to keep a menial attitude. "Oh, yeah!"

I wake up and answer the phone next to the bed. Where the hell am I? Why am I naked? Why does my head hurt like this?

"Hello?" I mumble, disoriented.

"Good morning, Ms. Vitali." I sit up in bed. Oooh, my head, my stomach. Shit! I start to get flashes of last night.

"Rob?"

"Were you expecting Prescott Nelson?"

"Well, actually, I was dreaming. Where are you? Where am I?"

"At work. At home."

"Not my home. What time is it?"

"My home. 10:30."

"Fuck."

"Well put. Don't worry, everyone will be in late today."

"Everyone but you. Why didn't you call me?"

"I tried, but I had a meeting at 10:00. I kept getting my machine. How do you feel?"

"Shitty."

"I'll have some breakfast delivered."

"No, I have to get to work. I'm late. Totally. This is bad."

"I'll call you in fifteen."

"No, I'll be fine. Don't worry. I'm getting up."

"I'll call you later," I hear him say as I hang up. Shit. I am going to die. Okay, I will give myself one minute and then, if I can, I will get out of bed. Just then I remember holding on to him tightly as we walked into his building, a doorman building. I look around the room, it's nice. The bed is big. I am wearing my bra and underwear. Oh, no, I think I pulled off my dress seductively while trying to get Rob to Latin dance with me. He was protesting, then he was helping me with my dress, but not dancing. Oh, my god, I am a slut. I am like a bad B movie on the USA channel. I have to get out of here. While I am washing my face in the huge bathroom with the sunken tub (I have no memories of the sunken tub, thank God) I remember putting the sushi plate aside at the party and (oh God, I'm cringing) kissing Rob. I keep getting images of these passionate kisses. What have I done? The bathroom is spinning. I spend two minutes on the toilet trying to compose myself. I hunt around in Rob's well-stocked fridge until I find (bingo!) orange juice. My dress is on the floor of a different bedroom. I assume this is Rob's room—it looks out onto the water. Where the hell am I? I should call him back.

No, I won't call him. I'll ask the doorman. Oh, shit, the doorman was smirking at me. I remember him holding open the elevator door as Rob practically carried me in.

"Do you want me to get something for the young lady?"

"No, don't worry, she does this all the time—" Rob smiled at me "—she isn't supposed to drink with her medicine." I thought that was the funniest thing....

No, I am not going to ask the doorman. I am going to go out on the street and start walking. I just need to sit for a second. I'm going to fall asleep, no, okay I have to get out of here. The phone's ringing and I ignore it.

I dash past the doorman. I feel like a high-class call girl in my red-beaded dress. Where the hell am I now? In the Cab of Shame.

"You are on West End and 86th Street, ma'am. You going to a party?"

"No, I just came from one."

It takes fifteen minutes to get to my apartment and costs thirteen dollars. We had to go through Times Square and I thought about sinking down in the back seat when we passed the Prescott Nelson building. At about 60th Street, I started worrying that we would get into an accident in front of the building, and I would have to get out onto the street in all my beaded glory. That reminded me of kissing Rob King on the couches. He was rubbing his hands all over my dress and he kept muttering how he didn't want to touch me because all my beads were coming off. He must have gotten over it, because there's definitely some bare spots.

I will not let myself fall asleep, although my bed looks so inviting. (Did Rob King tuck me in last night?) Then I hear something from the living room. Oh, my God. Someone broke into my apartment. They've probably been staking us out for weeks and didn't expect to find anyone home.

I decide to fight—if they've been watching the place, they won't expect me to be home and therefore are unarmed (that's logical, right?). There's nothing in my room that would be a suitable weapon, my heels will have to do. Shit! They are in bad shape someone must've spilled beer and (ugh!) puke—probably my own. I'll just have to get the right shot. I get into my best *Miami Vice* gun stance and *spring!!!*

I bump straight into Rosie and we both scream.

"What the heck are you doing here, Eve? I mean, thank goodness, you're okay, you should've called, but what are you doing?"

"I could say the same to you. It's almost eleven."

"I called in sick. Last I saw you were headed downstairs with that guy Tabitha says is your ticket to the good life. What happened with him?" I explain to her that I'm not sure what happened with Rob and I'm just glad she's not a vicious killer, but I have to get to work.

"Roseanne, do you think anyone noticed us going downstairs?"

"I doubt it. Tab and I just noticed because we weren't hooking up. Did you know she is going to Paris for New Year's?" It seems Roseanne and Tabitha are suddenly best friends. I change into my comfiest (there's that funny word again) jeans and hit the subway.

I get to work at 11:20. It's like a ghost town. No one but Brian, the intern, is around. Does he ever stop kissing ass?

"Rough night, Eve?" He is all smirk.

"Brian, do you see anyone else in here?"

"Everyone's sleeping off their bad behavior." Is he trying to tell me something? I ignore him. I start to check my messages. "I saw you with some guy last night."

"That's funny, Brian, because I thought I saw you with some guy last night."

"I wasn't. I—"

"In fact I was standing next to Herb, you know my boss, and I said, 'Isn't that Brian, our intern, flailing away with some guy from the photography department?' He seemed to think it was." Brian leaves me alone after that. Anyway, my messages.

"Eve, it's Tabitha. It's three o'clock in the morning and you were a very bad girl tonight. Just reminding you to call me the moment you get in." She manages not to sound too drunk. Delete.

"Eve, it's Lorraine. My dog is sick and I figured no one will be around, so I'm taking the day. You have my home number if anything major comes up." Delete.

"Eve, it's Tabitha. I just got up, it's ten o'clock, I'm headed into work. I checked my messages at work and you have yet to call. I am starting to worry. You're never late." Obsessed. Delete.

"Eve, it's Mom. Where were you two last night? I called your apartment several times. I hope you aren't going out on school nights. I hope you are planning on coming home this weekend for your sister. Are you sick? You know you don't even have insurance. This isn't good, Eve. Call me so I can stop worrying." Where does my mother get these stories? She of all people should know I went to the party. Delete.

"Ms. Vitali. I'm thinking of sending out a search party for you. You haven't picked up and I'm having a real hard time locating your home number. I think you were planning on going to work. Hope you are not pulling those elevator shenanigans again. Know how you love those. Call me when you get in, 3364." I listen to that one again. He sounds too intimate, we must've slept together. I save the number.

"Eve, it's Monica. Mom is so neurotic, she is forcing me to call you. I told her you went to that party last night. She wants you to call when you get in. She wants you to come home, but I think I'd rather crash with you guys this weekend. I can't bear to be with them any more than necessary. Call me." I don't think I can bear to be with Monica any more than necessary. Delete.

"Eve, it's me again. Where are you? I'm on my cell in the cab on the way over. This cab is making me nauseous. The cabbie's name has absolutely no vowels in it. What do you think of that? Have you talked to Rob yet?" Tabitha is out of control. One to go.

"Eve, it's Roseanne. Some guy, Rob King, oh, boy, I think that's the guy you hooked up with. Anyway, he just called here. He says to give him a call. I played dumb. I thought it was your boss. Sorry." How did he get my number? My phone beeps. I hope it's not him!

"Eve, why haven't you called me?" Tabitha needs psychiatric care. I spend the next hour trying to answer her questions in a low enough voice so eavesdropping Brian won't hear. We analyze everything I can remember about the evening, but Tabitha isn't really satisfied with my fragmented memory. She's in a pissy mood because the Big C was ready and waiting for her at eight and Lady Tabitha strolled in around noon. We stay on the phone until about 12:30. Most of my department (the people who decided to show) come in about one. Everyone is grumpy and whispering—they might as well have stayed home. It's amazing how few people can actually hold their liquor. I manage to be cheery and polite, despite the fact that there is no way I'm getting out of my chair. Lacey is noticeably out for the entire day (that can't be good for her image). I see Rob's number come up a couple of times on my Caller ID, but I don't answer, and he never leaves a message. Every time I realize that there isn't going to be a message, I regret not picking it up. I keep telling myself that if he calls back, I'll pick up. Then when he does, I don't.

At 4:30, people start sneaking off. I wait until quarter after five and then book it out of there. I have managed to avoid Rob King all day (well for the five hours I've been at work). I have yet to eat any solid food. As if she read my mind, Roseanne has a big vat of cream of wheat waiting. We have two servings each, feel sick and pass out on the couch watching some poor victim woman movie on Lifetime. Quite a Friday.

I must never drink again.

My sister shows up at around eleven on Saturday morning. She has decided to crash "for a few days." The sight of her overnight bag makes me a little queasy. I guess I'm not yet over my hangover.

It's not that I don't love my sister—I do. When we were little she wasn't one of those competitive older sisters that ruined my self-image, nor was she excessively mean to me. My sister was always sort of an oddball in school. She was a little too old for her age and a little too smart. She was going to demonstrations when most people were just going to football games. Even in high school, I tried to avoid the cheesy people (which is hard to do in Jersey) but not be too much of a geek. My sister was always getting nominated for "Most Original" and she is. I think I disappointed her a little because I never followed in her radical footsteps. In college, she declared herself a socialist. She named her kittens Sacco and Vanzetti. My father developed an ulcer.

For everything my sister is, she is also kind of a baby. I guess I tend to think of myself as more of an expert on the real world because I've held a full-time job for almost a year and my sister has always been at school or volunteering in some impoverished part of the world. She is good-hearted, if a little disillusioned. Sometimes it's hard to be patient with her. I know, I'm awful. She is flustered when she comes through the door, because she had trouble finding her way over from Penn Station (ten blocks!).

Roseanne comes out of the kitchen, wiping her hands on a dish-towel. She smiles at Monica, whom she's only met a few times. "How was your trip?"

"Hard. It was hard for me to leave Chuck." All of the sudden I get a quick flash that this entire visit is going to consist of Monica looking wistful and trying to engage me in conversations about Chuck.

"That's too bad," says Roseanne, who has suddenly turned into Ms. Compassionate.

"Wanna check out the rest of the apartment?" The last thing I want to do is talk about some over-the-hill folk singer all weekend. Monica plops her bag down and walks around. I can't read her expression.

"Wow! It's not so bad. I mean it's decent-size."

"Well, it's actually really big by New York standards."

"And cheap," Roseanne adds.

"No, honey, it's great." I hate it when she calls me honey. Monica is only five years older than me. I am vowing not to lose patience with her. I watch her staring out the window onto 7th Avenue. "It must get really loud though."

"Not bad," I lie. "It's a great apartment."

"Can you go out on this?" She means the fire escape.

"Well, we won't go out now, it's too cold, but we like to call it our veranda."

"Or balcony." Monica nods and stares out the window. I can tell she is thinking of Chuck. Whatever.

"So, Monica, what do you want to do today? Shopping? Want to go see the tree and shop?"

"Sure, that's fun. I'm never in New York. I'll feel like a tourist."

"Well, we'll see enough of those today. Let's eat first. Roseanne made breakfast."

"Yeah, I made honey walnut pancakes and fresh fruit toppings."

"Oh, that sounds good, but I'll just have fruit salad."

"Oh, I can make something else. Eggs?" Poor Roseanne.

"No, that's okay, I'm vegan." What?

"What?" I can't believe she's such a freak. "Why, Monica?"

"Well, Chuck is. I just think it's a better way to be. It's almost hypocritical of me to feel as I do about global ecology and then munch on animal products."

"Vegetarian?" Roseanne asks, confused.

"No, vegan," I tell her, "no animal products of any kind— milk, cheese, eggs, honey. Nothing that comes from an animal."

"Humans should not be drinking cow's milk, Eve."

"I'll keep that in mind. I just think that's a little drastic." Then it occurs to me. "What are you going to do Christmas Eve?" We have like seven different fish dishes on Christmas Eve.

"I'll just eat the pasta."

"Mom is going to flip. Dad is going to lose it. Aunt Sadie will take it as a personal insult if you don't eat her calamari salad. This could be a huge issue."

"Monica, here's your fruit. I have plenty." Roseanne is always chipper. Damn her!

"Thanks." Roseanne gives me a motherly look so I won't start a fight with Monica. When did I let Roseanne become my Jiminy Cricket?

We sit and eat. I ask for seconds on the pancakes. I only manage to get half a delicious pancake down because I'm stuffed and I'm probably only trying to eat to rub it in Monica's face. Monica chats away about Chuck (I can't handle it.) She assures me that I am going to love him—but that's what she said about the Marxist and about the religious freak she met while volunteering in Appalachia; in fact, that's what she says every time there's a new guy in her life. I'm trying to be patient.

Once we get out, it's hard to believe how crowded the city is. There are tourists everywhere, all walking at a snail's pace. It's so frustrating. Roseanne doesn't care; she eats up Fifth Avenue. I actually kind of get a warm feeling when we look at the tree in Rockefeller Center. It's Christmas, after all, and even with the crowds, there's something magical about it.

My sister tries to get me to go ice skating, although she knows my aversion to physical activity. She and Roseanne form some kind of tag team and after an hour of waiting on line, I am circling the rink, gripping the sides. Roseanne and Monica are busy doing figure eights in the center of the rink with the pros. Once in a while they remember me and skate over to try to coax me off the wall or to call to me from the center, but I refuse. I am making my way steadily around the rink. I keep running into the same children. They mock me, these kids, because eventually they all get the hang of it and start skating in the center of the rink. I hate kids. I hate looking stupid.

Being alone, I can't help but think about Rob King and kissing him at the party. When I think about it, I get that familiar queasy feeling. I try to imagine what it would be like to date someone like that. He's not your average guy—I mean he is, but, he isn't. It's a little scary, anyway, I shouldn't think about it. I won't get my hopes up.

Finally, the excruciating hour of skating is over and Monica and Roseanne help me off the rink. I notice some of the kids snickering at me. Monica and Roseanne are totally pumped about the whole thing, like those annoying writers at work who talk about the "biker's high." Whatever. If it isn't artificial it shouldn't affect my mood. Despite their obvious competency on the rink, they still defer to me about where we should go now. I suggest Tiffany's.

There's another line for that—just to get in! It feels like a club, where the security guard/bouncer looks us up and down and waits for some people to leave, before letting us in. The thing I like about Tiffany's, once inside, is the accessibility of it all. Who knows who you're shopping next to and how much money they have. You want to hate it for being so snobby, but it's not like you can't get in, so you have to sort of love it and wish you had enough money for several pretty blue packages.

I catch Roseanne talking to a real cute guy from Texas, so I steer clear of them. I look around for my sister and begin to think she got fed up with all the consumerism and left, but then I see her checking out the engagement rings. There is not an ounce of disdain on her face; in fact she looks relaxed and almost content. Even with all the social ills in the world, my sister manages to look content for a moment. I walk over quietly, but I hear my sister tell the sales assistant that she is just browsing. When she turns, our eyes meet and she smiles at me. We go up to look at silver.

I pick out a pendant for Tabitha for Christmas. It's about seventy dollars. I throw it on the plastic. As soon as I get out my card, my sister, who was momentarily an unknown beautiful and calm woman, turns back into the sister I know and tolerate.

"Eve, you are such a consumer, I can't believe you are going to get such an excessive gift for anyone. Never spend that much money on me—unless it's to donate to a charity."

"I won't spend that much money on you ever, Monica, don't

worry." Tabitha's pendant is in a box inside a tiny blue fuzzy pouch. I will keep the little bag for myself.

We decide to go to St. Patrick's Cathedral. It's Monica's idea, although she diffuses it by explaining to Roseanne her misgivings about the Catholic church. She says she just likes the aesthetics. I don't like church that much, either, but my grandmother used to always take us to St. Patrick's Cathedral at Christmas. She gave us money to light a candle and say a prayer. It used to be a few coins, but now it's a buck. I sit at one of the little alcoves with the statues.

I don't think prayers are like birthday cake wishes, I think you could pretty much tell people what you're prayers are. I mean don't people always say "I'll pray for you" and stuff like that (I would never say that). But anyway when I light my candle it seems pretty much fair ground to pray for whatever I want. I ask for pretty standard stuff, a new job, health for my family, my dad and grandma especially, health for my friends, no rodents in the apartment, a happy holiday, a better year, my sister to get some direction and not marry this bozo, and (then I'm trying to wrap it up), I know that I would be lying to myself and to who knows who else if I didn't at least mention Rob King calling me, so I pray for that, too.

"I didn't know you were so devout," Monica says when we are all sitting on the stairs of St. Patrick's. "Can we go soon? I'm cold." I ignore her.

Monica can't believe all the women who are wearing fur coats. "What are they gonna do, when the revolution comes and they are left out in the cold?"

I would like to ask her what revolution she is talking about and if it will conflict with her studies. I don't say anything because we are on the church steps and my sister is so sensitive, I think anything I say would throw her into a tirade.

We decide to get take-out and head home. We stop at a gourmet market and get some prepared stuff. Roseanne decides to buy some fresh pasta and have Tyler (Mr. Texas) over for dinner tomorrow. She'll have a little dinner party. Tabitha can come over and talk to Tyler (a soap opera name, if ever there was one) about The Lone Star State. She starts running down a list in her head.

"Ro, you shouldn't get all this stuff. We can get it right on 23rd. Just get the pasta if it's so great here, but really do you want to carry all this stuff home?" Suddenly my sister looks like she is about to expire, she is completely horrified.

"We're not walking, are we? It's so far."

"Monica." I take a tone I've heard my mother take when they are on the phone, I'm amazed I can do it so well. "It's twenty-eight blocks and a couple of avenues to our house. It's all flat land. Come on!"

"But it's cold." She rocks herself a little like a kid who has to pee. "Besides, we've been walking all over, all day." I cannot believe this is my sister.

"Monica, what are *you* gonna do when the revolution comes?" That said, we walk home in silence.

We are watching *COPS* on Fox, trying to decide where to go. Tabitha is over and she wants to go somewhere good. I realize that I'm going to be pretty poor by the end of December with all this spreading of Christmas cheer. Monica is also being a big baby (surprise!) about going out. She complains that everything is too expensive in New York. We decide to drink at home—we have some beer, vodka and Collins mix. If we are still functioning we'll go to Dusk, a bar on 24th where the English bartender calls us "sweetheart" and gives us every third drink free. It's swank enough for Tabitha, although I have to bribe Monica into going by promising to get her some drinks.

Roseanne isn't having much luck putting together her dinner party. Tabitha seems down with it until she hears Tyler is from Texas. It's strange the way she changes her mind suddenly. "I have no desire to trip down Memory Lane with a redneck."

It's beginning to look like Monica and I are going to have to make ourselves scarce during the dinner party.

COPS is taking place in a real white trash neighborhood in Texas. We ask Tabitha if that's her hometown. She doesn't laugh. An overzealous cop is handcuffing a potbellied criminal who is wearing dirty jeans. His partner is asking the guy in a black heavy metal concert T-shirt humiliating questions. Later these two sensitive guys are shown counseling the wife of one of the criminals. My sister is outraged.

"Do you realize how wrong this is?"

"Totally," Tabitha, to my surprise, agrees, "I mean when you think about it someone could just come in and wardrobe these people, it would be great product placement and we wouldn't have to be subjected to seeing these dirtbags."

I just start filling up everyone's glasses again. Maybe if I can get Monica drunk she won't be so hard to deal with. I actually think it's working because I start to hear a little Jersey accent come out in her voice.

We make it to the bar. It's dark and trendy and just small and selective enough to make us feel like we have our own exclusive place. We drink cosmopolitans—even Monica—and dance a little to the DJ's trip-hop. I know when my sister is totally drunk because she keeps twirling around and saying, "I'm so cosmopolitan."

She also calls Chuck from the pay phone on my mom's credit card. When she comes back she says she misses him a lot and wants to go home. We aren't very far from my apartment, but I have a feeling if I give her the keys and send her on her way, I might never see her again. I tell the girls to stay, but Roseanne says she wants to get beauty sleep for her date tomorrow. I assume Tabitha will leave, too, but she wants to stay and chat with the bartender about Paris. She is leaving in a week.

When we get back, my sister throws up all the vegetables she ate for dinner and I hold her hair and rub her back. I force her to drink water and remind her how cosmopolitan she is.

We go shopping in the village all day Sunday. I pick up a couple of presents for Adrian and Roseanne. For Adrian, a belt with an awesome buckle; for Rebecca, a cookbook and a sexy black shirt. My sister and I go in on a couple of appliances for our parents and decide that I will pick up some Broadway tickets. We also get some little things for our family. Monica buys Chuck a huge coffee table book on Frank Lloyd Wright architecture and a sweater.

"Are you sure you aren't spending too much money on him, Monica? You don't want to turn him into a consumer." I can't help but bring it up.

"How could I spend too much money? There is no way to place a value on all he's given me." When my sister says cheesy crap like that, I have to think she is not too far removed from all the people she looks down at.

My sister definitely has an agenda for our day, she wants to extract details about my sex life and insinuate nonstop the possibility of her marrying this Chuck guy.

"Are you being careful, Eve?" My sister got her major in public health. She has always considered herself an expert and maybe the only person on earth who knows about condoms. From the time I was fourteen, she has been trying to push condoms on me and extol their virtues. My sister's big quest in life is to find out how many sex partners I've had and if I'm having more satisfying sex than she is. She has an elaborate method for doing this. She doesn't come out and ask me what she wants to know; she hints at it. She also has a habit of asking me the wrong questions in the wrong places. "Eve, are you being careful with the boys you see?" she asks over tempeh burgers at lunch. "You can be creative, you know, you don't always have to have intercourse."

"I've been thinking about face painting or maybe setting up a piñata." I wish my sister would just ask me if I'm a slut instead of taking this tone of medical superiority.

"I'm serious, Eve, and so are STDs." I have to laugh at that one. This burger is misnamed, it's disgusting. "Are you in a relationship?" In spite of myself the name Rob King pops into my head. Damn! (Was I creative enough with him?)

"Monica, honestly I'm fine. I know everything I need to know. Don't get neurotic about that, too."

"Too? What do you mean? You think I'm neurotic like Mom?"

"I think Mom is an alarmist, I don't think she's all that neurotic. But, I guess it's a fine line. Don't get excited."

We go to some other stores and the sales are so good that I wind up buying stuff for myself. I love this season and I love the fact that Monica is giving me the silent treatment, so she can't tell me how tired she is from walking.

When we get back to the apartment, it smells really good. The dishes are still on the table and the food appears to have been picked at. I start to call out to Roseanne, but then I hear noises from Roseanne's cranny that lead me to believe that Roseanne is being very creative. You go girl! Monica decides to go back to my parents' house. I'd prefer not to have her pissed at me, but I don't think I can handle much more of her. I walk her to Penn Station and give her a big hug. Maybe I'm a bad sister—but don't forget about the puking. That makes me a kind sister.

On Wednesday, the Feed Meet is canceled because Herb's on vacation. I know I've been here too long, when I'm actually telling myself it's the hump day. I brought some of Roseanne's Christmas cookies in to work today, and everyone crowds around my desk and demands to know about the fat and sugar content. I confess that I have no idea, but it's probably a lot. They ravage the cookies anyway.

Roseanne is having an emotional crisis. She's happy (and relieved) that she finally got some booty but Tyler's business is finished in New York. There's a good chance he'll return in six weeks, but that's a long time and apparently they really clicked.

If only we could find a nice straight New Yorker that neither of us works with; we could even share him. Now, that's creative. Anyway, I take her out for sweet potato perogies at Veselka, this Ukrainian place on 2nd Avenue. It seems to make her feel better.

Tabitha is off to Paris this week until after the New Year. Luckily the Big C takes a cruise every Christmas time, so Tabitha was able to get all that time off.

December is a really slow time, so I spend time cruising the Net. Maybe I should start my own Web page about living in New York, and get Prescott to fund me. Pipe dreams. I won't make a resolution, but I vow this year will be different. This year I will actually do something that I enjoy. The phone rings.

"Eve Vitali."

"Eve, this is Sherman Mussey, Rob King's assistant. Rob told me he took a look at your proposal and thinks it a great idea—"

"He took a look at my what?"

"Proposal. He is pretty jammed up today, but he was wondering if he could meet you tonight around nine for a late dinner meeting."

"Is this a joke?"

"Is what? Isn't this Eve Vitali?" The guy seems genuinely confused and very serious. Is Rob King asking me out on a date through his assistant?

"So, ah, Sherman, did you read my proposal?"

"I have to confess, I haven't, but Rob seems very enthusiastic about it."

"Thanks." For a minute I actually believe I wrote some sort of proposal. "Can I call Rob directly?"

"Well he does answer his own phone, but today he has back-to-back meetings."

"Voice mail?"

"I have to check his messages, in case it's urgent I can find him and alert him."

"Alert him, huh? What about e-mail?"

"Same thing I'm afraid." He gives me the name of the restaurant and offers to send a car to my apartment to pick me up. I respectfully decline the car.

No one can believe it. I can't believe it. I can't believe I'm going out with Rob King and that his assistant asked me out. Tabitha insists she come over to help me plan my outfit. She can't believe I turned down the car. She and Roseanne entertain the notion of a surveillance operation while we are eating, but I quickly nix that idea. I don't want those girls anywhere near the restaurant.

Tabitha does my makeup. I remind her minimalist, only she can't help but mix the brown eye shadows with a sparkly yellow. I'm wearing black pants and a gray Asian shirt with frog fasteners. I think I might be doing it.

He picks a Russian place in midtown that's really close to the office. I stand kind of stupidly in the elegant foyer and try to look into the restaurant for him. I ask the host if he has arrived yet, but he hasn't. The host suggests I have a drink in the bar. I order a rum and Coke. I wish I had a magazine or something; the bartender isn't the friendliest and the other two guys alone seem like some kind of dorky salesmen waiting for their clients.

I am midway through my second drink and starting to wonder how much of a credit card bill I will have if I charge these, when he shows up. He is wearing a dark gray suit and it fits him well. I guess I sort of forgot what he looked like. We smile at each other a little awkwardly and then he kisses me on the cheek. I lean up into him. He smells good—it reminds of the party, but nothing concrete. He settles my bar tab and we go to our table.

"So, do you want to talk about my proposal?"

"Yes, I do, Ms. Vitali, I definitely like your idea about elevator game requirements, but I'm afraid I've talked with the board and we have voted against your policy of not alerting us of your progress. Communication is key if we want to—" he cocks his head to the side "—put this project to bed." He is so hot!

"Oh, that, well I've been busy."

"You know in the cab on the way home you told me all about how little you have to do and how bored you are at work." I did? "I think you've just plain been avoiding me, Ms. Vitali."

"It's not that—" I'm interrupted by the waitress who wants to take our order. Rob tells me to order the wine, I pick one of the more (but by no means most) expensive reds. Rob orders us two of these special Russian drinks he guarantees will "warm me up." I have a bad flash of Zeke, but ignore it.

"So continue." He looks over his menu at me, intensely.

"I just, you know, didn't know." I don't want to sound like a confused kid. I don't want to act like I think he is such a great catch. I want to be the catch. "I didn't know what was up."

"Have you thought about that night at all?" I wait while the waitress places our warming drinks on the table and lets him taste the wine. He tells her we'll need a few more minutes to mull over the menu. He smiles at me and leans closer. "I hope you're going to be a good girl and eat all your beets." Why is he so sexy?

"You know, you have really nice teeth. Did you have braces?"

"No. Just good breeding."

"I bet." We sit there until the waitress assumes we are ready to order. Rob gets a bunch of appetizers and I get some lamb dish that is really just the first thing I see.

"Look Rob, this is kind of a ridiculous thing to ask, but—" he is hinged on my every word "—did we..." I roll my hand over to imply.

"What?" He rolls his hand over faster.

"You know, do the deed, get nasty, slap skins, what have you?"

"Well there was quite a bit of 'what have you,' but I don't know about that other stuff." He shrugs, he is so cute.

"C'mon, tell me."

"Well—" he looks from side to side and then peeks under the table "—no." I don't know how to feel. "Believe me it wasn't for lack of encouragement on your part, but I figured when you almost walked into the closet, you weren't really in any shape to be making decisions. You were difficult for a while, but then you sort of conked out. I'd like to think if it did happen, you'd remember."

"My dress?"

"You took it off. Cute undies, by the way."

"Thanks." Our appetizers arrive. I focus on eating sexy, but not in an overt way.

"I figured it was kind of awkward, though," Rob continues. "I just wanted you to call me and not be freaked out."

"I wasn't freaked out. I wasn't." Lies. I was.

"Okay." I'm finding it hard to keep my cool with him and at the same time wondering if I have anything in my teeth. "Does that kind of stuff happen to you all the time?"

"Yeah," I'm too quick to answer. "Actually, no. I've never woken up in a strange bed with no immediate idea why. I think I forgot, or blocked a lot of that night out."

"You make it sound so traumatic."

"I don't mean to, it's just sort of a weird situation."

"Why?"

"Well there you are hanging out in the cool V.P. room and I mean, I'm an assistant. I don't even have benefits."

"Yeah, we're working on that. And you're not my assistant. How do you like that drink?" It's so good, and when our food comes it is also delicious. I like that Rob offers me some of his meal. I make sure not to have him feed me (not that he offers). He smiles when he sees that I like it. I feel a glow, not the alcohol one that I usually feel, but, a glow like I'm in a cosmetics ad. It's a perfect sort of romantic feeling. I can't help but smile. Rob doesn't ask me why I'm grinning like a dork, he just smiles back.

"You told me all about your plan to have your own magazine. I think it's a great idea."

"I guess I think about stuff like that all the time. It's funny that I actually said it."

"Why?"

"I mean it's so far-fetched. I don't have the capital or the experience. I have an entry level position that's supposed to be my foot in the door, but really just seems like a big waste of time. No offense."

"Why should I be offended?"

"Well, because you're one of the top guys. Guys like you are depressing."

"Why?"

"Because you're young and the company is supposed to be young and hip and cool. They want you to represent them. But beneath the image, it's still a business. There's the same shit at brokerage firms and other corporate businesses. We just get to wear what we want."

"And how does that apply to me?"

"Because you either skipped all these steps or you came in when there was a clearer path to where you are now. You're a reminder of the speed things should move, but it doesn't usually go that way."

"I don't know, Eve, I've worked really hard to get where I am. Maybe you should be more aggressive. Do you tell them that you want to do more? That you're bored out of your skull playing hangman all day?" Not a good idea to tell him my computer recreation activities.

"I think that whole aggressive thing is a lie. I mean, after a while you just start to annoy people. No one wants that."

"It seems like a waste of the company's money, of your talent. Part of the reason I'm there is to consult, to tell the board how they can make things run more efficiently." Ding! Duh! I've finally figured out his job.

"You're here to fire people." He looks away from me and examines the crease in his cloth napkin.

"Eve, I'm here to do research, to get a feel for all our lines of business. It may be that some of the fallout from my findings is termination, but if not me, someone else." I wish we hadn't gotten on this topic, I think Rob let me in on more than I should probably know. We sit in silence while the waitress takes our plates away and asks us if we want dessert. Rob asks me if I like chocolate (I do) and then orders this chocolate dessert they have. I get a cappuccino. I am remarkably sober, and while I don't exactly appreciate the tension, it's refreshing to talk to someone like Rob and have him relate to me like I was someone worth talking to.

"There, we got those nice teeth of yours back, Ms. Vitali. Do you like it here?"

"It's a great place. Do you come here a lot?"

"Actually, only one other time—some business meeting. I thought it would be a really nice place to go with a date. So what comes after dessert?"

"Whatever. It's only, shit, it's 11:30."

"What's that 'shit, it's 11:30'? I thought you were the young one. The night is young."

"You know I was never late until the day after the party. Even when I was hungover and coming from Jersey."

"You're a Jersey Girl? I'm from Cherry Hill."

"Yeah, but that's Philly, that's slightly respectable. I'm not too proud of Jersey."

"And now you live in Chelsea."

"How do you know?"

"I've got friends in high places."

"I thought that was confidential info."

"Right, but we're not going to talk business, we're just going to eat this delicious dessert and then…I guess we'll have to get you home so you can get up early tomorrow. Another day another dollar." He raises an eyebrow at me. He's got great brows. I tell him my Kevin story and he laughs.

"Very impressive, Ms. Vitali, you've got the pros fawning over you."

"Well, he wasn't exactly fawning. I never get fawned over." Again the eyebrow raise. I really want to go back to his apartment. I really want to practice different elevator activities with him and run my fingers along his eyebrows. This is getting too Spice Channel. "So how's your doorman?"

"Good, I guess." He laughs. "Why do you ask?" I could find a way to make it clear that I definitely want to remember tonight, but honestly I can't help feeling a little freaked out about all this. I need to confer with the girls before I proceed. I don't want to be the geeky girl who gets seduced by the captain of the football team and then stays moony over him. I know I'm getting carried away, but, as I recently discovered, he was a math major after all.

"Just wondering."

"Should we get the check?" I nod, although I don't really want to leave. "Maybe we could walk back to your place, if it's not too cold."

We decide to walk. We go past the Prescott Nelson building, and Rob senses me stiffen up. "You know we're not really doing anything wrong, Eve. I'm not your boss." But, once we get onto 40th, he puts his arm around me and I feel sort of tucked into him. There's nothing for me to do but put my hands around his waist. When we start getting close to my apartment, I wish we'd walked slower, because I don't want the night to end and I don't want to deal with the doorway etiquette.

"This is it." I stop and turn to him. Should I invite him up? No, he can't see my apartment, I can't remember the last time we cleaned.

"Eve, I have to go to the L.A. office until after the New Year." He probably has a girlfriend in L.A., some aspiring actress... "Don't look like that, I don't want to go, I hate L.A. I was hoping to spend Christmas with my parents for a change."

"When are you leaving?"

"Friday morning. I'll call you." Now I'm the one who is going to be waiting on a call from god knows where. I can't deal.

"No, Rob, don't call, you can just wait until you get back."

"Eve, c'mon, don't be upset. I had a great time with you to-night." He tips my chin up to look at him. I reach up and touch his sexy, arching brow and then we kiss for a while against the door. I can tell he is getting into it, and so am I.

"You can come up if you want."

"I want to, Eve, but..." I don't know what his "but" is, but I definitely have some "buts" of my own. I decide to just kiss him.

"All right, good night." I kiss him for a little bit longer and go upstairs. Tabitha and Roseanne are sitting on the couch, poised for interrogation.

"Why did he leave?"

"Are you going to get a promotion now?"

I cannot believe them.

"Were you guys spying on me?" They look at each other and

shrug. I want to tell them all about my date, but I'll let them sweat it out a little. I like being the one with the story. I take my time with my nightly rituals. I stare at my eyebrows in the mirror and examine my teeth.

When I get back out and I'm ready to talk, the lights are out and Roseanne is in her cranny and Tabitha is asleep on my bed. So much for their curiosity. Looks like I have to figure this out for myself. On the couch.

Rob doesn't call me on Thursday. I spend most of the day entering data, because the office will be closed a couple of days for the holidays. Tabitha can't hold out anymore and she invites me to hit Fifth Avenue with her for a few quick sprees before her trip. She's already spent far too much money on coordinated luggage, but she insists she just needs a few more things. She gets all the details out of me and is not as fascinated by our passionate kissing as she is with the reason for him being here.

"Wow! So heads are going to roll."

"Probably not our heads, we're too low."

"Yeah, but it could totally shake things up around here. You could be like a spy for all the people who suspect they're going down."

"Tabitha, I just want him to call again."

"He will, maybe when he gets back."

"I don't want us all to be pining away for these jet-setting guys. Our lives are exciting enough, I don't need to be waiting by the phone."

"Yeah, Roseanne is pretty into that Texan."

"He's a cutie. He said he's from right outside of Houston— near you. You guys should hang out."

"Yeah, we could share our Texan pride."

"He's got an accent, though. You don't have one at all."

"Thankfully."

"Is your family upset that you won't be spending Christmas with them?"

"I doubt they'll notice." Tabitha will never talk about her family. I imagine this really cold, rich family having no idea what to do with this crazy super-cool New York mover and shaker daughter.

"Do you want to come over tonight? We can exchange presents. I mean, I can give you your present."

"Don't worry, Eve, I got you something."

When I get back from shopping, there is one message. It's Lacey, who needs me to messenger something from her desk to her at home. She isn't feeling well today so she isn't coming in (can we say six-day weekend?). I do it and stare at the phone a while before I decide to call it a day. I'm looking forward to going to Jersey tomorrow. Even with my sister there, it will be nice to wake up at home.

I buy some apple cider and some spiced rum. Roseanne is home early and she has lambchops in the oven and is making some cranberry and wild rice side dish. Every day my apartment looks more and more like a gourmet magazine cover. I tell Roseanne that Tabitha and I are going to exchange presents, and to my surprise she says that she has something for Tabitha, too.

We have a pretty mellow night. After dinner, we eat some of the chocolate cake Tabitha made. It's awful, which to me, is a little comforting. Tabitha gives Roseanne her present first. It's a crepe pan, a pretty expensive one, too. Roseanne is so touched.

"I figured I would get used to eating them in 'Gay Paree' and no one else could make them for me. It's selfish really." Tabitha also gives Roseanne some MAC makeup. Roseanne is a little surprised, but seems to like the colors. It might be the start of a new Roseanne. Roseanne gives Tabitha a (get this) handmade porcelain ornament with her name on it. It's really delicate.

"Oooh, I hope Jaques has a tree." There is also a pillow for the airplane and a trashy novel. They hug again. It's almost too much for me. Tabitha gives me a sexy, yet classy silk nightie with a matching robe and some perfume, which I love. Tabitha adores her pendant from Tiffany's. Roseanne gives me a woolen scarf that she knit and a pair of short classy silver earrings that I was looking at in Tiffany's (now I have my own blue bag). She loves her cookbook and she declares her new shirt a New Year's "Eve" shirt. We talk for a while about what we are going to do for New Year's, but we don't dwell because Tabitha won't be with us. With all this love and Christmas cheer we are like the Three Musketeers.

After Tabitha leaves, I do the dishes. Roseanne and I discuss the possibility of having a New Year's party. Later, I lie in bed and think about Christmas for a while. I used to have a major countdown starting right after Thanksgiving. I'm not as aware of it anymore, but as cheesy as it can be, I still go for all that stuff. Especially the present part. I mean you can't say "Merry Christmas" or "Happy Holidays" enough. I'll be sad when the tree comes down in the lobby.

*   *   *

"Somebody has an admirer," Lorraine says. I look up from my computer and one of our messengers, Ben, is holding a big bouquet of flowers. I don't believe they're for me, but they are. Lorraine hovers around my desk. "Well, aren't you going to read the card?"

"No, don't get excited, they're probably from my mom."

"Looks like an awfully expensive bunch from your mom. I'll let you keep your admirer a secret." She leaves, but of course, now Brian needs to know.

"What are those?" he says, standing by my desk.

"Poisonous herbs that will fend off the unwanted stupid questions of those around me." He shuffles over to his desk. I open the card.

I'll miss you. Have a great holiday.
R.

The flowers are beautiful, but it would've been nice to get a phone call. It's going to be hell taking these home on the train and I can only imagine what my mom is going to say. I'm sure she will embarrass me in front of my entire family over Christmas dinner and then my sister will make some comment about the wastefulness of flowers.

I try calling Rob, just to thank him (it's the right thing to do). Sherman answers and makes me identify myself before he tells me that Rob is already out of the office. He won't confirm that he is in L.A.

Herb comes over to make sure I sent out the company Christmas cards. He actually asks about my holiday plans. I wonder if he's acting interested in me because somehow he found out I went out on a date with Rob. He takes out a small wrapped box and hands it to me.

"Just a thank you for all you do." Wow! I open it. It's a Christmas ornament that looks like something from the fifties.

"Wow! Thank you. Thanks a lot."

The nice thing about leaving for the holiday is that everyone is in a good mood. Despite how harried this time is, most people hug each other before they go. I go visit Joe and Adam and eat some Christmas cookies that are in their conference room. I tell them I'll let them know after the break if we are going to have a New Year's Eve party.

* * *

It's a relief to be on the train to Jersey, even though I get tons of dirty looks as I push on with my flowers. Everyone else is loaded up with packages, so I don't know how or why I should be singled out. Monica is waiting for me at the station. I can tell by her expression that it isn't going well. I attempt to be cheerful.

"What are those?" She nods to the flowers. I decide to practice my story.

"One of our advertisers sent them to the magazine and I was the only one who wanted to take them home. I thought Ma would like them for the table."

"Can you believe they're starting with the church thing again?" I know that's a lie. Every year it's the same. My sister comes home and, just to antagonize them, announces that there is no way in hell she is going to Christmas Eve mass. They fight, she cries, she complains to her friends, but she always winds up going and the next day, Christmas, there is all kinds of residual bitterness.

"Monica, I know you're the one starting it. I really want to enjoy my time at home. Do you think for a change you could just suck it up and be mature and go to church since you know you're going to wind up doing it anyway? We're not kids anymore."

She doesn't say a word to me for the rest of the day, she just mopes around her room. I help my mom with all the cooking (Roseanne is rubbing off on me). I spend a lot of time watching Christmas shows and just vegging. Monica finally breaks down on Christmas Eve when I lean across the pew and offer her my hand. The classic "peace be with you" thing.

"And also with you," she says, but I'm not sure she means it.

Christmas morning. Although the four of us are adults now, we like to feign surprise that Santa has actually visited us. We even put out cookies for Santa and carrots for the deer. We all sit in the living room in our pajamas and ooh and ahh over every gift. This year, since I've been sleeping in the living room, I'm awakened by my mother's squeal. I sit up on the couch and she looks at me and says, with all seriousness, "Eve, I can't believe Santa didn't wake you up."

My dad makes coffee and we have some leftover fish from last night (yes, it's only 10:30 a.m.) and thus the Christmas ritual begins. Even the gift tags are marked—some are from Santa and some from my parents. (Although it seems like everyone forgot me this year.) Everything is for Monica. My parents love the gifts we got them, but one after another, it's a wretched sweater for

Monica or a new comforter for Monica and I am trying not to be selfish, but it's Christmas, for Christ's sake, where are my gifts?

"I guess that's it," says my cold, heartless mother.

"More coffee anyone?" asks my mean, negligent father.

"I guess I'll have some." I might as well get something out of this whole thing. When my father comes back in he's is carrying a big box. The three of them are thrilled with themselves for fooling me and I rip off the paper and (oh, my God!) it's a computer.

"Wow! I can't believe it! This is awesome!"

"I'm glad you like it, it's from all of us and Santa." My dad encourages this Santa thing, too. I think it's so he can eat the extra cookies off Santa's plate.

"It'll help with your writing." I can't believe my parents know me so well, what I want and need and support me in what I want to do. "I just hope it won't get stolen out of your apartment."

I can't even get annoyed about that. I just hug all around and say, "This is the best Christmas ever." My sister hands me another wrapped box. "This is so you won't become a slave to the computer age. Don't forget that pens exist." It's this amazing journal and two really nice pens. There's a card inside that says, "So you can capture all your thoughts."

"Thanks, Monica." We women sit basking in gift glow and my dad goes to get more coffee. He answers the phone and it's for me. We never get calls so early on Christmas morning, but I figure it's Roseanne.

"Merry Christmas," says the warm male voice on the line.

"Rob?" I can't believe it.

"How's it going, Ms. Vitali? Was Santa good to you?"

"Yeah, great, I got a computer. Oh, and a little elf brought me some flowers on Friday. Thank you."

"Yeah, I'm sorry I couldn't call, Eve, I wanted to."

"That's okay, God, it must be what, 7:30 there, why are you up so early?"

"I went for a run. This is the first free time I've had since I got here. The weather's great, but I could go for some snow."

"Yeah, me, too. I love white Christmases. When are you coming back?"

"Not until the third. Listen, can we have dinner when I get back?"

"Of course." My mother comes into the kitchen and I can tell she's eavesdropping. I ignore her. "Your friends in high places must have worked real hard on this one."

"No, your parents are listed, you told me Oradell." Oh, right.

"Well, I should go, my relatives are coming over." My mother has decided now would be the best time to refill the sugar bowl.

"Well, have a great day and I'll call you when I get back."

I try to escape the kitchen right after I hang up, but it doesn't work. My mother asks me if I need more coffee, which means she is able to get me into a conversation with her. "Who was that boy?"

"Just someone from work." He is *so* not a boy.

"On Christmas." I give my mother a kiss and thank her for the computer again. I can tell she is not happy to let the boy subject drop. Any minute now she might tell me that I shouldn't give in to boys, I should be creative.

When I get back to my apartment Roseanne is already there. My dad is with me, so that he can set up my computer. As soon as she sees my father, Roseanne starts apologizing for not having made anything. It takes us about two hours to set the thing up. Surprisingly, my dad knows a lot more about computers than I do. I offer him a beer and we sit on my bed, as he shows me all the functions that the sales guy told him about in Computer World. It's kind of cool to see my dad so animated about something.

"Hey, Daddy, maybe you should get a computer."

"Yeah, we don't really have the money right now."

"Can't you write it off as a business expense?" My father gives me one of those looks he reserves for the times I bring up matters that he thinks are specifically adult, like rent, bills, taxes. He nods at me.

"Maybe, I could do that."

"Hey, do you want me to order pizza?"

"Thanks, kid, but I should go back for your mother." Chuck, Monica's new boyfriend, is arriving tomorrow night. "I can give you some money, though, if you're hungry." He fishes into his wallet for a ten.

"Dad, I really...okay." I take the ten, not because I need it, but because it's my dad and I think he would like to think that I could still use some cash every now and then. I walk him downstairs. "Get home safe."

"Yeah, you, too. Listen, kid, your mom and I are very proud of you. Don't be afraid to ask us if you need help. We know you can take care of yourself, but we like to help you." He pats me on the head.

"Thank you, Daddy."

I bring back one cheese slice and two cheeseless mushroom slices to share with Roseanne. "How was home?" I plop down beside her on the couch.

"Well, I think my mom is a little bitter at me for leaving. She's dating some asshole and she was kind of pissy. Christmas was just okay."

"Yeah, you seemed a little bummed yesterday on the phone. I'm sorry. Did you see your dad?"

"Well, we spent Christmas Eve together. He tries so hard, my dad, but I just can't help wondering how two people could've screwed up their lives so much. Still all they do is complain about each other. I don't know. I guess it's nice to feel removed from that, but at the same time I feel guilty about not being there." We chew on our pizza for a while. "That's a nice computer. Are you going to be hooked up?"

"Yep, we can check out tons of porn."

"Can't wait, let's have a New Year's party." We agree that this is the thing to do. Everyone is always searching for the perfect New Year's Eve plan and scrambling at the last minute. This way at least we'll know what we're doing. Roseanne is already thinking of appetizers.

The three days at work are slower than usual if you can believe that. Everyone is on vacation. I spend the time surfing the Net, checking out the after Christmas sales and calling people for the party. Somehow my sister manages to squirm herself onto the list with Chuck, as does Tabitha's friend, Nicole, who will only go under the stipulation that she has nothing better to do. When I call Pete, he mentions that Todd is going to be in town and they will probably come. It's so hard to actually have a conversation with Pete, you always think he is bored to tears.

Monica brings Chuck to the office. He is really excited about our party. Too excited. Right away, he acts like I've known him all my life. Monica beams about this. He also carries a guitar case. Neither he nor Monica gets it when I ask him if he's going to play on the subway.

"So, Eve, can we stay at your place tonight?" It's not easy for my bohemian sister to swallow her pride and admit she needs me to escape from our Italian Catholic household, but it seems easy for Chuck.

"Yeah, your sister and I aren't used to chaperones." Eww! Of course, he has to take it to the next level by rubbing my sister perversely and saying, "Or sleeping apart." Yuck! I can't believe my poor parents have to be subjected to this.

"No problem!" I guess this means I'll be hitting the couch tonight. I hope I can scrounge up an extra pair of sheets when they leave. I'm trying. Really. I give them five "bang for the buck" vegetarian restaurants straight out of Zagat's. Testament to what a good sister I can be.

We spend the entire day of the party cleaning. Roseanne has written herself a schedule for all the tasty treats that keep popping out of the oven. I run up and slip notes under the doors of our neighbors. We've invited maybe twelve people and told them they could bring whoever, but we don't want to make waves with the neighbors.

At around nine Pete and Todd show up. We freeze in horror when the bell rings. I have just gotten out of the shower and Roseanne still has to dry her hair. She begs me to let them in and entertain them while she gets ready (she is still holding out for Pete, I think, hoping she might ring in the New Year with him).

I am still in a pair of sweats and a T-shirt, but I've got no one to impress. I haven't seen Todd in forever, but he doesn't seem to notice my outfit. If there's one thing I can count on, it's that Todd will find me attractive. I make the guys drinks and we sit around the living room listening to Todd tell us about his travels all over Asia. He inspects clothing factories and tells them exactly how to set up. It's great to have him around to entertain Pete because I certainly can't. Todd picks up a picture of Roseanne, Adrian and me and says, "Who is this stud?"

"Adrian. He's gay." I purposely mention this so Pete will know Roseanne is not into him.

"He's not gay," Todd says, shaking his head like an idiot.

"What do you mean?"

"You believed that hype? Gay men—so safe." He starts talking in a high-pitched voice that's supposed to be me. "Let's move to Chelsea, Roseanne, it must be safe. Let's walk around in our underwear—they're gay, they don't care—actually we can walk around naked, it doesn't matter—they're gay." He gets off the couch and does an imitation of the seductive walk I would do and the "gay" men's reaction.

"You're ridiculous, I don't talk like that or walk like that."

"Of course not, not in front of me anyway, because I never said I was 'gay.'" He points to the picture. "But this guy, oh, my God, of course you can sleep next to me in my bed—you're gay. Want to have sex with me? It won't matter. Sure you're gay. That's the secret to New York. The New York Myth, that's what I call it.''

"You've given this a lot of thought. The Myth of the Gay Man. Thank God you're here to shatter it."

"Yeah, Pete, think of all the hot chicks we could get if we were just gay?"

"We could still watch lots of sports and drink beer," says Pete, for once funny.

"Maybe you should try it tonight," says Roseanne, who is looking good in a pair of remarkably trendy and tasteful pants and the shirt I gave her. She emerges with the spinach dip. I take a heap of spinach dip and duck into my room for my transformation. I throw on Tabitha's black BCBG dress that I wore to the Fashion Awards. No one has seen it yet. It might be a little much for a house party, but, it is after all New Year's Eve. I feel like a little flash tonight. When I reemerge Adam and Joe are there. We all kiss hello. Todd is staring at me. He looks embarrassed and gives me a goofy grin.

I bring out some more of Roseanne's appetizers and she sets up the chocolate fondue on the coffee table. Adrian and Anthony show up with some of Adrian's friends. Adrian immediately decides he is in control of the stereo—it's basically Marvin Gaye and Motown dance classics for the rest of the night (he brought his own CDs). There is barely any room in our kitchen for more alcohol. As I walk back in I notice that, with the exception of my co-hostess, there are only guys in our apartment.

"I never thought those two would show up," Roseanne whispers to me about guys from her job.

"Ro, we are the only women here." I grab a strawberry and dip into the fondue.

"That's okay, we should enjoy it while we've got the advantage. Even though some of the better ones are gay." Not according to Todd, an open heterosexual, who keeps ogling me. Every time I start to talk to someone, I notice someone else with an empty glass, so I run over to fill it. We have to keep freshening up the snacks. Anthony's friend, Kristen, comes over with three other females. Monica and Chuck show up, looking like they've just come back from following the Grateful Dead. He's got his guitar case. Mother of God!

By 11:00, the place is packed. We've developed a method of signing to each other when we need more stuff. I have not had time to realize that I'm getting drunk, but I do notice Todd talking to one of Kristen's perky blond friends. Whatever.

There are at least thirty people here. I'm noticing chocolate fondue and smashed strawberries on our hardwood floors, but I can't worry about it now. In addition to his CD collection, Adrian brought over a crazy colorful disco light. He shuts off all the lights and gets the music grooving. The place feels almost like a club and some people are starting to dance. Shit! It's getting loud. I sincerely hope our neighbors are away. We see them so rarely, we have no idea what their stories are. I look over at Roseanne, who has her hand on Pete's arm. He doesn't mind. Todd is still talking to the Stepford Girl. I hate her and her tiny tummy. Adrian gives me a big kiss.

"Great party. We're really turning the place out. I wanted to talk to you sooner and get the lowdown on that delectable guy you snagged at the Christmas party, but I myself have been wrapped in a lover's embrace."

"So, it's serious?"

"Who knows? All I know is that neither one of us has had time to see anyone else, because we've been together 24/7. We even spent Christmas together. I might be rushing it, but it's fun. Any chance of the big King man showing?"

"He's in L.A. I know, very bicoastal. Do me a favor and give me a kiss when the clock strikes 12? After you kiss Anthony, of course."

"Oh, Eve, look at all these men. They're going to be lining up to kiss you." The doorbell rings again. I've given up trying to figure out who it is so I buzz them in. It's ten minutes to the New Year. I see Roseanne's expression and for a moment think there is probably a psycho killer behind me. I hear Adrian make a high-pitched squeal. I turn around, expecting the worst, but it's Tabitha, looking coifed and dolled up. Her very presence makes the night seem like it's going to be okay.

"What are you doing here?" I don't really care what the circumstances are. She just rolls her eyes and shakes her head.

"It didn't work out. *C'est la vie.* At least I was able to exchange my ticket and come home as soon as possible. I could not have taken another moment of smelly Paris and dog shit all over the streets. It was gross!"

"Well," I say, happier to see her than I have ever been, "you are *doing it!*"

"It's two minutes!" We all huddle around my shitty TV. Some-

one else shouts that we should get a new tube and Tabitha, back
in effect, says, "Enough!" which shuts everyone up. I look around
and I begin to feel drunk, not just from whatever drinks I've been
pouring myself, but also from all the anticipation in the room.

We watch the ball drop. It's happening twenty blocks uptown,
right outside Prescott Nelson Inc. And then it's a new year and
even though we don't have noisemakers everyone is cheering and
kissing. Tabitha and I hug and we grab Roseanne, after she finishes
her tongue kiss with Pete (we'll get to that later) and the three of
us sway a little, psyched that we're here. I make the rounds kissing
everyone. I turn my face away from Adam, who looks like he is
going for more than a peck. All of the sudden I have to pee and
now is probably the best time. Todd comes out of the bathroom.

"Hey," he says.

"Happy New Year." I've seen Todd drunk many times. I can
tell he is now. His face turns serious.

"Already? Shit!"

"You look like you found a friend."

"Huh? Oh, yeah, she's okay."

"C'mon, she's cute." His lack of interest gives me the okay to
push this girl on him. "You could have kissed her when the ball
dropped."

"I could have—" he grins "—but I guess 'I dropped the ball.'"

"Oh, I'm sorry you missed the countdown. Here hold on." I
push him into the bathroom and close the door. What am I doing?

"What are you—? My watch." I take Todd's wrist and stare at
his watch.

"Okay, get ready for our own little countdown. Ten, nine,
eight—" he is leaning very close to my hair, I'm trying not to
look up at him in the mirror. "Seven, six, five—" he starts
breathing heavier. Boy, he smells good. "Four, three, two—"

"One. Happy New Year," he whispers, and he grabs my chin
and kisses me softly on the lips and I want more, but when I open
my eyes he is just holding my face and staring at me. My hands
are on his sides. He feels more muscular than I would have ever
thought.

"Wow. Happy New Year." He is still holding my face. I want
to kiss him again. Wait! He's Todd. I grab his hand. "Um, I have
to pee."

"Oh, okay." And he's back to being Todd, and I'm not quite
sure what just happened. He opens the door and Adrian is standing

here. He raises his eyebrow at me. He thinks I've made good on his boy-kissing prophecy.

"See what I mean, Eve? Is the bathroom suitable for use?"

"I just have to pee."

"Oh, I bet." Adrian is cocked. He gives Todd a once-over. "Nice ass."

"Hey," says Todd, "I know your secret, it's not going to work with her." I can't stop laughing even as I pee. I'm still grinning when I leave the bathroom.

"Was he that good?"

"No, Adrian, get your mind out of the gutter. If you're lucky I'll tell you his theory sometime, it will give you a good laugh."

"But, alas, I have more important matters. By the way, some people are going Scarface in your bedroom."

"What?" I rush to my room, some unidentifiable opens my door.

"I'm sorry you can't come in here."

"It's *my* fucking room!" I push past the guy and right atop my computer, some skinny girl is bending down to take a hit. There's about five people in here that I don't know, plus Adam. Where are Crockett and Tubbs when you need them?

"Look, I don't know who half of you are, and it's not cool that I can't even get into my room." Tabitha comes in behind me and shrieks.

"Oh, my God! Cocaine! What are you doing? These are not cocaine people!" Her voice has never been so shrill.

"Look, relax, we're almost done," says a girl I thought worked with Roseanne.

Roseanne is next to me and whispers, "Who is that?"

"I thought you knew." Fuck. I look back at the girl. "Not to inconvenience you, but finish your coke, get out of my house, find a subway, and take it straight to hell." Well, they clear out pretty fast. Everyone in my room, except Adam, leaves the party.

At some point the music stopped! I look at Adrian and shrug. Then the party gets hopping again. Todd passes out in the cranny and I take a quick peek at him. I think he's drooling. I feel no animal magnetism and I don't know what the thing in the bathroom was all about.

Monica keeps calling me "honey" and making sure I'm okay. She's real shaken up. To calm her down, I agree to shut off the stereo and the flashing lights and let Chuck strum his guitar. He does a folk rendition of "Auld Lang Syne." Horror of horrors!

All our drunken guests think it's wonderful and sing along, swaying. How can I associate with people that are so cheesy? Monica smiles proudly and rubs Chuck's shoulder. Somebody get this woman a tambourine.

I pull Tabitha into the kitchen. I'm starting to get the Paris story out of Tabitha—something about a size two model who was hanging out far too much for Tabitha's liking when Roseanne comes over to us. "Guess what? I think I managed to get Pete to stay over."

"Wow! What a feat! You guys will have to take my room, because Todd is long gone in the cranny."

"I can't even believe this party worked out. Are you guys drunk?"

"Completely," I say, and Tabitha nods.

"Let's toast the New Year." Roseanne is getting sentimental. "You guys are great, really, I'm glad I'm ringing the New Year in with both of you. Whoever you're with on the New Year is who you'll be with for the rest of the year."

"I'd heard it was whatever you were doing on New Year's Eve." Tabitha holds up her glass.

"Maybe it's whatever you are thinking about." I feel the sentimental wave catching me. "Maybe this year, we can think about doing something that makes us happy, something that will keep us living the fabulous life, but not as paupers. It's all going to happen this year."

"Sounds good to me."

"Me, too." We clink glasses. Happy New Year.

January

When I get to the lobby of Prescott Nelson on my first day back after the holiday, the tree is gone. You'd think they would have kept it up until at least the Feast of the Three Kings, but no more holiday reverie for us—it's time to get back to work. I know it's some kind of sign from the gods, a challenge, if you will.

There's an e-mail from a woman I've never heard of, Mabel Karavassian, called "Challenging Yourself For A New Year." I can tell you one thing about Mabel; she loves quotations. She offers solutions to the "the blahs" and to feelings of "inadequacy." She writes that the most important thing we can do this year is identify the challenges that lay ahead of us as best we can, the "knowns" versus the "unknowns." This way, we will be able to best "attack" all of our "obstacles" this year. How can Prescott allow this? I call Tabitha.

"Eve, I knew you were going to be upset about the tree."

"Well, I was, but I'm beyond that now. I am talking about this work propaganda cloaked in self-help rhetoric that was waiting for me on my e-mail this morning. How did Mabel Karavassian get a soapbox?"

"I don't know, but I'm certain I deleted that e-mail. Straight into the Waste Box with 'Johnny Q. Dork's Promotion' and 'Please Join Me In Welcoming April Ann Unqualified Aboard,' not to mention the ridiculous amount of chain e-mails and uninspired jokes that the assholes in my department think I am somehow interested in."

"But this is different, Prescott is cc'ed on this and so is—"

"Eve, you can't make 'cc' a verb. I can't stand by and let you murder the English language—it's bad enough that you say 'I rush-messengered the document to her.'"

"Guess who else is cc'ed on this e-mail?"

"Prescott and the Prescott Nelson mascot."

"Is there a mascot?" I ask.

"The water buffalo, of course."

"You are out of control. No, Rob King. Maybe he's the new mascot."

"No way this woman in HR cc'ed Prescott and Rob. That's huge. That sends a signal. Rob is in control. It's a new year, and Eve has got a new man of power. Have you heard from his majesty yet?"

"No, I'm convinced it was a dream, a Russian dream. Maybe I'm the lost czarina."

"You're losing me. Anyway, you know what you can tell him if he doesn't call?"

"What?"

"'Get on the subway and take it straight to hell.'" Tabitha cracks up and then hangs up. As if I never said anything even slightly funny before, my friends have held on to this little phrase. Adrian called me about five times yesterday to say only that. Todd said that's what he was going to do as he and Pete left our apartment yesterday. As she went to bed, Roseanne shouted it from her cranny. Is this the best I have to offer?

"Happy New Year, Eve," Herb says, sneaking up on me, startling me. "I didn't mean to scare you. I just wanted you to call an impromptu meeting for our department, say around one, and order from the Health Deli. The agenda is to discuss our challenges for the year."

"How original," I joke, but Herb nods and walks away, again amazed at himself.

Welcome back everyone. Don't worry about the effects of all those holiday cookies. There will be lunch today from the Health Deli at 1:00. The conference room to be determined. Thanks.
—Eve

I call the woman in charge of scheduling conference rooms throughout the building, Jennifer Hoya. Jen answers the phone with no amount of enthusiasm whatsoever. She must have the worst job in the world.

"Hi. My name is Eve Vitali and I work for *Bicycle Boy*. We're going to be having a meeting today and I was wondering if the thirty-sixth floor conference room was available." I hear Jen laughing. "Oh, is that booked already? Do you have anything available around there?" More laughter. "Okay, on that elevator bank?" Still laughing. "Hello?"

"Let me guess, honey, your boss just decided to call this meeting, because he can."

"Well," I say, "pretty much. Although, I don't want that to be my official statement."

"Right, well, your boss and every other director."

"So is there any hope of getting a room?"

"Let me check." She sighs and I can hear her ruffling through her book.

"Well, there's a room on the twenty-seventh floor." It's kind of a hike, because it's a different elevator bank and I can imagine all the writers grumbling, but I need a room.

"Yeah, that'll be great."

"Okay, how many are you?"

"Around thirty."

Jen makes a disturbing sound. "In that case, forget it. The room barely holds fifteen. Unfortunately that and another eight person conference room is all we have."

"Well, I need a room. What am I going to do?"

"I can't help you. I'm sorry." This is a woman who has no intention of facing the challenges that lie ahead.

"Listen, I really need a room. Can you call me if one makes itself available?"

"I sure will, but I'd think about maybe having it in your kitchen."

"Thanks." Having a meeting in the kitchen is like having it in the hall. Everyone gets annoyed because they have to stand and eat, and the few people who have seats seem to lord it over those who don't. In the meantime, I call the Health Deli. I grab an old bill and start to repeat what was on that one. Unfortunately, this guy can't speak English very well. It takes me forever to put in my order. It's 11:15 when I get off the phone. I check my responses. Adam:

Hey there, I hope my activities on New Year's Eve don't get me kicked out of the garden.

I delete it.

From Maggie, one of the graphics people:

We just got back, I am busy catching up on work, and do you think we could get more notice about meetings like this?

I think there are some fundamental issues that Maggie doesn't understand. I am merely the messenger and Maggie's comments are falling on deaf ears. If she wanted results she could have hit "reply all" or "cc'ed" Herb, but she wimped out and just wrote back to me. Whatever. I overheard Herb saying we needed to "freshen up" the graphics. Her days are numbered.

And from Jim, one of the most anal people on the planet with one of the easiest jobs (he's the head writer and I doubt he knows how to ride a bicycle).

Do we have to order from these ridiculous prissy pants places? Can we please just get a pizza or something? This isn't food, it's cardboard! Can we at least make sure one of the wraps doesn't have onions?

I don't e-mail Jim back. I dread opening the rest of my responses, but they're simply people letting me know they're coming and a few even say they love the Health Deli and I personally am great for ordering from there. (That's right, Jim!) I call Jennifer back.

"Honey, you better tell him to have the meeting in his office. It'll be good for him, he might get over some personal space issues."

"His office isn't close to big enough."

"Well, this will teach him to plan ahead."

"The only one who is going to look stupid is me if I have to send an e-mail canceling."

"You are letting this happen to yourself. In this day of e-mail you should be happy you could be quasi-anonymous in your cancellation at the same time working on your blame acceptance issues."

"I didn't know I had those, Jennifer. Please give me a call if you find any rooms."

"Don't wait to the eleventh hour to cancel." Jesus! I've decided to blame Jen if the meeting is canceled. I am almost beside myself and I get another shitty e-mail from Vickie in marketing, declining. Damn her and all her offspring! I call Tabitha.

"I'm having a shitty day."

"In just two hours. Sorry to hear that."

"And of course I got Jennifer Fucking Hoya analyzing me."

"You know what you can tell her—"

"Tabitha! Please! I am going to have to cancel a meeting!"

"You are toucheee!"

"I want to go back home and lie under the Christmas tree and stare up through the lights."

"And they say there's nothing to do in Jersey."

"How's your day?"

"Okay, the Big C is out today, so I am running the ship. I'm canceling meetings, checking her e-mail, going through her invites."

"What meetings?"

"She scheduled this stupid new year meeting for the department."

"Tabitha, what are you doing with the conference room?"

"Sitting on it."

"I can't believe it! What about when I said I needed a conference room?"

"You never said it!"

"Well, I said I was talking to Jennifer Hoya!"

"'Jennifer Fucking Hoya,' you said. I don't know. I thought there was actually more to why you were upset than canceling a meeting, but who am I to judge?"

"Well, why would you hold on to a conference room?"

"To do favors for unappreciative people like you."

"Tabitha, you are the best! What conference room?"

"The forty-third floor. It's got a river view."

"You're the best. I'm sorry I yelled."

"That's okay, Eve. Oh, Eve?"

"Yeah?"

"'Get on the subway and take it straight to hell!'" Again, she hangs up. I really hate when people get fixated on things.

I send another e-mail about the meeting conference room. I intend to personally sabotage the office supplies of anyone who complains about the conference room being on another elevator bank. Lucky for them, no one does.

I told Health Deli that my meeting was at 12:30, and it never fails they don't get there until 1:05. Since I told them to come to my floor with the food and the meeting is all the way across the building, I have to walk throughout the building with the two delivery boys, leaving a trail of healthy wholesome goodness in my wake.

I know when I walk into the meeting that no one has been able to concentrate on a word Herb is saying, they've all been waiting for the food, thus for me. (Don't think I don't realize how pitiful it is to power trip on such ridiculousness.) I have the guys put the food on the tables where the lions are ready to pounce. I go outside to settle up the bill and forge Herb's signature. As usual, the delivery guys try to get me to give them the tip in cash. I explain to them, as patiently as ever, that I don't have the cash. Sometimes I think that perhaps their employers are cruelly keeping their tips from them and I am aiding the process, but they're probably just scamming like everyone else in the city.

When I get back into the meeting most of the food has been ravaged. Luckily I manage to scrounge a salmon wrap, a few grilled veggies and some hummus. There isn't a sound in the room, except for the chewing and swallowing. Jim is breathing deeply. In protest, he brought McDonald's to the meeting. I am just glad that he paid for it himself.

"Now that everyone is ready," says Herb, even though people are still eating, "again, I hope everyone had a wonderful holiday. I wanted us to talk about the work we have to do to get more recognition. A lot of the promotional work that our partners in marketing have been helping us with has put us on the map. For as young a magazine as we are, our popularity rate is phenomenal."

After he says each sentence, Herb grins around the room. If he were a cartoon figure (which a lot of the time I think he is) the bubble coming out of his mouth would say, "This is tiring, I am tired of this, I should be sitting in my office writing, listening to my New Age music, practicing my breathing—in fact, maybe next time we could have this meeting on our bikes, a slow-paced, ten-mile trek downhill, anyone?" That would be a lot for a bubble. I feel myself zoning out of the meeting—it's a good thing I can concentrate on grilled eggplant.

"It doesn't mean we don't have a lot of work left to do. As you know, there's been talk of changing the format." I hear a few gasps. Herb takes a deep breath, this is spin control. "This is still in the discussion stage and I can't see changes like this happening anytime soon, but it's something I think we should all keep in mind as we start the new year. We want to keep ourselves open to new possibilities and work toward strengthening our relations with our fellow Prescott Nelson magazines in the sports division. As far as assignments and work to be done for ourselves..." Blah, blah blah.

Here's where (if you haven't guessed) not even my grilled tomato can keep me tethered to this meeting. I wonder if any one else can tell I'm orbiting the room or if they're lost in their own little dreamworlds. I keep trying to focus back on Herb and what he's saying, but only certain words and phrases come through: "I hate to use words like synergy," "the importance of our work," "staying true to our brand." I'm trying to follow clues from the rest of the people at the meeting. I laugh when they do, and when I see a couple of heads nodding, I work on looking positive. I am amazed at myself that I can give the impression of being so attentive without really paying attention. Of course, that's how I got through a lot of those business classes in school. I check my watch, covertly. I only have this room for an hour and a half. We're just past the hour mark. I start imagining Rob King's shoulders. I really like his height. It's so rare that you find a nice tall guy. I wonder if Rob King will like my poochie, if he ever sees my poochie. Shit! I think he's already seen it. I am a whore. I wonder if I can get Rob King to make sure that our magazine stays "true to our brand" while I run it.

"Thank you, Eve," Herb says in reality. What?

"Yeah, Eve." People are really saying this. What happened to my internal monologue? Uh-oh! Did they hear about Rob's chest, too?

"Eve always gets the best things." Rob *is* a pretty tasty morsel.

"Whatever," says Jim, eating his last fry. What's going on? Everyone is getting up to leave. Oh, the meeting is over. They are thanking me for the food.

"Sure," I say, starting to collect the trash, "no problem."

I get the trash together as much as possible as everyone leaves. Lorraine helps me a little. I tell her not to worry about it. She grumbles about everyone. "I thought that meeting was never going to end."

When I finish cleaning up the conference room, it's back to my desk and hangman for the rest of the afternoon.

I'm not expecting to see Rob at the Feed Meet on Wednesday. He's sitting there in his suit looking slightly out of place among the super casual writers. I consciously bring my bottom teeth to the top, so my mouth won't hang open. Of course there are no seats at the conference table and I wind up sitting on the floor. Rob cranes his neck to see me as he is taking his jacket off, and when our eyes meet he winks. Wow! I look away. Brian, the intern, sits next to me.

"It's the end of the semester, shouldn't you be back at school or something?"

"Well, we don't go back until February third. I was told I could get three credits if I came in every day of January in addition to the nine I got this semester for three days a week."

"Don't you think that's prostituting yourself for credits?"

"Are you kidding? I would do it for free to get to go to meetings like this." I think it's Brian who is kidding himself about this meeting. I hate him and wish there was a seat at the conference table so I could escape his annoyingness.

"Hi, everybody, some of you may already know Rob King." I wonder if that is directed at me and if Herb knows exactly how well I know Rob King. "He is joining us from corporate to see how we do things and understand our creative process."

I can tell that the writers feel that this in an unnecessary invasion from an outsider. They see it as symbolic of some kind of change to come. They don't want to be reminded of how much their "creativity" is dependent on a man like Rob King, a man in a suit. You can feel the tension—unless you're Brian. He starts applauding for Rob. Everyone awkwardly joins in.

"Thanks," says Rob, and I feel a little bad for him. "I'm totally interested in your creative process. This is a very successful magazine and I'm attending writer's meetings at some of our top magazines to understand the process and hopefully take it back to our less successful ones." They are warming up to him. I want to applaud him again.

The meeting proceeds. Instead of tuning out like I usually do, I finally have something to focus on, Rob King's hands. I am even more involved with those perfect, masculine hands than I usually am with my daydreams. I can't stop fantasizing about Rob and wish he would give me some idea that he was having trouble concentrating also. In the middle of the meeting he reaches his hand into the back waistband of his pants and just leaves it there. It's such a cute pose for a man who supposedly has all this power. I wish we were alone on the conference table.

"Why are you making that noise?" Brian whispers, ruining my life.

"What the fuck are you talking about?" I whisper back loudly as Lacey is reading her copy. He starts to moan low. Was I doing that? "Shut up!"

"Excuse me," says Lacey, and then continues to read. I am so embarrassed, I hope Rob didn't hear me moaning. Herb finishes his critique and we applaud. We've been here for almost two hours. I get up to get some water from the kitchen. If I take my time, maybe Rob will join me and we can have an encounter in the stairwell. I give him three minutes. I can only fill and drink my water cup so many times.

Horror of horrors! When I try to get back to the conference room, the door is locked. I have to knock to be let back in, thus interrupting Gary as he is reading one of the paragraphs of his article that Jim has a problem with. He isn't too happy about the interruption. I mutter a "Sorry" and catch Rob smiling at me. How embarrassing. Gary and Jim get into a fight over the use of the word "compulsion." They ask Rob, an objective third party, to settle it. He thinks the word works, Jim will hate him forever. We applaud and finally we are dismissed. I want to talk to Rob after the meeting, but Herb has him and I can't find a reason to stay so I go back to my desk and call Tabitha.

"You should have passed him a note."

"C'mon, Tabitha, I'm out of the first grade."

"Well, all that fantasizing sounds like you're in high school. Wanna go to an awful Brazilian dance performance tomorrow?"

"You make it sound so enticing."

"Well, you know those things. Everyone is entirely too pretentious."

"They could take a lesson or two from you, Tabitha."

"Honestly, I should give out my cards."

"Tabitha Milton, Pursuer of the Fabulous Life. That sounds good—" I look up and there is Rob King standing at my desk, grinning at me "—actually, Tab, let me call you back."

"Eve? Why does your voice sound so funny? What's up? Is he there?"

"Yep, great, thanks, 'bye." I hang up on her and smile up at Rob. "Hi."

"Hey there, too bad about that lock." He is teasing me. I think about mentioning his hands tucked into his waistband, but that might sound too obsessive.

"It's great the way you settled that compulsion problem. Now, I know why you make the big bucks." He laughs.

"Are you working late tonight?"

"I'm out of here when the clock says 5:55."

"Do you want to come over for dinner? I make a mean chicken marsala. I think it's good for a man to know how to make one dish."

"All he really needs is to have a woman over once, right?"

"Eve, if you'd rather go out, we can—"

"No, I was just being mean. What time?"

"How's 9:30? I should be home around then, and I'll start cooking."

"Do you want me to bring anything?" He grins so I think it might be true about having the woman over only once.

"Dessert, of course." He leaves and I call Tabitha to give her the play-by-play. She forgives me for dissing her. Then I have to call Rob back and get Sherman to give me directions to where his place is because I was in no condition to remember when I was last there.

At 9:45, Rob opens the door, smiling. He's got some Billie Holiday on and I can smell garlic. He seems a little harried as he leads me in and gives me a quick kiss. He's pretty cute with his shirt untucked and his sleeves rolled up. He's also barefoot. He is moving around the kitchen like he needs to remain in control of all the things that could go wrong with the chicken marsala. He hands me a glass of white wine and kisses my forehead.

"Can I help you with anything?" I say, walking into the living room.

"No, no, just got home a little later than I expected. Make yourself at home and relax." I hear a huge crash in the kitchen. I flip through his CDs. I sit on the couch and look through his coffee table books. Some nice art books. When I look up, he is staring at me. I slide over on the couch and he sits next to me. He fills my glass with more wine and puts his arm around me.

"So, do you like all these artists, or is this just for show?" He puts his hands in my hair, my neck starts to tingle.

"Um, well, they aren't my favorite artists, but I do respect their work and—" he kisses my ear "—I think they are entertaining if you're just—" my neck "—sitting on the couch—" my cheek "—better than TV, don't you agree?"

"Mmm." We wind up kissing on the couch and I barely have a chance to set my wineglass down. The book falls down as he kisses my shoulder, twisting up the fabric of my shirt to get to it. I want to just pull off my shirt but that might be too forward. I start to undo more of the buttons on his shirt.

"Maybe we should eat dinner first."

"Right," I say, moving my hands on his stomach.

"Okay wait, let me just shut the oven." He is back on the couch in a nanosecond...

Afterward, we smoke Dunhill Lights. We eat cold, delicious chicken marsala on the couch in our underwear. There really is an afterglow. I decide that my press release on the Act will be only to reveal a few telling things. I don't want to sound like a lovesick cheeseball.

He kissed the poochie for about a half hour and concentrated on that task like it was the most amazing thing in the world. He has an absolutely godlike chest, and more importantly, at the most crucial moment, he found a way to look in my eyes and say, "Say when." He settled for a sign (squeezing his shoulders). It really was triumphant and passionate, although I am skipping that part in my press release to the girls and Adrian because I know they would cling to that worse than my subway comment. After the chicken, we consider doing the dishes, but give it a go on the floor instead and then we eat the tiramisu I brought.

He is also a great cuddler, which can be alluded to, because that's a respectable thing. He doesn't let go at all in his sleep and wakes me up with some more lovin'. Nice.

"Why are you in such a great mood?" asks Tabitha, who actually pays me a personal visit in the morning. She is looking me up and down, hoping to discover my secret.

"No reason, isn't it Friday?"

"Those clothes look suspiciously new and generic."

"I stopped at the Gap on the way in."

"In, from where? Roseanne said you didn't come home last night." I cannot believe they were already on the horn gathering evidence.

"It's true."

"So?" I clear my throat and prepare to release my statement calmly and professionally, with the knowledge that every word I utter will be repeated in a higher pitch with much more enthusiasm. I can do it, I'm certain of it.

"Tabitha, it was wonderful. Oh, my God, in the vein of a romance novel, earth-shattering, the prototype for a *Cosmo* article. The man has a gift. He should patent himself, then clone himself. He is that good." I lower my voice a notch, "I am still trembling."

"Eww," says Tabitha, and then her eyes get wider. "Wow!"

"Yes," I say, "yes, yes, yes." Herb walks by and smiles. I hope he doesn't know.

"Do you need a Valium?" Tabitha asks with complete seriousness.

"No, I just need to calm down, honestly I need something mundane like this crappy data entry that has piled up. It will focus me, if you will.''

"Wanna have lunch?''

"Honestly, I don't think I can eat.'' Tabitha looks at me suspiciously. "I know exactly what you're thinking, believe me I'm not acting like this to him. I am cool as a cucumber. Honest. I've got my poker face all set.''

"Great, but don't use another shitty metaphor. I've got to get back, but you should call Roseanne. Next time, maybe she'll bring you some good clothes.''

I don't call Roseanne right away. I feel like I can't even talk about it. My stomach is tied in knots, and if I say a word to anyone I'm likely to just explode or something. I'm not usually this much of a sap. I could tell by Tabitha's concerned face she thinks it's a score, yes, but a one-time-only thing that I should just not expect too much from. And it's bad. He is too high up there for me not to feel like I'm violating some kind of employee code. I'm having a real hard time concentrating on anything. It takes me forty-five minutes to send an e-mail about the staff meeting being changed to Monday.

When I do finally call Roseanne an hour later, she is on her other line with Tabitha, getting the story. She'd rather hear it from the horse's mouth (what is it about booty that reduces me to these pitiful metaphors?) so she comes back on with me. I'm still trying to remain calm and it isn't easy to give the blow-by-blow (gasp!) at work.

"Next time give me a call, so I know he's not a psycho killer.''

"There probably won't be a next time. It's weird.''

"Morning weirdness?''

"No, not even, I don't know, it probably shouldn't have happened. It's a won't work weird.''

"Maybe it will. What should we do tonight? I've got post holiday blahs.''

"Me, too. I don't know. Shit, my other line, I'll call you in a bit.'' I switch over. It's him.

"What are you doing tonight?'' Play it cool, I tell myself. Keep him guessing.

"I don't know, nothing. I really want to see you.'' Foiled myself again.

"I know, Eve, I think I'm going to get out of here early tonight. No, I will. I should be able to clear out at 6:30. Everyone is still clinging to the holidays. Can you wait around?'' You are never supposed to wait, you are supposed to be picked up.

"Sure.'' When we hang up, I call the girls and tell them my plans. I feel a little bad about Roseanne because I know she's got the blahs.

I wind up waiting at my desk until 7:30. I'm getting pretty sick of surfing the Net when Rob comes to my desk. He looks stressed. I try my best to be pissed. I check my watch.

"I thought you had adjusted to New York time.''

"Funny, Eve. I'm sorry, I got caught up in something.'' I quietly shut my computer and gather my bags. Even though there isn't a soul around, I can tell he's nervous about someone busting us. Whatever. I walk to the elevators, leaving him to follow.

"You're pissed, Ms. Vitali. I'm sorry. I really wanted to see you tonight. I went as fast as I could. Does that help at all?'' It does, but he can't know that. I don't say anything; we get in the elevator. I stare at the wall and he starts humming a familiar song.

"Hey, you like Aerosmith?'' He looks so cute and he starts to sing off key and air guitar "Love in an Elevator.''

"Dork, don't even think about it,'' I say and laugh. He grabs me and gives me a big sweet hug. It shouldn't be this easy, but it is.

The weekend is a blur. I don't leave his side. I just keep buying new clothes or wearing his T-shirts. It honestly feels like one of those love montages, from all those eighties movies, except we don't have any rain scenes. We go out to dinner, we do the deed, we sleep in. There are cold walks in the park, lots of nastiness. We go to brunch on Sunday and hold hands over the table. We rush back to slap skins, and then it's Sunday night and we are lying on his couch reading the rest of the *Times*. I can't help but wonder if it's going to be strange at work.

"Are you done with 'The City'?'' he asks, kissing my hair. I hand him the section.

"Do you ever feel like your life is just Sunday nights? Like everything centers around certain sections of the Sunday *New York Times?*''

"No, I feel like it's one long meeting.''

"Do you like your job? I mean, is it fun?'' He shifts me around so he can look at me.

"Yeah, I like it. I like planning a project, implementing it, and seeing it succeed.''

"You like the power.'' He shrugs and looks back down at the

paper. I gather his job isn't something he wants to talk about with me. We read for a while longer and then go to bed.

On Monday, even the staff meeting doesn't get me down. I clap enthusiastically when Lacey reads the first installment of her four-part series on women and bikes. I cheerfully gather up the leftover bagels. I laugh when the writers hover by my desk and make fiber jokes. My messages:

"Eve, it's Tabitha. Are you still alive? I swear you and Adrian are lost in some kind of lover's wasteland. Why don't you call me at some point? I met an amazing Brazilian this weekend." Delete. Mother of God.

"It's me. Rob. What's up? I wish my life were a Sunday night. I'm in meeting hell. Wondering if you wanted to catch a late dinner and movie. Maybe ten. Will you be around?" Save. I'll listen to it at least five more times.

"Eve, it's Roseanne. Just calling to see if you are coming home for dinner tonight. I bought some salmon yesterday at Chelsea Market. I didn't make it because you didn't come home. Just let me know if you are coming home tonight. Okay, 'bye." She sounds really sad. Delete. I don't need to be reminded what a sucky friend I am.

"Eve, it's Lacey. Can I get a 4:00 with Herb today? I need to talk to him about my installment before the Feed Meet." I hate the way she says "need" like I should drop everything and hook her up. I hate her. Delete. Delete. Delete.

I tell Tab I will have lunch with her. I call Roseanne and say, yes, I'll be home for salmon, then I leave a message with Sherman saying I will meet Rob at ten, but not for dinner. I don't say what we're doing at ten, because I don't want Sherman to get the wrong idea. I don't even know Sherman, but I hope he doesn't think I am some kind of assistant traitor. I schedule a time for Lacey and Herb. I'm multi-tasking.

Tabitha and I meet in The Nook. She gets the chicken cordon bleu with two sides and I grab a California roll. She gives a good show of asking me about Rob. Since I don't really want to say too much, she starts right in about Joao, this Brazilian choreographer she met at the dance performance on Saturday. He is only in town for two weeks.

"Tabitha, do you ever think that maybe you have some reason for going after all these out-of-towners?"

"I certainly hope this quasi-domestic blissful relationship you are having with a totally unattainable and who-knows-how-reliable guy is not making you just a tad judgmental. But, yes, there is definitely a reason.'' She licks her chickeny fingers slowly. Always the drama mama.

"I give up, what is it?'' She takes another bite of her mashed potatoes and leans into the table, encouraging me to do the same.

"I get bored fucking one guy for too long.'' I laugh out loud. Tabitha is rarely so crass. "That's right, laugh. Monogamy is monotony.''

"Even Jaques? You were down for the long haul with Jaques.''

"I was slightly deluded by his fashion sense and the way he would encourage me to eat buttery things. You can't fault me for that. What you can fault me for is picking a friend—that would be yourself—who would not knock some sense into me when I started to get all mushy faced.'' She sips her iced coffee and scans The Nook. "But I can be strong-willed, so I guess I can forgive you not speaking up sooner. Although, I would like to think that in the future you will alert me to these strange behaviors.''

"Only if I get the feeling you want to be alerted.''

"Good plan. Hey—'' she looks past me "—isn't that a high-powered exec who is rumored to be having an affair with an underling?'' I see Rob having lunch with a very attractive woman. I decide I need some catsup for my sushi. I try to eavesdrop on my way up as I walk behind him. He has his all-business stance, which is slightly encouraging. I'm acting like a teenager. This is stupid. If he was screwing around with this very attractive woman, he wouldn't bring her to The Nook. He apparently doesn't see me at the condiment stand. I decide to sneak back behind him, to avoid suspicion of my suspicion.

"Hey, Eve,'' he says as I am walking behind him. There is a table full of people between us and I know his lunch companion is checking me out.

"Oh, hey, Rob.'' How cool am I?

"Did you get enough condiment?'' His face is serious, but he cocks an eyebrow up.

"I think so, see ya.'' He turns back to his lunch date or whatever. When I get back to the table, Tabitha has her analyzing face on.

"Interesting exchange?''

"I guess it's a business meeting.'' What am I doing? "Did you talk to Ro this weekend?''

"Not really. I invited her out to the dance performance, but she didn't want to go. I think she's mopey about Pete. He still hasn't called. Oh, God! The Big C is in our midst. Look at the skirt, it's like she plans her Monday outfit around the Sunday *Times* style section. What's she eating, Eve, can you see?''

''Not sure, looks like a salad.'' She stops to chat with Rob.

''Of course, probably no dressing. She's ridiculous. Let's get upstairs before she spots me. We have to start going to delis.'' It's a rare occurrence for us to see anyone we know in The Nook, but one Big C sighting and Tabitha will keep us out of there for a month.

Roseanne is sitting on the couch watching one of those gossip news shows when I get back to our apartment that night. Monday is usually her Spinning class at the gym. When I ask her why she isn't going she shrugs and tells me she will grill the salmon in twenty minutes.

When she gets up to make the salmon, I try to call Rob at work to tell him that I can't make the movie. Sherman keeps picking up. I can't believe he has to wait there until Rob gets out of his meeting. What a slave driver Rob is!

Roseanne's salmon is delicious and I tell her. I must be the worst roommate ever, because she is giving me the silent treatment without actually committing to it. I shouldn't have spent the whole weekend at Rob's. I hate conflict.

''Hey, Roseanne, are you mad at me?''

''Not at all.'' She sounds pretty convincing, but now that I've grabbed this confrontation thing, there's no turning back.

''Well, you're being really quiet. You didn't go to your Spinning class and here you are watching trash TV.''

''It's comfort TV.''

''Well, why do you need to be comforted?'' She doesn't say anything and has another bite of salmon. ''Ro?''

''My job has to be the most boring ever,'' Roseanne spills. ''Not like your kind of boring where I can surf the Net or go shopping or talk to my friends. No, there is work to be done—boring work. Every hour lasts an eternity and it's numbers, numbers, and numbers. Big surprise, that's what I majored in. My mother is upset that I won't give her my work number. The reason I won't is because I don't want her to call and complain about my father from dusk till dawn, but not for the reason you might think. No. I don't want her to have my number, because I think the sound of her voice might actually comfort me when I'm hanging out with my numbers. Like these shitty shows. I'm bored with working out. The past two boys I had sex with haven't called back. Well, I should make that one and a half, because Pete was too drunk to get it up and keep it up, despite my valiant efforts. Of course, he won't call me back, even though we've been friends for like five years or something. I keep thinking I can have enough fun after work with you guys, but honestly, I don't know if I can make it. I keep telling myself that the summer is coming and I'll have summer hours and I'll get to do what I want. But that's five fucking months away. That's the other thing. I'm talking like a sailor. I never swore this much before. My parents used to hurl curses at each other and I swore I'd never do it. But, fuck it, now I do!''

"Wow!" What do you say to that?

"Eve, don't. I know you are going to try and say the most sensitive thing. And you will. I mean you always do, you listen to people and you help them. I guess I just want to revel in my own self-pity for a while and then figure it out. I don't want to bring you down, because I can see you're happy. I know you already feel bad about spending time with Rob, but don't worry about it, please. Shucks! I never used to be such a drama queen.''

The thing that makes it hard to be friends with Roseanne is that when she's like this she doesn't turn into a witch and make you hate her for a while before she clues you in on the problem. She knows what's wrong and she doesn't ask you to fix it. When my friends have problems, I like to be the one that interprets it for them. The last thing I need is a self-sufficient friend. Then my one skill will be futile.

"Do you like this guy? Rob?"

"Maybe. I don't really want to. I mean we're not cut from the same cloth. I can't help feeling like I'm sleeping my way to the top, although I haven't gotten anywhere and probably won't. I'm not doing anything wrong, but I feel like I have to keep this hush-hush.''

"Eve, just do what you want. If he's cool, go for it.''

"Pete hasn't called, huh?'' Roseanne just shakes her head. The phone rings. It's Rob asking me to meet him at the movie theater in an hour. I almost tell him I can't make it, but I want to see him too badly. I feel like a big shit when I say good-night to Roseanne.

"Hey it's only another hour to Letterman,'' I say as I'm leaving. She smiles, but it doesn't seem to reassure her.

The job listings come out every Tuesday. Now they are available via e-mail. There is never anything good that I am considered qualified for. I once applied for a copyright position in *NY By*

Night marketing. Tabitha told me about it. I could tell that the woman who interviewed me was really impressed. I was proactive about staying on top and keeping myself "fresh in her mind." I called her once a week, but she never returned my calls. I didn't want to be a nag, I just wanted to know. Finally, after four weeks of waiting by the phone, she told me that although she thought I would be "great for the department," I just didn't have enough experience.

"Did you see the listings?" Tabitha says almost breathlessly when I answer the phone.

"No, but, let me guess, executive assistant to some crappy finance guy."

"No, a coordinator position for *Food and Fun,* the travel/restaurant mag. Listen to the responsibilities— 'Coordinator will be responsible for the attachment of photos to copy and often attend photo shoots to assist in brand conveyance—' if that's even a word '—for a deadline. Coordinator will be expected to attend creative meetings and assist in magazine development.' Development is awesome, it's so flaky, but actually cool. Travel and restaurants. Awesome."

"Sounds like a major they offered at my school. Are you going to apply?"

"No, Eve, are you crazy? I am in the zone here at *NY By Night.* I am a proverbial rung away from the Big C's job. I think this would be a great job for you, and sort of a test."

"It sounds pretty cool, but what is it a test of?"

"The strength of your blossoming love."

"Tabitha, is this Brazilian supplying you with some crazy South American drug?"

"It's more of a love juice, actually."

"You are foul."

"You're no nun. Honestly. Rob needs to put his money where his mouth is."

"That would make me a literal whore."

"Right, but honestly, it's all who you know. You just know him better than most."

"I appreciate your support, but it lacks integrity and ethics."

"Mother of God! Eve, you aren't writing a journalism thesis, you are trying to get a goddamn job. Look at the Big C, where are her ethics?"

"I don't know, but I don't want to put a price tag on it. Who knows if he can even help me get the job?"

"The way I hear it, he's got everyone quaking in their boots. I assure you, Rob King can get anything in the company he wants. Including the assistants."

"Thanks for the reassurance. I am not going to give him an ultimatum or anything. I'm going to apply fair and square. Okay? My phone is beeping."

"If it's him, you should ask." I hang up and it is Rob asking me if I want to come have lunch in his office. He's getting wraps. I order a spinach wrap with portobellos and goat cheese. There is no way I'm going to mention that job. Instead, I e-mail my résumé to the appropriate person.

I have to wait for Rob in his office. Sherman assures me he is finishing up a meeting. Our wraps and fruit smoothies (a special treat I didn't know about) are sitting on Rob's desk, taunting me. I am starving. If only Sherman would stop checking on me.

I hear the door close behind me and feel Rob kissing my neck. I reach my arms up around him and we start kissing. I can't believe it, but I notice he has the shades drawn on his windows. He is putting his hands into my sweater. I try to stop him. I'm thinking of poor Sherman.

"I locked the door," he whispers, trying to lift me onto the desk.

"Rob, I don't think it's a good idea." He pulls back panting and goes to sit on his side of the desk. He looks across at me like I might be some other exec.

"Well, Eve, if that's the way it has to be, we're going to have to establish some rules. You can't cross over to my side. This is my side, this is your side—"

"Just like *Dirty Dancing.*"

"Eve, please, these are important rules." His sexy eyebrows are arching all over the place. "You may not do anything overtly suggestive, like licking your fingers, tilting your head or lowering your gaze to my unmentionable areas. It may be torture, but remember this is what you wanted, not me. Now. Let's eat." My wrap is not what I ordered, it's lamb and some kind of chutney. Rob catches my grimace. There is nothing I hate more than people who kick a gift lunch in the mouth or however that saying goes. Every time I order food for the people in my department, there is always one person who has to ruin it by complaining about something, "They didn't send enough plates, I need a separate one for dessert" or "I can't eat this, this has cilantro in it, I will not stomach cilantro." So I feel a little guilty that Rob takes my wrap out to Sherman. I can't hear or see the exchange, because the door is closed. When Rob comes back in he is wrapless. I would have eaten the lamb—I like lamb as much as any carnivore (I've actually started to like it more since I started working with so many vegetarians), and I was really hungry. He sits back down on his side.

"Well, looks like we are going to have to sit here staring at each other until your new lunch gets here."

"You could eat your wrap."

"That would be rude and besides, I prefer to stare at you and think about what might have come from our lunchtime rendez-vous." I guess there is something that would take my mind of my stomach—his stomach.

"You are filthy." He nods and drums his fingertips. "Did you lock the door?" I know, I am turning into such a whore. To think I was so staunchly opposed to an office romance and here I am struggling to get my tights off without ripping them. We are getting very caught up in the moment and his wrap, which is open, almost gets all over the back of my sweater (which would suck because it's Roseanne's sweater and this might push her over the edge). We almost don't hear the knock on the door. He mutters a curse and waits for me to untwist my skirt before opening the door to Sherman.

Sherman, whom I am convinced is on to us, comes in looking cold and red. He places my wrap in my hands and leaves. I can't believe Rob made him go get it. It's the middle of January, he must be frozen. Rob thinks that we should pick up right where we left off, but I'm hungry. Besides, it just isn't right that Sherman had to walk out in the cold so we could be unprofessional in the office. I try to explain this and he doesn't get it.

Rob asks me out for a late dinner, but I suspect it's just because he's all worked up about the thwarted lunchtime efforts. I decline, for a lot of reasons. I figure it's a good idea to keep Roseanne company and I've been out so late with him this past week, I need some sleep. Besides, if I deny him, I'm still the one in control.

Roseanne and I rent a movie and I fall asleep half an hour into it.

When the weekend rolls around, I break my "control," and spend it with Rob. I am getting a little sick of myself and how cheesily happy I am. I tried to go out drinking with the girls on Friday night, but Tabitha dissed to hang out with Joao. I have to admit that I really wanted to hang out with Rob, but I was glad

Tabitha was the one to diss so I wouldn't get the blame. I suspect Roseanne didn't see it that way.

Roseanne and I never let another guy in between us in college. If there is one thing I can't stand, it's a girl who doesn't realize the importance of a friend over a guy. I'm afraid I'm turning into the kind of girl who is putting her boyfriend first. I hate that. What's worse despite all the nasty fun we've been having and the habit he has of arching his eyebrow or curling his lip at the perfect moment, I'm not sure Rob King would consider me his girlfriend.

By Monday, Isabelle Chambers, the Human Resources Recruiter, has set up an interview with me to discuss the *Food and Fun* position. Tabitha is convinced that I got such speedy service because of Rob, but I assure her that I haven't even told him I was interested in the job. She says he has ways of finding out.

Tabitha helps me pick my outfit. She tells me right away I should wear the Jackie-O suit and insists through each of my twelve outfit changes that Jackie is the way to go. Roseanne puts tea bags on my eyes to bring down the swelling and tells me that I haven't been getting enough sleep. That's the thing about Roseanne that can be infuriating. You wish she'd get bitter sometimes, when you feel bad about something, but she doesn't. She tells me I need to get more sleep because I do, not because she's getting her digs in. I wish I were a better friend because I know, even though she's been getting lots of sleep, her eyes are looking as puffy as mine. She won't talk about her job.

Roseanne shoots a zillion practice questions at me. After going on all these interviews, she is an expert on the questions they ask. She asks me to tell her what my best and worst qualities are. I have trouble thinking of my worst quality (can you believe?). For my best quality, Tabitha says I can't use "excellent hand job" at all in the interview. Then, she leaves to go to some Brazilian music concert with Joao.

"Now, the biggie, the one they all ask, and the one that's the most ridiculous bull doo is, 'Where do you see yourself in five years?'"

"Sitting on the couch watching Springer with my thumb up my ass."

"You don't want to come off too ambitious, Eve. C'mon think about it. Just say something that applies to the magazine position."

"I want to be the best coordinator for *Food and Fun* ever. *And* I want to travel and have fun, of course, and fight world hunger."

"Hey, Eve, I'm going to watch *Dateline* if you aren't going to take this seriously."

"Okay, in five years, I guess I really would like to do a lot of traveling. I don't want to be a big stress case, I want to enjoy my job, which, I think I would if I worked for this magazine, because it's something I like. Ideally, I want to have my own magazine, which might metamorphose from this one and most importantly, I would like to have the respect of those around me, because that is how I will gauge the job I've done."

"Not bad, but you might want to curb the part about your own magazine. They want you to be theirs. F—your own ambition."

I suppose I got sidetracked by *Dateline,* because I never figure out how I am going to answer the question.

The interview goes fabulously. I describe my current position in a glowing way. I make myself out to be much more important and a lot less bitter than I actually am. I identify my weakness as being the inability to say "no" to people (not in the dirty sense) and my strengths as the way I can focus on a project and still manage all my other duties. I can see that Isabelle Chambers is eating this all up. I can virtually read her mind and I know she thinks she's found the one. Isabelle Chambers is getting ready to type "Prospect Identified" in the listing to deter all the other hacks who think they've got a chance. Sorry! It's my game now.

"So, Eve, where do you see yourself in five years?" Shit! What was I not supposed to say? Isabelle leans in a little, waiting for my next perfect answer. Was I supposed to mention my own magazine or not? Fuck! Then it occurs to me, five years is a long time and what if—oh fuck—what if I'm still sitting in the same desk, surfing the Net and watching the world move around me? What if I run into someone I used to work with on the school paper and they ask me what I do? What will I say as they smirk when they discover all I do is order lunch and talk on the phone. Who am I kidding? My own magazine at twenty-eight? My sister is almost twenty-eight, she doesn't even know what she wants to be when she grows up. It's not my fault, it's my genes, of course, my parents are both very motivated. But it was a different time. No one asked my parents where they wanted to be in five years, because they knew it was a stupid question. Nobody gets where they want to be. They just get somewhere. Is *Food and Fun* where I want to be? Oh, God, who knows?

"I realize it's a tough question, it's hard to see the future, but I'm asking for your ideal."

"Well—" I clear my throat and try (unsuccessfully) not to sound like a ditz. "I really just want to travel and have a lot of fun." Isabelle Chambers sits back in her chair. I can tell all her hopes for me as the perfect candidate have just crashed, but she is the pro. She smiles at me—she definitely had braces—and thanks me for interviewing. She holds her hand out to shake.

"I really want this job," I say with a hint of desperation, "that's where I see myself, at *Food and Fun*."

"Okay, Eve, thank you. I'll give you a call in a couple of weeks. Thanks." She gets up and leads me out. When I get into the elevator lobby, I am slightly in shock. Tabitha is only two floors up. I let about six elevators pass before deciding if I want to go up and talk to her or down and mope at my desk. I go up. Luckily, the Big C is in a meeting. As soon as Tabitha looks up at me, I know I must look like shit.

"Great suit, Eve, but you've got to start getting some sleep. What time is the interview?"

"It's done." I plop into a chair next to her desk. She must be busy because she keeps looking back to her computer screen. "I don't want to bother you."

"No, Eve, you look icky. Are you all right?"

"No, I don't know." The very last thing I want to do is have a breakdown at Tabitha's desk. I feel like I'm about to cry so I get up to go. "I'll call you later." I notice as I walk past her desk that she was on the Net. It's a fine feeling when one of your best friends would sooner surf the Net than be your shoulder to cry on.

"Eve, this is just—" she calls to me as I'm going out into the elevator bank.

When I get back to my desk, there's a message from Roseanne. I nip Intern Brian's incessant annoying chatter in the bud by making him alphabetize the freelance files. I listen politely to Lorraine telling me about her dog's pregnancy. I want to crawl into a cave and die. I am feeling so low that I stare at the delivery guy in disbelief when he brings a huge bouquet of flowers over to my desk. I rip off the card.

Just wanted to brighten your day, like you brighten mine.

I beg Sherman to tell Rob thank you. I wish more than anything I could tell him myself, but he's in a meeting. I can't believe the timing. Maybe I will spend the next five years wrapped up in Rob's loving wonderfully muscled arms. I think I might be in love.

I decide to tell Rob the next time we are intimate that I'm in love with him. In the past this has usually signaled the end of my relationships. I have actually said in the past "I love you, but you're a loser. I think we should end it." You see, the guys I've gone out with in the past have been scared of commitment or just drunk most of the time, so it was no big deal. Rob is different. He's a man, and this could be it. I wouldn't be such a loser and need to hang out with him nonstop if it wasn't. Besides, he has this uncanny ability to do the right thing. Those flowers came at the perfect time. Lucky me, so young and I found the one. What a catch. My e-mail dings, new message. It's from Sherman and titled "Rob King Out of the Office." What?

Rob King will be out of the office at the Georgia Convention from now through Tuesday of next week. He will be checking in with me, so please call me at 7761 with any scheduling requests or other questions.

Thanks.
Sherman

I have to say that Sherman lacks the e-mail writing panache that I pride myself on. Of course, he may not want to be so casual with this distribution list, which includes people like Joe Sullivan and (gasp!) Prescott Nelson himself. In many ways it's a personal victory to be on a distribution list with those big guys. Almost like they might check their e-mails and say to themselves "Well, I know Joe Sullivan, but who is Eve Vitali? What a cool name."

Of course I'm sure that their secretaries (assistants) will be checking the e-mail and probably not give a shit. So my victory is marred by the fact that my significant someone (or whatever the hell I'm supposed to call him at this point) is letting me know via group e-mail and his assistant that he isn't going to be around to fuck me this weekend. I should Reply All:

Does that mean he's not going to be able to fuck me this weekend?

The e-mail patrol would certainly be at my desk in a nanosecond, and I would never be heard from again. My ID would immediately stop working, and I could kiss those cool Prescott T-shirts goodbye. Also, after all I put Sherman through, he would probably take it as some kind of embarrassment and disgrace to him. He might commit hara-kiri.

I should look on the bright side of all this. I'll have a weekend to spend with the girls. Yes, some hard-core quality time. Although I feel kind of guilty that it takes Rob going away to get me to have some much-needed girl bonding. But no, I've only been out of commission for two weekends. Don't I deserve some fun, too?

On Sunday afternoon, we are drunk. We went out too late Friday night and wound up getting a heavy post-clubbing breakfast at Florent at like five in the morning. Of course, we couldn't find it at first, so we traipsed around the meatpacking district in heels and sexy skirts. We didn't get in until 7:30, because, still drunk, we decided to walk back. Tabitha spent most of Saturday puking, as Roseanne and I slept through our hangovers. We woke up just in time for *COPS* and decided it was too cold to leave the apartment, so we ordered Indian delivery and watched a lot of Saturday night TV.

On Sunday morning, we woke up early. We woke up bored. I brought margarita stuff and movies back to the apartment when I dropped off my laundry. We had a Richard Gere film fest with *Pretty Woman, Internal Affairs* and of course, my personal fave, *An Officer and a Gentleman.* (I'm a product of the eighties, what can I say?) By 4:30 we were toasted and having a heated discussions over various urban myths. Of course the natural progression was to discuss blow jobs. Roseanne told the story of the time she gave a blow job to that guy in the bathroom (like I haven't heard that one a million times). What he said afterward is always dependent on the mood Roseanne is in when she tells the story and how drunk she is. This time she claims he said, ''That was beautiful.''

Tabitha claims to hate blow jobs (big surprise) but to love getting oral sex. She wishes men were born with penises on their forehead so they could just ''do it all in one exciting shot.''

''Do you guys ever wish you could get flavored cum?'' Roseanne asks. Tabitha is disgusted by the idea that Roseanne actually swallows.

''Even that guy in the bathroom, the one you barely knew?''

''Especially him. Mmm.'' Roseanne licks margarita off her lips. She is dirty today. ''Anyway, sometimes when I'm giving a blow job all I want for is a nice shot of chocolate sauce. As a chaser you know?'' Roseanne does a little shot-taking motion and I almost pee my pants laughing.

"Alcohol definitely helps,'' says Tabitha, "I mean if I am going to do that, I might as well be drunk.''

"Yeah there are two things I like to do when I'm drunk. I like to fight and I like to fuck.''

"Eve, I don't think I've ever seen you get into a fight.'' Roseanne seems very concerned that she might have missed something crucial all these years.

"Eve, I don't think I've ever seen you fuck,'' Tabitha chimes in. They both find this hysterical, as if I never get laid.

"I'll have you both note that I—yes, yours truly—am the one getting the most regular sex right now. Thank you very much.''

"So how is it? Is it fun to sleep with all that power?'' Tabitha is on the edge of the couch. She almost spills her margarita as she leans forward.

"Yeah, is he that good? You definitely seem more...chipper lately.'' I can tell just by the way Tabitha cracks up that they've been having discussions about my sex life.

"It's great,'' I say, reveling in it. "I can honestly say that I have never been more attracted to anyone in my life.'' They are impressed, I can tell. Then of course, as I expected, Roseanne holds up her two hands about four inches apart. I jack my thumb up, her palms get wider, I jack my thumb again, and her palms get a lot wider. I shrug and make a circle with both my hands.

"No way,'' says Tabitha, in disbelief. "Eve, it just isn't fair, I don't believe it.''

"Neither did I at first, but it's true.''

"Wait, wait,'' Roseanne says, struggling to make sense of it all, "the most important thing and, Eve, tell the truth, does he know how to use it?''

"Yes, that's it, he does *and* it's not just that. He isn't afraid to get down and dirty and do what I love. He goes nuts. He's unstoppable.''

Roseanne holds up her glass. "A toast to Rob King, a prince among men.''

"Hey, Roseanne, that's great. Wow!'' Roseanne has no idea about her pun, but Tabitha laughs because nothing escapes her even when she's drunk. I figure now is a good time as any to ask about Pete. I can tell it's a painful subject, but what bugs me the most is that Tabitha already seems to know. Tabitha, who criticized everything about Roseanne right up to her earrings, is now rubbing Roseanne's back in a "Go ahead it's okay, just let it out, honey" way. Don't they realize that I am the one who brought them together, that there should be no fraternizing when I am not involved?

"He fell asleep while he was, you know, going down on me."

"No fucking way." I am horrified, and Tabitha nods like she's heard it all before. Whatever.

"Yeah, I thought he was just getting some air, but it took a while. I tried to encourage him, but he just stopped, that was it. So what do you do? I mean I couldn't let him sleep there. I mean it would've been kind of a traumatic wake-up don't you think?" Of course her new best friend Tabitha chimes in.

"I said she should have left him there, maybe he would have gone back to business."

"So, what did you do, Roseanne?"

"Well, I kind of scooted around as carefully as I could, and slept next to him. It wasn't very comfortable, but I think I saved some embarrassment. In the morning, he was back to the old Pete, you know quiet, sort of surprised he actually wound up with a girl. Of course not a call since." I want to ask her if he said anything about Todd, as in Todd and me. But I am in love with Rob and I shouldn't care and this is Roseanne's story, not mine.

"You know Pete. We've known him for what, five years, now?" That part is for Tabitha. "He's just quiet like that. He's probably so into you, but he can't show it because he still doesn't know how to talk to girls."

"I'd like to think that, but I think I'd be lying to myself. I'd sooner just get drunk. Anyone need a refresher? I think we're done with margaritas. Luckily I got some Absolut. I'll pop in *Internal Affairs.*"

"Yeah, get me another drink, I'm never going to get to the laundry away. I don't know what it is, but every time I do laundry it seems like I have less and less underwear. Maybe I should get some of yours, Tabitha."

"What does that mean?" Tabitha is suddenly all touchy.

"Nothing, you just have a lot of underwear. I mean you're always buying it. Everywhere we go you get underwear."

"Yeah," says Roseanne, coming back in with the drinks, "you do have a lot. What's the deal?"

"Hey, I don't really think we need to be talking about my underwear. It's my business."

"Well, excuse us, Tab, Roseanne just told us about swallowing a shitload of cum, and now we can't mention your penchant for underwear?''

"No, we certainly can't and I don't have a penchant for underwear, all right? So are we going to put the movie on or do I have to leave?''

I can't believe her. Roseanne shakes her head as she puts in the movie. She mouths the word "Wow." There is definite tension until I mention how much I like Andy Garcia in this and Tabitha tells me I like him because he's hairy. I do not like hairy men, I merely wind up with hairy men, but since she is being so (dare I say?) pissy today I let it slide.

Eventually we're done with all the movies and it's eleven. Tabitha is passed out on the couch and I'm feeling pretty dizzy when I get up. Roseanne and I wash up in the bathroom together and whisper about what is up Tabitha's butt.

"She is really touchy when it comes to her underwear. Actually underwear in general—one time she picked up a dirty pair of mine that was on the floor."

"Eww."

"That's what I said, and she just said they were cute. They were plain cotton underwear, I think they were hot pink."

"That's totally bizarre. Do you think she's got some kind of compulsive disorder?''

"No, I think you're drunk and you've been reading too many of Prescott's women's magazines," Roseanne concludes. I don't say anything. I'm sick of her and Tabitha's condescension.

"Hey, Eve, I was just kidding."

"I know. I know." I sit down on the toilet. "Roseanne, are you sick of living with me?''

"Eve, I like living with you, it's one of the few things that I like about my life right now. Really."

"But, I haven't been around much."

"So? I mean you're not supposed to hang out with me and help me feel sorry for myself. I just gotta get my shit together."

"Well, you're making scads of money. I don't know what more you need to get together."

"I just want to go to work and not believe that if I keep going this will be my life, you know."

"Yeah, I had that feeling the other day at the interview that I could be doing the same, old *nothing* for the rest of my life."

"At least you have ideas—you know, the magazine."

"What are you talking about? I told you about that, too?''

"Whenever you get really drunk, starting back in college, you talk about it. You get so passionate about it, sometimes you even get teary-eyed."

"Please tell me I don't sit around bars weeping about a magazine I can barely remember when I'm sober."

"It isn't that bad. I mean it sounds good—a magazine for people our age in our predicament. A magazine about getting the most out of your lot. I'd read it. I can't believe you never realized."

"God, I can't believe I'm such a lush. Do I do anything else when I'm drunk that I should know about?"

"No, actually it kind of makes me wish that I had something I dreamed about. I go to work, I exercise, I watch just about every sitcom, and I'm so typical. Here I am in New York with you two, who like, know about everything."

"But we totally don't. I mean there's so much shit we want to do that we can't, that we don't even know about."

"Yeah, but what about me?" Roseanne asks.

"When we do it, you'll do it."

"Do I want to do it?"

"I don't even know what 'it' is." I laugh.

"Right." Roseanne nods. I feel bad about not being around and even worse about being jealous that she's been hanging out with Tabitha.

"Ro, I'm sorry if I've been a bad friend."

"Eve, you are a great friend." She kisses my forehead. "You took me in when I got here, you kept my spirits up, and you always tuck me in when I'm drunk. Don't ever feel like you're a bad friend." It's a touching bathroom moment, which is a testament to our blood alcohol level. We both realize this and go to bed.

In the morning, Tabitha has a huge hangover. Neither one of us can seem to get moving with enough time to walk to work, so we take the subway.

"Tabitha, do we always talk about starting a magazine when we're drunk?"

"Of course."

"How come we never talk about it when we're sober?"

"Because alcohol gives us balls. I don't know."

"Maybe we should start writing it down."

"Eve, oh, God, I have such a headache. I'm not going to start scribbling away in the middle of a night out. I hate those pretentious people."

"It wouldn't be like that, Tabitha. Maybe we've got some good ideas."

"They're definitely good, Eve. So good you can't remember them."

"Well, Roseanne says they're good."

"Eve, no offense, because I am really starting to like her, but Roseanne thinks Lifetime, that is, Television for Women, is good."

So I guess we're done with that conversation. Still, I'm intrigued at this other, less inhibited, me who goes around shooting my mouth off about a dream that I can't remember or won't let myself think about in my normal life. I feel the train approaching by the wind in the tunnel. I rarely take the train, but whenever I do, whenever I first feel the wind in my hair and start to hear the train, I can't help but feel like it's the beginning of a movie about my life, like somehow my fate is going to change. I manage to hold on to this feeling all the way into work until I have to go to the shitty meeting and listen to the asshole Gary complain about there not being any light cream cheese.

As usual Rob is getting out of work a lot later than I am. It's too soon to ask for a key, so I decide to get my hair cut. I have the best hairdresser (stylist) ever. His name is Ed and he is what I think should be the standard for hairdressers—gay and Asian. I don't know too much about Ed, because he never talks to me. He's only concerned with my hair and making me look good. I try to make conversation with him and he answers me with a series of nods and monosyllables. Tabitha turned me on to Ed and I'm working on convincing Roseanne to go there. It's about time she stopped looking a little too much like a country singer.

When Ed is done with his masterpiece, he hands me a mirror and turns me around in the chair so I can see his work from all angles. He gives me a few tips on how to do it, as if, standing in my bathroom, I have one-tenth of the artistry he does over my head. I let him delude himself, and nod.

"Nice hair," says Rob as he opens the door. I'm want to tell him all about my wizard, Ed, but I don't get a chance because he slams the door and the next thing I know we are on the floor, reacquainting. "I missed you," he keeps saying over and over, and I almost (but don't) tell him that I love him, because it's barely been a month and I vowed it needs to be at least two. When we're done, I toss on his shirt and he orders some Italian from the place around the corner. I watch him on the phone, naked. That's my man.

When the food is delivered, we eat and lounge around all lovey-dovey. I think I might be able to stay at Rob's forever just having sex and eating. He is so easy to be around that I sometimes forget who he is.

"So, how's your job going? Firing anyone yet?" I'm trying to be whimsical, but I should've probably kept my mouth closed.

"Eve, that's not what my job is about. Look, we really shouldn't be talking about this." I've managed to annoy him.

"C'mon, you can trust me, I'm not a company spy."

"Are you sure, you have vays of making me talk?" He pulls me close. He wants the subject to drop, so I let it. He pulls his shirt off me and suggests we "go to sleep."

Later, when we are cuddling and talking quietly, I remember about the flowers. I tell him how much they made my day. I don't mention the interview to him, because I don't want him to know about it if I don't get the job.

"Thanks, Rob, I loved them. They got there at the perfect time. How did you know?"

"Eve," he says into my ear as he kisses me, "how do you think you got the interview?"

February

Somehow, Adrian gets me to go to some show in the East Village. It's starring some guy (Jason, I think) that Adrian used to see when he first got to the city. He and Anthony have been fighting for three days and Anthony hung up on him. Oh the drama!

When we get to the theater, there's a huge line outside. Adrian tells me that he's had reservations for weeks. I wait patiently while Adrian kisses just about every guy on the line. A ton of names go by me and I'm sure I'll never see half of these people again, so I just smile and nod as I get introduced.

"Yeah, my boyfriend Anthony was being a drama queen, so Eve agreed to play fag hag tonight." The guys love this. I'm a little concerned about how high Adrian's voice is getting. He's putting on some act, like he is Super Gay, a new superhero.

Finally, we push our way into the place. Surprisingly, it's full of middle-aged women and quite a few young, trendy hetero couples. Adrian explains in a more normal voice that Jason works in the finance department of Sony, so he knows tons of people.

"But, does he really want to be a singer?"

"No, I mean I think it's a little too late for that. He just does this a couple of times a year for his friends. Tons of people show up."

We wait an inordinate amount of time for the show to start. At least we can drink, although everything is sort of watered down. Adrian keeps getting up to greet all these older guys I've never seen before. They are so openly checking him out. Now, I see why it's better for him that I came. Anthony would flip out.

Finally the show starts and the crowd goes wild when Jason is introduced. I'm expecting this hot young guy, but Jason is older with gray hair and a little bit of a paunch. I look at Adrian, to see if maybe this is just the opening act, but he's clapping fiendishly so I know it's Jason. I try to imagine Adrian and this guy having sex. Yuck.

Jason opens up with the song "Too Darn Hot." Show tunes?

There is no way I would have been down with this if I knew about
the show tunes. Jason is getting really into it, though. What he
lacks in vocal talent (which is a lot), he makes up for in dramatic
presentation. This is pretty wretched. I keep glancing at Adrian,
waiting for him to realize, but he, along with the rest of the crowd,
loves it. I can't believe Tabitha went out with her new Russian
boy, Vlad, tonight. How do I get myself into these things?

What's worse than Jason's singing are the ridiculous mono-
logues he goes into before each song. I mean it's all about himself,
but why? Why would anyone allude to their first love affair in
front of people they work with? And he's got all these cheesy
effects happening, so when he sings ''Stormy Weather'' the lights
flicker as he's leaning against the wall of the stage and you hear
thunder piped in. I can't help but laugh. I'm so embarrassed, but
I realize it looks like I'm crying, because that is what most of the
audience is doing. Am I missing something?

When the show is over Adrian insists we have to stay to con-
gratulate Jason. Jason emerges like a star and I watch all these
people run up and hug him. I'm convinced they're deaf and blind.
Jason accepts all these well-wishers like a diva. He keeps eyeing
Adrian. He tries to get over to us, but keeps getting stopped by
his crowd of adoring fans. I can't believe this.

Finally, Jason is in front of us and he grabs Adrian and kisses
him on the lips. Adrian introduces me, and tells Jason what a great
job he did. I try to be positive. I tell Jason that he had a great
show, but he doesn't take his eyes off Adrian. What a lech! I can't
believe Adrian would tolerate this pawing. Worse, Jason invites
Adrian out for (horror of horrors!) a drink. I want to hug Adrian
when he declines. He tells Jason to give him a call to talk about
the show. Yuck, yuck, eww!

Then we're out of there. I agree and we head over to this place
we like on Greenwich Avenue. I study him for a while over our
tea, waiting to gauge his reaction about the show.

''Well, that was pretty bad,'' I say. I can't take it anymore. He
looks shocked.

''What do you mean?''

''C'mon, show tunes! And when he sang that Michael Bolton
song—what the hell was that? It was pretty campy.''

''Well, he is gay.''

''Yeah, but that doesn't mean his show has to be clichéd and
bad.'' Suddenly, there's something weird with Adrian, and I feel
like I've done something wrong.

"Eve, didn't you see how into it everyone was?"

"Yeah, but they were all..."

"What? A bunch of queens?" What is he trying to say?

"No, *his friends*. This isn't about sexuality."

"I didn't realize you were such a theater critic, Eve."

"Adrian, why are you getting so harsh? I'm not a theater critic, but I know when something's bad."

"So, how do you explain those people crying?"

"Well, I was surprised, because you said that they all work for Sony, so you'd think they'd know better, but honestly, I think sometimes people look for sentimentality. I think those crying people wanted to be moved."

"And it was nothing Jason did?"

"I mean he picked a couple of cheesy songs and people reacted, that's all."

"They came to see a friend, to support a friend. They felt his experiences, I mean whatever talent he has is inconsequential, as far as I'm concerned, because he got up there and he sang about things that mattered to him. It wasn't glamorous, it wasn't great, it was just a guy singing from his heart, doing his best. You talk about a lot of things, Eve, and you're critical of a lot of people and things, but I never see you act on anything.

"Jason is never going to make a career out of being a singer, but he's brave enough to stand before his peers and just be who he's always dreamed of being. It takes courage, Eve, to put yourself out there to give it a go. It's so easy to laugh when you sit in your life and don't take a risk."

Wow! Now there's a tension between us. This is the wrong place to be having a fight. It's too small; the other customers have stopped talking in their groups. Now they're all busy listening to Adrian and his Oscar scene. I hate that.

"Well, I never realized you thought I was such a loser, Adrian, but, I have to admit, I was a little shocked to see you letting this guy paw you. Was that part of being courageous, too?" Sometimes I say something and hope that it doesn't come out as bad as it sounds, but in this case it does. I know I've said something I can never take back, just by the way Adrian looks at me. I try to remember exactly what he said to deserve that; to give myself an excuse for being so angry.

Adrian stares into his tea and shakes his head. The rest of the people in the café are holding their breath, waiting for his reply. I wonder how long they will stay like that, hinged on our conversation. They probably think he's my boyfriend and this is even more scandalous than it is. But it would be almost more excusable to talk to a boyfriend like that. It's never cool to cut that deep on a friend. When Adrian speaks to me again, his voice is low and thick.

"I don't know what you think of me, Eve. I guess it's cool for you to have a gay friend. It's chic, and you aren't one to miss a trend. Jason and I saw each other when I first got to the city. Maybe he seems like, I don't know, some campy buffoon to you— don't roll your eyes, just listen. He is a smart and fun guy and my relationship with him wasn't too different from your relationship with Rob King. The older man thing. And believe it or not, Jason broke my heart. I hate to say this, but I think you don't like him because he is a bit too flamboyant for your taste. It's cool to have a gay friend, but not too gay, right?" It's really hard to be having this conversation with him here, because I know we're on display and I really just want to scream at him. I try to be calm and think about what I am going to say.

"I don't know where you get off basically saying I'm homophobic, like my friendship with you is built on superficial reasons other than true friendship. It offends me. I'm sorry, I just didn't think the show was all that good. That doesn't really reflect my cowardice or my homophobia. I think you're upset about something else, maybe seeing Jason, or your fight with Anthony, I don't know, but, I don't think it's fair for you to take it out on me." Adrian shakes his head again and sips his tea. I can see people leaning over slightly to try to catch our conversation.

"You finished your tea, Eve. Do you want to get out of here?" I nod. We settle up the check and leave.

We don't say a word to each other as we walk back. It's so cold out, so we're walking fast. When we get to 18th, Adrian's street, he stops and turns to me.

"So, um, have a good night. Say hi to Roseanne."

"I will, take care." That's it.

No New York Kiss. No nothing.

Roseanne is up watching David Letterman when I get in. She is sitting on the couch with a blanket around her. I can't see her hands and I could swear she was, never mind, I don't want to think about it, she hasn't gotten any in a while. Maybe I'm a prude.

"How was the thing?"

"Shitty! Adrian thinks I'm a coward and a homophobe. Our friendship is most likely over. I guess it doesn't matter because apparently I was only using him to be a chic trendy woman. You know, because it's cool to have gay friends.''

"Wow!" says Roseanne. She isn't really listening to me, because Dave is in the middle of his monologue. We say our goodnights (she'd probably rather be alone). I try calling Tabitha, who isn't answering. She was going out with Vlad, her February. I toy with the idea of calling Rob, but I don't know if we have that kind of relationship yet. It's too soon for him to see my weaknesses and have a glimpse of what my friends think of me.

So the worst possible fate: I get left alone with myself. I don't think I'm homophobic and I don't want to believe that Adrian does. Maybe I am too much of a critic (God, maybe I am a wretched person). I guess it's pretty cool to pack a place with a bunch of your friends (there were like seventy people there) and just sing, no matter how bad or good you sound. Maybe Adrian's right about taking a chance, maybe I should.

No, that's ridiculous, I'm twenty-three, I'm too young. I'm not going to let Adrian affect me that much. I wouldn't even know where to begin on my so-called dream. I just hope I haven't lost him as a friend forever. That would suck.

I'm having a shitty day at work. There is a lot to be done for some reason. In reality, it's nothing, but relative to this job, it's probably two weeks' work packed into one day. Lorraine is having me do some of her work, Herb has me plan about eight meetings, and there must be some supply demon stealing everyone's supplies. Everyone keeps coming up to me wanting their special pens and multicolored Post-its and guess what underqualified writer is hassling me to help her do her crappy expense report. It's all super boring.

Tabitha is also having a crisis about Vlad, which I can't seem to stay on the phone long enough to understand. I am contemplating sending Adrian some stupid office humor. It might help reopen lines of communication. Calgon take me away. I haven't seen Rob in three days so I decide to take a little visit to his floor. I deserve a break.

"Sherman, how's it going?" I sneak up behind him.

"Great, great." He has no idea who I am until he turns around, but, I've got to give him credit for having his "greats" practiced. "Oh, it's you. Rob is in a meeting, can I schedule something else for you?"

"Well, when is this one getting out?" I pick up the printed out page of SchedulePlus that's in Sherman's mailbox. I can tell Sherman doesn't like the idea. "Relax, Sher, it's only his schedule, not a company secret."

Sherman is kind of a dork, I have to admit. I mean I want to like the guy, especially after the whole wrap incident. It's just that I think he's the kind of guy who gets really jazzed about being an assistant, who honestly believes he can work his way to the top. I catch myself being critical. Again.

"What's this reorganization meeting he's at?" Sherman shrugs and looks nervous. I like feeling like the cheerleader talking to the geek. For some reason Todd pops into my head, but then so does our bathroom interlude, so I suppress it. "Well, it gets out at two, which is in like one minute, and he has an hour window."

"But those meetings always run late."

"Well, I'll just wait in his office until he gets back."

"Ms. Vitali, I'd rather you didn't."

"C'mon, Sher, it's only for like a second and you know you don't want me hanging out at your desk listening to your personal calls." Sherman is pretty horrified at the idea of that.

"I never make personal calls at work." That's what I'm talking about, too into his job.

So, I shut the door in Rob's office. It's a pretty good size and he scammed a great view of the river. I sit in his chair. If only I knew he wasn't bringing anyone back to his office or Sherman wasn't going to pop in any minute to check on me, I'd be a naughty Goldilocks, but I don't do anything. Once again, I'm not taking any risks.

I decide that I will find the last file that Rob was working on in his computer and leave a giant erotic message at the top. That's risky, right? I mean there's always the chance that it's a company wide memo that he isn't going to check before distributing. It will give him a little thrill when he sits down to work on it.

I open up Rob's last file and try to think of something juicy. It's a memo to Prescott with only two other people cc'ed. It's a lot of bullshit about branding ourselves as Prescott Nelson Inc. and giving all of our magazines a distinct image. Right in the middle, Rob starts talking about cost efficiency and how a lot of the magazines are overlapping some of their operations responsibilities. I'm starting to feel guilty about reading this. It's not the usual garbage e-mail with lots of pro-Prescott rhetoric.

Rob suggests that certain divisions are merged. The superfluous staff will be transferred to other positions or terminated. Now, I *know* I'm not supposed to be reading the memo. It looks like *Anna,* the women's magazine, *Angry Beavers,* the feminist magazine I once coveted, and *Banana,* the health magazine, are losing quite a few people. I know if I scroll down, I'll see the *Bicycle Boy* list. I shouldn't be doing this.

I practically scream when Rob opens the door. He's alone and smiling, so I know Sherman told him I was in here. He doesn't seem surprised that I'm at his computer; from his vantage point, he can't see where I'm looking.

"Ms. Vitali." He starts adjusting the closed blinds. My hand is still hovering over the mouse. I should just close the file, but I'm frozen. My heart is racing.

"Hi," I say, trying to keep my voice level.

"Are you trying to steal my job?"

"No." I think it comes out too defensive. He leans over the desk and kisses me. He grabs my hand and walks around the desk, kneeling before me.

"You look like a dark-haired Goldilocks. Who's been sitting in my chair?" He is trying to be cute, but, I can't relax. "Do you think I can get you to call me Papa Bear? What's going on?"

"Just stopping by, you know."

"I thought you were still upset about that job. I've missed you."

"Me, too. I'm not mad or anything, I'm fine."

"Good, I locked the door. I have a half hour and I intend to use it." I am not sure how I feel about being scheduled in. I am still blocking his view of the screen. He doesn't kiss me right away, he looks at me for a little while, plays with my hair. "You're really pretty, Ms. Vitali."

I should tell him. I should turn around and point to the screen and say, "I know you're some kind of corporate grim reaper," but I want to just forget it and kiss him. I can't help liking him when he's kneeling in front of me in his office, staring at me with those sexy eyes. We start kissing. Thank God the door is locked because for a little while I forget where I am. His hands are moving up under my shirt and we are both in his chair pushing it back. Sherman is a very distant thought.

Rob realizes as he is kissing my neck. In all the excitement, I forgot to keep blocking the screen. It takes me only a second to figure out why he's stopped.

He is disheveled when he pulls away. He looks back and forth from me to the computer, like I'm some kind of awful traitor. My lipstick is smeared all over his mouth. He sits back on the floor and stares at me, waiting for me to say something.

"I was just leaving you a note, I swear I wasn't snooping."

"Eve, this isn't cool. I mean all that information is totally confidential. There are maybe five people in the company who know we are going to do something like this. Did you see the *Bicycle Boy* list?"

"So there is one? Am I on it?"

"Eve, c'mon."

"Why aren't I on it, because of you?"

"No, Eve. We always need assistants."

"Well, that's comforting. I may hate my job, but I love the job security." He doesn't say anything. He just stares at me. I want to wipe his mouth off and forget about everything but the kissing parts, but, I can't. "So who is it? Who's getting fired?"

"Eve—" he's shaking his head "—we can't do this. I was spoken to about it—"

"What? You were talked to about me?"

"You need to relax." He is up now; I don't mention the lipstick.

"What, is our half hour window over?"

He doesn't answer me and I hate being ignored. He stops at the door and looks at me. "I have a meeting I can't miss, Eve. I'll call you later." I hate the way he talked down to me. I wish he would come back and we could give it another go to make everything seem normal. He might be thinking that, too, but he's late for a meeting and so he shuts the door behind him and leaves me sitting in his chair, still disheveled with the stupid file still open.

I hate everyone.

Except Roseanne. She makes me ribolita for dinner—it's my grandmother's recipe. She doesn't ask me why I'm being so quiet, she just gives me a second helping. Roseanne will be a wonderful grandmother someday.

Rob calls me that night. He's still at the office. The conversation is a little tense, especially when he tells me he is going to another conference early tomorrow. He'll be out of town for a week and he doesn't seem to realize that means he won't be around for Valentine's Day.

"Eve, I don't know what's wrong with you. You were snooping around my office and that's not cool. I have a million things to do and I have to go home and pack. I'll call you from Jacksonville, okay?" Again, he's talking to me like I'm someone he needs to be patient with. Whatever.

We have no heat on one of the coldest days in the past two years. I'm trying to sleep through it, but I wake up in the middle of the night to Roseanne standing over my bed with all her blankets.

"I think my pee just froze on the way into the toilet. There's a draft in the window. My body temperature is rapidly dropping. I have to get up in three hours."

"Climb in," I say, rolling over in my bed. She gets in and scrunches up to me. I miss having someone sleep in my bed. It's kind of cozy. I need to work it out with Rob.

We arrange the covers so that only the very tops of our heads are exposed to the elements. Roseanne cannot stop whining and moaning. "This is the worst, ever!"

"C'mon, it's cozy! Besides, at least we have a home. Just think, one day we'll look back on this like our starving artist phase. We'll remember it fondly."

"Starving artist? More like poor low-level functionaries. I beeped that fix-it guy Frank today. Twice. He never called me back. Can you please call Yakimoto?"

When I agree, Roseanne rolls over and goes to sleep. I can't help but feel used.

It's very hard to get a hold of Yakimoto in the morning. First one of her kids, who seems unimpressed when I mention that I am the Little Nell lady, gives me the number to a restaurant. Some guy who doesn't speak English answers, and after a lot of confusion, which is exacerbated by the fact that I don't want to talk too loud, I get her.

"Hi, Mrs. Yakimoto. It's Eve. Listen, our heat isn't working. I would call my dad, but we don't have keys to the basement. Roseanne beeped Frank yesterday, but he never called back. Do you think you can call him?"

"I will give you his number at his shop. You girls should just try calling him again. Be really as cute and nice as you can be. You can do it."

"Well, okay. So, what's this restaurant you're at?" Every time I call Mrs. Yakimoto, I try to be as friendly and interested in her as possible. I think she likes me.

"Well, I opened a restaurant. It's a theme restaurant close to the mall out here. It's a lot of work and very expensive. You should get a man to take you here."

"Well, you're quite the entrepreneur, Mrs. Yakimoto." I can tell she's thrilled. It never hurts to butter up the landlady.

I call Roseanne back and give her the news. We have decided that I will always deal with Yakimoto and she will always call Frank (I think it has a lot to do with her being cuter and nicer). I also share with her Yakimoto's advice for getting optimum results from Frank.

"So, basically she wants us to prostitute ourselves to get the heat fixed. Heat, which we are, by law, entitled to. Heat, for which we pay."

"They're making you file, huh?"

"Yes. Oh, my God! I think it's sexist. The office assistant is out and I am the lowest on the totem pole. There is nothing I hate more than filing. My suit is filthy, at least they could have told me this is what I'd be doing." Roseanne is never happy when she has to file.

"What are you doing tonight? Tabitha's friend Nicole got us tickets to an indie flick and the reception."

"I'll be too busy showering the dust off and freezing in the apartment."

"Well, don't suffer in silence."

"I'll try not to. See you later."

I jump at the phone when it rings the next day. It's only my sister warning me not to be suckered into the consumerist holiday. As usual I patiently explain to her that I am not the enemy, I do not encompass the evils of corporate America, nor, despite appearances, am I "the man." She informs me that she *loves* Chuck. I remind her of how greeting card that word is. (I'm not exactly in the best of moods. Last night, even though Tabitha assured me that the film swept Sundance, it sucked. The after party wasn't so bad. We got drunk on vodka drinks because Stoli was the sponsor and I watched Tabitha dance into the night with the director's grandfather.)

"Boy, Eve, you're bitter about men. That Todd guy looked so cute."

"Monica, Todd is in fucking India, for all I know. We are just friends. We were never seeing each other. I don't know where you got your info."

"Well, I read the Eve Vitali fan letter, of course." Sometimes, I have got to give my sister credit, she may be Ms. Social Redistribution or whatever, but she can be a real smart-ass. I toy with the idea of telling her about Rob, but I can't just tell my sister about a guy without her bugging me about my sex life and defining for me (again) power issues between men and women. She would go nuts with the power issues between Rob and me. My sister tells me how she wants to scrap this whole Women's Studies thing, "how practical is it?" and maybe go to some holistic medical school out west with Chuck.

"Okay, Monica, my suggestion, which you probably won't accept, is that you wait to tell our parents this new plan." I can hear Monica stirring with this, I know she is ready to unleash the fires of the underappreciated older child, but lucky for me my other line beeps. "Oh, Monica, I'll have to call you back, I need to take this call." I switch over before she can tell me how I always take our parents' side.

"Eve, this is Isabelle Chambers. I'm sorry, I haven't been able to return any of your calls. We've been busy going over candidates for a lot of positions."

"I understand." I'm searching for the acceptance or rejection tone in her voice, but it's level and flat.

"So, we decided to go with someone with a little more publication experience."

"Oh. Okay. Thanks." Why am I thanking her? She does not deserve my thanks. I don't want to believe it's got anything to do with Rob.

"You're welcome, Eve. I thought you were great and I'll definitely keep you in mind for anything else that comes up."

"Please do. Thanks a lot." When I hang up, I realize that I'm not ever going to have another job. My destiny is to be an assistant at this desk.

"Stop being ridiculous, what about our magazine?" Tabitha must believe I really will be an assistant forever, because she would never bring up the magazine otherwise. "Honestly, Eve, I've been thinking about it. It isn't a bad idea. We should start looking into it. I wonder if we could put it out ourselves or if we need a backer. I mean, I'm sure we need a backer, because we don't have enough capital, but you never know."

"What about your father?" I don't know why I'm asking her this, she never talks about her father or her family, but she always gets money from somewhere, so maybe it's her dad. I know it's a sexist assumption, but maybe Tabitha will open up a little more.

"Yeah, I can probably get money from somewhere, I'm not sure if I have as much as we would need, but we can talk about it. More importantly, Vlad is dissing me on Valentine's Day for some wrestling match. I'm not sure about this one, of course, it might be Cold War child anxiety.''

''Remember that episode of *Silver Spoons* where he met Andropov? Terrifying.''

''Right. So, are you flying solo?''

''The King is dead. Actually, just pissed at me and I don't even know what city he's in. Planless for V-Day and it's a Friday. So it's even more disgusting.''

''Shall we have a girls night out? You get Roseanne, I'll get Adrian.''

''Adrian? What about Anthony?''

''Too much drama. They're done, just in time for the holiday. C'mon, we'll go to that cheap soul food place in the East Village.''

''Fine, but can it just be a real girls night out?''

''Oh, right, the fight. You know, you can't fight forever.''

''I don't know, we probably can fight forever. And we'll still be pissy on Friday. Besides that place is really small—we're never getting reservations.''

''Okay, no Adrian. I'll call for reservations now.'' Sometimes, there's no talking to Tabitha. She's thriving on the hustle-bustle. At least I won't have to see Adrian.

I keep hoping that Rob will come back in time for V-Day. I have the urge to be wrapped up in his loving arms. For some reason I think this out loud to Tabitha and she makes vomiting noises.

Valentine's Day. Roseanne and I arrive first at our Valentine's Day fete, and, sure enough, the waiter is a doll. When we thank him for seating us he says, ''My pleasure.'' Roseanne is smitten with him, so she orders wine right away. We're mostly through the bottle by the time Tabitha shows up. Tabitha immediately flags the waiter over for more wine.

There aren't too many lovey-dovey couples to remind us of our solitude. There's one couple in the corner, so we put Tabitha in the seat facing them, because she's had sex most recently, so as Roseanne says, ''She can deal.''

The food is delicious. We make a silent pact to get the waiter over as often as possible so we can gawk at him and hear him say, ''My pleasure.'' Roseanne asks him if he has a Valentine and the rest of us try to explain her, which makes Mr. Sexy Waiter giggle and Roseanne gets belligerent.

''Where are you from?'' she asks the waiter.

"Texas." Roseanne and I get excited because now we have a reason to keep him here. I wish I knew something about Texas, but I just want to look at him. We tell him Tabitha is from Texas. He asks Tabitha where she's from and she looks annoyed.

"Can we get another bottle of wine?"

"My pleasure." Tabitha turns to us, repeating, "My pleasure."

"Tabitha, you guys were *paisan,* you should have talked to him."

"I know, but who wants to talk about Texas?"

"Not you, obviously," Roseanne says. "You were acting like you'd never even heard of it."

"Well, I was overcome by his hotness." I didn't think that happened to Tabitha, I've never seen her seem so nervous. "Besides, I've blocked out Texas, it was a traumatic time."

"Why?" Roseanne thinks she's the only one who hasn't heard about Tabitha's family.

"Just childhood, I don't know." Tabitha picks at her mashed potatoes and doesn't say anything. I know Roseanne isn't satisfied with that, but I shake my head at her.

After dinner we decide to go to a bar around the corner. It usually has shitty live bands. The bar is loud and shaking, it's a country band. We all get drinks. Roseanne hasn't quite let the Lone Star State go, because she keeps trying to sing along to the music and saying, "It's your music, Tabitha, the music of your past. If you don't like it, kiss my—" but of course she doesn't finish. She's pretty entertaining for the two of us, who somehow aren't quite as drunk yet. Roseanne meanders through the crowd.

After a time, Tabitha looks over my head toward the bar. "Is that who I think it is, talking to Roseanne?"

I turn to look. "Zeke." Of course he has to be looking my way that very minute, and our eyes meet. We both look away. It's stupid. Of all days, today.

"You have to save her, Eve." Sadly, Roseanne looks like she's enjoying talking to him. It hurts me more than it will hurt her, knowing the bad luck she's had lately. "You can do it, Eve, you're the woman. Besides, it'll be good for him to see what he missed out on. You're doing it tonight, Mommy." I walk up to Zeke and Roseanne.

"Hey, Zeke." He does a poor job of feigning surprise.

"Oh, hi, uh, Eve." He needs to stop pretending he can't remember my name.

"Hey, you know my roommate?" Roseanne asks. "Oh, my

gosh, oh, my gosh, I know who this is. Oh, wow!'' Exactly what I didn't want—like I've been pining for him all this time.

"Roseanne, Tabitha needs to talk to you right away about macramé.''

"Really,'' Roseanne says, truly shocked. I watch her stumble away.

"So, what's up?'' I turn my attention back to Zeke. I can tell his wanna-be friends are intrigued. He is plainly enjoying this.

"You know, just catching some tunes.'' Eww, he may be cute, but was he always this much cheese? "My friend's the drummer in this band.''

"Exciting.'' I think that was a little too sarcastic. "So what have you been up to?''

"Just writing, you know, everything else is useless.''

"Yeah, the book, right.'' I'm waiting for him to ask me about myself because, you know, that's what people do. I should set an example. "Are you still working in A&R?''

"Oh, no, that was taking too much out of me. I'm somewhere else. It's just a day job, finance. I get to write all day and that's what I need to be an artist.''

"An artist, huh?'' He shakes his head at me, like he's remembering my ignorance and pities me for being this way. But, I've got him all figured out, he was just temping for some A&R place, creating himself, like I do. I can't fault him for that, but I can for actually *believing* he's an artist.

"My art is what defines me.'' I laugh, because, c'mon, has he listened to himself sound so obnoxious?

"Well, have you sold anything, Zeke?''

"Eve, it isn't about money, you just don't get it.''

"Whatever, Zeke, I'm doing okay, thanks for asking. Have fun with your art.'' I walk away. When I get back to the table I recount the story, for some reason, I guess alcohol, we start talking about the suffix "ist.'' We name all the professions we know that end in "ist'' thrilling each other with words like "anesthesiologist'' and "linguist'' which no one is sure about (hey, sometimes, these things are funny).

"I don't care, maybe I'm dense,'' I say, cracking them both up, "but, I don't think anyone can be an artist unless they are somehow getting paid or recognition or something other than a pat on the back from their own hand. Otherwise, everyone would be an artist. Do you think I'm being too critical? Adrian thinks I'm too critical." I'm beginning to feel bitterness and an alcohol flood coming on.

"Mother of God." Tabitha puffs her cigarette.

"A criticist," says Roseanne, giggling uncontrollably.

"Eve, it's New York. Everyone thinks they're an artist, you almost have to be."

"So is that an excuse?" I'm talking to Tabitha because Roseanne is too busy saying "criticist, criticist" over and over. "I don't think you can consider yourself something unless you get paid. Well, if I had a job like a bartender and I painted on the side, I would say I was a bartender and I painted. Not a painter."

"A paintist," says Roseanne.

"Right," I say. "I think all these artists need to get a dose of reality and realize that they aren't artists, they actually suck. And some might wonder who am I to say these things, because I may want to be a writer, but I haven't written in a million years. But I admit it and I don't know who I am. Hopefully more than an assistant, although I guess my own definition has come back to bite me in the ass. So what am I?"

"Mother of God. Look, enough of this heavy conversation, I'm going to go to Krispy Kreme. I need something I can count on."

"But, Tabitha," says Roseanne, finally serious, "what are we?" Tabitha looks at us and puts her hands on our arms. She leans into the table and we do the same.

"All right, I'll tell you, but I swear, I'm going to Krispy Kreme after that. We," she shouts, "are fabulists."

Herb asks me to see about ordering lunch for a meeting on Monday. Right away, I start to imagine my conversation with a laughing Jennifer Hoya, but Herb assures me that we already have a meeting space available. He suggests I order lunch for a larger number than I usually have, because the folks from *Yoga for Life* are going to be with us. That's kind of strange. The man wants me to work miracles, but of course I tell him I can do it. I get an e-mail from some random YFL assistant.

Please clear your schedules for a very important meeting about our magazine. Today at noon in the MESS HALL on 43. I apologize for the short notice. Lunch will be served.

I guess I should have been tipped off when Herb was wearing a suit instead of his usual khakis, but I wasn't. I've been trying to pay less attention to him. My first clue that something's wrong is that Rob King is cc'ed. As far as I know he's still in Jackson-fuckingville, probably forcing some woman to call him "Papa Bear." Maybe it's going to be a public outing of our relationship. Maybe he's gathering everyone together, so he can declare his love for me, in front of everyone. More likely it has to do with the list I almost saw, but didn't. For some reason, everyone keeps coming up to me throughout the morning and asking me what the meeting is about. Lacey Matthews is the most obnoxious one.

"Well, aren't you friends with Rob King?" She's proud of her-self, like she's busted me.

"Don't you aspire to be friends with Herb? Ask him." That sends her away. I'm all set to tell Jim that I don't know anything about the meeting when he comes up to me, but all he wants is to see if he can expense a meatball sandwich from the Italian deli. I tell him that he should be grateful he gets his lunch paid for and if he doesn't like the "prissy pants" food that we have, he can look elsewhere for lunch. I don't mind being rude anymore, it's kind of fun.

There is a sense of urgency in the meeting room, demonstrated by the slight restraint people use in getting their food. The *Bicycle Boy* staff and the *Yoga for Life* staff look at each other suspi-ciously. People are whispering to each other about people they know who were recently canned. The women from *Angry Beavers* got very angry and apparently threatened some huge lawsuit at Prescott himself if any changes took place.

The *Yoga for Life* assistant is a very pregnant woman named Elise. She and I shrug at each other. When we are opening up more of the food, she whispers in my ear, "I could give a rat's ass about what they say, my maternity leave starts next week."

"I could just give," I say. It makes me wish I had a baby or some other excuse for being so disinterested. Herb comes in with Rob. I haven't seen him since he was standing at his door with my lipstick smeared on his face. He looks good. Our eyes meet and he sort of nods at me. I want him, I can't help it. I take a bite of my pita.

Jarvis Mitchell, who's in charge of all the sports division mag-azines, comes in with a woman I don't recognize—it isn't his assistant. His presence means it's serious. You can feel the col-lective concern. Everyone falls quiet.

Jarvis is a guy with longish graying hair and a beard. He is a thinker, everyone says, like so many other men in power at Prescott, he likes to imagine procedures that he thinks would work and then implement them without really considering the people they affect. He is usually very removed from the situations and people he makes policy for.

"Hi, everyone. First of all, I want to say that despite a lot of rumors, no one is losing their jobs. You're all doing great work, circulation is up tenfold, our advertisers are happy. The sweepstakes we did in *Yoga for Life* gave us a much better handle on our readers and although it's a new magazine, we are quite pleased with how its doing. In fact, I can assure all of you that it's been noted all the way up to the top of Prescott Nelson. Let's give *Yoga for Life* a round of applause." Everyone starts clapping. If I were them, and it were my career on the line, I would be a lot more careful with how I tossed out my applause. I notice that the woman who came in with Jarvis is clapping most enthusiastically. I think he is setting them up for the big shock. I look over at Rob. He is staring down at his papers, but looks up and catches me. He knows what's really going on.

"Of course a blueprint for success was set up by *Bicycle Boy*. If you want to talk about a magazine with a huge circulation and a great look, with critical acclaim for presenting information that is intelligent and thought-provoking, it's *Bicycle Boy*. We manage to get the information out there and that's got a lot to do with Herb, who commandeers the magazine in such an original way. We've definitely gone for an edgier feel and started including a lot more issues pertaining to women into the magazine. With some publications, changes like this cause readers to be confused for a while. In this case it hasn't hurt our circulation at all. In fact our demographic has opened up quite a bit.

"I know a lot of people in this room have been feeling anxious about these changes. It's never easy to see something you take pride in going through such a big change. But, it's a lot like a cocooning process." Oh, no, I smell acid flashback. Am I going to be subjected to boring analogies? I look over at Rob, he's transfixed until he catches my eye. I quickly look away and try to emulate his look. Why am I such an asshole?

"A lot of women who were reading us initially are even more thrilled to discover that now we're talking to them. We haven't suffered a bit for the changes. That truly is a victory." The woman with Jarvis Mitchell starts clapping immediately. (Who is she?) She is outdone in enthusiasm by Lacey Matthews, who believes that she is single-handedly responsible for attracting those women readers.

"Also, I think, it's important for us to start thinking globally. The sales of our international *Bicycle Boy* branches are down, this may be because they don't have as fearless or talented a leader abroad as we do here." Jarvis takes a moment to look over at Herb, who eats it up. I'm going to get sick, but no matter what I won't look at Rob again.

"What we've got planned is very exciting. Before I get to it, I'd like to introduce Mabel to everyone. Mabel Karavassian, meet our group." I hate when people give the impression that we are like one huge collective or one big happy family. "Mabel is here to help us understand some of the changes we'll be going through." No one is too keen on the word "changes" and I wish Jarvis would get to it. I've got to call Tabitha.

"Hi, everyone," says Mabel, looking at each and every one of us before she continues. Then her face breaks in to a smile. "We've got a lot to discuss before the end of today. We've been doing a lot of thinking throughout the company to try and centralize everything that's going on. I know a lot of these changes are going to seem..." she pauses for a long time as if she hasn't already thought this all out in her head "...strange, but I can tell you with a lot of honesty and integrity—" more looking around "—that it's a very positive step."

"What we're going to do is visionary," says Jarvis, taking back the focus. It's like they went to some kind of meeting school. "We're going to start a new magazine."

Jarvis lets that sink in a moment. It's kind of like one of those courtroom dramas where everybody starts buzzing because they disagree with the verdict. Everybody is all excited and starts talking. Except, no one is talking to me and of course I have to sneak a peak at Rob, who's staring at me. I feel like an even bigger loser for not having any friends to buzz to.

"We expect lots of questions and concerns. We hope this new magazine will be a hybrid of the spirit of the magazine we've already got. We have no intention of taking either of the magazines out of circulation; in fact, we know the magazines will evolve as this new one does. We have decided to call the magazine *Breathe*. We want it to be that intrinsic." What the hell is he talking about?

"We expect a transition period, but I am confident that you will be pleased with the eventual result. By year end, we should all be quite adjusted." Year end? That's ten months away. There is no way it's going to take that long. Jarvis looks over at Mabel, who smiles at him. "Mabel, thank you."

Mabel puts a chart on the projector. Jarvis steps up immediately to prevent any misconceptions. The chart is pretty dramatic. A lot of people's names are on it in different places than one might think. In addition to everyone's current jobs, there are new responsibilities. It appears that some of the *Yoga for Life* people will have more senior roles than *Bicycle Boy*'s staff.

"In reality, we've just put a lot of the creative names in slots that we think would be ideal. Some of you have been stuck in a creative rut for a while and we hoped this would breathe some new life into our jobs. We are just trying to set the groundwork up for you. We plan on meeting with you several times over the next few weeks to iron out the processes. Now I think we should open it up for questions."

The rest of the afternoon is like this. Things get pretty heated. It's not a meeting I can tune out of. There is anger on all sides. Everyone's complaining about the workload and I can totally tell the *Bicycle Boy* staff is not pleased with having to share any kind of spotlight. I want to write it off, but even Lorraine is getting emotional. Jarvis and Rob are clearly not surprised by everyone's reactions. Mabel is thriving on all the drama. She nods at everyone's comments and writes them down on the white walls so we can "capture" our emotions.

Although Lacey should be happy that she is sitting pretty, she is getting fired up with questions. I think she is setting herself up to be an advocate for the people. Jim just keeps making obnoxious comments and I'm surprised that he hasn't bitched about lunch. Gary, who has been put under Lacey and some other writer from *Yoga for Life,* asks a question in a high-pitched voice on the verge of cracking. I keep waiting for Herb to make some stupid joke that everyone will laugh at, but he doesn't.

We wind up there until—get this—about 4:30. (Rob left at 3:00.) And, no, the brownies and cookies didn't help. Mabel stands at the door and finds out all of our names. She wants us to sign up for change management workshops. "Nice to meet you, Eve." She pumps my hand and looks straight into my eyes. "When would you like to come in and talk to me?"

"That's okay, it doesn't seem like my job is going to be affected that much," I say, trying to get by. Mabel is not a small woman, she almost blocks the door to prevent me from getting through. She doesn't stop smiling though.

"Eve, a lot of times, the best thing for us is to deal with things head-on. Now, I know you're swamped, everyone is, but it's important to get your concerns out in the open." Now I'm holding up the line. I don't want to make a big deal out of this.

"How about I just call you later when I'm not busy and see if we can work it in?"

"Eve, how about you sign up for a time, then if you absolutely can't make it we'll reschedule." She actually puts her arm on my shoulder as if she truly pities me for being so overworked. I feel guilty. I bend down and sign up for a time in two weeks, one of the last possible days. With any luck the building may burn down by then or I'll find a new job. Rob may not have been able to help me get a new job, but maybe he can use his pull to get me out of this meeting. If he ever talks to me again.

"Okay, I'll be sure and call you a few days ahead to see if you're too busy." She will because Mabel is one of those people who never suspects that her actions might annoy. There's a purpose for everything she does.

"Great," I say, finally slipping by. "Thanks."

Back at my desk, I have a zillion messages from Tabitha trying to figure out how many of us have been fired. She knows I haven't been because "assistants are golden at this company since they aren't supposed to have any brains." Tabitha has a whole conversation with herself on my voice mail about this, and how maybe we are bad assistants because we do have brains. There's also a strange one from Rob. He speaks very quietly like his dog is dying or something.

"Hey, Eve, just wanted to make sure everything is okay. Give me a call if you need to." Well, when he puts it like that, how can I ever call him? Any phone call would mean that I need to call. I call Tabitha and tell her the story.

"I think it's only the beginning," she says.

"They said that we, I mean they, were chosen to 'spearhead' (eww!) this new magazine, because the readers had similar lifestyles."

"Yeah, boring, healthy lifestyles."

"Exactly. Rob was there and he looked cute. Should I call him?"

"Eve, you might want to because you've been slightly nunnish lately."

"Tabitha, it's been like three weeks. How's Vlad?"

"On his way out, but he doesn't know it, so he's still being pretty wonderful."

"Wonderful. Anyway, I have to go clean up."

"Let's kick off the week with some cocktails? You in? I might ask Vlad."

"Am I going to have to watch you fawn all night? You know I can't stand it."

"Hey, I'm just trying to freshen the crowd a little, girl. You oughtta welcome the change. With any luck he can bring one of his sexy friends."

"As far as I know I'm still taken."

"Debatable."

"Thanks. Stop by around ten. I'll talk to Roseanne. 'Bye."

I head down to the conference room to check on the status of the food. With any luck they'll have ravaged everything and I'll just have to throw away the serving trays. The food is mostly all done, but they made quite a mess, so I'm a little annoyed. I start to clean up and I don't realize right away that Gary, the writer, is sitting there in the dark.

"Oh, hey," I say, covering my embarrassment. "Didn't see you in here. Are you done with this?"

"Sure." He is disconcertingly quiet. I start carrying the trays out to the garbage cans near the freight elevators, so I have to keep coming back in. He is acting strange. I feel like I should talk to him.

"Are you okay, Gary?" He waits a long time before he answers me.

"It's just the beginning, when they do this. They start by just making one change, but the next thing you know it's three months later and your job is nothing like it was. They'll package this like a promotion, but the magazine is dying. When it sinks, they'll have someone to blame."

I have no idea what the right thing to say in this situation is, so I sit down across from him. "Change is hard, I mean maybe after a while you'll like this magazine. I'm sure this magazine will take off." He nods, but I don't think he thinks so.

"I'm one of the only people who believes in the product. I'm the demographic. That's what got me in trouble, I was too resistant to all the new things they wanted to do, now I am out!" He makes a kill motion across his neck. He is starting to get worked up.

"Well, it's not like you got fired." I'm trying to be encouraging.

"No, not yet, anyway, but it'll happen. Dammit!" I kind of

think Gary needs to just calm down a bit and give it a chance. I start to tell him this, but he puts his head down on the table and I think he starts to cry.

Shit! I'm not good at these kinds of things. I mean, it's one thing to comfort my friends, but I don't even think I like Gary. I try to reach across the conference table, but it's too big. I get up and walk around the table.

I hesitate a second, before sitting next to Gary and touching his shoulder. Almost immediately he starts hugging me, sobbing. I try to be soothing, but it's Gary, an annoying writer, it's not like I can pat his back and say, "There, there."

After three really long minutes, Gary sits up. He squeezes my hand. "Thanks, Eve, you're very kind. I guess I let myself get comfortable in a situation and now I'm realizing that it was never the situation I ever imagined myself being in. Eve, if I could do it all again, I would have just concentrated on my own writing or cycling professionally. Let this be a lesson to you, you're still young. Don't let your day job get in the way of whatever it is you want to do." Then Gary gets up to leave.

That episode and the way Tabitha said "debatable" about Rob are really bugging me, so instead of going right home, I head up to Rob's area. Sherman is surfing the Net, I'm sure of it, but real quick, he switches to his SchedulePlus.

"What's going on, Sher?"

"Nothing, Rob isn't here and I can't let you in his office."

"Hey, Sherman, relax, I was just in the area and I wanted to see if he was around." I eye his SchedulePlus. Sherman gets flustered and switches it off back onto the Net. He puts his hands up by the screen, not wanting me to see what he's looking at.

"Easy there, Sherman, soon you're going to be making personal phone calls."

"Never." What a dork.

"Okay, can you tell Rob I came by? When did he get back from Jacksonville?"

"I can't give that kind of information out. Sorry."

"Well, thanks, Sherman. Have a good night."

"Ah, yeah, good night." I walk away slowly, hoping Rob will be on his way back up. This is pathetic.

I don't bother to mention Gary's crying episode or anything about Rob to the girls when we're out that night. I'm not sure why. Maybe Gary deserves to have a little dignity. But, not telling them about Rob? I don't know, maybe *I* need a little dignity. We do wind up talking about the changes going on in the company. Roseanne is getting bored with all this talk, but she takes off running with the work-for-yourself topic. She starts off talking about Tabitha and me and how we want more out of life than what our job is giving us, but somehow winds up complaining for a half hour about her job. Now I can tell Tabitha is losing interest and in the meantime, we smoke all of her cigarettes. I kick her so she won't get up during Roseanne's diatribe.

"I just hate it. Every day I sit there and I stare at my computer and all those numbers and they start to blend together and I actually start zoning out."

"Fascinating," says Tabitha as I kick her harder under the table. "No, really, it is, it just goes to show how everyone our age, even the people we'd like to believe are happy with themselves, are miserable at their jobs."

"Maybe we are the only ones and we attract each other, because we know we can feed off our misery?"

"I don't know, Eve, you would think people at my job would be the type who would just accept their fate, because they are making good money. No one really feels sorry for themselves, but no one is having fun."

"Are you supposed to have fun at work?"

"Tab, you're the one who absolutely needs to like what you're doing! You are probably the most into your job."

"Because of all the perks, sure. *NY By Night* is high profile, its success is crucial. But I know there's been a few slips in advertising, and it's going to affect us. I bet we get reorg'ed."

"Nice grammar. But, you really think you are supposed to have fun at work?"

"Okay, maybe fun is the wrong word, but I think you need to be doing something that gives you a purpose instead of sitting from nine-to-five bullshitting with your co-workers like Johnny Q. America, not giving a shit. Content with your paycheck and wondering if there's anything good on TV. Does anyone really believe in what they produce?"

"I don't even produce anything—I crunch numbers. In theory it is kind of fun, 'cause I like math, but at the end of a day, will all those papers mean anything?"

"If you believe in your company." I think we are starting to have a talk my sister Monica would love. She would come into it with all kinds of theories and try to show us up with all her knowledge.

"I think Eve's right," says Tabitha, "we should think about starting a magazine."

"Exactly what kind of magazine, though? Eve never really says." They both look at me.

"I guess just one that we would want to read," I suggest. "I mean one for people our age, not exactly kids anymore, but nowhere near adults."

"But making adult decisions."

"And pursuing the fabulous life," Tabitha adds.

"Right," I say, "although the fabulous life would be anything from the coolest club in New York to pursuing your dreams or having a weird, cool job. We'd be inspiring but not creepy. Fun but not fluffy. There'd be gossip and stuff, too, but articles that you wouldn't want to just skim, you know?"

"What kind of articles?" Tabitha is taking this seriously and so is Roseanne. I don't like being the focus of attention when I don't have things decided. It would be one thing if I had a good story, but now I'm just tossing out ideas.

"Articles that wouldn't make you say 'why bother?' when you finished reading them. I mean your occasional celebrity profile, but more of a lifestyle magazine, I guess, with stuff people want to read. Everything from like making it on your own to debunking advertising myths to joining the circus."

"The circus?"

"I don't know, Ro, forget it, I'm getting carried away. It's too ambitious."

"No, Mommy, you're doing it," says Tabitha. They both look at me, waiting to hear more, but I tell them I need another drink. I realize when I'm standing at the bar how excited I'm getting. I mean it's strange to actually let these ideas come out. When I get back to the table with our cosmopolitans, Roseanne is smiling at me like I've done something amazing.

"Is Tabby getting cigarettes?" She nods. "What's up?"

"It's a good idea, Eve, I'd read it."

"C'mon, it's just talk, besides, you'd write for it. You'd write the money and cooking sections." She starts laughing. "Anyway, it's drunk talk. I'm only just beginning to realize. Some girls get drunk and talk about the one that got away, not me, I want to start a magazine."

"You're no average woman, Eve Vitali." Roseanne gives me a kiss on the cheek.

"Perhaps you can write an exposé on the myth of the New York

Kiss.'' When Tabitha gets back, we smoke another pack of cigarettes and drink many more cosmopolitans. We do a little dancing,
even though it isn't that kind of place. Our friend the British bartender, Clive, encourages us, shouting, ''There you go, sweet-
hearts.'' I drink myself into oblivion and forget about the magazine. For a little while.

Rob is the only one in the elevator when I get in the next day.
Hungover, the only thing I had on my mind was getting to my
desk as quickly as possible. I am wearing my most comfy pair of
pants and pale lipstick that won't be too harsh against my color-
less, dehydrated skin. He raises an eyebrow at me. I lean against
the back wall of the elevator and wait for someone else to come
running in, screaming, ''Hold the elevator.'' Someone always
does, but not today. ''So, um, what's up?''

''Not much. How was Jacksonville?''

''Hot. I've been crazy busy since I got back.''

''So what are you doing in this elevator bank, reorganizing some
more people?'' He looks at me and somehow manages to make
me feel like a shit.

''I doubt you even cared that much, Eve. I'm sure you were
somewhere else during the whole thing. As usual.'' The ''as
usual'' kills me. I am too tired to get into it with him. Silence is
always a better approach in these situations. After a little while he
says, ''I miss you.''

''You miss me? But, you're 'crazy busy,' right? And I guess
that's the reason you didn't call? No time whatsoever.''

''Eve, c'mon.''

''C'mon, what? I thought we were seeing each other.''

''Eve, I just don't know if it's a good idea.'' I don't want to
hear this. I mean, I want to know what's up, but I don't want it
to be this. I still feel like he's into me, though. At least I've got
that on my side.

I watch the numbers ascending. We haven't stopped at a single
floor, but it's taking forever. It would be wonderful to be stuck in
the elevator with him, eventually we'd have to start hooking up.
There's got to be cameras in the elevator though, and he'd probably never go for it. Our rescue crew would watch encouragingly,
happy that we weren't freaking out.

We are two slow floors away from mine. Fuck it! I grab him
and sort of push him against the wall. I have to get on my tiptoes
and reach up. We wind up bumping chins, but he settles into the
kiss quick enough. I look him in the eyes right as we get to my

floor. I hold on to him daringly, the doors are about to open, but he doesn't push me away. If anything, he holds me closer.

"Let me know if you figure out whether or not it's a good idea." I get out of the elevator. I love feeling like I'm in a movie. I stop in the bathroom on the way to my desk to switch lipsticks. The color has definitely returned to my face.

I feel a little high until I head to the kitchen for my morning coffee. Everyone is gathered around whispering. I am not going to cater to this craziness, I've got my own life, my own agenda. I grab for my Prescott cup, but to my surprise, all the cups have been replaced by wretched cups that say *Breathe*. Wow! These people work fast.

"What do you think of that, Eve?" says Gary, my new best friend. "They must have put in that order at least three weeks ago. By the way, they've canceled today's meeting. So much for keeping us up to date on what's going on." Thankfully, a fellow disgruntled employee is right there to chime in with complaints. It's a *Yoga for Life*-er. I'm psyched that they can find a common bond. I sneak away.

This morning is already turning into too much of an emotional roller coaster. I need someone who can comfort me with their tone. I call my mom. It's been a while since I spoke to her. She hasn't been checking up on me that much. Maybe she thinks I'm growing up. I'm not sure if I like that. The phone rings a bunch of times before my dad picks up.

"Hey, Daddy. What are you doing home today?"

"Oh, you know, I just thought I'd take the day off." I hear him exhale cigarette smoke. I think the whole idea of phones makes him uncomfortable.

"So, is Mom around?" He exhales again.

"Actually, your mother is lying down."

"Why? Is she sick?"

"Allergies or something. I don't know." My father, typically uninvolved.

"Okay, Daddy, just tell her I called. No big deal. She can call me whenever. And tell her I hope she feels better."

"Okay, 'bye." Weird.

That afternoon something wonderful happens that, unfortunately, I can only attribute to my relationship with Rob King and the strangeness of the day. Apparently, Prescott gets a new staff member. She's not his direct assistant, but she's got something to do with arranging his schedule. She must have got my name off the e-mail that Sherman sent out regarding Rob being out of the office. This new coordinator or whatever dubious title she has, is obviously a dingbat, because she has included me on a list of people I don't recognize. She wants to arrange a meeting with us and Prescott to discuss our jobs and the future of Prescott Nelson Inc.

It's not like Herb is on it and I am just cc'ed as his assistant. No, I am on it with no assistant. This woman must think I am someone who deserves a meeting with Prescott, in May of all times. I call Tabitha. "Why do you torment me with the drink?"

"You do it to yourself, sweetheart."

"Next time I do this to myself, you need to take action. Aren't you hungover?"

"Well, I was until I mauled Rob King in the elevator and got an e from one of Prescott's assistants about meeting the man in May."

"You're doing too many of those tongue twisters you love to do. There are cameras in the elevators, I can't believe Rob let himself be mauled. Please tell me you are not meeting Prescott. Remember when he smiled at you?"

"All too well. It was the happiest day of my working life."

"I don't get this meeting, though."

"Neither do I. It's just a mistake. Eventually, they'll realize how low I am."

"Wait, so you're *not* going to meet with him?"

"Not if he wants to meet with a division leader. I can't just worm my way in."

"Why the hell not? You got an invite. Please, Eve, don't let me get too excited. Every time I talk I feel like I am going to throw up. Respond that you would love to go. C'mon, Eve, you somehow lucked into this. It's not even something you can be morally opposed to for whatever fucked reason you were opposed to the job at *Food and Fun*, this is just a fluke."

"I don't appreciate the job comment, Tabitha, especially when I didn't get it. And for the record, it wasn't the job I was opposed to, it was asking Rob for help."

"Well, Eve, looks like you are going to have deal with it while I go throw up." She hangs up on me. Nice.

I read the e-mail over again. It's funny how human error and simple language can bring a thrill to your life. Of course, I can't respond right away—that would be a tip-off. Maybe, most people do respond right away because it's Prescott and he commands respect. Maybe it's a tip-off if I *don't* respond right away. If I was a vice-president I would be in meetings all day, I wouldn't even check my e-mails, my assistant would. I wouldn't find out about this e-mail (although it would most likely be on the top of a stack) until tonight and then I would have to take some time to check my schedule and make sure everything was cool.

I will respond tomorrow. It doesn't stop me from reading the e-mail over and over again all day and imagining the response and then the meeting and then Prescott asking me to join his secret think tank, because I represent the confused post college Generation X that is so underrepresented at board meetings.

The next day, without too much analyzing or thought about the proper etiquette, I shoot off an e-mail to Prescott Nelson's confused coordinator asking her how May 16 would be. It's a week before my twenty-fourth birthday and I think it'll be lucky.

By the end of the day I have an e-mail back (I swear I hadn't even started to worry) that confirms my appointment for 3:00 p.m.

I print out the e-mail confirmation and vow to save the e-mail in its own special folder forever. I have proof now and there's no way they can stop me.

But, I have this weird nagging feeling all day. Everyone is uptight and on edge and I hate to think I feel this way, because of this whole "transition." Tabitha can't talk to me because the Big C is out sick and Roseanne is right in the middle of an audit, whatever that means. I call Monica, but she has no answering machine. It sucks.

I break down and try my mom again. My dad answers once again.

"Dad? You're home again? What's going on? How's Mom?"

"Eve—" I hear my dad exhaling smoke "—I think you better come home this weekend."

March

My father managed to give me no details about what was going on, just that my mom was okay and they didn't want or need me to come home before Friday. He put my mom on the phone. She sounded slightly feeble, but did her best to assure me that everything was really fine and they would tell me all about it on Friday. I couldn't get in touch with my sister all week, which wasn't very comforting. I imagined her camped out with Chuck somewhere, removed from all forms of civilization.

I pumped my dad for details in the car on the way home from the bus station. He wasn't saying a word, he was just chewing a lot of gum. I kept waiting for him to pull out a cigarette, but he didn't. Although I had never seen it before, I knew as soon as we pulled into the driveway that the van parked in front of the house was Chuck's.

"Monica's home? How long has Monica been home?" I try to ask my dad, but he is already barreling up to the house.

Chuck is the first person I see when I get in. He gives me this huge hug. Chuck isn't a small guy, he could have at least waited for me to take my backpack off.

"How are you doing, Eve? Are you hanging in there?" Chuck looks into my eyes like he's a counselor. Any minute now, he's going to pull out his guitar and start singing.

"So, where's my mom?" Then, I hear her come in with Monica behind her.

"Hi, honey." Mom hugs me. She feels skinnier. She keeps smiling at me. It feels forced. I have a sick feeling in my stomach.

"What's going on, Mommy, are you sick?"

"No, I'm going to be fine, just fine, I made snacks. You like artichoke dip right, Eve?" She scurries into the kitchen. I glare at Monica.

"How long have you been here?"

"Hi, Eve, how are you?"

"Cut the shit, Monica, since when?" Chuck starts to say something and Monica puts her hand on his shoulder.

"Wednesday." Wednesday? I turn to my father, who is fingering his shirt pocket. He would usually have his cigarettes there, but today he has none.

"How come I had to wait till Friday, but Monica was here on Wednesday?"

"Eve, don't be such a baby," shitty Monica says.

"Times like this can be very trying on families, but the important thing is that you stick together," shitty Chuck says. Thanks for the update. My dad opens a drawer.

"Dad, don't do it," squeals, Monica, "you are doing so well."

"What's going on, Dad? Why aren't you smoking?"

"Eve, it's a good thing. Why don't you leave him alone?" I haven't smacked my sister since I was seven years old, but I have a feeling I'm going to any minute. Of course, my mother, who is trying to harness the sun in her smile, comes back with her dip and some bread. Monica and I both reach to grab stuff out of her hands.

"I'm fine, I got it." My mom starts chattering away. She asks me about Roseanne.

"Roseanne's fine. Maybe I should have brought her, but I thought this was a family meeting." I stare at Monica and Chuck.

"Eve, grow up." I hate my sister. Now is the time to get in touch with my inner child. I clench my fist. My father clears his throat. We quiet down.

"Mom, can you tell me what's wrong?" I can tell by Monica's face that she knows already, which means—worse—Chuck knows already. It's easy for her to pretend to be mature and supportive when all her questions have been answered.

"Well, honey, first of all, I'm feeling fine, truly." She drops her voice an octave. "A while back I found a lump in my breast."

"What? When?"

"Well, it was just before Christmas."

"Just before Christmas? That was over two months ago! How come you didn't say a word to anyone?"

"Well," says my mom. Then I realize that she told Monica. I can't believe this. She told Monica two months ago. That means this stranger hippie jerk knew the status of my mother's health before I did. That stings. "Eve, we just didn't want to worry you, you've got a lot going on with your job."

"Oh, like I don't," says Monica, annoyed.

"Hey, at least someone let you in on this. So you could alert the hippie community and think about all the ways it affects your mental health."

"Eve, shut up!"

"Monica, can you even go to the bathroom without an audience?"

"What the hell is that supposed to mean?" Monica stands up, and I stand up, too.

"This is supposed to be a family thing, yet we have to have an audience. Mom doesn't even like saying the word 'breast' in front of Dad, let alone Art Garfunkel, here."

"Eve, you are out of control." I can tell my mom is trying to talk to us, but I'm too mad to stop yelling at Monica. Finally, Chuck, who gives the impression he is the embodiment of a Tibetan buddhist, yells "Hey!" loud enough to shock everyone, including my dad, who needs a cigarette now more than ever. We all turn to him.

"Eve, you've got a point. I would like to be considered a part of this family, but maybe it's best if you all deal with this on your own for a while. I'll be out in the van."

I manage a quiet, "Thanks." My parents go into the details of her lumpectomy and how she is getting chemo treatments now, but it's going to be a little while before they realize if all the cancer is gone.

Then it hits me, just how serious it is. It's the way my father rests his arm lightly around my mother's shoulder and how she kind of leans into him. They never really show that much affection. They always just seem to exist around each other, instead of for each other. Is she going to be okay? She has to be, she's my mom.

"I'm going to be okay, Eve. The doctors caught it just in time. They are very optimistic, but I'm not going to be myself for a while and I thought that now would be a good time to tell you." She puts her hands on my shoulders. "Are you okay, Eve?"

"I'm fine, Mom. I'm just worried about you." She smiles again. "Don't worry, I'm going to be fine." Easier said than believed.

I'm mad at my dad for not telling me. I try to stay clear of him all weekend, which usually isn't a problem, because he stays clear of me. But this weekend it seems like he is making the attempt to talk to me. Monica and I scowl at each other the whole time and seem to be in competition for who can be more doting. It's tough because my parents are enforcing celibacy on Chuck and Monica, so Monica and I have to sleep together in the den. She sticks me with the recliner. We argue over who is making each meal and Chuck steps in to be diplomatic. I should have known he would be like this when Monica told me he was once a social work student.

Chuck makes all these little schedules for how we should divvy up the responsibilities, right down to cutting carrots. I'd like to tell him to go fuck himself, but my mom seems to think it's great that we're all working together. She can see into the kitchen from her chair in the living room and she keeps saying, "My girls." It would be the perfect picture of familial bliss if I didn't hate all of them, except of course my mom. Every time I look at her I want to cry.

Monica takes the week off (yeah, so much to do, Monica, real full life). I take a personal day on Monday. Lorraine, who seems to have more and more work piling up, sounds annoyed about my timing. She takes two days when her dog vomits on her rug.

On Monday, Monica goes for a long drive with Chuck. My mom and I finally have a chance to chill and we play cards and watch soaps. But once we're alone, I feel like I'm walking on eggshells, like I don't really want to look at her. Her wrists seem really tiny to me. I can't believe they've always been that small.

Monday night Rob calls me at home. He called me in the city and Roseanne told him what was going on. Monica hovers around me in the kitchen as I'm talking to him. I'm so glad we aren't talking to each other, because I know it's killing her now.

"Are you doing okay, Ms. Vitali?" he asks after I explain the situation.

"I don't know, this is all too weird. My mom seems fine, like the doctors have got it all under control, but she's not herself. She's just different."

"I think stuff like this is always an adjustment. It's going to change her life *and* yours for a while. Maybe you should talk to her doctors." I can't believe he is being so awesome. I wish I could really enjoy it, but more than anything it's just nice to have someone that I can tell all my worries to. I certainly can't tell my parents and I don't want to tell Monica.

"What bothers me the most is that they just took care of it without ever telling me."

"Eve, sometimes, I think people tend to see you as this little self-sufficient being, who needs to have her space." What?

"I don't see that. I love having my space invaded, especially if it's done right."

"Yeah, and you always say the perfect thing to deflect it, too. You've always got that faraway look in your eye."

"Well, I'm not sure what that's supposed to mean, but I don't know if now is the best time to get into it. I've been exerting enough bad energy onto Monica, I don't think I have the strength to get pissy with you."

"Well, that's refreshing. Hey, want to have dinner tomorrow?"

"I'll have to see if I have the space. Don't call me, I'll call you."

"You are too much, Ms. Vitali." We start kidding around. It's all good—so what if he's the harbinger of doom for all Prescott Nelson employees? They would understand if only they had him invade their space.

On Tuesday, my mom doesn't get out of bed to say goodbye to me. I come into her room and she raises herself up on her arms to kiss me. I can tell she wants to get up, but she can't. The worst is she never stops smiling. I mutter a goodbye to Monica as I collect my bag from the den, but she turns over into the couch. Whatever.

My dad is out in the car to drive me to the station. He has one of those no smoking devices that looks like a tampon between his lips. I can't believe my dad doesn't have more self-respect. Chuck jumps out of his van as I'm about to get in the car.

"Hey, Eve, have a great day at work." He walks over to me. Is he going to—? Yes, sure enough, another bear hug. I can't deal.

"Thanks, Chuck, have a great rest of the week."

"And listen, if there is anything you need to talk to me about, I'm here." I want to think, Eww, gross, why would I talk to him? but I give him another hug. This whole thing is making me soft.

"Thanks," he says, "I'll give that one to Monica. Peace."

"Not a bad guy," my dad says, sucking on his tampon. I can't believe Chuck, with his hippie band and his Birkenstocks, is winning my sweet, unsuspecting family over. I'm becoming a victim, too. My dad drops me off at the station and I feel like he wants to say something important so I wait there.

"Hey, Dad, it's okay. I'll call, okay?"

"Yeah, right, take care, kid." I give him a kiss and bound up the stairs to the bus.

Thankfully, the journey isn't too bad.

My mother calls me during the day to explain that she's fine, she was just a little tired this morning. Monica is out with Chuck grocery shopping (yeah right!).

"Honey, you've got such a great job. I got beautiful flowers from someone named Rob King. You know him?''

No surprise, Sherman is playing Adult Tetris when I go up to see Rob. I can see Rob is on the phone; we smile at each other, but I'm working on my relationship with Sherman. I stand near his desk. He jumps when he realizes I'm next to him.

"Hey, relax, Sherman. It's a good thing you got the volume turned down. That's usually half the fun, right?'' Sherman isn't amused. He looks nervously at Rob.

"Hi, Rob." I wave. I run into his office. I wish I could just shut the blinds and throw my arms around him, but I behave with the utmost decorum. I sit in the chair facing him at his desk. I only hike my skirt up a little. I've got class.

"Ms. Vitali, we meet again.''

"It sure looks that way. My mother loved her flowers. Thanks, that was nice.''

"Hey, the way to a girl's heart is through her mom, I hear. How is she?''

"Fine, I guess. I don't know. I don't want to talk about it.'' He shakes his head like he was expecting that.

"Well, um, you can.''

"I know, thanks. Are we still on for dinner tonight?''

"Yeah, where should we go?''

"I had a hankering for that cold chicken marsala special you make.'' Then he smiles and I know it's going to be a great night.

I offered Rob one sexual favor after another to have him help me get out of Mabel's wretched change workshop class. Tabitha told me I needed to start making this relationship work for me, but I informed her that I was just happy to be getting the booty again. This was proven by the way Rob collected on all bribes, without actually holding up his part of the deal. He found other ways to make me happy. As far as my love life was concerned, it was a blissful week.

In the meantime, I planned Roseanne's birthday bash. I invited Pete, Todd, Tabitha, Tabitha's Mr. March (Blake) and Adrian. I have Tabitha call Adrian. I am just excited that Pete is going to come. I don't tell Roseanne who's going to be there, just that we are going out. Tabitha and I chip in to get her a dress from miu miu.

We drink (a lot) at our apartment as we get ready. We turn the music on really high because we never hear a peep out of our neighbors, so who cares. Roseanne keeps twirling around in her dress and begging us to tell her where we are going. Tabitha keeps saying "American Eclectic" over and over again because that's how *NY By Night* described this hot spot. Roseanne is frantically searching Zagat's, hoping for a sign.

Tabitha slices her thumb with Roseanne's boning knife as she's cutting up a lime. All the blood makes me woozy. Tabitha is already too drunk to care, so she holds up her finger and says, "Look, I'm devolving."

We catch a cab down to Soho. This restaurant is pretty flashy. Adrian, Pete, and Todd are already at the bar. I'm glad to see Todd made it, which means Pete has no reason to beg off. They've been drinking and I wonder if Adrian has heard Todd's theory on the gay man, yet. We all exchange New York Kisses. Adrian is putting on a good show and kisses me quickly. Roseanne keeps her arm around Pete. I hope she gets her birthday present from him.

"I hope Blake shows up," says Tabitha. The sight of physical affection between anyone makes her need to have her own man present. Blake is some British actor.

"I hope Matt shows up," says Adrian. Of course I haven't heard anything about him and I guess he's being tight-lipped with Tabitha, too. Tabitha looks at me, waiting to see if I mention Rob.

"I invited him, but he's working late."

"Who's that?" Todd asks. I am sitting between him and Roseanne.

"It's Eve's sugar daddy!" Roseanne gets too excited. I hoist up her neckline. It's her birthday, I guess she's entitled.

"Is that what you like, Eve?" Todd looks so serious. I don't know what to say.

"He's not even rich, they're just being stupid."

"Oh, is this the guy that didn't come to the New Year's Eve party?" Why must Todd be such a dick? I have to believe it's just because he's still holding a torch for me.

"He happened to be away on business that day." Blake shows up and so does Adrian's boyfriend, Matt. Todd bumps my knee under the table.

"All a farce, trust me."

"Well, you *are* the expert on the gay man."

We've been ordering bottles of wine left and right and I'm starting to lose track of how much I'm drinking. I notice that it seems like everyone is kind of paired up, which puts me in with Todd, which is totally weird. I wonder if he notices it, too.

We decide to go dancing, we are all drunk enough to think this a good idea. I borrow Tabitha's phone to leave Rob a message. I half expect to get Sherman, but it's too late on a Friday. Todd is listening to me.

I hop in the cab with Pete, Roseanne and Todd. Adrian and I have been staying clear of each other all night. I wonder what he's told his new man about me. I sit in the front with the driver and ask him how his night is going. He's from Tunisia. He tells me he owns several cabs, he's an entrepreneur. Maybe I should set him up with Tabitha.

When we get to the place Tabitha is waiting for us. The rest already got in because Matt knew the bouncer. "I think he's a keeper," Tabitha says, referring to Matt. "Did you know he's a party planner?"

We know we'll have no trouble getting in, but because we're with the boys we have to wait on the line. Tabitha sweet-talks the bouncer. He is stoned, but she whispers something in his ear. He smiles.

"Okay guys, you five." He lifts up the rope and waves us in, as only a bouncer can do. Tabitha tells us she'll be in in a minute. The bouncer yells in to the cashier, pointing at Roseanne, "Comp this girl in the black dress!"

Blake scored a big table, with cushy couches, which Roseanne plops into immediately. Adrian and Matt are already dancing. Matt's pretty hot. Tabitha comes out holding a big drink tray covered with Krispy Kreme donuts and burning candles. It just might be the cutest thing I've ever seen. Adrian and Matt jump behind her singing "Happy Birthday" and we all join in louder than the music.

"How did you get these?" I ask Tabitha after Roseanne blows out the candles.

"I told the cabbie to step on it," Tabitha says, starting her second donut.

"Let's dance," says Roseanne, pulling us both onto the dance floor. Okay, I know I'm drunk because I don't give a shit, I'm flailing my arms and getting low and before I know it's a reggae song. When I look up, I realize that the girls are now dancing with their respective partners and Todd is still at the table with a cuddling Adrian and Matt.

I gesture Todd over and he puts his hand on his chest and

mouths, "Me?" I nod and wink at him. We laugh. When he comes over, I dance around him thinking I can shock him a little, but he grabs me and starts moving like he's in control. It's just like when I was dancing with Joe at the Christmas party. I feel myself letting go, but Todd is looking into my eyes and I can't help but be embarrassed.

"Where did you learn to dance like this?" He shrugs. I am flirting with Todd. This is too easy and it's not fair to Todd. But, I'm such a sucker for attention. There is a way he has of looking at me that like wraps up all this history. Like I'm still the girl who lived down the hall from him freshman year, only much much more. It's not easy to have someone hang on your every word, except he's dancing with me like he doesn't care, like he's sure of himself, like he knows he can wow me. He is.

We shut the place down. We've all bought Roseanne at least two shots each and she has her head in Pete's lap. I am going to have to give her (them?) my bedroom.

Adrian and Matt are ready to go home. Matt gives me a big hug before he gets in the cab. He's super smooth, I doubt he'll remember my name tomorrow, unless of course Adrian rants about what a bitch I am. Adrian lowers himself to give me another official New York Kiss, much like you might give a co-worker you absolutely despise. Whatever. I wave goodbye to the cab.

Tabitha wants to stop at Cafeteria for some late-night grub, so I drop Rosie and Pete off at our place and walk down 7th Avenue with Todd. Everything is sort of fuzzy, I can't really remember the cab ride. At some point I realize we are holding hands. I don't know why and I let go as soon as we get to the restaurant.

"I shouldn't be eating this late," I keep saying. I could swear Tabitha is giving Blake a hand job under the table. What's going on? I am going to try calling Rob again. Wait! I can't do it in front of Todd.

"Tabitha, want to hit the bathroom?"

"Yeah, I need to wash my hands." She smiles at Blake. I can't believe her.

In the bathroom, I try Rob's numbers, home and work, but I keep getting the numbers mixed up. I'm having trouble seeing. Tabitha keeps chattering about her new lipsticks, she mixed two together and she loves the way it looks.

"What are you going to do, Eve, go all the way up to his place? You're in no condition to do that. I thought you were working it with Todd."

"No, we are just friends. I feel sick."

"Oh, Mother of God, are you okay?" Tabitha starts splashing water in my face getting it all over the sink and my shirt. Never let a drunk person assist another drunk.

"Okay, okay, Tabitha, I got it. Relax." She is holding on to the sink.

"Let's eat our burgers and go." Shit! I totally forgot about the burger. I can't eat mine. I take two bites and give it to Todd.

"I got to go," Tabitha, says throwing some money on the table and grabbing Blake. "It's 5:30."

We watch from the window as she hops in a cab. We get the check and stumble the five blocks back home. Todd lies down on the couch. I pull off my shoes and he starts to rub my feet. I'm just going to sit here a minute.

I wake up to Todd moving his hands over my back. Shit! Where are we? Okay on the couch. We're still in our clothes. What the hell? Things start coming back to me. After he rubbed my feet I said that I just wanted to lay down on the couch for a minute. I must have passed out. Then, at some point, I remember he got up and got a blanket and he came back and lay down next to me.

What the fuck am I doing? Oh, my God! He keeps rubbing my back. I half open an eye, and he looks really cute. He's holding me so tight and it's nice. But, why?

I know if I get up my head will be pounding, so I lay there. I entertain the idea of hooking up with him. More and more of the night keeps coming back to me. I think about how we were dancing, how much fun it was. But I got a man, right? I never got in touch with Rob. But if I kiss Todd now, that's a big deal. He likes me, but it's not a good idea. It will fuck everything else, besides, he lives in Atlanta. I am not going to do a long distance thing and I can't cheat on Rob. I don't even know what our status is, last month I was ready to use the big commercialized L word with him, and now Todd's hands are so nice.

It's too much for me. Too many drunk thoughts. I go back to sleep.

When I next open my eyes, Todd is staring at me. It's pretty bright in the living room. I feel sort of nauseated. I should have had water before I went to bed.

"Hey," he says.

"Hi." This is too weird. He tugs my hair and then we sort of have to disengage. Now we're sober there's no excuse for this. "What time is it?"

"It's like 3:00."

"So, last night was pretty crazy, huh?" He's testing the waters. This is why it's bad to get involved (or even think about getting involved) with your friends. You have to act stupid and make like everything was the result of some drunken mistake.

"Yeah, from what I can remember of it." I'd say that puts me in the clear.

"Hey, guys." Roseanne comes out wearing my robe. Todd and I sit up.

"Wow, you guys are still in your clothes, when did you get in?"

"Pretty late," I say, ignoring her look. "I didn't really think I could make it up to the sleep loft."

"Good plan. I was totally sick this morning." Pete comes out like the cat who ate the canary. I'm just glad we didn't get as far as they did. That's got to mean some super banal conversation. Pete seems a little more talkative than usual. Apparently, he had water last night.

"So, should we get a birthday breakfast?"

This of course turns out to be an early dinner. Then we get a video and crash until Tabitha calls us at 8:30. She wants us up and out by 10:00. She is cracking the whip because Matt is hosting a party for some company at a club in midtown. Not my idea of fun, but Tabitha promises that everything will be free. I doubt Todd wants to spend his weekend in New York asleep on our living room floor watching TV. Pete wants to head back to his house to change and shower and he takes Todd with him. We all agree to meet up at the place at 10:30 and screw Tabitha if she gets pissed.

The sketchy thing is Todd and I kind of stagger out so Roseanne can walk Pete down and they have a chance to have a proper goodbye. "You're definitely going later, right?" Todd asks.

"Yeah, definitely." I smile. What am I committing myself to? This is weird. It's like he wants to kiss me, but he goes downstairs. If only Rob would call me.

Roseanne returns from her Big Red kiss goodbye with Pete. She is glowing. I laugh at her. "Is this how it feels to be twenty-four?"

"No." She does this little twirl. "Being twenty-four makes me feel sick to my stomach. Or maybe it was all that tequila, but this, this is how it feels to finally get the goods from the guy. Shoot, I'm starting to talk like you. I can't wait to see him later. What's going on with you...and Todd?"

"Nothing. We just passed out, that's all."

*   *   *

This party is like a million other parties we've been to—a bunch of people we don't know, most of whom we don't care to know, while we scarf up as much free food and drink as we can get our hands on.

On most nights, I'm happy to just be chilling with my group, but tonight I feel off my game somehow. I don't have any bad premonitions, but just this sad feeling, like everyone around me is happy and I can't find it. Todd is into me, asking me how I'm feeling and telling me he likes my outfit. I just want to be left alone. Plus, Tabitha's friend Nicole is there and I have to be all fake, like I give a shit. Todd keeps saying things that everyone finds hysterical. I can't stand to hear Nicole laughing at him. I excuse myself and go to one of the phone booths. The best thing about cell phones is that there is rarely a line for the public phones anymore. I want to call Rob, but I forgot to bring any change so I sit there.

Tabitha comes by on the way to the bathroom. If I thought any quicker I would have picked up the phone and pretended to be talking, but instead I look like a dork. "Hey, what are you doing, Eve?"

"Nothing, Tabitha, I'm fine, really, I just wanted to be alone, you know."

"What's wrong?"

"Nothing, just getting a little sick of all the people, probably because I partied too much last night." It's always easier to blame everything on alcohol.

"Yeah, we're leaving soon. Maybe hit another bar, if you're up for it. Are you worrying about your mom?"

"Look I just want to sit in here for a minute. Quietly." I am the biggest bitch ever, but Tabitha, who once held that title, accepts it. It is so unlike her to be nurturing. I sit there for a while watching all the skinny girls in tight black dresses go by me. I used to think those bars on the Upper East Side were all full of people who looked the same way, but tonight it seems I'm crowded by cool people clones. I can't stay in here anymore, I don't want to be alone.

When I get back to my group of cool people clones, it's only Todd and Tabitha who notice I've been gone. I can't blame Rose-anne because it's apparent that she and Pete are getting along really well; I'm not going to bust up their groove with my unexplained depression. Todd puts his hand on my shoulder and squeezes.

"I think we're going to go somewhere quieter," he yells in my ear.

"Cool."

We head to a bar nearby. Among all the dives, we head straight for the most upscale bar/restaurant. The hostess tells us we can sit at a large round table even though we aren't getting food.

I feel like I can relax here, because now it's just us. Again, we all seem to be paired up. This time it's Roseanne and Pete, Nicole and her new man Drew, and Tabitha and Blake. Once again, Todd and I are paired up together.

"So, how's work treating you?"

"Like a dog treats a fire hydrant. We're going through all these changes. I don't even know what they mean—and honestly I don't even care. We're 'reorganizing.'"

"Have you let anyone see your stuff?" Great question, Todd.

"Well, not in a while. At first I sent article proposals to like every magazine, but lately I haven't exactly been proactive. They all use the freelancers they know. Anyway, it's tough to break in."

"Yeah, I'm really glad I'm not creative. I just get a task and do it." It occurs to me that Todd sees me as a creative type, because of all those articles I used to write for our school newspaper. Anyone who met me in New York would see me as just another schmuck living on another stupid dream. I don't see why I can't find the positive tonight but I can't. Pete hands me a drink.

"Todd, sometimes I sit at work and I can feel my brain slowly being sucked out of my head." I'm getting sadder and sadder. I sense that he can see it.

"Yeah, but it's like the song. If you can make it here you'll make it anywhere."

"I'm not sure if I'm actually *making* it."

"Yes, you are. You've got a cool apartment, you earn a good amount of money and you go to all these cool parties. You're successful, especially for your age." Todd is talking to me like I'm about to jump off a cliff. That makes me even more depressed. I look away from him. Maybe I need to find another phone booth.

"Eve, I'm sorry about your mom." I turn around and look at Tabitha and Roseanne. I can just imagine them sitting Todd and everyone I know down and saying, "Now, Eve's a little testy because her mom is sick. Let's just carry on like nothing's wrong and get her as drunk as possible."

I'm about to confront the whole lot of them for treating me like a child, when the waiter comes back over to us and says to Pete, "Do you think this is a good tip that you gave the bartender?"

"It's three dollars. All she did was open some beers and make two drinks."

"You are not supposed to sit here if you are just drinking."

"The hostess told us we could," Tabitha says.

"Well you aren't supposed to and this tip is ridiculous."

"Well, that's the only tip she's getting," says Tabitha. She turns to us. "We're leaving after this. So much for friendly atmosphere."

"Good." The waiter walks away.

"I didn't think I had to leave much more of a tip than that," Pete says. Something like this could force him into another bout of silence.

"You don't," Roseanne says, obviously worried about the same thing.

"Excuse me." I get up and walk over to the waiter. I'm not sure what comes over me.

"What the hell was that? You don't have to be so rude. We were told we could sit there and now you're being a dick because we won't order food from you? That's shitty." The waiter is unmoved. "I have never been so insulted at a restaurant in my life. I have friends visiting, and it's another friend's birthday. Let me see the manager."

He sends the manager over. The asshole manager keeps insisting that we weren't supposed to sit there and I'm getting louder and louder, demanding an apology.

"Whatever! I'm filing a complaint against this place," I say, and stomp away. Back at the table Adrian and Matt have joined us. Tabitha is filling them in.

"Wow, Eve, you went nuts!" Tabitha smiles at me. The manager comes back.

"Look," he says to me, "can we get you all some appetizers?"

"We just ate delicious food. I want our money back for these drinks and I want that asshole to apologize." The manager walks away shaking his head. The hostess comes over to us now, it's like a receiving line.

"I'm talking to the owner. I want an apology." I get up and the manager directs me to a woman sitting on a barstool.

"I want our money back and I want the asshole waiter to apologize."

"I'm not giving you your money back."

"Your dicky waiter insulted my friends over a tip he and the bartender obviously didn't deserve. I have never been so insulted in my life. What about customer service? That obviously means nothing to you. Your staff is a bunch of idiots."

"Miss, that's your opinion." Now, I'm seething. I'm staring at her and she has to look away. I would give me a refund, just because I would know that I'm losing control.

"Fine, I hope you're doing everything right at this restaurant because I'm going to file a ton of complaints. I'm going to call the Health Department and my favorite, the Better Business Bureau."

"Do it!"

"I will!" I go back to the table. My friends are laughing and applauding, even Adrian, but I'm mad. I grab my jacket. "Let's go."

I let them go out of the restaurant first, taking a long time putting my jacket on. Only Todd is waiting for me. There's a vase of flowers on the bar and I grab it, tossing the flowers onto the floor. It's heavy. Todd doesn't say a word. We just start walking.

In a second the asshole waiter is outside. He puts his hand on my arm.

"Let go of me!"

"Hey, buddy, just relax," Todd says. He puts his arm around me, tugs me close.

"Now you are stealing, I'm going to call the police. Call the police!" He yells to another waiter who's watching from outside the restaurant. "Give that back."

"Call the police. I want you to." I look right into his eyes. I am not giving the vase back. Nothing has given me such a purpose in quite some time. Both he and Todd tighten their grip around me. I tighten up on the vase. My friends have stopped now, they are farther up the street. The manager comes out.

"She is stealing, I told her I would call the police," the waiter explains. I know the manager is looking at me, but I don't take my eyes off the waiter. We are staring each other down.

"Call them. I want you to. I've got a lot to tell them, too."

"Look," says the manager, doing a good job of assessing all the stories I might tell, "she wants the vase, let her have it."

I am still glaring at the waiter. Slowly he lets go of me and I nod. I have won this small, empty victory. I have the vase.

When they go back inside, Todd puts his hand softly where the waiter had his. He looks into my hardened face. I must look so angry. "Eve, are you okay?" His voice is so quiet. I nod, quickly. "No, Eve, I mean, *are you okay?*"

I take a deep breath in and when I let it out Todd is holding me. I know if I keep exhaling I'll start sobbing. My body is so tense. I can't let it go, but Todd is trying. He is trying to rub some happiness back into me. I pull away. I have to. He pushes my hair back and kisses my forehead. "Eve."

"Todd, I can't."

"You don't have to do anything, Eve." I don't want to think about what he's saying, what he is offering me. Roseanne calls to me from up the street.

"I'm fine," I yell back weakly.

"You've got a phone call," Tabitha says, holding up her phone. It's got to be Rob. I look at Todd. He has already pulled away a little. Tabitha and I walk toward each other and meet in the middle. She hands me the phone. I have to keep walking in circles, because I'm having trouble getting a signal.

"I've been trying to get in touch with you. I thought this was the wrong number," Rob says through static.

"I think the battery's low. What are you up to?"

"Nothing. Been working. Are you in any condition to come over?" No.

"Yeah, I'll catch a cab now." I look at all my friends except Todd. They are still waiting for an explanation. I hand Roseanne the vase. "Happy Birthday, girl. I'll get you some flowers tomorrow."

"Are you okay?"

"Yeah, I'm fine. I'm going to go uptown." Everyone looks at me a little skeptically. "I'm fine, everybody. Nothing to see here. Have a good rest of the night."

I get a cab right away. I don't look at Todd until the cab starts pulling away, but when I do, when I see how disappointed he is in me, I sink into my seat and cry. I hope Yuval will understand why I'm not talking to him.

The doorman lets me right up. Rob opens the door smiling. I don't let him say a word to me. I just start kissing him. We wind up bumping around on the floor.

"Do you want some water?" he asks as we're lying there.

"No, I just want to go to bed."

"You're a little fiend tonight, Ms. Vitali. I have to check one thing on my computer. I'll be in before you fall asleep." I gather my clothes and throw on one of his T-shirts. I lie down, waiting, trying not to think about tonight or the way Todd held on to me all last night. I want to be awake when Rob comes in, but it doesn't happen. I am asleep when I feel his side of the bed sink down.

The next day I bring Roseanne a bunch of flowers when I get home. She tells me that Todd left on an early plane to Atlanta. He said to say goodbye.

Try as I might to reschedule, Mabel winds up getting me into her change workshop. Gary, Lorraine, and two women from *Yoga for Life* are in my "class." Elise was supposed to be here, too, but apparently she's on maternity leave. How's that for an excuse? If only I had some forethought.

We do some stupid team building exercise. Mabel was really pissed, because we were supposed to be split up into two teams of three, but instead it was three and two. Gary and I were a team. We had to work on some kind of weird magnet construction. Mabel kept coming over with pointers. It was ridiculous.

I did my best to help out Gary. Ever since the day in the conference room, I've felt like he needs a little special care. The other day in the recently enlarged Staff Meeting, I found myself buttering a bagel for him.

When we finish constructing our magnet, which seems to take an eternity, Mabel gushes. She doesn't do a sweeping "you guys are great" gush. She looks into everyone's eyes and tells us how wonderful we are for working together and "recognizing this exercise."

The next task we have is to sit around and just shoot the shit about how we are about to be affected by the new magazine. Mabel doesn't want anyone to feel forced to speak, but she reminds us repeatedly that this is "our forum." Gary barely looks up from his chair. Lorraine and the two women from *Yoga for Life* have no trouble dutifully coming up with changes in their everyday lives.

To every gripe, Mabel nods as if she's never heard anything so true. "That's huge," she says over and over as she writes down each of the complaints. I got to hand it to this lady, I may be able to ridicule her in my thoughts, but when she's around, I honestly believe everything she says. I know she wants Gary and me to speak, because of the way she keeps looking at us with an inviting smile. Gary doesn't even look up, but I feel the pressure of Mabel's pearly whites.

I search my mind for possibilities. Why do I really care about this merge? Maybe because I wanted to hear it from Rob first and I didn't. That's not a good one. Honestly, I wish I had more ties to these people. Truthfully, I do care. I just don't care about my job. I've settled into it now. Shit! But what if the change means I have to do more yucky administration work, order more lunches, dole out more supplies? Now that Elise is on maternity leave, what if they don't get a temp? What if they give it all to me, and by the time Elise comes back they forget to redistribute? Oh, my God! Am I still going to be here in three months? That is so depressing!

"So is there anyone else who has any other issues to bring up in this safe environment?" She's looking right at me. I shouldn't fight it anymore, but what do I say? I hate it here and can't wait to get out?

"Well." I take a big swallow, I suddenly feel like I'm back in a college discussion section after not going to the lecture all semester. Shit. "I'm not concerned about anything specific, but just change in general. Change is frightening."

I swear I think Mabel is going to come out of her skin. She told us from the beginning that there were no right answers, that she just wanted to "capture" our feelings so that we could talk about it in the "safe environment." When I voice my answer, she clasps her hands together and her eyes almost roll back in her head. I have a brief disturbing image of her having an orgasm.

"Eve, yes," she says. "I think you've really got something there. That 'change' is an ugly word for everyone. Sometimes we're not exactly sure what the 'changes' are going to be." Keep in mind that she is pausing after every fifth word so that she can make eye contact with everyone except Gary, who still isn't looking up. She is not making those quotation marks in her hands, but intoning her voice so we know that if we get an e-mail transcript, we will find quotation marks around these words.

"What Eve just said is huge. She's really captured all our fears, and the big fear that is change. Change of the 'knowns,' our everyday responsibilities. Even scarier, change of the 'unknowns,' those things that we are only aware of on the peripheral. I really want to thank Eve for speaking to that."

My grandmother has an expression for all of this and that is "gobbledygook" and I know that when my grandmother said it there would be no quotes around it. But, I still feel like the golden child for saying the "hugest" answer. I wink at Lorraine, who laughs. She's probably dreaming of her dogs right now.

Anyway, Mabel figures that my huge answer is a great way to

end this workshop, we all have private meetings with her this afternoon where we'll touch on more of these "knowns" and "unknowns." I tap Gary on the shoulder, he looks up at me, teary-eyed.

I walk back to my cube with Lorraine, who tells me that upper management seems to have a whole new plan for administration, feeding into my fear that I'm going to have a lot more to do.

"It might be an exciting time for you, Eve, you might get a lot more responsibility, even though you are afraid of change."

"Oh, Lorraine, that's all so ridiculous, but honestly I don't want more administrative duties."

"I know you want to write." Lorraine doesn't get it. She thinks I'm ridiculous and fickle. Lorraine is from an older school that believes one should be happy to have a job.

When the time comes for me to have my meeting with Mabel I go down to the "space" she's set up on the floor between our offices and the YFL offices. She smiles radiantly when she sees me. Now might not be the best time to ask her what exactly she does and how she managed to find someone to pay her for looking so sincere.

"Eve, how are you?"

"I'm okay."

"Yes, I know it's an adjustment, but you are on the right track, by facing up to the changes and your fear of them. You are one very young woman." Wow! I could really get to like Mabel, she's not all bad. "Where exactly did you see yourself going with your job? How do you feel that's going to be affected by the merge?"

"Well, I don't know. I guess it wasn't quite going the way I wanted it to." Mabel nods, I know she understands better than Lorraine ever could. "I suppose now I feel like I'm going to get stuck with more administrative duties and then, you know, never do what it is I want, which is write."

"Well, Eve, I think the most important thing you are going to have to do is to challenge yourself about writing. This new magazine will be good for you, there are going to be a lot more opportunities."

"It's just hard because everyone is so depressed."

"Luckily, no one got fired. Unfortunately we've been doing these types of—" she pauses as if searching for the proper word (I want to offer "massive overhauls") "—transitions for the past two weeks, and we'll continue to do them. There have been a lot of casualties, but certain changes have been made because those people were no longer serving the brand. You need to make your-self a beacon of this positivity that you possess, your courage will be an example to others. You may be a little younger, but, you aren't afraid. And another thing—'' Mabel's lip starts to quiver ''—I know you care about the brand.''

"Well, yes." At this moment I do. I care about the brand more than anything. There are possibilities here for me, stuff I never dreamed. I am equipped to deal with all of the issues. It is my "career." I want to tell Mabel about how Prescott smiled at me. And that when I meet him, he will see all my qualities and how much I love the brand.

"Oh, Eve, our work has only just begun. I am going to go back to Herb and to Lev, who is the new editor for *Breathe,* and impress upon them the talent that's being wasted here. I commit that to you, if you commit to me that you will not give up until you feel that they have heard you." She waits for me to say something. I feel like we're about to get married.

"Uh, well, yes, Mabel, I do."

"Thank you, Eve." Mabel stands up, which is my cue to stand. She shakes my hand vigorously. I think I see a halo around her or a ray of light. I know she is going to go forth and champion me. As I turn to go, she is still smiling at me, amazed by my bravery. Mabel has instilled something in me that I never imag-ined. This could be what being in love feels like. Mabel and I have committed to each other to further me along in my career. Maybe Mabel is love. She is certainly an angel.

I barely notice the armed guards that are on my floor when I get back to my desk, I'm still kind of gliding. I sit down and start to dial Tabitha's number. Wait! Maybe Tabitha isn't ready to deal with my bravery and my long-hidden brand love. Poor Tabitha! Gary comes up to me as I am gloating at my desk. When I see him, I know it's a test for me, I have to be a beacon.

"You see, Eve, you see how they lie? I knew it. They said no one was fired. Eve, they've fired Lorraine."

"What!" He's got to be lying. "I just talked to...never mind." I go to Lorraine's office past the guards and sure enough, most of her office is in a box and she is packing up the pictures of her dogs.

"Lorraine," I say hesitating, "what's going on?"

"Well," she says, sniffling, but in some kind of haze, "I'm fired. They want to make some administrative changes. Don't ask me who is going to be the coordinator. Maybe you'll get a promotion.''

''No.'' I shake my head, not really understanding. ''No! Lorraine, it's not fair.'' She smiles at me. It's probably the most ridiculous thing anyone has said to her today.

''It's okay, Eve.'' She says this like she's talking to a small child, which I can't help but feeling like. I'm an asshole. ''I might be better off. I hated the commute anyway. It'll be okay. I'll call you.''

I nod as she kisses my cheek and rubs my shoulder. She is comforting me, when I'm not the one who got fired. I'm just the one who was stupid enough to believe them. She leaves the floor with the guards. Guards? God, I can't believe this. Like Lorraine was going to fight them or something. I wonder who fired her.

Suddenly I realize who ultimately must have known about it, who ultimately sat there and let it happen. I hurry down to the lobby and then back up in the other elevator bank (why can't anything be simple?).

Sherman tries to stop me, but it's now or never. I fling open the door and he is sitting at his desk with a guy. They are speaking very seriously.

''What? Are you firing him, too?''

''Eve, what's going on? Calm down.'' Then, he looks at his watch and nods his head.

''What? You knew what time it was going to happen? I can't believe this.''

''Frank, can you give us a moment?'' Frank had already stood up, uncomfortably.

''Yeah, Frank, just be happy you're leaving with your job.'' When Frank's gone, Rob motions for me to sit. I stand.

''C'mon, Eve, don't get carried away. Do you have any idea who that was?''

''Carried away? What the fuck, Rob?''

''Eve, what do you want me to say? You're acting like a child.''

''I just can't believe you could do this.''

''Eve, I didn't do it. I don't know who you think I am or what you think I could have stopped. Will you just sit down? Please.''

''I prefer to stand.'' I can't believe I date this guy.

''Look, I assess situations, that's all.''

''On paper! You assess them on paper! You don't know about the people!''

''Theoretically, you're right, that's the way it's done.''

"It's people, people and their jobs, their life, Rob!"

"Okay, everything is not as black and white as you want it to be, Eve. I'm sorry. This is business. Someday, you'll understand."

"How did Lorraine impede the business process? Why did you say no one was getting fired? Are there more?" Rob swallows and stares at me. When he speaks to me again, his voice is quiet.

"Eve, I don't want to fight with you. I don't like this whole situation. C'mon, will you just sit, please?" I shrug and sit down. "Now, I agree it was wrong for them to say that no one was getting terminated. I make recommendations, Eve, and that wasn't one of my recommendations. Firing Lorraine was somebody else's call. They needed to find a job for someone Lev wanted to bring over."

"That's ridiculous, she could sue."

"Well, only if you spread it around, which I wish you wouldn't. I've spoken to you in confidence. These things happen in business. It wasn't my call, but, Eve, even if I had made that decision that wouldn't make me a bad guy. You're infuriated with me and I don't think that's fair. It's been an issue with us from the beginning. Maybe it's time to..."

"What? Now are you going to break up with me?"

"Eve, you react to everything I do, like it's some testament to how I feel about you. It isn't all about you, you know. I really shouldn't be involved with you. For a lot of reasons, but mostly because you don't get the business part of this. You think these things make people awful and they are unfortunate, but it's business, it happens."

"Then Mabel gets sent in for spin control. Maybe she can put a better spin on our split. Maybe she can transition me out of this. Make me a beacon for solitude."

"Damn! Stop being so bitter. Half the time, I don't even know where you are."

"What is that supposed to mean?"

"Look, one issue at a time please. What is upsetting you so much?"

"I don't know, it just doesn't seem fair. I know it makes me sound like a child. I hate this. I actually believed for five minutes today that the company wasn't bad. I believed in the brand."

"Oh, that's right, you had your meeting with Mabel today."

"Yeah, that woman is unbelievable." We smile at each other, it's nice for a second. I (of course) can't let it last. "You see, it bugs me that you know that stuff, when I had my meeting, when Lorraine got fired. It's hard to deal with.''

"You could forget about it, pretend I'm unemployed." He cocks an eyebrow.

"How would you explain all the late dinners and the nice apartment?" I can't believe we're talking calmly for a moment. It's probably just a trick to disarm me that he learned from Mabel. Sherman buzzes him about a meeting. Rob looks disappointed that he has to go.

"You see why we can never pretend you're unemployed?" I'm trying to make light of the situation. Rob stands up and looks upset.

"God, Eve, it's so hard to argue with you. Half of me wants to tell you to just grow up and the other half thinks you should feel this way, that you shouldn't accept any less. My advice to you is to try and work for yourself somehow." He stands up and gets his papers together. I start to move away from the door, but he shakes his head a little and grabs some of my hair between his fingertips. If only he wasn't so cute. "Eve, I know you think I'm evil now, but I don't know how to make sense out of this. I think you need someone else.''

"Oh, sure, make this all about me." He shakes his head.

"You always have to make a joke. I can't even tell if it really bothers you. I can't tell what really upsets you.''

"Lots of things. Lots.''

"If you want to talk, all you have to do is call.''

"By the time Sherman transferred me to you I might lose my nerve.''

"Yeah." He lets my hair go and leaves. He is always leaving me alone in his office with only the temptation to do bad things. I guess we're broken up now.

I call Tabitha right away and tell her I need a drink. She suggests this new spot on 9th Avenue with lots of theater types. She's working late, but there is no way I'm staying in the office a nanosecond longer, so I tell her I'll meet her there. I spit outside Helena's restaurant when I pass it.

The place seems a lot like a dive to me, but I take advantage of the happy hour special while I wait. When Tabitha arrives, she is a bundle of energy. She is all decked out in pale pink (I'll never figure out how she pulls these colors off). She's giving me the New York Euro Kiss (both cheeks) and recognizing my alcohol zeal. "Starting it out right, Eve, I see. *Garçon,* cosmopolitan for me."

"Tabitha, are you sure it will be good here? I'm not sure that this is what you had in mind."

"It is, Eve. It is. Hell's Kitchen is rising. Just give it a chance. It's still early." The bartender comes over to ask Tabitha what's in a cosmopolitan.

"Oh, you have got to be kidding me. It's just pink goodness. How do I know? I'm paying you to figure out these things. Don't you have a little manual back there?"

"Absolut Currant, cranberry, lime juice, Cointreau, maybe," I say to help him out. Tabitha snorts as he starts to make it.

"Eve, you're so sweet. Of course I knew what was in it, but really the man ought to figure it out for himself. This is supposed to be a service country. Anyway, how was your meeting with Mabel? She is the Big C's nemesis by the way. Apparently she wants to talk to the Big C about reorganizing and I overheard the Big C saying 'Frankly, it's my magazine, and when you start seeing drops in circulation then, and only then, can you talk to me about reorganization.' Can you believe it? Then when she got off the phone she screamed, 'Reorganize this!'"

"That Big C, quite the crusader."

"Eww, Eve, you've been in such an icky mood. Let's get you another cocktail. I'm in the mood to spend money. Let's get a fabulous overpriced meal on Restaurant Row. What do you say?"

"Let's drink these and see how we feel, Ms. Golightly."

"Come now, I'm much too robust." I think about trying to explain my day to Tabitha, but I wouldn't know where to begin. I also can't exactly get a handle on which part bothered me the most. I basically brief her on Lorriane's termination.

"Wow! They're not handling this well at all. Morale is going to plummet. I'm so glad the Big C is holding off the dogs. I hate when people start making changes."

"I don't know how long the Big C can hold anyone off for."

"Poor Eve, so worried. How's Rob?"

"Done. He basically fired me. I cried in the handicapped bathroom a little."

"Oh, Eve, how dehumanizing. I didn't know. Drink up, let's go get a meal."

"Like that's going to improve my disposition."

"Well, getting laid might, but a meal is the first step."

We walk down Restaurant Row and Tabitha picks an Italian

place because she "needs carbs." The doorman ushers us in. We get seated between two tables of businessmen who can't stop staring at Tabitha.

"I hate it here," I say to a smiling Tabitha.

"Mother of God! All the drama. Think of Tuscany. It's inspiring."

"It isn't inspiring, but we're on 46th Street. Yards away from our office. Next door to where Rob and I had our first date." Tabitha ignores me and reads the menu with the appropriate hunger/orgasm noises.

"I know I want a meat dish." She giggles, aware how that must sound to the males who are practically sitting at our table. "What should I get, grumpy puss?"

I shrug when she looks up at me. The businessmen are silent, listening.

"Excuse me," she says to the one sitting farthest from us (he has on the nicest suit), "Is that the tagliatelle with truffles?"

"It is." Tabitha is on her feet and strides over to him. I can't believe this. She peers into his plate.

"I hate when these restaurants get all excited about al dente— know what I mean?" He nods, hanging on her every word. She picks up his fork and (I can't believe this) "Do you mind if I just..." She is twirling his pasta onto a fork and eating it. She closes her eyes as she does it, transported to heaven, by the bite. I have to start laughing. All of the guys have their napkins in their laps.

"Thank you, that's what I'll get," she says, opening her eyes. She grins down at the man and says, "Not too hard." It's going to be a long night.

I creep into the apartment and Roseanne is asleep on the couch with the TV on and a cookbook across her chest. I shut off the TV and she wakes up right away, startled. I am full of wine and pasta. I apologize for not calling her.

"No, it's fine. Pete called. We are going to go to lunch tomorrow. Your sister's boyfriend called, too. He says everything is okay, he was just checking up on you."

Herb calls me into his office when he gets to work (I got there on time, thank you very much). He's got the New Age music going full blast.

"How are you?" I ask.

"Doing okay, Eve, doing okay. I know most of the staff is

unhappy about the changes, but we have to move on. We have to think of the product.''

"And the brand," I offer, knowing it's what he wants to hear.

"Exactly, it's going to be an exciting time of growth and..."

"Synergy."

"Exactly." He nods, pleased. I'm getting used to playing this game. Any minute now, I think he is going to bust into a Mabel doublespeak. "So, I hear you're being very positive about the changes. It says a lot to your youth, but also, I think you can set an example with your attitude. There are going to be opportunities. Mabel expressed to me that you were interested in writing and I had a great idea that might utilize your skills.''

"Really?" Is he going to give me my own column? I know nothing about *Breathe* as a brand, either, but I could learn. I'll learn.

"Yes, there are certain duties that aren't being filled to my satisfaction. They're small things, really, but I think you could be integral in helping." Integral? Did he say integral? "And also it might interest you, because of your desire to write.''

"What is it?"

"Correspondence. You could open the correspondence from our readers. Select the ones that you think are worthy of going into Letters to the Editor and which ones should go into the You Asked Us section. You would separate them by magazine and decide which ones could be used for *Breathe*. Then you would research and write the answers for You Asked Us which, with my approval, would go into the magazine.

"The mail? You want me to do the mail?"

"It's more than the mail, Eve. It's a great way to familiarize yourself with the style of writing we want. It's quite a stepping stone." Isn't my shitty job enough of a damn stepping stone? Aren't I already familiar enough with the magazine?

"That sounds great," I say as Herb hands me a box from underneath his desk.

"You can see there's quite a bit of mail. It's a testament to our popularity. So go through it at your leisure and pick out ten letters you're thinking of responding to and twenty that are suitable for Letters to the Editor. I'll review them and we'll get cracking.''

"Thanks, Herb." I'm trying to sound as cheerful as possible.

"Oh, Eve, try to get them to me by Wednesday." What about my leisure?

"Great," I say, not wanting to look at the hundreds of letters in the box. "I definitely will.''

April

I'm eating, sleeping and breathing these shitty letters. You would not believe the kinds of things people write in about. I guess I understand e-mailing, sort of. I mean, that takes a second and if you really have something to say you can just whip it off and be done with it. But to actually write a letter, get a stamp, mail it out? I think that's a little crazy. Don't these people have lives?

People either write ridiculous questions about their bodies and nutrition, or try to plan our magazine for us. Like we're going to listen to these crackpots. The worst are the *Yoga for Life* letters which go on and on about all this enlightenment crap. It's disgusting.

I think I am going to explode if I read another fucking letter. I can't call Roseanne, she is in the middle of yet another audit. I'm still not exactly sure what that means, just that she's busy and cranky and stays at work till way past midnight. I suspect she hasn't been eating properly. She's got no time to deal with me.

My mom is getting treatment all this week. I would really like to go home and be with her, but she and my dad insist that there wouldn't be much for me to do other than hang out in the hospital with my dad and worry. My mom asks me if I've talked to Monica lately and I have to lie and say I have. I think it makes her feel better.

"Hi, Eve, what's going on?" Lacey is hanging over my desk. It's a little early in the season for the shirt she's wearing and I know she's already sporting open toe shoes.

"You know, Lacey, just going through the mail."

"How fun," she says, not having heard me. She slips into her English—this-is-my-way-of-trying-to-be-funny-and-friendly, you-serf-in-my-kingdom—accent. She hands me a small shoebox full of receipts. What is this? "Anyway, I was wondering if you could help me organize these."

"What exactly do you expect me to do with these?"

"Well—" she's back to her American accent and taking a tone, as well "—I was under the impression that with this new—" she pulls her spread hands apart "—entity, we, that is the writers, are not going to be dealing with the administration as much. It's really been impeding my creative process." I'm going to lose it. I can feel myself losing it. I'm certain she's had expensive dental work, and I'm going to ruin it. Why am I so violent lately?

"Look, Lacey." I can take a tone, too. "We are still transition-ing. We don't even know when our new magazine is being launched or what it's even going to be about. But, I'll tell you one thing, Lacey, I don't care what decisions are made. There's no way in hell I am ever going to do your expense reports. If you take issue with that you can bring it up with Herb and I will bring it up with my human resources representative."

She is speechless. I'm kind of surprised myself. "I certainly wasn't trying to insult you. I just thought it was your job."

"Did you really think cataloging all the ways you've sucked off the company was in my job description?"

"I don't know what you're trying to say?" But I can tell by her face that she does. She's sure not slipping into her faux British accent now. "I understand that everyone is a little stressed with this whole thing. I'm sure it will all work itself out."

The nice thing about this transition is that it's the perfect excuse for hostility. It's a get-out-of-jail-free card. In a way, I love it. I turn back to my computer, it's just my screen saver, but I look at it like it's the most important document in the world. That makes her go away. I can't wait to tell Tabitha about this, but she is also too busy for me.

The Big C is on jury duty, which is absolutely killing her be-cause it's such a bad time with this crazy reorganization thing. She is counting on Tabitha to hold down the fort. They have nightly meetings where Tabitha goes over every detail of the day. The Big C screams and yells about how they are trying to take away all her power and Tabitha supplies her with cigarettes by the car-ton. Tabitha is thriving from it. The other day she bought me lunch that we ate in the Big C's office answering phone call after phone call. It's kind of sick that she's so busy.

I call Todd. I know he is out of the country right now, though I don't know where. We haven't talked since Roseanne's birthday. I try not to think about his face when I took the cab to Rob's place. It's the last thing I need. I get his voice mail, which says he will be out of the office, traveling, but checking his voice mail.

I hate leaving messages, especially because I know he'll probably roll his eyes when he gets it.

"Hey, it's me. It's Eve. Just kind of bored and sick of work. I, um, wanted to see how you were. How are you? You can call me back when you get a chance. Or not. Whatever. Take care." I hang up. That was stupid.

"Eve, how's it going?" It's Herb. He is really getting into this whole YFL thing. He is wearing an Indian print cotton shirt. "Are those letters coming along?"

"Oh, yeah, it's going great. I'll definitely have them done by Wednesday." It's Monday. I've barely gotten through forty. I am so screwed.

"Wonderful, Eve. Terrific. And you've been separating them into piles. How's the *Breathe* pile?"

"Well, it's a little ambiguous because, you know, we haven't really nailed down exactly what this *Breathe* thing is." He nods, thoughtfully.

"But, Eve, I'm sure you'll do your best."

"Oh, yeah, as always."

I call my mom and tell her I am coming home for dinner tonight. I want to check up on her, now that this part of the treatment's over. She protests for a while, but I won't give up. I want to see her.

"Okay, honey…but I just want you to realize that I'm losing some of my hair. It's not awful, but I'm wearing a lot of hats. Just don't be alarmed."

"Mom, it's fine, I don't care about your hair, just relax and don't make anything for dinner. I'll bring home some pizza or Chinese or something."

"Okay, honey. I don't have much of an appetite. I've been having lots of soup."

"I'll pick up some soup on the way home at one of those soup places. They're really good." I am trying to sound happy and excited for her, so she won't worry about me when she's already got so much else on her mind.

I stop at Macy's. They're having a sale so I get a bunch of scarves for my mom.

My dad meets me at the train station in New Jersey. I don't want to be annoyed at him anymore, but I feel like I can't let go. He keeps nervously drumming his fingers on the steering wheel. I decide to try, for my mother's sake, to be civil. "How's the not smoking coming, Dad?"

"Well, I got the patch, but I miss the habit. You know?"

"Yeah, I know. So, how do you think Mom is?"

"The doctors are still optimistic. The chemotherapy is working well on the cancer. It's just a shame she can't feel better, you know, she gets queasy." I feel a little queasy when we pull into my driveway. My mother is standing in the doorway, like she used to do when I was in high school.

"Hi, honey." She gives me a big hug. She's got on a baseball hat, but I can see there is some hair under it. My house smells different, like sickness.

"Hey, Mom. I got four different kinds of soup and here—" I give her the Macy's bag. "Those are for you, so you can be fashionable, even when you don't feel so good." My mom oohs and ahhs over every scarf like it's Christmas morning.

We all sit around the dining room table and my mom keeps chatting like she usually does. For once, I'm actually into it. I study her for signs of what's going on. She hardly eats any of her soup. My dad and I both offer her some of ours.

"No, I'm just not very hungry," she says. She puts her hands up to her head and closes her eyes. I look at my father, who is calmly checking his watch.

"Mom, what's wrong?"

"Nothing, honey. Just time for my pills." She tries to smile. My father is up getting her pill bottles. I go to the kitchen and fill up a glass of water. When I return to the table my father is laying out five sets of pills. I watch my mother take each one.

"Make sure you drink lots of water," my dad says calmly. They are huge horse pills. I go get my mother another glass of water. I stand in the doorway, watching my parents. My mom has her head on my dad's shoulder. It would be sweet if it wasn't so sad. At first, they don't see me, but then my mom does. She smiles at me.

"I think I'm going to go lie down, honey. I'm getting really old." She tries to make a joke out of it. "Are you staying over?"

"No, Mom, I think I'm going to head back into the city. If Dad can drive me to the bus station. If you can be alone." My mom laughs.

"I'm not a baby, honey, I can be left alone."

"Okay, well, at least let me help you to bed." I don't really want to. I want to run out of the house, go home and not think about this. I don't want to come back until my mom is making crappy dinners and my dad is chain-smoking.

I tuck my mom in and give her a kiss on the forehead. She

looks so tired. She closes her eyes right away. My dad and I don't say too much to each other the whole way to the station. I have to take the bus in at this time. He offers to drive me into the city, but I'd rather sit on the bus alone. "I'm okay, Dad. You should get back to Mom. Just give me a call if anything changes or the doctor's give you any news. Please."

My dad nods. "You should talk to your sister."

"I have." My dad shakes his head at me. Thankfully, we're at the station. I give him a kiss goodbye.

I'm super tired by the time I get home and I am just falling asleep when Todd calls. He's in Sri Lanka. He sounds tired and faraway. There is this weird delay between us, so we keep talking over each other.

"I thought you forgot about me," I say at the end of his description of the factory.

"No, I was just really busy. I meant to call before." We are silent for a minute.

"This call is costing you too much money to be quiet," I say as I hear him telling me that its a good thing his company pays for everything. I picture him in his impersonal hotel room and I think about how we danced.

"What are you doing right now?" He is already telling me that he's bored just sitting on this bed wondering about what TV is on. At least we are on the same wavelength. I take a deep breath.

"I keep thinking about you," I say a little too quickly because it just overlaps—

"I met a girl in Atlanta."

It seems like we both say "Oh" at the same time. I resolve not to say another word until he does.

"Eve." His voice is so soft and I think about when we fell asleep on the futon and what a coward I am. "I wish...fuck."

"Well, maybe you should have called the girl in Atlanta then. It's late and I have to work tomorrow." I don't mean that how it comes out. I wish I wasn't bitter.

"Oh, Eve," he says, and he sounds so lonely and I feel like the biggest shit in the world. "I'll let you go." There is nothing to say to that except goodbye and I try to convey an apology in that word, but I can't.

Just before he hangs up, I hear him say, "I miss you, too."

Here's the part where you think I'm a big baby and even though I hate to blame PMS for things, I must be getting my period. I start to cry and I fall asleep thinking about that stupid rhyme I learned in kindergarten and would say over and over again. "April showers bring May flowers."

Mabel comes to visit me the next morning. I'm still bitter about the way she almost pulled me over to the dark side of loving my job. She's all smiles and concerned looks. YFL just let go of two of its staff. I wish I had her ability to feign sincerity.

"So, Eve, how are you transitioning?"

"Well, Mabel, it isn't very easy when the person who was the closest thing I had to a mentor was unexpectedly fired and now everyone else is worried. It's not a happy time here on this floor." It doesn't faze her. The thing about Mabel is she doesn't hear anything she doesn't want to hear. She nods thoughtfully, then turns it around.

"Well, Eve, you are going to be integral in so many parts of these changes." She is looking deep into my eyes, she's smiling. "You are going to be helping us with the interview process."

"So, let me get this straight, now we're hiring new people when we just fired a bunch? It doesn't make any sense."

"Eve, there are going to be lots of new groundbreaking positions and we are going to begin working creatively, and in many regards, on the cutting edge. This is the time to adapt to these changes or relocate." She smiles and lets that sink in. "I think you'll see the benefits to Prescott Nelson as a whole as we move into the future and diversify."

"What does that mean, Mabel?" She hands me a folder of résumés.

"Eve, can you set up interviews for these people with Herb and Lev? That would be so helpful. Oh, they need to be scheduled by Tuesday." Great. "Have a terrific day, Eve. Call me if you need any support." Mother of God! As if on cue, Tabitha calls me.

"The Big C's trial is recessed until Monday. I can totally tell she's threatened by how well I've been handling everything. I think she wants me out of here. I'll petty cash a lunch at Carmine's. Want to make our way through the screaming throngs?"

We order two family-style meals. We're eating like fiends, like we've never eaten before. Tabitha is so excited about her week as an editor that she is talking with her mouth open and spilling little bits of food out of her mouth. It's kind of gross, but also funny to see how oblivious she is to all the tourists and suits around us. I keep waiting for her to ask about me, but she just goes on, heaping huge portions of chicken parmesan onto her plate. I want to scream and yell and tell her about my mom and Mabel and Todd, but she's almost high on this whole thing.

"Eve, this is what we've been waiting for. Now, I know I can do it. I don't need a man, I don't need anyone. I did it all, I worked it, on my own." I can't stand this.

"How's Blake?" Tabitha laughs and picks up some mozzarella cheese.

"Honey, he had to go."

"Why, he didn't fit into the plan?" I don't know why Tabitha of all people is annoying me so much. She ignores me and launches into the saga. I'd rather hear about this than how awesome she is for single-handedly ruling *NY By Night* for a week.

"And, Eve, I had to say, 'working at Medieval Times doesn't make you an actor.'"

"Wait! What? That's what he did?"

"Yes, can you believe it? How embarrassing! I really liked him, too."

"Apparently not that much." She sits back a little in her chair.

"What's that supposed to mean?"

"Well, you couldn't have liked him that much if you just nixed him because he wasn't a serious thespian. Everybody's scraping by."

"Are you out of your mind? There is no way I was going to go out with someone who told me those kinds of lies."

"Lies? Tabitha, how many lies did you tell him?" She shakes her head. "None? Give me a break, Tabitha. Give me a fucking break! How many lies do you tell me? I don't know the first thing about you! Do you realize that? Doesn't it seem strange that you never talk about anything real?" I'm yelling now. I'm losing it.

"Eve, it's fucking New York. Everyone's got a story. You're from New Jersey. The Big C's a dropout. Roseanne had an eating disorder. What difference does it make?"

"None, unless you work at Medieval Times and your girlfriend breaks up with you because you can't take her to only the finest establishments. None, unless your friends wonder why you never talk about Texas or why you always have so much money or how come you buy tons of underwear once a week."

"You want to know what, Eve, you're ridiculous. That's why Adrian won't talk to you! That's why Rob broke up with you! You are out of control! Keep judging everyone else from your dreamworld. Keep wanting to be a writer and not writing anything.

This is New York, you know. College newspaper writing just doesn't cut it. Check, please.''

"So that's it, Tabitha? We're getting the check and going. You think I'm ridiculous, too." I'm getting too upset.

Tabitha doesn't say a word. She starts fishing out her Dunhills and puts her sunglasses on. This is it, she's writing me off. I can't believe it. Of all the blows. Now, I'm going to have to avoid her elevator bank, too. I leave the restaurant. Fuck her!

I go back up to the office. I can't believe it! My heart is pounding and I feel like I am going to start crying and never stop. I need to go cry in the handicapped person bathroom, but I stop at my desk to leave my stuff. There is a huge bouquet of flowers. I can't believe it. Could it be Rob? He's got perfect timing, but how could he know? Todd? No, he's wooing a Georgia peach. I read the card.

Dear Eve,
Thanks for all your hard work. Happy Secretaries Day.

Herb

I can't stay here. I shut down my computer. I don't know who to tell that I'm leaving. There is no more Lorraine. I e-mail Herb that I don't feel well and I have to leave. I don't bother to spell check it before I flee the building.

I'm running through the streets crying. I feel ridiculous. I am trembling when I get to the apartment. I lay on the couch and cry. I haven't cried like this in so long and I'm not sure how long it lasts, but I must fall asleep crying. When I wake up, Roseanne is hovering over me in her blue suit, looking concerned.

"Eve, it's okay." She's hugging me. She's bringing me soup.

So it finally happens, that fateful night. I have my breakdown. I cry all through the night and into the next afternoon. Roseanne sleeps in my bed and keeps smoothing my hair and telling me it's going to be okay. She calls Herb in the morning for me and actually gets him on the phone. She tells him I have bad stomach flu and haven't been able to leave the bathroom. I hear her laughing and I can only imagine what asinine thing he is saying to her.

"He doesn't seem like a bad guy," Roseanne says when she hangs up. This makes me cry harder. Somehow, I manage to assure her that I'm all right being alone. It's not like I have to go on suicide watch or anything, I just can't seem to stop crying. I tell her that my period is on the way. I want to believe that's all it is.

I spend the next two days on the couch; crying and watching trash TV. It's liberating, really. I smoke cigarettes in the house, knowing Roseanne isn't going to say anything. She is still in the midst of her audit, so she gets home real late and is working through the weekend. She tries to make me eat when she's home, but I'll only have soup and tea. I should have done this long ago.

Yep, I've been going along too easily, no more trying to be nice to anyone else. From now on, it's all about me. All about Eve. That's right. Just me and my bed and my sofa and my comfort TV. Happy together. I could stay like this forever. I check my messages at work. There's one from Chuck.

"Hey, Eve, it's Chuck. I just wanted to call and leave you my number, in case you wanted to talk. I'm around. I know you haven't talked to your sister and you probably don't really feel comfortable talking to me, but sometimes it's easier to talk to a stranger than anyone else, and anything you say to me is totally between us." That sounds creepy, right? But, it's not, he sounds sincere (not like Mabel sincere, like kind sincere). I write down his number and delete.

I start to cry again. I know I should call my mom, but I don't need her to worry about me on top of everything. Besides, if anything were really wrong with her, someone would have called me, right? Maybe not.

When Roseanne comes home Monday night she stands over my bed with her hands on her hips. I assume her audit is over because she is home at five-thirty. "Eve, you smell. Do you realize that? This can't go on. You have to get up."

"I'm having a breakdown, Roseanne, leave me alone."

"You are not having a breakdown, Eve, no one has breakdowns anymore. Everyone takes Prozac, which I know you don't want. You are just feeling sorry for yourself and it has to stop. Stop the drama. Now, get up, take a shower, tweeze your eyebrows, do your hair and eat some solid food!"

"Don't you yell at me!" I scream as snot flies out of my nose.

"That's real attractive, Eve."

"I don't care, I don't have anyone to impress. I liked you better when you had your audit." Roseanne sighs and then the doorbell rings. I sit up in bed.

"Who is that? Who did you invite over? Your new sane room-mate? I don't want to see anyone! Do you understand? Shut my door!" I hear Roseanne talking to Tabitha on the intercom. "I especially don't want to see her! Shut my door!"

"Shut it your damn self," says Roseanne, sweet as pie. She opens the door for Tabitha. "She's in there and she don't look pretty."

"Fuck off, the both of you!" I scream and roll over to face the wall. I hear Tabitha come into my room. I pull the covers over my head. She sits down on my bed.

"I'm sorry, Eve." I wish I couldn't hear her. "I was really pissed that you questioned my life. Wanna hear something funny? The Big C is leaving at the end of May. She wants to devote her time to writing crime novels. Can you imagine? That's so not her. One fucking stint of jury duty and she thinks she's John Grisham.

"She called me into her office to tell me. It's what she always wanted to do, she says, and she feels like it's now or never. Want to hear something funnier? She said she wanted to take care of me before she left. I thought she was going to offer me her position because I had done such a bang-up job while she was out. Not quite. But she did offer me a coordinator position. She went on and on about what a good position it would be for me and how much room there would be for advancement. She told me I had a lot of potential and that she trusted me and how important trust is.

"I kept thinking that the Big C doesn't really know too much about me, although I knew so much shit about her. I believed her when she said that she trusted me. She even said she thought of me as a good friend. Then, I couldn't help but feel bad for her. I think she really does think I'm a friend. It's sort of lonely, I mean it sucks when you've got to think of your employees as your friends, especially when they're really not.

"When I left her office, I was psyched, kind of about my promotion, even though it wasn't the big one. I wanted to call all my friends and tell them, all the people I trusted. Who should I call? Adrian? Okay, yeah, he's a friend, but what does he know about me? Nicole, come on, she'll start thinking of even more ways to get her clients in *NY By Night*. And I couldn't stop thinking about you and what you said. I guess you just wanted me to trust you, and that pissed me off for some reason.

"All this time, I've been trying to be this person and that's fine, I mean it's New York, you know, but you need to have someone whose going to get your back, whose going to like you, no matter what.

"I'm from somewhere worse than Jersey. I'm from a little town upstate that you've never even heard of." What? "And while

I'm giving this Oscar speech, I might as well tell you that my family has like no money and there were times I could barely support myself. So I set up a Web page, which I bet you didn't know I could do. I sell my underwear on the Net. It's sort of sketchy. You would never believe how much money you can make doing it. That's it. That's me. Now you know. Now I guess I can trust you and Roseanne, who's been listening to this whole thing. Hi, Rosie.''

"Hi," says Roseanne from my doorway. "Wow!"

I sit up in bed and turn to look at both of them. Tabitha is in sweats and has her hair up in a scrunchee. I can't believe it. She looks so different all of a sudden. Not any less glamorous or anything or trashy in lieu of what she just said, but less like a Tabitha and more like a friend.

"So that's my story, Eve. What's yours? Why are you like this, right now? Why are you crying and snotting all over yourself in a way that is so unlike you?" I'm a little shocked by everything Tabitha just told me, I have to admit. I figure I might as well just talk to her and see what comes.

"I honestly don't know. I feel like if I start talking I might never stop." Roseanne comes in and sits down on my bed, too.

"So what is it? It seems like you've got a million reasons to be upset."

"It does, doesn't it?" I can feel my lips trembling. "I'm sure all the reasons you can think of are probably true, but to single any one of them out would be an excuse. I don't want to use my mom as an excuse."

"So, what is it?" Tabitha is being so matter-of-fact.

"It's me. I guess it's everything. It's how I'm becoming. A lot of what you said the other day was true, Tabitha. I know I should have done this long ago. I should have gotten out this good cry years ago. Maybe I should have planned for this in college, but this is it. This is my life."

"Eve, what are you saying? I don't think we understand."

"On top of everything, my mom, my shitty sister, the end of the whatever I had with Rob, ruining a five-year friendship with Todd, in addition to all that, I've come to a shocking realization. This is it, guys, I'm going to be an assistant for the rest of my life. I got fucking flowers for Secretaries Day. There are worse things I guess, but I just can't stand that I'm defined that way.

"Do I want to have my life, my emotions, ruled by these stupid meetings and decisions other people make based on how things look on paper? The highest I can go is to become a Lacey, a Mabel or a Big C who thinks that this is it. And for what? For some stupid sports magazine?''

''Eve, you're not even twenty-four, this isn't your life, it can't be! You won't let it be!''

''Why the fuck not? I am letting it be! I have gotten so complacent! I've been sitting there playing hangman, surfing the Net, slowly losing any ambition I ever had to do something else. Something that I don't even know. I am like a pseudo slacker. I am a slacker on the down low! I am the worst!''

Tabitha shakes her head and looks around the room. It's really strange to see her with so little makeup. Roseanne rubs my foot and says, ''Shoot.''

''Why don't you quit?''

''Tabitha, let's not go crazy, she's in a bad state as it is.'' I am sure Roseanne is thinking about the rent, too. ''It doesn't seem like this staying at home stuff is working.''

''Besides, I'm never ever going to be able to find a better job. Part of me really believes that's my in. I don't want to leave my foot-in-the-door position until I've actually gotten in.'' Tabitha rolls her eyes at me.

''I'm not talking about getting another job. I'm talking about taking a risk. I'm talking about really doing it. Starting a magazine, giving it a go.''

''Oh, right, the magazine tree that grows outside this window is due to blossom anyday now, all this rain is going to do it.''

''Do you have any savings?''

''I have about four thousand dollars, I started saving it in like kindergarten. That would last me maybe three months. Maybe.''

''Listen, maybe it's time we all took a risk. I'll give Eve money. I've saved fifteen thousand. I'll invest it, I might as well.''

''You've saved that much from selling your skivvies?''

''Your used panties?''

''Yes, and sometimes—'' she covers up her face ''—yours, too.''

''Eww!'' We both scream in unison, hitting her.

''I definitely want a cut of that!'' I say. ''Honestly, though you'd be out of your mind if you gave me fifteen thousand bucks for a pipe dream that I haven't even fleshed out. You were right when you said college newspapers didn't mean anything.''

''Eve, flesh it out a little. It's New York, anything can work. Sorry about what I said. You're young, you're hip, I have imparted a great deal of fashion sense onto you. This is the way it works here. Look at the Styles section! Who are those people? They are just people who got a good spin! They have got no more luck or talent than you do.''

"Probably got a hell of a lot more discipline than I do, though. I have barely turned on that computer since I got it and if I did I'd probably surf the Net. Maybe, I'd check out your site." Roseanne and I laugh; I still kind of can't believe this.

"I've come clean now, and I feel better," Tabitha says. "Skeletons out of the closet. You both know where I stand."

"Yeah, we got your back, girlfriend," Roseanne says like she's a hip-hop sistah.

"True that," I say, mocking.

"So, what are you going to do, Eve? You going to do it or not?"

"Tabitha, I feel a little bombarded, right now. I'm not going to make this kind of decision with any sanity."

"But what's your gut telling you?"

"Roseanne, I thought you were against this?"

"I was, but I like living vicariously, and besides, that was before the money."

"That's the craziest part of it all. I am not going to lose your money."

"But you wouldn't. I guarantee, if you took my money you'd do your best to get it back for me. You wouldn't be on your own, we'd help. Right, Roseanne?"

"Sure, I do the money and cooking sections!"

"I'm not sure anyone wants a cooking section," says Tabitha, shaking her head, "but we'll see."

"Yeah, we'll see about everything, I'm still in the midst of my breakdown."

"Whatever. You have until your birthday to decide."

"That sounds like a pretty expensive birthday present."

"It is. All this unburdening—let's go get some cigarettes and a drink."

"You guys, I haven't had solid food in like four days."

"The liquid diet won't be affected. We'll get some late night Krispy Kreme."

"Fine. Twist my arm. Let me just wash my face." They both give me a disgusted look. "Okay, all right, I'll shower, too."

I decide to take another couple of days off. I leave the message on Herb's voice mail. Let the temp handle all the new wretched

scheduling. I need the mental health time—I'm having a breakdown. I don't really feel like crying anymore. Now I can finally
enjoy it.

Tabitha's first assignment in her new coordinator position is to
gather all the facts on some East Village restaurant that *NY By
Night* is doing a major story on. Tabitha has to go down there and
do a little research. She invites me to come down for lunch with
her and Raj, the photographer. After last night's debauchery with
the girls and now this little outing, I am definitely deviating off
the breakdown course.

Tabitha is totally eating up the way the staff of the restaurant
is kissing her ass, so she'll portray them in the most fantastic light.

Any evidence of the vulnerable Tabitha who showed up at my
place is totally gone. She is dressed to the hilt in Dana Buchman.
I ask her how much of a dent she put into that infamous savings
by purchasing the shoes she's wearing.

"Let's get at least four entrées. I want to see what Raj makes
of my appetite," she says, ignoring me. The food here is great,
but Tabitha has warned me not to show too much approval.

"We want to keep them on their toes." She's expressionless as
she jots things down in her little notebook, but not as she flirts
with Raj, who looks like an Indian mobster to me.

"Do you girls want to get a drink after this?" I can tell it's my
cue to exit.

"No, actually, I ought to get back, but thanks."

"Sounds fabulous," Tabitha says, winking at me. "Do you
need cab fare, Eve?"

"I think I'm going to walk."

"It's a pretty good walk back up," Raj says.

I walk up Avenue A for a while and along the way, I'm amazed
by how much is going on around me. There's people unloading
instruments, a rally going on in Thompson Square Park, crowded
ethnic cafés, upscale restaurants cleaning up after the lunch
crowds, a student film being shot, and tons of people on the streets
performing or begging for money.

The weather really is starting to get warmer and if I were up at
college, this would be the time that I pulled out my sandals and
sat up on the hill near my dorm. But I'm not at school anymore,
I'm here. I'm in New York with a little bit of money in my pocket
and not much more certainty about the future. But it's as if all the
reasons I love it here and all the possibilities have set them-

selves up for me today. I breathe it in. I inhale it and feel a little hopeful.

I promise to give myself one more day. I just can't go to work yet. I can't until I put my life in order. I start with the easiest parts. Rob. I don't miss him. All right, I guess I miss part of him—the good parts. I just don't feel like we were ever on equal footing. It's not easy to date someone who has influence over whether or not you get a job. You can't have that relationship without feeling like a bit of a ho.

Then there's Todd (I am going backward from easiest to hardest). I can't quite put my finger on why I've been thinking about him so much. Why am I nervous to leave him messages? Why, when I close my eyes and want to think about the random guy in the elevator or Rob, or anyone but Todd, do I find myself getting this strange feeling in my stomach? I can't explain it. I don't like it. I've known this guy for like, forever; I can't be attracted to him.

Besides, he's got a girlfriend and he's in Atlanta. I just need a diversion. Then of course there's my mom and my sister. I decide to call Chuck. I don't know why. I hope my sister won't be there. Luckily, she isn't, she has a class. He sounds super happy. "Are you at work, Eve?"

"No, I'm taking the day off."

"Everyone needs a day off now and then." Of course, if you're Chuck, then it's always a day off. "I'm really glad you called, Eve."

"Really?"

"Yes, how are you doing with your mom's sickness?"

"I guess okay. I went home for dinner last week, and it wasn't that much fun. I didn't stay over. She told me she was feeling fine."

"And you didn't believe her?"

"I wanted to, but you know, they haven't exactly been the most up front with me."

"That really bugs you, huh?" I notice that Chuck is just kind of reacting to what I'm saying and encouraging me to say more. He may think he's got me fooled somehow, but I am totally aware of what he's doing.

"Chuck, it's my family. I'm really pissed that they told Monica about this but not me. No offense."

"Look, Eve, it's not about Monica now, I want you to think of me as your friend."

"Why?" The question seems to stump him.

"Well, because I guess I'd like to be a part of your family someday, and I don't want you hate me because you feel as if, somehow, I was untruthful with you."

"I see."

"I know you aren't getting along with your sister right now, and I know it's painful for her and I'm sure it's painful for you. It's times like this when families get polarized, unfortunately."

"Well, why do you think they told her and not me?"

"I don't know, Eve." Some help he is. "Maybe, since you live a lot closer to them, they thought perhaps it would take too much out of your life if you felt like you had to be with them all the time. Monica is far enough away that there really wasn't too much she could do, unless she wanted to drop out of school, which they made her promise not to do."

"Well, how come *she* didn't tell me?"

"That's something you should ask her. Eve, I don't really have any family right now, my mother died when I was young and my father and I don't get along too well. The sad thing is that try as you might to avoid this, no matter how much better she feels, she and your family are never going to be the same."

"That's encouraging."

"Eve, please don't be so cynical with me. I'm just being honest with you."

"Look, I'm trying not to be. I've cried for about four days straight and only now do I have a handle on things. If I start again, I might not stop. I thought I was doing okay." I'm not, because I start to cry. Chuck sings me a funny little song over the phone and it makes me laugh, just because of the sheer cheesiness and sweetness. I'm amazed that I can actually stop and laugh, but I can.

"Thanks for talking to me, Eve. It's nice to get to know you. Your sister has told me a lot of great stories about you. She loves you a lot and I'm glad to have this opportunity to get to know you myself."

"I think she loves you a lot, too. Thank you for talking to me."

I don't know if I was expecting the building to have burned down or what, but it's still there when I go into work. Everything is pretty much the same on my floor, except my desk is a lot neater and the temp left me a long note about all the things she did in my absence, so I will have the "heads up."

Gary comes over to me right away to update me on all the meetings and the ways they've been lying to us while I was gone. I clear my throat to let him know that Mabel is standing right behind him. He looks at her defiantly.

"Also, Jim quit." He nods at Mabel. "I doubt he'll be the last one, either."

He goes back into his office and Mabel smiles down on me. "Hey there, Mabel."

"What's going on, Eve? I heard you were sick, are you better, now?"

"Yep, it was a nasty stomach flu. Believe me, you don't want to hear about it."

"I'm sure I don't. I wanted to urge you to check the postings. There might be some positions right here in this department that you would be suitable for. We are provided by law to post these positions, but I think you might have an in." I can't believe Mabel is looking out for me like this. I thought she would hate me for not being a good enough beacon, for getting sick right in the thick of things.

"Writing positions?" Her smile doesn't falter. She is unsinkable.

"Well, actually, these are administrative positions, but I think you'll find a lot of growth there." I bet it's Lorraine's position repackaged.

"Oh." Thanks, I guess. Luckily, my phone rings.

"I'll talk to you later, Eve."

"How's your first day back?" It's Tabitha.

"Oh, you know, the usual. How's it going for you?"

"I've been interviewing my replacement. You would not believe the awful candidates the staffing people have sent up so far. You would not believe it." I have a feeling Tabitha is going to make this poor assistant's life a living hell anyway. "But, I had a great night with Raj. It's true what they say about Indian men."

"Really?" I have no idea what she's talking about, better not to ask.

"Eve, gotta run, I have a 10:30. A Brown graduate. I noticed two spelling errors on her résumé. They expect these people to fill my shoes? I don't think so. 'Bye."

I decide to check on Herb. He's got the incense going particularly strong and he is sitting cross-legged in his chair, staring out the window. I knock on the door and he turns slowly toward me and smiles.

"Oh, hello, Eve," I want to believe he smokes weed a lot or something, because I can't understand how he can appear so calm all the time. I wait for him to ask me how I'm feeling, but he doesn't say a word.

"I'm feeling a lot better," I offer finally. "Just wanted to see how you were." Again we stare at each other. "How are you?"

"Oh, I'm well, Eve, I'm optimistic about everything. The merger just has to be approached the right way. We plan on having meetings to help everyone adapt a bit better than they have been."

"To help them think properly?"

"Exactly." He smiles at me, reassured it's a simple concept if even the assistant can grasp it.

"Great," I say. It's so easy to slip back into the bowing and scraping. "Did you need anything?"

"Actually, we're getting a new coordinator, her name is Erica Rutt. I was hoping maybe we could have all the files in order for her when she gets here."

"The files?"

"Yes, you know, the ones in the file room." I wasn't even sure we still used those. We have another file drawer near my desk where most of the old issues are, but, the file room...I don't even think I've ever been in it. Lorraine told me it was a mess.

"Lorraine told me it was a mess in there."

"Lorraine?" Is he for real? "Oh, right, Lorraine. Yes, I'm sure it is, that's why this is a very important project, considering Erica starts in a week."

"Okay, great, I'll get it done." I guess that means I'm dismissed.

When I get back to my desk, there's a message from Roseanne. I ask her about Pete when I call her back.

"He mentioned a play he is in, which I think means he wants me to go with him. We're on our way to becoming a real couple." I can practically hear her swooning. "But the reason I called you is because I saw this thing for a breast cancer fund-raiser. It's a run/walk. I thought it would be good for us to do, raise some money for a worthy cause."

"That sounds good, but I don't really run."

"That's why it's a run/walk. I run, you walk. We could see if Tab will do it, too."

"She never will."

"You'd be surprised. I bet there'll be all kinds of giveaways and a lot of good contacts, besides she's softening now that we know she's from upstate.'' Roseanne says she's a little embarrassed by the whole thing, but happy that she knows Tabitha is a little less glam than she pretends to be.

"All right, as long as we can walk."

So it looks like I'm back into the old routine. I'm toying with the idea of calling Todd. I wish someone could give me advice. Adrian gave great advice. I decide to just suck it up and end the conflict.

It's been a long time since I've been on this elevator bank. *Little Nell*'s floor looks totally different. They are totally reorganized, but from what I hear Adrian made out like a bandit and got promoted. I come up behind him and fidget for a while before I say his name. He turns around and looks kind of shocked to see me.

"Hey, Eve, how are you? I heard you weren't feeling so well." This is good, he's not cursing at me or giving me an attitude.

"Yeah, but I'm better, now."

"How's your mom?"

"She's fine," I smile at him. "Congrats on your promotion!"

"Thanks, I see Tabitha's been briefing both of us."

"Yep, so are you busy?" He laughs.

"In general swamped and I don't use that word lightly, believe me. Right now, I have a little time."

"Can I, uh, take you to lunch and work on begging your forgiveness?"

He studies me for a second and then says, "Honey, I'm there."

And that's that.

May

I don't know about flowers, but it definitely is a nice day in Central Park. We're standing on the Great Lawn listening to the celebs talk about what a good cause we're running for. Everyone is cheering. All three of us have my mother's name pinned on our cool new Prescott T-shirts. We were encouraged to pin the names of people we know who've had or have breast cancer on our shirts. I also have the name of one of my high school teachers who died while I was in college and Tabitha has the name of one of her cousins. But, it's amazing how many people are covered with names, many of them dead.

We all raised a lot of money. Many of the YFL people gave me a ton of cash. I think it was a political gesture but I didn't care. I was just happy to turn in my pledge sheet. Tabitha agreed to walk, but we had to assure her that Krispy Kreme was a sponsor. I haven't seen any of those melty delicious treats yet, so I hope she's not going to get pissy.

"So, we'll meet at the finish line, okay?" Roseanne is pulling her knees up to her chest. I nod. I kind of wish I told my sister I was doing this. Not to rub it in her face, but because it's totally her crowd, and would have loved it. There's a joyous whoop from the crowd when we take off. Roseanne waves and we watch her jog off.

"It's hot," Tabitha says.

"It's cool, and breezy! It's a good day, Tabitha, come on, I heard Halle Berry was here." She feigns indifference, but I know her eyes are darting behind her sunglasses. Suddenly, she pulls me closer to her and points.

"Look. Oh, Mother of God." I watch as Lacey and the Big C jog by, chatting. They look all together too designer fit, they are decked out.

"Wow, Lacey didn't mention she was running in this. Of course she didn't give me money, but I just assumed it was because she's a bitch. What do you think they're talking about?"

"How little they eat," Tabitha says. "They're congratulating each other for being the most fit any female could possibly be. It's their only joy." She might be right, but, I can tell after we walk a while that she's getting into it. She's complaining less and smiling a little. She's softening, but still has to maintain an image.

"Is it much farther now?"

"No, c'mon, we're doing good."

"I just hope this party is as good as the Aids Walk one was."

"Tabitha, I didn't know you did the Aids Walk. Are you doing it again this year?"

"Maybe."

"You're a regular philanthropist."

"Whatever."

I'm a little disappointed when the walk is over. The press is there and people are clapping and waving when we walk through the finish line. I stand for a little bit and cheer others through, while Tabitha looks for Roseanne. Not everyone who is running or walking is totally healthy; you can tell that some of these women are running to find a cure for themselves as much as for anyone else. I can't help but feel a little proud of these women that I don't even know. And I clap for them, imagining all the times I've wasted my applause at the Feed Meet, clapping automatically at articles on Scottish cyclists.

"Hey, Eve." I turn and see Roseanne and Tabitha standing with my parents. Oh, my God! They are both in jogging suits. She's wearing one of the scarves I got her. I run over to them.

"Did you guys do this?"

"What do you think, I quit smoking for nothing?" My dad pats his slightly smaller belly.

"But, Mom, do you feel okay?"

"Honey, I feel great. A lot of the women in my survivor's group were doing this and I thought it was a good idea. I didn't tell you, because I wasn't sure I'd do it, but when I got up this morning I knew I had to. I left you a message this morning, but I guess you had already left. Let's go get our totes of goodies."

Afterward, we sit on the grass and eat cheese nips and ice cream bars. We got a lot of good loot—makeup and magazines—and stuff from all the sponsors.

"You did really well, Mrs. Vitali," says Tabitha, going through my mom's bag, "I'm a little jealous."

"Yes, we survivors make out like bandits."

Roseanne is stretching out in the grass. I lie on one of the mag-

azines and put my new Breast Cancer Awareness shirt over my
eyes and fall asleep.

"Eve, honey." My mom is standing over me and I have no idea
how much time has passed. I think she looks younger with no hair.
I fell asleep, I guess on the grass, my butt feels wet. Great, grass
stains. "Daddy and I are going to drive home. Want us to give
you a lift back to the apartment?"

I sit up. Roseanne and Tabitha weren't sleeping. I wonder what
they were talking about with my parents. We all decide to head
back. My mom reminds me (and I guess my friends) that my
birthday is coming up in two weeks. Luckily, it's a weeknight, so
I can go home and have dinner with the 'rents and maybe, if
anyone is planning anything, I can celebrate the weekend with my
friends.

My parents hug my friends goodbye. Roseanne and Tabitha con-
gratulate my mom on her run (that's right, she ran—I walked).
After they're gone, we go home and sit out on the veranda for a
while. Roseanne makes lemonade. Tabitha doesn't smoke.

"You guys, I think I'm going to have an early night tonight,"
Tabitha declares.

"Tabitha, did you get too much sun?"

"I'm fine really, I just think I want to go home and take a bath
and try on my new lipsticks and maybe drink some cognac."

"Cognac?" We both say in unison.

"Tab, it's May. Pull out the mint juleps. Summer's on the
way."

"Eve, don't think in my overheated state you are going to get
away with calling me Tab. Now, I'll give you guys a call tomorrow. Maybe we'll grab a fatty brunch. I think I worked off too
many calories today. The last thing I want to do is lose my ass."

She let's herself out. Roseanne and I watch her hail a cab.

"Not much danger of her losing that ass."

"How much money will you give me if she's going to see a
guy now?"

"How much money will you give me if she stops at Krispy
Kreme first?"

"Eve, think it's strange that we're okay with the fact that she
stole, then sold, our underwear—used underwear—to men who are
probably using it to pleasure themselves?"

"I think what bothers me more is that she's from upstate."
Roseanne looks at me, shocked. "Kidding. Just kidding. I don't
mind, really. I wouldn't mind a percentage and I'm kind of sorry

that I didn't come up with the idea but, if it keeps another loser off the street and Tabitha occupied, what's the harm?''

"I guess you're right. Do you want to have an early night to-night?''

"Not a chance.''

On Monday, Tabitha pressures me about what I'm going to wear to my meeting with Prescott. I had been trying not to think about it. I'm still considering canceling.

"Eve, I bought you a very smart suit at one of those sales, a Max Mara, for this very occasion. C'mon. Do it for me! Please.''

"As if I didn't know. Don't you remember *GoodFellas* when they were all excited about Joe Pesci becoming a made man, be-cause they could never be made? He was the only true Italian. But when Joe Pesci got there, there was plastic on the floor and he knew right away. Pow!''

Wednesday comes before I know it. Tabitha's idea of prepping me is forcing me to spend over a hundred dollars on conservative sandals. These sandals still manage to show the pedicure she also included in her grand scheme prepping. Tabitha insists that not having the right shoes or toenail polish will destroy my credibility.

"Well, don't you think my credibility will be affected by the whole suspicious circumstances under which I'm meeting with him?''

"Eve, calm down, I can see you getting in one of your states. Just don't start talking about obscure films or anything.''

I wind up getting the suit from her. I must say I look pretty smart. I take the subway to work and when the train comes and the wind pushes back my hair, I definitely feel like my life is starting over. This feeling lasts me through the morning all the way up until I get on the elevator to Prescott's floor. I've never been on these elevators before. They are so hard core. The very first floor they stop on is forty-five. There is a certain distinction between the people that get on this elevator and the staff I'm used to. No one here bought their pants at Urban Outfitter.

I get to his floor, sixty. The receptionist looks me up and down—I know she can see through me. "Hi, I've got an appoint-ment with Prescott, that is, Prescott Nelson.''

"Go right through.'' I walk past a huge kitchen, an amazing oak conference room and (get this) a gym. There's a well-dressed older woman at a big desk.

"Hi, I am Colleen Brandes. You must be Eve Vitali,'' she says.

She's figured it out. She is going to tell me that there has been an awful mistake, and could I please return to the lower floors with the rest of the peons. If not, she'll call the armed guards.

"Yes, that's me."

"What a lovely name. Mr. Nelson is just finishing up a meeting, but we'll bring you in in a moment." She gestures to a plush sofa. I sit. I grab a magazine from the stack they have. The only other advice Tabitha did give me was to be aware of everything I did; all my body language, all my choices. Shit! Shit! Shit! I should have taken the financial magazine. I would have been taken seriously, then. Shit! What's the name of our financial magazine? What if Prescott tests me on the names of all his magazines?

"Ms. Vitali, he can see you now, come with me." Oh, my God! I toss the magazine back on the table. Why did I toss? Why couldn't I have placed? What is wrong with me?

I follow Prescott's assistant down the hall. She is walking softly; why do these wretched sandals make so much noise? What if Prescott is sensitive to noise? Why haven't they figured out my awful secret yet? I am destined to suffer for this. How could my friends not talk some sense in to me? We get to Prescott's door. It's closed. Colleen opens the door and puts her hand on my back to guide me in. No! No! I can't do this. I resist her hand, but she is firm. She closes the door behind me.

Then we are alone in the office, just him and me. There seems like miles between us. The office is amazing. It takes me a second to realize the low hum is Prescott talking on the phone. He looks up and gestures me over. There is only one chair for me to sit on directly in front of his desk. I stare out past him at the large view of the Hudson. This is living! He is talking so softly I can't make out what he's saying. Finally, he hangs up, writes something down in his book and smiles at me.

"Hi, Eve. I suppose you know why I wanted to speak with you." He's got a Chicago accent.

"Look, I know, I'm sure it was a big mistake. I understand." I look pleadingly at him. I am conscious of my pleading look. I tried it out in the mirror.

"Well, Eve, I randomly picked a sample of our temp force to speak with. Temporary and freelance employees are making up a larger part of our workforce and I wanted to talk to a bunch of you, personally, about ways we can make it easier for you."

"That's why?"

"Well, of course, didn't you inquire when you got the e-mail?"
I'm a dork.

"No, I didn't. I thought it was some kind of mistake. If it was,
I didn't want to correct it. I thought it would be cool to have an
audience with you." Prescott laughs, it's one of those gaspy laughs
you expect from men down south who sit on porches and smoke
too much. Any moment I expect him to slap his knees.

"An audience? Who am I? A king? A pope?" He laughs so
hard, he actually wipes his eyes. Prescott must not get out much.
Maybe I should tell him my "get on the subway and go straight
to hell" line. That would really have him in stitches. Maybe I
should see if he wants to come out for a drink with Tabitha and
me.

"It's just that I'm really excited to meet you. This is going to
sound really brownnosey, but I admire you, my friends and I think
you're really cool."

"Why, thank you." He is still recovering a little from the laughing attack. He opens up a thick folder on his desk.

"Is that a folder about all the temps?"

"No, this is your folder."

"My folder? How could you have that much stuff about me?
Oh, my God, do you have copies of my e-mails in there?" He
laughs again. I'm cracking this guy up.

"Your e-mails? Of course not." But then he composes himself.
"But, I would advise you to only use e-mails for official business.
And be aware that anything that you write on e-mail is owned by
the company."

"Yeah, well you might want to start with all those people who
think I'm interested in chain letters and dirty jokes." He nods,
considering this, I can't believe I am sitting here talking to Prescott
like a normal person. He laughs again.

"So all right then, Eve. Do you like working for Prescott Nelson
Inc? How are things going down at *Bicycle Boy* with all the
changes we have been implementing?"

"I guess okay. I think it's going to take some getting used to,
but we'll do it."

"Very nice, Eve, very diplomatic. You can be entirely truthful,
this is to benefit you, not hinder your progress in any way. You
can say whatever is on your mind. You have carte blanche." Carte
blanche, huh?

"I don't know where to begin." He looks at me, I think he

must dye his hair. I can't believe it's naturally silver. I'm trying to remember everything so I can tell Tabitha.

"I see here that you've applied for staff positions in quite a few of our magazines, most recently *Food and Fun*. You even sent story ideas to a few."

"Now, you're going way back."

"Yes, it's interesting that you stopped sending ideas into magazines around August of last year."

"Wow! You did some thorough research on me. This is how you make the big bucks." Prescott laughs some more about this, although not as maniacally.

"You know, a lot of good writers get rejected in the beginning. It's never easy."

"But it seems kind of fake, kind of wrong."

"What does?"

"I was sending in all these ideas to magazines I didn't really care about, to get a break, but what then, continue working on something I didn't really care about?"

"And being an assistant is better?"

"No, worse. I hate it." Maybe I should calm down, Prescott's not my therapist. He closes the folder and leans back in the chair. "Look, I'm sorry." So much for decorum. "I'm sure you didn't intend to listen to all my gripes. My parents always taught me to be happy about getting paid. It didn't work on my sister Monica, now here I am, complaining to you. My dad would kill me."

"No, I find this more interesting than anything my research could tell me. I'm not a creative person, so it's beneficial to hear this side." When he says that I think of Todd.

"I'm not creative, either, that's the problem. I can't remember the last time I was creative. No, I can, it was probably a week before I graduated college. I'm learning a harsh reality, that creativity falls by the wayside once you get out of school. There's no time to be creative anymore. No one cares. And you, you must be creative. Look at everything you own."

"Creativity comes in different ways. I'm more of a creative thinker, that's my secret." Is Prescott really letting me in on his secret? "Eve, what is it you want to do?"

"I don't know. I mean, I like to write, I like to go out, I like to believe there is more out there than what's in my life. I would love to encompass that in a magazine."

"What kind of magazine?"

"I don't know. I always know when I'm drunk. Got any mar-

garita mix?'' He shakes his head. Maybe I'm getting too familiar.
''I guess just something that was fun and cool and made you laugh
as you realized that you were slowly becoming an adult. A magazine about people who take chances and have fun, but for people
who are stuck in a rut. A magazine that shows you the possibilities.
A magazine for people my age, not just women. People who are
waiting for the better thing, you know. For people who are on the
verge. Of what? I don't know, neither will they. Does that sound
totally naive?'' He shakes his head.

''So why don't you start it?''

''How am I going to start it? I don't have capital. My parents
aren't rich. I've got no real connections—I went to a state school.
It's just something we talk about when we're drunk. I think it's
easier to let my brain be sucked out while I sit at my computer
inputting names or staring at the screen saver. I actually changed
it, finally. I put the New York skyline. I don't know why I am
talking so much. I'm not making any sense. That's the problem. I
don't know the first thing about starting a magazine. I totally lack
discipline to do anything like that anyway.'' Prescott nods at me.

''Sounds like a convenient excuse, Eve.'' I feel super small. ''If
this is something you want, you have to go for it. It isn't going to
fall into your lap. Not in this town. There's money to be made,
Eve, and fun to be had, but you have to work for it. And I suggest
you not work for me if that isn't where your heart is.''

I look down at my hands. I can't believe I'm admitting what a
failure I am to the head of the company. I have lost all subtlety.

''Do you want it, Eve? Do you want to work for yourself and
not for me? Do you want to not have your 'brain sucked out of
your head,' as you say? Do you want to see what it is you're on
the verge of, even if it's scary?

''When I bought this company I was running a few small printing presses in Chicago. Everyone told me not to do it. I didn't
listen. I believed in my vision, but I knew I was taking a risk. Ten
years later...'' He holds his hands up around him.

''It's all about determination and discipline, Eve. Do you know
what the most important thing is?'' Sounds like it's going to be
another D-word. I shake my head.

''Um, just doing it?'' He laughs.

''No, Eve. Courage. That's the most important thing.''

''I see.'' Maybe it's his intent blue-eyed stare or just plain
nerves, but I believe it.

"Well?" I wasn't expecting to be put on the spot. I take a deep breath.

"Yes." He nods and reaches into his desk. He opens up a large blue book and writes something down. Then he rips out a check and hands it to me. It's a check for ten thousand dollars.

"You're a temp so you can't get severance pay, but you can cash this if—" and he looks at me hard "—and only if, you decide to take that leap. Consider it severance pay. Consider it capital. The rest you have to do on your own."

"Can you do this?" I stare at the check, amazed. It looks real.

"I can do anything, I'm the president."

"But, why? I mean I could be a loser. I could go quit and go shopping."

"Well, I'll take that risk. Also, you went to a state school. Everyone needs a little push. Consider it an investment. You don't seem like you'd want to let me down and I like taking risks. These days, I can blame senility."

"Thank you, I mean, wow, thanks." He smiles.

"Besides, if the magazine ever does do so well it's a threat, I will have the canceled check as proof that I invested." He kind of lets that slide over my head, but I realize for all his claims of senility, he is still pretty sharp. "So anyway, my purpose in talking to you was also to find out about getting temps health care, but hopefully, you won't be eligible for that soon. So I guess we're done."

"Done? Wow! I can't believe it. I've been wanting to meet you for so long and now, well, now you gave me money." He laughs again.

"Well you should've come up here sooner."

I don't tell anyone about the check. It's too weird, too much pressure. I put the check in my room under my computer, which is gathering a lot of dust. I tell Tabitha that Prescott only cared about temp health care and that he was a sly old fox. I describe the office to her, relieved that we are on the phone, because I don't want to see her drool.

It's my birthday before I know it. I wake up with a little gift from Mother Nature—my period (I bet you thought I was going to wind up pregnant or something. Sorry, not that kind of story). I go home to my parents' house for the night. My mom makes a big dinner and my dad actually helps. My mom seems happy about everything. She tells me she is optimistic about not losing her breast and makes some kind of sex joke about my father that I block from my mind immediately. My parents are acting like people I don't even know, but it's sort of good in a way. I should be glad that they can pick up the pieces without their children.

My sister calls during dinner. She always has to get in on everything. My mom chats with her for a little while and then calls me over to talk to her

"Well, Eve—" she's going to have an attitude, I can tell "—I just wanted to say happy birthday, you know. Hope you're having a good day. I'll be home in a couple of weeks to bring you your present. I just want to say also that I'm sorry about the fact that we haven't talked in a couple of months. I hope to make up for that when we come home."

"We?"

"Chuck is coming home with me. I think we should have a little announcement by the end of the summer."

"What? Are you guys getting married? I thought you didn't believe in that."

"Eve, don't say it too loud. I don't want them to get too excited. We'll probably just have a commitment ceremony." I look over at my parents, who are holding hands and cuddling. I don't know how much of this I can take.

"Monica, believe me, that's the last thing you have to worry about. Besides, I'm surprised you don't just announce it today so you can attempt to ruin my birthday."

"Eve! Look, we really need to repair our relationship. This can be healed."

"Repair our what? *You* look, Monica, we just have to hang out, okay? Let's not get crazy. It doesn't have to be a big deal!"

"Eve! You have anger issues!" I'm going to try not to raise my voice at her so my parents won't get involved. At this point I think I could hop up on the table and do my "Lord of the Dance" impression without them taking their eyes off each other.

"Monica, I don't want to fight with you now, okay? Let's not write your master's thesis on this. We'll just hang out when you get back."

"Okay, Eve, I hope so, because I value you and respect you." Oh, the drama! "I want you to know I love you, honey."

"Yeah, me, too, honey." Help! Finally, I get her off the phone.

After dinner, my mom brings out a big cake. She and my dad sing "Happy Birthday" to me off key. It's sort of cute. We all laugh. I hate to say this and I never thought I would, but seeing

my parents all lovey-dovey makes me kind of wish I had a man.
I hate feeling lonely, especially on my birthday. It's not even like
I want to call Rob or anything. I guess I sort of wish he would
have remembered it was my birthday, but I honestly don't miss
him as much as I thought I would. I'd just like to have someone
to crawl into bed with on my birthday and get a good nasty present
from.

Instead, I'm stuck in the den with the TV really loud, so I won't
have to imagine what the noises are from my parents' bedroom.

Tabitha and Roseanne pretty much told me to make no plans
for the weekend of my birthday. They claim to have something
"fabulous" planned. I can't wait.

I didn't get a cake at work. That was the old regime. A cake
for every birthday. Now, we're lucky we get a happy birthday
e-mail. I started in this department just after my birthday last year,
so I missed out then. Always a bridesmaid, never a bride.

The first event of my fabulous weekend is a downtown spa. We
are all led to separate rooms. A large Eastern European woman
starts giving me a relaxing facial. She puts all kinds of heat on
my face and I feel like I'm going to fall into the best sleep.

It doesn't last. She takes off the warm wonderful stuff and is
torturing the hell out of my face. It lasts an eternity. Is this the
same thing happening to Tabitha and Roseanne? When it's finally
over the woman slathers moisturizer on me. Finally, she leaves,
and she's gone for a long amount of time. Is this a joke? Maybe
I should get up and go. Just as I am about to get up, another
woman comes in. She is Asian. She smiles at me sweetly, but now
I'm really scared. I look at the woman, helplessly.

"Waxy, waxy," she says. Oh, my God! Is she going to wax
me? They never told me! Why are they trying to torture me?
Hasn't anyone told them that it's my birthday?

The woman peels back my blanket with force. Suddenly, the
calming music that was once playing has turned into a samba. Why
is the score of my life so devastating?

"Off, off," she says insistently. How could my so-called friends
put me through this kind of torture? I take off my underwear. She
is staring at my crotch. This is awful.

"Oh," she nods, "what is your father?"

"Italian?" Is this what she means? It must be, because she nods.

"Yes, yes, Italian fathers make very hairy." Hello! It's my
fucking birthday present! Do I need to be insulted on this the most

wondrous of weekends? I can't believe these beauty regimes are making me feel so inadequate.

She then proceeds to rip the hairs off my most sensitive areas with no rhyme, reason, or consideration. Now, it's personal. In the middle of all of it, her friend comes in. They start speaking rapidly in another language as my beauty care "professional" continues to rip the hair off of my inner thigh. Hey, ladies! Guess who's not wearing any underwear? Can we maybe have this conversation over a drink *after* work? The worst part is I feel like they are talking about how hairy I am. Maybe I am just being paranoid, but this experience is not exactly something I want to share with the world.

"Lot of hair, lot of hair, almost finish." It's killing me. She does my legs next. It isn't as bad, but I have a feeling she is smirking at me the whole time for having an Italian father. I hate her. Finally she slaps me down with cream and powder.

"Finishy, finishy," she says. Great, thanks a lot. Maybe it's return karma. Maybe I should have been kinder to Zeke. Finally, I get my robe back on. Just as I leave Tabitha is coming out of her little room. We look at each other, then touch each other's faces. We head into the lounge where Roseanne is already sitting in her robe with a glass of wine, smiling like a superstar with glowing skin. Sometimes I forget how pretty she is.

"Wasn't it great?" We sit on the couch next to her and pour some wine. We both take a swipe at her skin. It's even smoother than Tabitha's or mine.

"It was great except for the torturing parts," says Tabitha.

Roseanne looks at us blankly. "Torturing parts? She said I had really great skin." I think Tabitha is going to pummel her. We sit around and drink a bottle of wine. When we get back into the locker room, Tabitha and Roseanne are putting on little black dresses. They hand me one, too. It's one of my dresses that they got out of my closet. I try to gauge their bikini areas—have they been waxed, too? Were they made to feel like part of a zoo?

"Where are we going?" I ask in the cab, but they ignore me. I can tell we are going farther and farther west. It's exciting. When we finally stop, it looks like we are in a dark, seedy part of the village. It smells like the meat-packing district.

It may seem like we are in the middle of nowhere, but they both head down a staircase and then, we are in a funky little restaurant with a long bar. Sitting at the bar are some of my favorite people. Adrian, Anthony, Todd and Pete.

I start giggling for no reason and feel embarrassed all of a sudden. Everyone is kissing me and saying happy birthday and of course, Tab orders us shots. It's some kind of strong whiskey. "Happy birthday, girl," Tabitha says. "We need to catch up with those guys." I look at Todd. He puts his arm around me.

"Yep, I got in at eight o'clock, haven't slept in two days. I'm still on Australian time, but it's all good." I hug him, I don't know why. It's so nice to see him. I look over at Pete and Roseanne, they are starting to look like a real couple.

We are seated at a big table in the back. I am sort of in the middle of everyone.

Todd is next to me. His eyes are already drunk and so is his smile. Before I know it there is wine on the table and appetizers. The food comes and I can't really concentrate on anyone's conversation. I keep smiling at Todd without really being able to hear what he is telling me. I feel like we are spectacles for all of the rest of the patrons and the restaurant staff, too. Are we being too loud?

Todd is feeding me some garlic mashed potatoes. I can feel my face is flushed. Everything is hitting me too fast. I get up to pee.

"Nice, Eve," says Adrian, "get up, so we can order your dessert." Everyone laughs except Roseanne. She follows me to the bathroom.

"Eve, it's your birthday—you are the star. No one expects anything from you. Have a good time! Don't worry about anything else."

"I am having a great time, really. Thanks for setting this up." We hug.

"Tabitha deserves some thanks, too, you know. She is going to be pretty pissed if she doesn't get it."

When I head back upstairs, there seems to be more wine than before. My glass, of course, is full. As soon as I sit down, a waiter comes over with a piece of tiramisu with candles in it. Everyone at the table sings "Happy Birthday" to me.

"Speech, speech!" yells Todd. I want to kick him.

"I just want to thank you all for coming out here tonight. It's been a kind of strange year. What am I saying? It's nice to have you all, you know, around. That's it, I guess. Oh, and please don't clap again. We're about to get booted out of this restaurant."

"Mother of God!" Of course Tabitha ruins our moment. "Let's pay the check and get to the bar."

"Oh, there's more," I say.

"Look at her being coy now," Adrian says to Tabitha.

"Watch her act all cute when she offers to pay the check," Roseanne says jumping in.

"Yeah, *offers*." Todd makes quotation marks with his fingers.

"Guys, it's my birthday, quit the ridicule."

We're waiting for the L train to take us across town. There's a guy with one of those pan flutes. Tabitha gives him a bunch of change and asks him to play "Happy Birthday." They all sing drunkenly. Todd smiles at me. I have to keep telling myself that he is just a friend and not to do anything stupid.

When the guy finishes he launches into the pan flute version of the Carpenters' "We've Only Just Begun." Todd just kind of smiles at me. I look around, but no one in my party seems to notice. When the train comes, I see the wind blowing up through his hair. He smiles at me, like his life is just beginning.

What do I know, I can't feel my nose?

We are going dancing in the East Village. The city is alive and I imagine it won't be for much longer. It will be summer soon and the city will empty out because people have better offers— summer houses, vacations and more air-conditioning. But right now, the city is at its peak. I am holding on to Roseanne so that I won't have to hold on to Todd. She needs to hold on to someone as badly as I do, but I think she would prefer her someone was Pete.

I am in the perfect condition to dance. I balance my large blue drink in my hand and start to sway. Roseanne and Tabitha sort of corral me onto the floor. I am spilling a little, but trying not to get too messy.

I feel someone touching my shoulder. I whip around, thinking it's some stupid guy, but it isn't, it's my sister Monica, and Chuck. I can't believe it! I give Monica a big hug. "Oh, my God! What are you guys doing here?"

"Well, I had talked to Roseanne and figured it would be a nice surprise."

"It's great, I can't believe it." I am even happy to see Chuck. I can tell they're stoned and want to cuddle and chill on the couches so I head over to Todd, who is smoking. "Hey, what are you doing? You don't smoke."

"Come on, I'm in New York." The music changes then to a loungey reggae song and everyone on the dance floor starts bumping and grinding. Todd and I look at each other, not sure what we're supposed to do. He raises an eyebrow at me and says, "Better me than any of these other losers, Ms. Vitali."

We dance and I drop my drink on the floor. He holds me close, laughing. I look over at Roseanne, who is literally making out with Pete on the dance floor, but comes up for air long enough to say very loudly, "Aren't you glad we got you that wax?"

I'm embarrassed until I realize that Todd has no idea what we are talking about. We dance some more and then he kisses my neck. "Todd! Hey!"

"Listen, I'm sorry about that."

"No big deal, just took me by surprise." I don't want to make an issue out of it.

"Me, too." We all dance for a while. The crowd swells at one point and the room feels hotter, but we hold our frozen drinks against our faces and keep dancing.

The crowd thins out a little and it gets cooler. Monica and Chuck decide to leave, so I give them my key and urge them to take my bed. I can't help smiling at everyone, including Tabitha. I know she's thrilled that I am having such a good time.

The next thing I know, the lights come on and the place is shutting down. I can't believe it, four o'clock already.

"I am going to be sick," says Roseanne. Pete rubs her belly and she kisses him. Wow, I guess they are turning into a real couple.

"I'm sure you'll be okay," Tabitha says. Her tone makes me laugh.

"Tabitha, are you staying with us tonight?" I'm having trouble focusing on her face, but when I do I see her do the once-over to the guy she's been talking to. I've seen it all before. It makes me laugh so hard I almost pee my pants. "Oh, I get it, I get it. You've already found a place to stay."

"I think someone needs to take the birthday girl home," she says.

"Tabitha, it's your birthday, too." Everyone laughs at me, except Tabitha.

The cab ride is quick. I fall asleep on Roseanne, who is in turn asleep on Pete, who is drooling and snoring against the window. I wake up when I hear Todd in the front asking me if I'm awake. I nod, kind of startled, and he pays the fare.

It's a tough flight up the stairs, but easier because I'm holding Todd's hands, tight. When we get into the apartment, I remember that Monica and Chuck are here, so I drag the futon onto the floor. Roseanne and Pete pass out on the couch.

I can't stay in my tight black dress, so I head into my room to try to see if I've left any pajamas on the floor. It's dark in there, but I can hear breathing and the sounds of moving sheets. Eww! It's not something I want to hear or think about. I rub my feet around on the floor until I remember that I cleaned up my room on Wednesday. Shit! Why did I pick this week to be neat? The only way I am going to find my pajamas is if I turn on the light. I am not too drunk to realize that would be a bad idea.

I go back out into the living room. Todd is watching me from the futon. I smile down at him. Once again we are forced to sleep together. "Are you all set with the light?"

"Yeah." I switch it off and quickly peel off my dress. I hope he can't see my bra or underwear. I lay stiffly on the other side of the futon. I will not cross over to his side.

"Eve, are you awake?" says Roseanne, shaking me out of dreams. She is all dressed in workout clothes. Pete is standing up next to her. I look down and realize I am only in my see-through black lace bra. I pull the sheet up. I look at Todd, who is sleeping underneath the sheet, he is holding my hand.

"What time is it?"

"It's noon. I just wanted to let you know that Pete and I are going to Central Park for a jog."

"What? Why?" There is no way I can understand how anyone would want to do any kind of physical activity.

"It's a beautiful day out. Your sister and Chuck already left. They left a note. You can go sleep in your bed, if you want." I can't move.

"That's okay. Roseanne, can you just get me a T-shirt or something and some Aleve?" Roseanne comes back with everything and some water. Pete is looking real uncomfortable, so I am as discreet as possible as I slip my T-shirt over my head.

"I'm going to wait downstairs," Pete says. "Happy Birthday, again, Eve."

"Thanks, Pete, take care." Some day that kid has to loosen up.

"I'm probably going to hang out at Pete's tonight. I hope you feel better and—" she looks at Todd and winks at me "—have fun."

"Whatever. Give me a call later."

"I will." She leaves and I fall back asleep for another two hours.

When I wake up, Todd is staring at me. Weird. Luckily, we're not holding hands anymore. "What's up, birthday girl? We slept a long time."

"Yes, we did. Roseanne and Pete have been gone for a while. Maybe we should go for a walk and seize the remainder of the day. I hear it's nice out."

"Yeah, I could go for some coffee, maybe some aspirin." As I get out of the futon, I am aware how short my T-shirt is. I tug it down and run to my room for some shorts.

After Todd has about four aspirin and I have two more for good measure, we get dressed and head over to 10th Avenue for some outdoor breakfast. It's really beautiful out. I feel like Todd and I are on a date. I totally think he thinks so, too.

"You know, here we are chomping on bacon and eggs and Pete and Roseanne were up at what seemed like the crack of dawn this morning to go for a run. Crazy."

"Yeah, we'll never be one of those couples," he says. We look at each other awkwardly. "I mean, not that we are a couple or anything." We spend the rest of breakfast gossiping about Roseanne and Pete and other couples we know. We stay far away from anything that could be about us.

When we get up after paying the check I decide to ask him what I've been curious about. "So, whatever happened with that girl in Atlanta?"

"Oh, um, it didn't really work out. I was away too much, which they tell me is an occupational hazard. Probably why I shouldn't get involved with anyone else for a while." We head over toward the pier. Everyone and their mother is outside today. Bikers and roller-bladers whiz by us.

"What about you and that guy?"

"Guy? He was a man. Nothing happened. I don't even know what happened. I think I liked him too much."

"He didn't like you back?"

"He did. I mean I guess he did, but you know, he liked his job a lot, too. I didn't really like his job and that was a problem. It's strange that we're at an age where our jobs could even play a part in our relationships. I feel like it's too bad I don't like my job more, then it might be worth it."

"I like my job and I don't think it's worth it. You shouldn't have to sacrifice things for it." We settle onto the edge of the pier.

"Did you really like that girl?"

"I don't know. I don't think so. I think I was hung up on someone else."

"Oh." For me to not ask who it is, means I think I know. For him to not tell me, means I'm right. We sit looking at the Hudson River for a while. A dog on a long leash comes over and we pet it a while, getting slobbered on.

Todd tells me to hang out while he goes to get something. He's gone for almost a half hour. It's not bad, though, I lean on my elbows and throw my head back, enjoying the sun. He comes back carrying two paper bags. From one he pulls out cheese and crackers. From the other, he pulls out a bottle of wine and tiny paper cups.

"Nice." We cut up the cheese with his pocketknife and drink the tiny shotlike cups of wine. "Definitely unhealthy." We sit there till the sun sets, later than usual. The summer is that much closer to us.

"What do you want to do tonight?"

"Well, it's still your birthday weekend, you decide."

"Do you want to just rent a movie or something? Or is that lame?"

"Eve, I've been here enough times. You don't have to impress me anymore."

"That's reassuring."

Back at home, we start watching the movie and get through the first bottle of wine (there are two). It seems like we are sitting closer on the couch than we ever would have before. I am more aware of him than usual. It's strange to be so conscious of him and every move he makes. I find myself staring at his hands as he scratches his knee. I am positioning myself so he can take my hand if he decides to.

"I wish we had some more of that cheese," he says.

"Oh, you know what we do have?" I don't know why I am so excited.

"What?" He's laughing.

"Peanut butter, I love spoons of peanut butter. Come on." I almost knock the wine over as I get up to pause the movie. He follows me to the kitchen, laughing. I search the cabinets. Where is it? Then I think about Roseanne's crazy fear of mice. I fling open the fridge. "Eureka!"

Todd is holding on to the Eat in Kitchen table, he is laughing so hard. I can't get the lid open fast enough. "It's really good, it's delicious. You're going to want some, I guarantee it.'' I dip in a big spoonful. ''Mmm!''

''Well come on,'' he says, grabbing my hand, ''let me get some of that.'' I turn back toward the peanut butter. It was a mistake to drink all that wine in the sun. Todd comes up close behind me. I turn around and we're really close. I hold the peanut butter spoon up to him, unsure of whether or not to feed him. He kind of laughs as I sort of shove the spoon in his mouth, hitting teeth on the way.

''Oh, I'm sorry.'' He shakes his head, holding his mouth. ''But, wait, wait, isn't it good?'' He nods.

Then something weird happens, something that's been coming. He puts his hands on my waist. I can feel his fingers on my skin. He is holding me tightly; he seems to be holding me down on the floor. I reach behind me to put the spoon down. Our faces get closer and I can smell the peanut butter and wine on his breath.

''What's up?'' I say like an asshole. We put our foreheads together. And then, we kiss. His mouth is warm and, damn! He can kiss. The nicest part is that we keep kissing, and then we stop and hug and kiss some more.

Then we're in my bed. I'm on my stomach and he's kissing my back. I'm still kind of drunk, but the room isn't spinning or anything so I can really enjoy this. Who knew? How could Todd have been this good, and the whole time right under my nose? I can't believe it. I'm going to be really loud.

But, wait! I can't do that. I can't wreck my image. I have to keep my mystique (besides I have my period). I need to turn the tables. I sit up and push Todd back on the bed. He deserves a little treat for sticking it out, for being down for the long haul. He kept the faith, all the while holding a candle for me. You got to love this guy and I am going to love him good.

Now, I'm no expert on these matters. I definitely think getting is better than giving, but I'm going to do it. I pin Todd's hands up and shake my hair over his chest (I have to believe he's been working out a lot since freshman year) and then I decide to just go for it. I am going to be so good Todd will never get me out of his head. The biggest obstacle is just getting his boxers off without hurting anything in the process. I kiss his belly for a while, urged on by his heavy breathing, and then I go for it. I think it's going smoothly until I feel him tugging my hair and careening me back to reality.

''Eve, Eve, come here.'' Shit! I must have done something wrong.

"What? I'm kind of in the groove here."

"I know, but I think maybe we should take this slow." Slow?

"Are you serious? Are you sure? I mean I thought this is what you wanted."

"Well, it is, but I just want to go slow."

"Oh, okay." I can only see his face in the shadows. "Why?"

"Well, for one thing, because you're drunk."

"Only a little." He laughs.

"Right. And also, two months ago you were all about some other guy. Don't get me wrong, I like it, but I want to make sure I'm not just some kind of rebound. I've kind of been imagining something like this for a while and I don't want it to be for the wrong reasons."

I stare at him in the dark. All this time, I've thought of Todd as just this kid who used to watch me make microwave cookies in the dorm kitchen and now I realize he's a man, a mature man. Scary. I don't know what to say. "Oh."

"Besides, Eve, I don't know if we should get all up in this when I'm going back to Atlanta. I mean I never planned to have a long-distance relationship."

"You mean, you just want me to hold you?"

"No, you can talk to me, too." So I do and then we fall asleep. Sometime in the middle of the night we wake up kissing again and then doze off again. It's nice.

I get up and make us coffee in the morning (look at me being domestic!). I run out to get the *Times*. He has a one o'clock flight. We sit in my bed drinking coffee and reading the paper. He doesn't get as into the *Times* as I do. He only cares about the sports section, which is good because we don't have any section conflicts. I don't want him to leave. I half expected to not be into him once we got up this morning, but I still am. We lie around kissing for as long as possible.

When it's time to go, he kisses the top of my head. "I hope you had a happy birthday, little Eve."

"I did. I'm really glad you were here."

"Me, too." He pulls me back for another kiss, then gets into the cab. He leans out the window. "I'll call you."

"Okay," I say, and put my hand up to wave. I watch his cab drive away.

When I get to work on Monday, I'm a tad depressed. I am twenty-four. I'm supposed to be mature now. I just want to stop thinking about everything and accept that it's normal that people my age aren't supposed to know what they want to do, but I can never seem to shake the feeling that I'm being sucked in.

When I get off the elevator, there are two cops and one security guard in the lobby. Did I do anything illegal this weekend? Is someone else getting fired? When Lorraine got fired there were security guards, but this is for real. This is New York's finest.

"What's up?" I ask Lacey, who is hanging out at my desk.

"It's Gary." Oh, my God! Gary is being taken out of his office in handcuffs.

"Gary!" I scream, and the cops give me a funny look. "What's going on?"

"Take care of yourself, Eve. You're a sweet kid." I'm a little in shock, but I can't really think about it, because one of the boys in blue starts asking me questions.

"We're going to want to talk to you further, miss. Is this where you'll be all day?"

"This is my job, of course I'll be here."

"Good, I wouldn't plan on making any sudden trips."

"What?" I yell at the officer. Soon there is another one next to us and Lacey has backed away from my desk, no doubt deciding her supply needs can wait. "Why are you talking to me like that? I don't even know what's going on! I just got here and I see cops carting off one of my co-workers."

"We'll be by a little later to talk to everyone."

"Great, I'll cancel my trip to the Cayman Islands." A disbelieving crowd gathers around my desk. They are buzzing about what Gary could have possibly done. I wish they would get away from my desk. I still have to answer these crappy letters every month and I can't do it with all the noise.

They don't stop talking about it. They're throwing out theories. Someone suspects embezzlement, but I get involved enough to announce that Gary didn't really handle any money and I would know if he had any sketchy expense reports. Everyone nods at me solemnly when I say this like I'm some sleuth or something.

"I know what it was," says Lacey, strolling over. Of course she has to steal my spotlight. Everyone turns to her, waiting. "He was selling drugs. Had been for months. He was doing illegal steroids, too. Hadn't anyone noticed how big his calves had gotten?"

"How do you know?" I ask, but she sort of waves her hand at me.

"It was common knowledge." Whatever, I suspect Lacey's got

some secrets herself. She seems like she would be a cocaine person or a secret diet pill junkie.

I keep forgetting that the staff meeting has been officially switched to Monday to accommodate the *Yoga for Life* people. It happened while I was out for mental health reasons. Every Monday since then I've been forgetting about the meetings. I like to have moments to unwind, Monday morning especially, but instead I have to hurry down to the meeting at 11:00 and listen to a lot of boring announcements. Today everyone is whispering about Gary, but the only official word is that we will be advised when more is revealed. Herb even reads a piece that Gary wrote, which I think is a little strange.

When I get back from the meeting, I call Tabitha, who has some news of her own. She wants to tell me in person, but the Big C is breathing down her neck, trying to get ready for her impending departure. We agree to meet in The Nook at 1:30. That means I have two hours to make a serious dent in these letters that have become my nemesis.

I don't get a chance to tell Tabitha about Gary, because as she is furiously eating The Nook's version of chicken cordon bleu, she is talking hyperspeed about Elliot, the guy she wound up with this weekend. I can see all the cheese in her mouth as she chews and talks. I hate when she gets like this. I suppose it is kind of worth it, because this news is so amazing and shocking; Elliot works at (and Tabitha takes a big deep breath before she says this) Krispy Kreme.

"But, Tabitha, I thought you were through with service industry types."

"Eve, that was ages ago."

"Well, Elliot is American. If he's American and works at Krispy Kreme he can't have all that much money. Summer's here, does he even have an air conditioner?"

"That's the thing, Eve, I don't need his money, I have enough money and you and I are going to make more money as soon as we get this magazine off the ground. Don't make that face, you have until the end of the month to decide, and I might just do it without you if you aren't in. Anyway, maybe I was looking for the wrong things in my men. Whatever I was looking for, I've found it in Elliott." She's talking crazy now. Any second the food is going to come flying out of her mouth. It only gets worse. "I think he's got everything I need."

"Why? Because he can get you unlimited Krispy Kreme?"

"Eve, don't be ridiculous. I'm sure that's part of it, but, it's more I don't know. I feel complete after this weekend. Did you know he's in a band?"

"No, Tabitha, I never met him before my birthday. Are you sure it wasn't just—?" I punch my hand in the air.

"Eve, are you kidding? Of course that was fabulous, but it's everything else. It's not about that anymore. I, too, am maturing."

"Great. Did you tell him about your little side business?"

"Yes. I told you, I'm all about honesty."

"You mean to tell me that he was okay with you selling your bloomers?"

"Of course he was a little taken aback at first, but then I think he saw it as an assertion of my independence."

"How progressive of him."

"Come on, Eve. Be happy for me. Don't be suspect. If I can get over his social strata so can you. He only works in Krispy Kreme so he won't have to get a real job and take time away from making his music. The fact that I love Krispy Kreme is just an added bit of fabulousness."

"Well, when you put it that way…"

"Come on, Eve." I guess she's right. She does seem super (almost sickeningly) happy. I should support her, regardless of what's going on in my love life. I am too confused by it to even go there with her or Roseanne. When Roseanne asked me Sunday how the rest of my time with Todd was I just left it at fine. Here Tabitha is, excited about a guy and not being a snob about it and not only into the booty—maybe she is the one who is really serious about maturing.

I decide to abandon her happiness for a moment and tell her my big news. "You'll never believe what happened this morning when I got to work."

"The writer Gary was arrested."

"How did you know?"

"It's common knowledge."

"That's what Lacey said. She said it was drug related."

"It was. He was not only selling drugs but using the Prescott Nelson courier, Eagle Express, to messenger them all over the city."

"I can't believe it. Now it looks like Prescott was responsible somehow."

"That's right, that's why they had to arrest him at work. They didn't want any ties to it."

"I can't believe you know so much about this."

"I've got my ear to the ground, Eve, and I've got the right connections." She is super proud of herself now. "Tonight there is a gala event at a Soho loft for some celebrity-endorsed charity. Our names are on the guest list."

"Is it going to be fun?"

"It's going to be fabulous! It's Monday night, we're going to get drunk and smoke lots of cigarettes. We're going to kick off the summer." And we do.

"Eve, you look great, I'm glad you wore that lipstick." Rose-anne was going on a date with Pete, so she didn't come. I think I'm going to have a hard time dealing with the both of them, if they are going to be locked in their lovers' embrace all summer.

We give our name to the people at the front, just as a famous actress is whisked in. There is a paparazzi line again, which gives the party a whole new dimension. Tabitha doesn't look at them, so I know they must think that with her sunglasses she might be someone. We rush in, laughing as soon as we get inside.

It's quite the setup. Our job now is to get as drunk as possible. We grab drinks. Tabitha sees the *NY By Night* press photographer and asks her to get a photo of us. I set my glass down and suck my stomach in.

"I love my new job," says Tabitha when we're getting some food. "I'll make sure to put one of the pictures of us in. I know I can slip it in under the wire, just as the Big C is about to leave. We'll get a little buzz going about us. We don't even need talent, just curiosity." I love Tabitha when she talks like this, it's easy to play along.

There are celebrities everywhere, they hang out among the public for a little while before heading off to their roped-off room. "Tabitha, can we get in there?"

"Eve, I don't know. I don't think this press pass covers it."

"Well let's grab a drink and try." I can tell the room is tiny, but the bouncers are being pretty strict about who gets in. They are checking names. There is a balding guy in front of me with a long white ponytail. Two scantily clad girls run up and kiss him.

"John, can you get us in here?" He puts his arm around them and guides them in. I tug his ponytail and smile when he turns around. I am trying to emulate the scantily clad girls without getting scantily clad.

"John, can you let us in, too?" He shrugs, and then guides Tabitha and me inside the room.

"Let them in," he says to the bouncers, and they do.

So we're in. It's a tiny smoky room, but we scam the couches. We sit, casually, like we belong, and can't help feeling like we scored. We smile at each other. The girls on the couches next to us are around our age, only more expensively dressed. We try to figure out who they are. One of them is the ex-girlfriend of some sitcom celebrity.

"Look who just walked in." I look up and see this totally famous actress approaching. Oh, my God! It's big. She is actually a celebrity in her own right. She waves at the women next to us and smiles at us in case we might be with them. She brings her entourage over and stands by the couches next to us.

"There is no way we're ever giving up these couches," Tabitha says. She is thrilled that we have something a celebrity covets. Tabitha motions to a sexy waiter and orders us two more drinks. We hold on to our fabulous couch for another hour; Tabitha smiles wickedly as she orders drink after drink. The actress has to sit awkwardly on the coffee table as she chats with the ex-girlfriend. They both went to the same expensive Manhattan girls' school. This justifies Tabitha's actions. She is totally smug.

Finally, I propose something radical. "Tabitha, we've held out long enough, what say we relinquish and mingle? Maybe there's someone else we might want to scope out."

We get up. I can tell Tabitha is a little wobbly, but she has her dignity. We walk around. The place is star-studded. E! Entertainment Television has a camera set up and their obnoxious host eyes us, not sure if we should be interviewed. It's the second time tonight someone has thought we could be worthy of being photographed.

"Oh, great, look," says Tabitha, stopping dead in her tracks. It's Kevin, the makeup artist she loves. "I suppose you're going to go and buddy up with him again."

"Tabitha, I doubt he'll remember me."

"Well, you might as well go see, Eve. Prove it to me one more time that I am destined to watch you woo away all my idols." We walk over to Kevin.

"Hi," I say, "how are you?" He smiles, but I doubt he remembers me.

"Okay, you?" He smiles at Tabitha, too.

"Good. Drinking."

"That's always fun." I can't believe we are actually having a conversation with him. Then his cell phone rings. He checks the number. He looks at us almost (dare I say) apologetically. "I'm having a little drama tonight. I've got to take this."

"Sure," I say. "Good luck." Tabitha and I walk around some more. By one o'clock the party is dying out. We don't want to be the last ones to leave, so we decide to head out, too. In the cab we are drunk and victorious. Tabitha's only problem is that Krispy Kreme is closed.

"You know," I say to Tabitha, "those people all just have luck and a good publicist."

"But, Eve, we've got talent and determination."

"Do we?"

"I sure hope so." I roll down the window in the cab and let the wind blow my hair as we head up 8th Avenue. I turn to tell Tabitha that I've made my decision, that I'm going to quit and as they say, give it a go, but she is sleeping and smiling in her sleep, which is sort of sweet. So, instead I chat with Amhal, my driver, for a while and then help Tabitha up the stairs when we get to my apartment.

The next day, I head into Herb's office at ten o'clock. There is no sense putting it off. Of course, I should have known he was in a meeting (I planned it), so I have to wait until 11:00. He's listening to monks chant when I go in. It is sort of a religious experience for me.

"You've been doing a great job with the letters, Eve," Herb says right away. I am not going to be foiled.

"Thanks." I am going to wait to see if I get any more compliments.

"I know it isn't the most challenging of projects, but it is invaluable. We are all still transitioning, but I think you're doing wonderfully." He pauses for so long that I almost help him with the words.

"Thanks." Stay strong. "But I'm quitting." The chant music swells to the climax as I say that, it works out just perfectly. I can tell Herb didn't hear me.

"It's great to have someone like you on the team. Someone with your youth and—" here's that pause again "—enthusiasm."

"Thanks a lot. But I'm quitting." This time he hears me.

"Excuse me?"

"Quitting. This is my two weeks' notice."

"Well, Eve, naturally, I'm surprised."

"Why?"

"Excuse me?"

"Why are you surprised? I mean I'm just wondering what you know about my character that makes you surprised?" I'm proud of myself for asking this question. It points out the fact that Herb doesn't really know anything about me. I've been his assistant—secretary—whatever—for almost a year and he has no clue why. It makes us both a little uncomfortable, but I'm secretly enjoying it, too. A lot.

"I thought you liked your job." He is talking much faster now, searching for something he knows about me. "You wanted to write, and I thought we were both in agreement that this correspondence was a step in the right direction."

"Well—" I am going to be as polite and matter-of-fact as possible "—I guess it could be considered a very baby step, but I think I've been here long enough to deserve a chance at a bigger step. Honestly, it just seemed to me like work that no one else had the patience to do."

Herb looks genuinely shocked by that. "Are you leaving the department or Prescott Nelson altogether?"

"I'm leaving altogether." This seems to appease him.

"What are you going to do?" Tabitha and I have discussed not mentioning what we want to do to anyone at work. I guess it was sort of silly for me to go straight to the top and tell Prescott, but Tabitha doesn't know I did. She intends to keep her job if I quit mine and use it for any office supplies and long distance calls we need. She feels it would be ultra-subversive and somehow similar to Gary's use of the Prescott Nelson messenger to transport drugs. Although it kills me not to tell Herb that I plan to start a magazine, I don't want to. Even though I don't want him to think that I'm some stupid kid with no ambition, I want him to know I have it in me to do more, because now I am starting to believe it myself. But, it's mine and I want to keep it that way, for now.

"I'm going to do something I love," I say finally, very proud of myself.

"Well, we'll need to train someone to replace you. You're giving us two weeks, aren't you?" He is all business, suddenly concerned about who'll keep his schedule.

"Yes, two weeks."

"Thanks, Eve." I stand up and he holds his hand out for me. I don't think we've ever shook hands before, I squeeze hard, just because. "I'm sorry we couldn't make it work better."

I feel great when I walk out of his office. It's amazing. I thought I would be scared, but I feel free. It's incredible. I call Tabitha to give her the news.

"Hi, Eve. I can't talk, the Big C is interviewing editors—I have to be an intimidating presence. I'll call you back."

I phone Roseanne, but get her machine. I decide maybe it's best not to play favorites and tell them together. So I call Human Resources Harry instead and arrange to have a temp train to replace me, starting next Monday.

The next week is sort of weird. I keep trying to get Roseanne and Tabitha together, but one's too busy with her man when the other one is free. I know I should be happy for them. I mean I've been pretty selfish about boys in the past, every dog should have her day, whatever, but it also kind of makes me miss Todd. He gives me a call on Wednesday and I tell him the news. He's the first person to know that matters.

"Eve, that's awesome. I'm proud of you. How are you going to get started?"

"I have no idea. This is the scary part. I bought a couple of books and I'm enrolling in a class at the New School. I don't know anything about the practicality of it, I just know what I want the content to be. How does that sound?"

"It sounds great to me. My own little magazine maker." We laugh. He is heading to the Philippines in the morning. He promises to e-mail or call when he can.

"Any chance you'll be in New York anytime soon?"

"I was thinking of stopping over there for a few days on my way back."

"There is nothing I would rather see than you, all jet-lagged and grumpy. Come on down, you'll get to see me unemployed and a nervous wreck."

"Great. I miss you. I really do."

"I miss you, too. I guess I didn't think too much about the practicality of this, either. I guess I'm just sort of going with things."

"Me, too." We get off the phone before I can get positively giddy, but I do feel a lot better about finally getting it off my chest.

I haven't even told anyone at work yet. Everyone is still so freaked out about Gary's drug bust. I'd like my own spotlight, my own fanfare. I decide to make a date with the girls for brunch on

Sunday. "It'll be great," I tell them separately. "We'll read the *Times,* I'll make a frittata, it'll be fabulous."

"Eve, you don't cook," says Roseanne.

"I'll bring the alcohol and the Krispy Kremes," says Tabitha.

I get up early on Sunday and pick up the paper. I buy the best ingredients and the freshest produce so Roseanne will have nothing to say but "delicious." The cooking goes off without a hitch and at 12:30 sharp, Tabitha arrives. I think she suspects something, she's never prompt. I open the door and she pushes mimosa ingredients at me.

"Hi, Tabitha. Why don't you work on those while I finish this stuff up?"

"Great, I thought I was going to be catered to. Had I known, I would have stayed in bed with Elliot." She and Roseanne kiss hello.

It takes me a few more minutes to get everything ready and then I bring it into the living room. We sit with the papers spread out in front of us and start to eat. I watch them chew carefully.

"It's pretty good, Eve."

"Yeah," says Tabitha, "I didn't know you could be domestic."

I am convinced now that I can, in fact, do anything. I give them a few more minutes to enjoy my frittata deliciousness, before telling them. I clear my throat as they start to look through sections of the paper. Tabitha has the Styles section, Roseanne has the City section. "So, um, the reason I wanted to make brunch for both of you guys is not because I think I can cook or anything, but because I've been doing a lot of thinking—"

"Oh, my God!" Tabitha doesn't look up from her paper, but I know I was right in thinking that she was onto me.

"I'm sorry, it's taken me so long to come to this, but—"

"Roseanne, it's us!" Tabitha is shrieking at Roseanne and holding up the paper. "It's Eve's elbow and my neck, shoulder and hair—it's unmistakable."

"Oh, my God, Tabitha! Oh, my God!" Roseanne is shrieking, too, and staring at the paper. "It is you, I can't make out Eve, but that's totally you."

"It is me! It is! I can't believe I am in the Styles section on the *Times!* I've arrived! I've really arrived!" She is jumping up and down now, screaming with Roseanne.

The floor is shaking from their jumping, the walls are echoing from their shrill voices. Finally I scream louder than they are, if that's imaginable. "Hey! I'm trying to tell a story! Can anyone listen to me?"

They stop immediately and look at me like I'm a big baby. Then they look at each other like they did when they tried my frittata. I feel like I'm dealing with a two-headed monster. Again, Roseanne speaks first. "God, Eve, you should be happy, you're in it, too."

"Barely," says Tabitha, smirking. This is her payback for my brushes with greatness. She is a bitter, bitter girl.

"Look, you guys, I'm glad parts of us are in the Styles section. It's great. It's better than being at the wedding they base the Vows column on, but I have some important news that I've been waiting almost a week to share with you."

They are doing it again, looking at each other. I've created a monster, I fully blame myself. Tabitha takes a deep breath. "Eve, what?"

"I did it."

"Did what?"

"Quit." They look at each other again. This is getting ridiculous. They shake their heads. The next I know they are grabbing me and hugging me and shrieking louder than ever. That is the one thing I'm sure of, but it's fun. I'm jumping up and down with them.

"You know what this means?" Tabitha asks.

"More mimosas," offers Roseanne.

"Yes, in the immediate sense, but in the long run, the big picture—" this time Roseanne and I shrug at each other "—that we are going to be in the Styles section again. This time it's going to be one of those 'A Night Out With' things they do. It's going to be a night out with us. It will bring back a celebration of the full-figured woman. This is going to happen for us. Oh, my God! We have to call Adrian! We need more liquor. It's Sunday, we have to go to a bar. We'll expense it. It'll be our first company celebration."

I get up later than I planned to Monday morning. It's muggy, I can feel that already. I want to get everything ready for the temp, so I decide to take the subway. It's waiting at the station as I rush down the stairs. I'm lucky. On the way to work, I compose the e-mail I'm going to send out on Friday. It will have to be meaningful and not sappy. I want to leave a good impression on everyone.

Of course, I forgot *again* that Monday is now meeting day. I'm worried that the temp is going to be sitting up here waiting for me while I'm at the meeting, but I guess I should go because they are probably going to announce my impending departure. I have to have my swan song.

I head down there and grab a whole wheat bagel with some veggie cream cheese. I look around the room. No one suspects I am going to leave them and move onto greener pastures. (I know what you're thinking—does anyone care?) Lev, the *Yoga for Life* editor, starts the announcements. Some guy on his staff, whom I haven't really met, is leaving to work on a dairy farm in Massachusetts. I'm kind of bummed that he got to go first, all the YFL people get all upset. But maybe it will work to my advantage, maybe the *Bicycle Boy* crew will feel they have to outdo YFL with their sadness. After a respectable amount of silence Herb gets up and clears his throat. Here we go.

"I'm sorry to say that we have another departure. I know, it seems like everyone is leaving us for one reason or another." He is referring to Gary, which I think is a cheap attempt to get a laugh. "This woman hasn't been here long enough. I think she's changed the way a lot of people think and she's brought her own individuality to every project she's worked on. She really shook things up around here. I know you'll miss her as much as I will, but she's going on to bigger and better things."

I can't believe he's saying all this about me. Is this because we had the talk? I didn't realize I made such an impact on everyone. I vowed not to have any regrets about this, but I wish he had said all these things sooner. Maybe I should stand up or something, he's making it sound like I ran the magazine. I focus back in on him and get ready to feel the waves of sadness in the room, "I know you'll all join me in wishing Lacey Matthews all the best—" (what?) "—as she joins another team and becomes editor of *NY By Night.*"

Oh, my God!!!

How could she do this? How could Lacey steal this moment from me? How could Tabitha keep this to herself? Is he even going to announce me?

"We also have another departure. Of course, this one affects me a lot. This woman has served the magazine so well for just over a year. Her work has been quite valuable and I know her e-mails have put smiles on many faces. I'm sure you'll all join me in saying all the best to Eve Vitali." I get applause that, in my opinion, is a bit heartier. I sort of do a little half wave at everyone and mouth, "Thank you."

I know a lot of the YFL people still don't know who I am, even though we've played those stupid getting-to-know-you games a zillion times since we merged. One of the breathy YFL writers looks around the room and then sees me. "Oh, it's you, you're leaving. You're so sweet, that's too bad."

This makes me feel better, I guess, but only a little bit. I'm still seething. I am going to kill Tabitha. I wait in agony for the meeting to be over, then I rush back to my desk to call her. This deserves an in-person visit, but I'm scared I'll totally lose it when I find out she kept this a secret.

The young temp is waiting for me when I get back to my desk. She can't be more than twenty-one. She is all smiles and cheerful. Shit! I totally forgot. I practice being nice. "Hi, you must be Jennifer. Sorry, we had a meeting this morning that I keep spacing out about. I can't wait to start training you, but I have to take care of some business first."

If I were her, I would hate me. That's a nice way of telling someone to fuck off, but I'm dying to call Tabitha.

"Good morning, Eve." Tabitha answers, cool as ever.

"Why didn't you tell me about Lacey?"

"Are you hungover or something?" Is it possible she doesn't know?

"Meet me downstairs for a cigarette in five."

"Eve, it isn't the most convenient time, and you aren't being very polite."

"Tabitha, you are going to want to meet me."

"Fine, in ten. Bring a better attitude." She hangs up on me. I hadn't meant to be so aggressive, I'm just pissed that not even my leaving this hellhole could be sacred. Now I have to go find jovial Jennifer and haul her back to the desk to cover for me. I find her standing obediently by the soda machines. She smiles when she sees me.

"Hi, Jennifer. I need to run out for a couple of minutes. Could you, maybe, I don't know, cover for me?" Her smile fades and she looks scared. I am successfully managing to intimidate her; I am an awful person to be training her.

"But, we haven't gone over anything yet. I'm not sure what I'm supposed to do." I take her arm and start leading her back to the desk.

"Jennifer, you are going to be fine, all you have to do is hang out at my desk and familiarize yourself with it. Don't answer the phone or anything. Just sit tight, and if anyone asks you anything, just tell them I will be back in five."

I am waiting for Tabitha when she gets downstairs. In addition to a better attitude, I brought a lighter, which I hold up to her cigarette. This news is going to upset her, too. She takes the light and gives me a bitchy look. "Okay, Tabitha, sorry I was a bitch. I thought you were holding out on me, but now I think you are just as ignorant as I was."

"Nice, Eve." I wait a minute, letting her get a couple of good puffs in. This isn't going to be easy.

"Have you been involved any more in the interview process for the new editor?"

"Well, we've had a few interviews, but no decisions have been made. When the Big C told me about her new plan, she assured me I would have a say in approval."

"How big a say?"

"Eve, what's up? Could you stop looking at me like you just got proposed to by Prescott!"

"Tabitha, it's Lacey Matthews. She's the new editor. They announced it in our meeting this morning." Tabitha's mouth forms a perfect "O" and she starts to step away from me, around the side of the building. I follow her. "I thought you knew when I called this morning."

Tabitha leans against the side of the building. She is turning white. Her mouth forms a tight line. She can't stop saying, "I can't believe this." I've never seen Tabitha this upset and I'm not sure how to deal with it. I've seen her pissed off, but now she looks downright defeated. I grab her arms and look at her face.

"I know you're pissed off, Tabitha, but you know what? It isn't going to matter, soon enough. It'll just be us. We will make our own decisions, we will be the ones with influence in our lives." She shakes her head, her eyes are filling up with tears.

"But we don't know, Eve, we don't know for sure."

"No, we don't, but I believed enough to quit. Even if we're being stupid, you have to think we'll do it and not let anything in this building make you lose sight of it." I am not sure if it's working. She pulls a pair of sunglasses out of her jacket pocket. I can't tell if she is crying behind them.

"It seems like a dream, Eve—your dream. And I guess I just wanted to believe that I would still have something here if things didn't work out."

"Well, you do, just because I don't get along with Lacey doesn't mean you won't." She pulls her sunglasses down her nose and raises an eyebrow over red eyes. "Okay, you probably won't. I know you're pissed that the Big C didn't keep you in the loop, but you have to start thinking that our thing will work out. Come on, believe in it. I'm starting that class in three weeks that will give me something to do other than sit on my ass. It's got to work, Tabitha—come on. Remember when your shoulder was in Styles?"

"Oh, you bring that up!"

"Yes, because there's more to come. It's only the beginning. We made the first step. And, Tabitha, it's not just about me, you know, it's your dream, too." She nods like it's sinking in a little, so I feel comfortable in saying, "Besides, I need to be consoled because the Big C stole my shining moment."

She laughs and then we hug against the side of the building. I'm not sure how she feels, but I feel a lot more confident about what we are going to do.

I have to. It's sink or swim.

When I get back to my desk, I notice that Jennifer is sitting up very straight. She seems embarrassed when I look at her. She better not be reading my e-mails. I have to remember to print anything important and delete everything when I leave.

"So, it was pretty quiet, huh, Jennifer?"

"Well, kind of. Eve, are you in some kind of trouble?" Trouble?

"Trouble? Why?"

"A cop from NYPD called." Her lip is quivering. "I told them I thought you were coming back, but I didn't know, you ran out so quickly."

"Do you mean to tell me that the coppers think I'm on the run?" I start giggling.

"I'm sorry if I gave them the wrong info."

"Jennifer, this may be one of the most exciting days in your entire career as an assistant here." I can tell Jennifer is still a little worried. I know after about a month or so, she'll truly believe this is the most exciting day of her working life.

I call the number and speak to the obnoxious Agent (or whatever cops call themselves) Shinners. He assures me that I checked out okay. He's got a whole new tone than he did last week.

"So what's going on with Gary? Is he going to go to jail?"

"Ms. Vitali, I'm afraid I am not at liberty to discuss that. But I would just advise you to not have any contact with him."

"Well, thanks for calling me."

"Yes, and again, I apologize for any inconvenience. We're the NYPD, we're here to serve."

Jennifer must really think I'm a freak. Her eyes are huge when I get off the phone. I know I should play this up more, but I don't want her to quit or anythng. Who knows, maybe they'll try to keep me here longer if she does? I try to act more normal.

"Well, looks like they're aren't going to be arresting me this week."

"What did you do?"

"I did nothing. I am innocent." When I explain to her about Gary, she keeps nodding, her smile getting smaller and smaller. I reassure her that stuff like that never happens, but I can tell she doesn't believe me.

I decide to put her at ease by making small talk with her for the remainder of Monday. She keeps asking me if there's stuff she is supposed to be learning, but I assure her we can get to that later in the week. I wish they hadn't forced me to have a week's transition period with the temp, it's literally a day's worth of teaching, and that's if I stretch it.

Wednesday morning I decide I should make Jennifer feel like she is learning something, so I give her a little overview of the departments, the history, the merge, other corporate folklore. She listens in wonderment. Then I show her where I keep all the supplies and how to get more. As I am showing her, Lacey comes up and stands by my desk. As I look at her muscular calves and her round little boobs revealed in her too-soon-in-the-season summer dress, I decide that I don't care about burning the proverbial bridge with her.

"Lacey, how appropriate that you would come now that I am going over supplies."

"Yes, Eve. I need to get packing supplies and someone to assist me in moving my stuff."

"Well, Lacey, this is Jennifer, my replacement. She has just learned how to fill out the supply request forms." I smile at Jennifer encouragingly. I hope she is up for the challenge. "Also, we have the Yellow Pages, and I'm sure you can find listings in there for a personal assistant—maybe they can help you pack."

I smile. I can tell by the way Lacey's nostrils (surgically enhanced?) flare that she doesn't appreciate that. Jennifer is beginning to cower, but I've got to hand it to her, she does a good job of diffusing the situation by dutifully going through the ordering procedure I taught her.

"Well, good luck to you, Eve," Lacey says, turning her attention back to me. "It isn't easy out there."

"You know, I'm young, I can bounce back. No real roots yet."

"Despite that, nothing comes on a silver platter." I will not let her rain on my parting parade.

"Not even an editor position." She glares at me. With any luck, I will never have to see her again, let alone be in a position where she can help me. But I'm taking that chance. I know she is unfazed. Like Herb, she is happy living in her ignorance. She waves to me and turns on the heel of her cute sandal. Jenny looks at me in disbelief.

I tell her to organize the supply shelves while I begin the arduous process of deleting all my e-mails and saving my incriminating files to disk.

Thursday, I head over to Rob King's floor. Sherman has a huge picture of a man having sex with a chicken up. He tries desperately to escape when he sees me coming, but his computer freezes.

"Sherman, you should call the help desk ASAP, you don't want that stuff on your computer forever. Not a very Prescott Nelson image." I look past him into Rob's office. Rob is sitting at his desk, on the phone.

"Yeah, I don't know how I wound up on this page, I was looking up my stocks."

"Happens all the time, I'm sure." Rob has gotten up and is standing in his doorway. "Got a minute?"

He smiles at me and steps back into his office, so I follow. "I was wondering if you would see me before you left."

"I'm not even going to ask how you know that." He must enjoy telling me things that piss me off, but I'm not going to make an issue.

"So you're going to do it, Ms. Vitali. You are going to be the enemy."

"With Prescott's blessing. Thank you, but I bet you know that, too." He doesn't say anything. "So, what's up with you?"

"I'm going to finish out the summer and then it's off to Dallas to help set up some new offices." Still not sure what he does? Me, either.

"Oh."

"Yeah, I'm glad I got to see you before you left. I didn't know if I would." I nod. "Maybe when you get your e-mail and stuff set up, you could e me."

"Yeah, I may need some business advice."

He nods. "Or whatever else."

"Yeah." We look at each other for a while. I am proud that my stomach is stabilizing as opposed to flip-flopping. It shows I'm maturing.

"Happy birthday, by the way."

"Thanks! The big two-four. I am mature at twenty-four." He laughs. I'm not sure what more to say to him. Have we always had so little to talk about? "Well, take care of yourself."

"Oh, yeah, I guess that's it. Take care of yourself, too." Then I walk toward the door. I stop in front of him and lean up. We kiss lightly on the lips. When I open the door Sherman is staring up at us from his desk.

"Good luck with your computer, Sherman." I turn back to Rob. "Thanks, Rob, for everything. Take care."

"You, too, Ms. Vitali. Watch out for elevator sports." As I leave, I hear him ask Sherman what's wrong with his computer.

So that was the big relationship. Sigh!

Had I waited one more Friday, early release Fridays would have started, but Memorial Day comes late this year so I am forced to stay the whole horrid day. Yesterday, I started teaching Jennifer the Excel program that I use to enter all the data. She is not picking it up very easily, so as I clean out my drawers, I give her pointers.

"I'm not sure I'm ready to do this alone."

"Trust me, Jennifer, you'll have plenty of time to get ready, it's a long way until that point. I'll never need all these folders again. No one cares about old T and Es." I dump huge folders into my trash bin. I smile at Jennifer. "This is super liberating."

I have a large shopping bag, full of stuff I'm taking home—my pictures, old funny e-mails printed out, a couple of Prescott Nelson T-shirts, a handful of sugar packs that have Prescott's name on it. Jennifer stares at me in disbelief. She is so fresh-faced, out of school. You wouldn't think that the year and a half between us would make such a difference. We stare at each other blankly.

"Well, I guess I should go say goodbye to Herb." I walk down the hall to his office. Enya is playing and Herb is leaning back in his chair with his eyes closed. I almost leave, but I really don't want to prolong this anymore. I knock softly on his door, and when he doesn't hear me, I bang.

"Oh, Eve, didn't hear you there. Are you getting ready?"

"Yep, I've cleaned out my desk and trained Jennifer. I think she'll be fine."

"She's got a tough act to follow."

"Thanks." I guess.

"I'm sorry we didn't get to do more for your departure. If time had allowed we would have had a separate lunch for you and Lacey. Now, you're lucky, you get our fondest wishes."

I can't believe he's gone this long without making a stupid joke, but I guess since I'm not a crowd of his underlings, I'm just me, he doesn't feel the need to impress. "I guess I just wanted to say 'bye and thanks for everything."

"I hope it wasn't too terrible, Eve." He looks up at me hopefully. I don't say anything. "Well, keep in touch."

"I will."

I take a little walk around the floor. I stop at only the desks of people who I think will really care. Some of the YFL people actually stop me and are very sweet. When I get back to my desk, Jennifer appears to be on the verge of tears.

"What's up?"

"You can't leave until you explain this Excel thing to me again. I don't get it. I'm not going to be able to do it." She is almost angry.

"All right, I'll show you again, but, first let me send out my goodbye e-mail." Jennifer doesn't seem too happy to wait, but this is the lasting impression I want to leave. The final e-mail to put a smile on people's faces:

Hi all,
So this is it, my last day. I'll try not to be too sentimental.
Save your tears for your summer subway commutes. This was my first real job out of school and I've learned a lot from everyone. Best of luck to all of you and have a great summer.
I'll be in touch as soon as I get my e-mail up and running.
Take care.
—Eve

There. Short and sweet. I spell-check and send. Now back to the matter at hand. Jennifer is breathing down my neck waiting to unlock the knowledge only I can provide. We switch places so she can sit at the computer and I can lead her through it. Tabitha calls in the middle of my lesson.

"Is it tragic?" she asks.

"No, I'm doing okay."

"Want to have a final smoke break?" I look up at Jennifer, who is biting her lip and staring intently at the computer screen.

"Tabitha, I can't, I'm teaching Jennifer something. I'll call you tonight when I get home."

"Are we going out for drinks?"

"Maybe later on—I'm going to need a little time to decompress."

"Whatever. Call me when you're over it."

Jennifer has messed up and seems as if she is about to hyperventilate. I put my hand over hers on the mouse and lead her through the entry. We do it a couple of times and then I take my hand away and she does it herself. She smiles at me, calm now. I smile back. "You see, Jennifer, it's all going to be okay."

Later I'm ready to leave the building. I swear I'm not being dramatic, but my heart is racing as I ride down the elevator. I almost feel like I can't walk out through the revolving doors. I stop for a second and watch the other people do it. Is this it? Is this what I want to do? Leave? Forever? I look at the expressions of the people who walk by. Some are a little annoyed that I have stopped right in their path, but the rest are smiling, thrilled that they have been released for a weekend. How will I ever appreciate anything without having a job that reminds me of how boring life can be? People are meant to hate their jobs, aren't they? Isn't that part of life? The part that makes everything else so sweet?

"Miss, can I help you?" The uniform guard is looking in my face.

"No, I was just standing."

"Do you work here?" I open my mouth and take a deep breath. He is waiting for an answer.

"No, not anymore."

When I leave the building I feel light and free. It isn't like the last day of school or an awful class, it is even more intense. I turn and look up at the massive building. It won't be the last time I see it, I'm sure, but it will be the last time it means this much. Eventually, it will just represent all the things that I group into "my first job." I start walking home. I am floating even happier than those around me. I haven't just been released for the weekend, I have been released.

When I get home, Roseanne is grilling tuna in the kitchen.

"Hey, Eve. I want you to taste this in a sec and tell me if it needs more lemon. So, the last day, how was it?"

"Well, weird. It's over."

"No, Eve," she says, feeding me a lemony delicious piece of tuna, "it's only just begun."

Epilogue

And then it's summer, and much like the days of my school career, I'm off. I'm taking a magazine publishing class one night a week; most other times, I'm sitting in front of my computer in our hot apartment. Tabitha set up a Web site and we've already had all these hits from people who want to contribute to or advertise in our magazine.

We are calling it *On the Verge*. It'll be a magazine about "holding on to your youth and creativity post-college without sacrificing the dream of what you want to be." It will have a "very New York sensibility but still appeal to young people all over." We developed this to tell all the people who are trying to invest in us. We have these meetings where Roseanne gets all decked out in her cool new summer suits and talks numbers and percentages with other guys in suits who are fascinated by the buying power of our demographic.

I sit around looking urban and young (as dressed by Tabitha) and being as aloof as possible. Tabitha thinks the less I say, the better—"we don't want to be boxed in creatively." (I mostly just support Roseanne and enjoy the air-conditioning.) I keep feeling like someone is going to figure out that we have no idea what we are doing, that we are just winging it, but they seem to enjoy how naive we are. They describe us as thinking "out of the box." Roseanne likes to quote that a lot. She refuses to put money in the jar now, claiming that we are a business and thus, we can use those terms. I think she's scared I'll spend the money on snacks or smokes during the day.

Roseanne got Yakimoto to invest with us. Her husband wasn't too jazzed about it, but she worked some great deal with Roseanne where we don't have to pay rent for six months or something. Our relationship has changed from landlord-tenant to something more business related.

It's a lot of pressure.

Somedays I sit staring at the blinking cursor and switch back to the Web site, noticing no hits. Some days, I can't stop writing articles and thinking of ideas and calling people and imagining a cover for our first issue.

When I was at Prescott, I would pick up the phone and call whoever I wanted to, now I can't believe the phone bill. Roseanne keeps telling me not to worry, it's a business expense, but it seems like a real expensive business expense.

Also, it seems like my days don't ever end. Roseanne and Tabitha both do their other jobs and sometimes make calls and have meetings during the day. For me, it's my whole life now. But, it's what I wanted. I'm in control for now. We're projecting that the magazine will hit newsstands in November and I guess that will be the true test. We're all about expectation.

I didn't tell my parents that I quit right away. My mother got sort of sick of her chemo at one point and it just didn't seem like the best time. Unfortunately, my dad called me at work soon after and discovered my big lie. He wasn't too pleased. When my mother was feeling better he told her, because this therapist they are working with said they have to be completely honest and supportive with each other. My mom was surprisingly mellow about it. She's taking everything in stride. I think it's got a lot to do with these survivors meetings she's going to. She's all about self-actualization now.

My sister thinks it's great, too. She believes I am making some kind of anti-corporate statement and wants to have a "discourse" with me about making the "publication truly subversive." She was calling me up every day with ideas. Lucky for me she and Chuck mutually agreed (meaning no one proposed) to have a commitment ceremony Labor Day weekend. They want to have it at my parents' place and make it (get this) a potluck party. Can you believe it? I begged my sister to not let any of her friends bring bongo drums. Also, to my father's dismay, not only will they not be married in a church, they are not having any kind of officiator. I can't imagine what this party is going to be like, but I do know that the potluck is going to have a whole new meaning for a lot of her friends. And I secretly think that my mom might be all about "medicinal purpose marijuana," which will be even more scandalous to some of the relatives. Anyway, it's a long way away.

Stuff at Prescott Nelson seems to be moving right along. I have yet to cash his check. I am waiting until I'm absolutely down and out. I haven't told anyone about it, but I think it would be a mistake to cash it. I probably shouldn't even have accepted. Prescott's no fool; I'm sure it could be considered an investment and then he could have some say in our magazine. Maybe he was just a test to see if I could stand on my own. I won't cash it, but having it reassures me that I can never be too impoverished—I'll always have a little money for a rainy day. I know it's weird that even though I feel so far from that office world, Prescott still manages to be my security blanket. But I don't miss my job at all.

Gary was indicted by a grand jury and his trial is set for early next year. His lawyer has contacted me about being a character witness. Lorraine is back working at Prescott Nelson for the animal magazine, *Bark!,* which I think is perfect for her. We are supposed to have lunch any day now. I suspect it will never happen. Jennifer, to my annoyance, has not only mastered Excel, but been promoted in less than two months to coordinator. It seems the magazines re'orged again and she was at the right place at the right time. It makes me sick in a way, but I guess it should just tell me that fate didn't want me there or something. I don't know.

Herb won some kind of journalist award and Tabitha got a copy of his acceptance speech. It was all about being a mentor and encouraging youth to meet their potential.

Lacey Matthews continues to wreak havoc, but this time on Tabitha. I have to console her on a daily basis and urge her not to poison Lacey's decaf cappuccino. In retaliation she makes flagrant non-business-related phone calls and steals Lacey's supplies whenever she gets a chance.

The Big C has actually become kind of a resource for us. She advises us on the magazine and makes an attempt to introduce us to the right people. I tend to call her the Big C now more as a term of endearment (although, not to her face). She is never pushy about her ideas, but having her name attached in any way to our magazine has been an asset to us, created a buzz, if you will.

Tabitha and Roseanne never neglect the magazine, but they spend every other minute with their respective others. It's sort of good for me as I don't have all the disposable cash I used to. The boys help me out a lot in my pauper stage. There's always Krispy Kremes around to nourish me from Elliot and I always go to the bar Pete works at to get a few stiffies on the house. Otherwise, I tend to feel like I'm on allowance from Roseanne or Tabitha. Even though we are all in this together, it's hard not making any money anymore.

Things with Todd are as good as they can be with him jetting all over the place. He stops over in New York after each trip and buys me dinner and denies me sex. It's an interesting take on a relationship for me, but I sort of like being the pursuer. We are taking our time with it, because there is residual weirdness from being friends for so long. It's working, though, in its own little funny celibate way. I am heading down to Atlanta soon for a weekend. Maybe I'll get some booty then.

That's it. I wish I could tell you it worked, that the magazine was a success, but I'm not sure if it will. You'll have to pick up a copy in November or whenever it comes out. Keep your fingers crossed.

In a lot of ways it's been a lonely summer, but also the hardest I've worked in a while. While I'm not completely productive every day, I never feel like my brain is seeping out of my head. That's good, right?

Some nights, the girls's boys have work to do and the three of us throw on our black dresses and go to a club or a bar with mega-air-conditioning. We grab big fruity drinks and dance around the bar till it closes. We smile at each other and accept that we don't know what lies ahead. We could be wasting our time and our energy, but if we are, we know that now is the best time to do it. Youth is on our side and our brains are sharp. We have no responsibilities and we let the concerns go as we shake our hips and giggle. We laugh at the lack of certainty. We are still confident and won't be discouraged. We wink at each other knowing what no one else in the bar knows.

We are on the verge.

Coming next month from Red Dress Ink...

Strapless

Leigh Riker

Australia or Bust!

Darcie Baxter is given a once-in-a-lifetime
chance to open a new lingerie shop in Sydney.
So she packs up and moves to Australia,
leaving New York City, her grandmother and
her possessed cat behind. A whirlwind affair
with an Australian sheep rancher sends her into
panic mode, fleeing Australia with a bad case of
the noncommittals. Who wants to be barefoot
and pregnant in the Outback? But don't worry—
she won't get away that easily!

Also available from Red Dress Ink...

Milkrun

Sarah Mlynowski

Hip and hilarious, MILKRUN is a must-read for anyone
who longs for the express—but is stuck on the local....

"...This entertaining debut represents [the Bridget Jones
genre] with both humor and substance."
—*Publishers Weekly*

"Mlynowski is acutely aware of the plight of the
20-something single woman. She offers funny dialogue
and several slices of reality.... Mlynowski may not be
able to provide all the solutions, but she certainly
makes the problems fun."
—*Publishers Weekly*

"I thought it was just wonderful—funny and
heartbreaking and true, true, true."
—Jennifer Weiner, author of *Good in Bed*

RED DRESS INK
™

Visit us at www.reddressink.com

Also available from Red Dress Ink…

See Jane Date

Melissa Senate

Debut author Melissa Senate has captured the essence
of being single in NYC, wryly portraying all the fun
and the annoyances that come with the title!

"Senate's debut, part of a hip new line of romances
aimed at young single women, is both witty and snappy."
—*Booklist*

"You could almost imagine a star like Renée Zellweger
being interested in playing a character like this."
—*Entertainment Weekly* on *See Jane Date*

"Senate's prose is fresh and lively."
—*Boston Globe*